Suffer Little Children

By the same author

Mother Love
Gemini

Suffer Little Children

Domini Taylor

Hamish Hamilton London

First published in Great Britain 1987
by Hamish Hamilton Ltd
27 Wrights Lane London W8 5TZ

British Library Cataloguing in Publication Data

Taylor, Domini
  Suffer little children.
  Rn: Roger Longrigg   I. Title
  823′.914[F]   PR6070.A913

ISBN 0–241–12068–3

Printed and bound in Great Britain by
Butler and Tanner Ltd., Frome

CHAPTER ONE

Ramona Charnley sat at the desk on the little dais at
one end of the school library. In front of her stretched
two rows of trestle tables, three tables to a row. Two or
three girls sat at each side of each of the tables, and there
were girls at the ends of some of the tables. Ramona could
more or less see what the girls at the sides of the tables
were doing. It was to enable the supervising teacher to see
what was going on that the desk had been raised those few
inches on its dais. It worked, up to a point. Ramona could
see also what the girls were doing who were sitting at the
ends of the tables so that they faced her. She could not
see what was in front of the girls who had their backs to
her. She could not see what books, if any, they had in
front of them; what they were writing or drawing, if they
were doing those things; what they were doing with their
hands. The system broke down, in regard to the girls who
had their backs to the teacher. The system had broken
down anyway, a long time before. Few of the girls were
in the school to learn anything. They were there because
their parents were in Saudi Arabia.

There had been, before Ramona's time, a rule forbid-
ding girls who were working in the library to sit with their
backs to the teacher. It was not forgotten, but it was not
often enforced. One or two of the older and grimmer
teachers claimed, in the Staff Common Room, to enforce
this sensible rule. For Ramona to have tried to enforce it

would have destroyed, probably for the rest of the hour of study, the studious atmosphere which, to a cursory glance, seemed to rule the room. Girls would have said that there was no room elsewhere, that they had been told to sit always with the light over their right shoulders, that kind of thing. They would have taken the mickey out of Ramona, more and more brazenly as her authority slipped away. It had all happened before. The game was not worth the candle. Ramona accused herself of moral cowardice: but the Headmistress would be better pleased by a silent library than by a doomed attempt to enforce a minor rule.

The desk was raised not only for practical reasons connected with the teacher's line of vision. It was raised also, perhaps, by way of symbol, to make visible the moral authority of teacher over pupils. This part of the system had not so much broken down as failed even to start. Teachers who had authority did not need physical elevation. Teachers without it did not acquire it by dint of a few inches of pinewood planking.

There were tall windows in one wall of the library, with bookshelves between them. On the wall facing the windows there were more bookshelves. The shelves were not full of books. Even from a distance, it was evident that here were no cherished sets of the English classics. The books were schoolbooks, primers, dog-eared and much bedoodled, survivors of generations of pupils who were not interested in their contents. Ramona and sometimes other teachers had tried to bring order to the tatty chaos of the library shelves. New systems were devised whereby books were signed out and in, and their condition scrutinised. These efforts had the apathetic approval of the Headmistress, herself not much interested in books; the brave new systems were ignored after a few days.

Ramona felt a sense of betrayal, looking at the books. It was not herself that was being betrayed, but the children who should have been fed on great literature. At least offered it, given a sniff of it, given a chance to sample it. She herself, at a much better school than the one at which she taught, had been introduced to Scott, Dickens, Thackeray, Trollope. For years that had been an important part of her life. Now she no longer had such books, and she did not know how to come by them. She could not have afforded to buy them; she was miles from a public library; if she could have found leisure to read she would have been too tired to read.

Facing Ramona's important desk, at the far end of the long room, was an important fireplace. It was made of marble, inlaid with marble of a different colour. It was intended to be classical in taste, even Palladian, but its designer in 1905 had somehow debased the style so that it became ostentatious and vulgar. Ramona had been brought up with the real thing, and educated to see the difference. Within weeks of starting at the school she had realised that there was no one there with whom she could discuss such a thing. In the Staff Common Room, any remark on the subject would have been dismissed as a pretentious attempt to acquire status, or greeted with blank incomprehension. Still the fireplace was important. It was the feature of the room. It was one of the things always shown to prospective parents who were visiting the school. For this reason, it was cleared out every day. But it was always full of the rubbish of the schoolgirls – wrappers of candy-bars, torn pages out of the dismal little books, sometimes blatant cigarette-packets. Such a sight, at home, would have thrown Ramona's father into a paroxysm of rage. It threw Ramona into a kind of echoed rage. There were plenty of bins for rubbish, but the squalid little girls flung their filth into the fireplace. Perhaps all little girls nowadays were as careless, as thoughtless, as indifferent to their surroundings. Ramona thought not.

Over the fireplace was the room's single picture, a repro-duction of a Gainsborough portrait of a family in the midst of their estate, their dogs about them and their lovely house in the distance. The frame was of yellow wood, varnished so as to resemble plastic. Ramona tried, had always tried, to stop herself staring at it. It was almost impossible, as she was obliged to sit directly facing it. The life Gainsborough had painted was the life she herself had

7

been brought up to. The house in the picture was like her father's house, and the dogs were like his dogs. He had had good pictures, too – not at the Gainsborough level, but decent sporting oils ascribed to Alken, Sartorius, Ben Marshall. Ramona had been brought up to know about these pictures and to love them: to despise the hanging of reproductions. She had been brought up to know about the subjects of her father's pictures, too – racing at Newmarket, foxhunting in High Leicestershire, the life of stables and farmyard and smithy. None of them were things she could discuss with anybody she now saw from year's end to year's end.

The picture was the gift of a grateful parent, or of somebody who had no further use for it. It was not a thing the Headmistress would have spent money on. There were some attractive, inherited, amateur water-colours in the Headmistress's study. Otherwise there were no pictures in the school at all, except those produced in art classes, which festooned the corridors on Speech Day in midsummer.

Speech Day was a long way off. The autumn term was only into its third week. Another year loomed ahead, like an ocean that had to be rowed across.

The time was seven-thirty. The rest of the evening loomed ahead, like the jumps Ramona's father had made her ride at on her pony. It was dark outside the shuttered windows. Ramona was supervising Evening Study Period, in which the older girls prepared for the next day or the next decade, three times a week, after supper. She did not teach these girls. Even at Malham House School, some qualifications were required for the teachers of sixteen-year-olds. She could have taught them about art and literature, but she was not allowed to do so, and would have been frightened of trying to do so. She only taught the very youngest children, the ones who should not have been at a boarding school at all, whose parents used Malham House not as a school but as a crèche for six months of the year. The tools of her teaching were paper cut-outs, crayons, building blocks. They did not equip her to supervise bored and rebellious teenagers. Nothing in her life or character equipped her to frighten them or earn their respect. They knew it, and they knew she knew they knew it. But her duties included the supervision of meals and Study Periods and walks.

She was only ten years older than the girls she was supervising. Sometimes she felt younger. They had knowledge and experience in areas in which she was completely ignorant – the Middle East, discos and pop concerts, the various Scenes which it was their whole ambition to adorn. They had better clothes than Ramona's and they wore them better. They had better legs and figures. They had much, much better eyesight. She was at a disadvantage with them. They knew it, and they knew she knew they knew it.

She was known as The Moaner. They knew she knew that, too.

One of the girls with her back to Ramona was a sixteen-year-old called Rosalind Tuck. Her mane of brilliant blond hair was quite distinctive, the brightest in a school with many blond children. The colour was too good to be true. A lot of things about Rosalind Tuck were too good to be true, but her precocious figure, her large pale-blue eyes, her bee-stung lower lip, these were all true. She was a newcomer to the school. In many ways she was typical of its pupils. Her father had been offered a job in the Persian Gulf, at a huge salary, at short notice. A boarding-school for his daughter became both a possibility and an immediate necessity. They were not people who would normally have considered either the expense or the social pretension of a boarding school, but they reacted rapidly to rapid changes. Very few schools could accept a girl of that age at a few weeks' notice, and very few would have accepted an entrant with such low academic achievement.

Malham House School might have been invented for Rosalind Tuck. It certainly now existed for Rosalind Tuck, and would have ceased to exist without her.

Her parents had come to see the school, bringing the child, five weeks before term began. Ramona was called on to show them round and answer their questions; she was the only member of the teaching staff who lived in the school during the holidays, except the Headmistress and her husband, who were going out to lunch. Rosalind's father was an oil-man. He was big, beginning to run to fat, with thinning hair worn long, a leather coat, and pale-coloured shoes with tassels on the laces. He seemed to Ramona not a qualified engineer but a technician, a skilled mechanic. Though no figure was mentioned – though he did not crudely boast – he made it clear that he was about to be paid a large number of tax-free dollars in the Gulf. It was obvious that he would contrive to evade the laws against alcohol. It was obvious that he was intensely proud of his only child, and that he spoiled her.

Ramona predicted an absurdly large allowance. She thought with despondency about the things it would be spent on.

The parents had brought reports of a kind on Rosalind, written in a hurry by teachers at her Comprehensive in Sussex. They were meaningless. Mr Tuck took the view that if Malham House had room for his daughter, and he was prepared to pay its bills, it was stupid to fool around with reports from another school. He was quite right.

Mrs Tuck seemed overawed by the school, by her beautiful and precocious daughter, and even by Ramona. She left it all to Derek and Ros. She said she always left everything to Derek and Ros.

Rosalind herself seemed resigned to coming to the school. She was not interested in any of the questions Ramona asked her. She was not interested in any school subject or any game. She played no musical instrument; she was not interested in drawing or painting. She showed a spark of response when Ramona mentioned music: but it was immediately clear that by 'music' she and Ramona meant different things. She was glad she was not going to be made to wear a uniform.

Five weeks later she arrived alone in a taxi, her parents having already gone abroad. Ramona, flustered by the onset of girls of all ages, familiar and unfamiliar, was

10

shuffling lists and telling them what dormitories they were all in. Rosalind appeared in the front hall, entirely self possessed. She was wearing skin-tight jeans, high heels, and a floppy sweater. Ramona told her that she could not, during term-time, wear jeans or high heels. A mulish look came into Rosalind's lovely little face. Her lower lip jutted. She turned and clopped off, on those ridiculous heels, without a word. Ramona had not invented the rule about clothes, but Rosalind seemed to blame her for it because hers had been the voice of authority. It was the beginning of trouble between them, and it happened within two minutes of Rosalind's arrival.

Well, she was quiet this evening. They were all quiet. It was a good evening. It was as good as anything could be in a hateful place among hateful people.

There was, of course, no way that Ramona could see what Rosalind was doing. It was certain that she was not studying French or history or the sociology which had become such a soft option. It was doubtful if she were writing to her mother. It was doubtful if she were drawing. It was possible that she was reading one of the new books by best-selling ladies which circulated semi-secretly round the school. It was certainly possible that she was doing absolutely nothing. A voice told Ramona to go and see what Rosalind was doing with her Study Period. Another and louder voice told her to let well alone. If she talked to Rosalind, Rosalind would reply, other girls would chime in, and the floodgates would be opened. There were still twenty minutes until the bell rang.

On Rosalind's left, sitting so that Ramona could see her, was Amanda Loring. Amanda had been at Malham House for six years, and she seemed to have come to life for the first time in the previous three weeks. She was Rosalind's age and identically placed, although she had been so placed six years longer. She had pale red hair, green eyes, and a hint of Scots in her voice. She had been, for six years, a lump, a pudding, pushed up through the school not by any achievement but simply by getting older. Ramona had only seen the last three years of this career, but she had heard

11

about the previous three from her colleagues in the Common Room. Rosalind's arrival seemed to have switched on a light that had never before been seen. Amanda had suddenly become an almost vivid personality, presumably brought to life by Rosalind. This was the theory of the Common Room; Ramona supposed it must be true. It was impossible for an adult to know – at least at this early stage – what the influence was that Rosalind had over Amanda: but the consensus of the Common Room was to welcome the change. Amanda was one of Rosalind's particular friends. She might not be so next term – she might not be so at bedtime – but she was now, and had been almost from the moment of Rosalind's arrival.

Amanda was reading. Ramona could not see what she was reading, and told herself not to care.

On Rosalind's right, and equally predictably, was Colette Davies. She was a year younger than the other two, but far ahead of them academically. Her father was a doctor, with a job in public health that took him all over the world. From what Ramona had heard about Dr Davies, Malham House was a surprising choice for him to have made for his daughter's schooling. (A man like Rosalind's father had very little choice.) It was expected that Colette's O-Level results would be something for the Headmistress to boast about to prospective parents. She was getting special coaching, to this end. Ramona had no part in any of this, but she was at the receiving end of grumbles in the Common Room – of grumbles and a certain excitement, too. It was gratifying even for the Malham House staff to have at least one really promising and motivated pupil. It was odd that Colette should have become – not within minutes, like Amanda, but certainly within days – Rosalind's other most particular friend. The Common Room saw this as a sign of grace in Rosalind, who otherwise seemed likely to present certain problems. There must be more to her than there seemed, for a girl like Colette to latch on to her so closely. Ramona was doubtful about this, and had said so. She was told to mind her own business, to stick to her crayons and building-blocks.

Near Rosalind, but at another table, sat a little creature called Sara Corderey. Like Rosalind, Sara was a newcomer. Like Colette, she was said to be clever, but nobody could yet be quite sure because she was painfully shy and miserably homesick. She was a year younger than Colette, two years younger than Rosalind and Amanda, but on the strength of her reports and of some papers the school had set her, she had been put in the same form as them. Ramona thought this a mistake, but that was another thing which was none of her business. Sara's misery was none of her business, either – the child had a form-mistress and a house-mistress and a tutor, and if her pillow was nightly wet with tears it was their privilege to concern themselves about it.

Ramona worried about Sara Corderey, although she had a sense that in doing so she was trespassing.

Sara Corderey worried about The Moaner. She worried about herself, lost and snubbed among older girls who resented her; she worried about her parents, just arrived in Central Africa, her father a medical missionary and her mother working for a relief organisation; she worried about her small brother Thomas, sent to board with a parson's family in Dorset and going to a local day-school; and she worried about the young teacher in thick spectacles who looked a little bit frightened all the time.

The form had been set to learn any poem from the little green readers which were what Malham House had in the way of poetry. Sara was learning the *Ode to the Nightingale*, which bewitched her from her first quick reading. She found it easy to learn, not only because she was quick at learning but also because the great images followed one another like battleships, in perfect order, glorious and unforgettable. She raised her eyes from the page, in order to say the poem over to herself in her head. She found herself staring, as she internally recited, at The Moaner. As though conscious of the stare, The Moaner raised her eyes, meeting Sara's. Astonishingly, The Moaner blushed.

13

A vivid, painful blush, as though her knickers had fallen off in the middle of Waterloo Station.

In pity and puzzlement, Sara dropped her own eyes to her book.

Ramona felt herself blush. She did not know why she blushed, but she did it often and it was one of the things people mocked her for. Sara Corderey had seen the blush, because her stare had for some reason caused it. Ramona did not think any of the other girls had seen it.

Sara saw that Amanda Loring had seen The Moaner blush. Amanda whispered to Rosalind Tuck, who was reading a paperback with a purple cover instead of learning a poem. Rosalind turned right round in her chair to look at The Moaner. The Moaner seemed to Sara to pretend not to see Rosalind. Rosalind gave a sort of little laugh, which could hardly be heard but could be sort of heard because the library was so quiet. Rosalind stared at The Moaner, and then turned round and went on with her book.

The Moaner blushed worse, so that it was painful for Sara to see her.

The bell rang. The library exploded into movement and chatter. Most of the girls scraped their chairs back and jumped to their feet, gathering up books and notebooks and pencils. Rosalind Tuck, Amanda Loring and Colette Davies sat where they were, heads close together, whispering and giggling. They all turned to look at Ramona. Once again, Rosalind had to turn right round to do so. There was nothing furtive about their stares. They just sat staring at Ramona. It was not like the lumpish Amanda of the old days to do something so brazen, so rude. It was not at all like the brainy and studious Colette. They continued to whisper and giggle as they stared.

They had not said anything impertinent, or done

anything for which they could be punished or even ticked off.

The room was emptying. It was almost empty.

Ramona felt the onset of another blush.

She forced herself to say, 'Are you going to sit there all night?'

'Are you, Miss Charnley?' said Rosalind.

Amanda caught Colette's eyes, and they both giggled.

Ramona stood up. She made a business of collecting her own books and papers, putting them together with quite unnecessary care so that she had an excuse to avoid those three pairs of pitiless eyes.

Rosalind's reply had been pert, but you could hardly call it rude. If she reported it they would think she was crazy, overreacting, unfair, persecuting Rosalind Tuck. There was nothing to report. They were looking at her. It was a sort of dumb insolence and they knew it, but there was still nothing to report. There was no rule against looking at teachers. You could say that there was a rule requiring pupils, in many circumstances, to look at their teachers.

Ramona stepped off the little dais and walked towards the door. She heard half-stifled giggles behind her. She knew that she was intended to hear them. There was no rule against laughing.

In the door Ramona turned. Rosalind had stood up at last, and gone to the fireplace. The fireplace had been cleaned out at tea-time: there was no litter in it. Rosalind was carrying a paperback book from which the garish cover had come loose. The cover was torn. It was one of the books that went from hand to hand, so that half the school read hundreds of pages of steaming, explicit sex. Rosalind tossed the disgusting cover into the fireplace.

Sudden anger gave Ramona courage. She felt her hands tremble with her unaccustomed rage. She was angry not only because Rosalind was being lazy, squalid, uncaring, inconsiderate, but also because the girl was showing blatant contempt for Ramona's authority.

'Pick that up,' said Ramona loudly.

15

For a moment, a long moment, Ramona thought Rosalind was going to disobey. Then she could be reported. For that sort of insubordination, for the refusal to obey a reasonable order, she would be punished. Nobody could overlook such a thing, even if it were done by a beautiful girl like Rosalind whose father had plenty of money.

Expressionless, Rosalind bent and picked up her litter. She rolled it into a ball. She threw it at a litter-bin in the corner of the library. She missed the bin; the purple ball of paper landed with a pattering sound on the floorboards.

Amanda Loring darted forward to pick up the ball of paper. She seemed to be Rosalind's slave. If this was indeed their relationship, it was very bad for both of them.

'Let her do it,' said Ramona sharply to Amanda.

'I don't mind doing it,' said Amanda.

'Let Rosalind pick up her own filth,' said Ramona, in a shriller voice than she meant.

She was not hysterical. She would not become hysterical. There were no reasons for hysteria. What was at issue was the placing of a small piece of litter in a litter-bin. Sense of proportion reduced the episode to the most minor of confrontations.

For another long moment Ramona thought Rosalind was going to refuse to stoop, to obey, to admit defeat. Her lower lip jutted, that lovely bee-stung lip which was probably already more experienced in kissing than Ramona's lips would ever be. Rosalind walked slowly to the litter-bin, exaggerating the movement of her hips. She was doing a Marilyn Monroe wiggle. It was another piece of dumb insolence, but it was not breaking any rules and there was nothing Ramona could do about it. Rosalind stood over the ball of paper, motionless. Then, instead of stooping, she knelt. She assumed an attitude of prayer, of abasement. Amanda Loring giggled. Rosalind picked up the bit of paper and, still on her knees, made an elaborate, mocking performance of dropping it into the bin. There was no rule against kneeling.

Ramona turned and went out. She was shaking with

rage and a kind of shock, as though she had been subjected to violence. Laughter followed her down the corridor.

Described, the episode would sound like absolutely nothing. It was absolutely nothing. Ramona had nearly stopped the shaking of her hands by the time she reached the door of the Staff Common Room.

Marigold Kent, alone of the four women in the Common Room, looked up when Ramona came in. Two of the others were reading; one was writing a letter. If there had been a TV in the room, they would all no doubt have been watching it, although they would all have said they despised it. The TV was, as Marigold Kent knew from the school holidays, the lonely woman's opiate.

She was ten years older than Ramona by a strict reading of the calendar; she was thirty years older on any meaningful scale. She did this job because her husband had run off with his secretary, and with two children of school age she had to have her holidays free. Teaching was the only option. Teaching at a school like Malham House was her only option. She found it pretty easy. She taught the middle school, nine to twelve-year-olds, and she had no trouble controlling them. She liked them. She thought they liked her; at any rate they behaved well for her, and came to her with their problems. Their problems were sometimes about school-work, sometimes about other girls who had been their best friends and were suddenly their cruel enemies, often about their families. There were some pretty rum families represented at Malham, even by Marigold's standards, and she knew her own family was a bit rum.

'How did Evening Purgatory go, Ramona?' she asked.
'All right. I had a dust-up with Rosalind Tuck.'
'My God, that's a pretty girl.'
'Yes.'
'You met the parents, didn't you? Which none of the rest of us have. What are they like?'
Ramona was about to tell Marigold what Rosalind's

17

father was like, and how far that went to explaining Rosalind. She saw that Hilda Joy had raised her eyes from her book. She remembered that Hilda Joy was Rosalind's tutor, responsible for most aspects of the child's whole school career. Hilda was fifty – just turned fifty, that last summer, occasion of a garden party which was rained off – and for that reason or for some other she had a sort of furious possessiveness about the pupils she called 'her' girls. She was allowed to criticise them, but nobody else was, feeling about 'her' girls as people are apt to feel about their families or countries. Hilda was also exceptionally close to the Headmistress; and she had, it was said, a financial interest in the school.

Ramona said, 'I couldn't really judge in such a short time.'

'You're quite right to be careful, dear,' said Marigold Kent.

Hilda Joy returned to her book. The others had not looked up.

Marigold Kent plugged in the electric kettle which, apart from the jar of instant coffee, was the only object in the Common Room, Ramona thought, younger than herself. The cream paint had yellowed to the colour of an old-fashioned London fog; the curtains dangled unintentional fringes of loose threads; the armchairs had aggressive springs and the upright chairs uneven legs. There were no pictures on the walls. The books on the shelf were schoolbooks.

The kettle boiled. Marigold gave Ramona instant coffee in a mug. Thanking her, Ramona was glad it was a mug. She thought her hands might still be trembling enough for a cup and saucer to betray her. Marigold would be full of matey concern, full of goodwill but unable to understand the problems of being a person like Ramona in a world full of people like Rosalind Tuck. Her sympathy would be genuine and worse than useless. On the subject of discipline she said, 'If they step out of line, sock it to them.' To her the issue simplified itself. For her the issue *was* simple, because none of the girls would try dumb insolence

18

on her, not even Rosalind Tuck. They wouldn't dare to and they wouldn't want to. There were things about Marigold Kent that Ramona bitterly envied, as there were things about Rosalind Tuck that she bitterly envied.

As it happened, there were things about Ramona that Marigold envied, as Marigold often said. Ramona's glorious childhood was a far cry from Marigold's middle-middle-class background in Beaconsfield. Nobody could take that away from her, whatever problems she ran into. Nobody could take away Ramona's intimacy – fruit of that wonderful childhood – with pictures and books and music, in all of which Marigold regretfully declared herself a non-starter.

Ramona would have exchanged the whole artistic achievement of Western civilisation for a thicker skin, an air of authority, and the ability not to blush. She would have liked good eyesight, too, and a few other physical changes in herself.

Marigold gave herself a cup of coffee, and sat with a sigh in an armchair. She yelped and shifted as a spring bit into her. She had brown hair, a high colour, a comfortable bosom, and a taste for clothes in bold checks. She looked as though she played golf every day and bridge every night, and drank white ladies at weekends in the bars of provincial hotels. She was often a surprise to visiting parents, who expected a schoolmistress to look different.

Hilda Joy had never been a surprise to any visiting parent. She was exactly what they expected. She was also indifferent to the arts, but from the way she did her hair no one would have guessed it.

Colette Davies, already in bed, watched Rosalind Tuck undress. It made her ashamed of her own underclothes, and of a mother who sent her to school with such woolly, childish, all-concealing horrors. There was nothing childish about Rosalind's bra and bikini pants, and nothing concealing about them either.

Colette had obediently believed, as she had been

19

brought up all her life to believe, that what mattered was work, achievement, success gained by effort, the full use of whatever God or genetics had given you by way of brains and talent. It came with the force of revelation that other things could be held to matter. To matter far, far more. The way you looked. The effect you had. The fun you had because of the effect you had. Rosalind quite agreed with Colette's father – the thing to do was to make the most of yourself. But she was talking about hair and a bee-stung lip, bosom and hips and legs. She would not be more attractive, more successful, if she knew about algebra, but less so.

Probably if they had not chanced to have beds side by side in the dormitory, Colette would have been less struck by Rosalind's underclothes and her simple philosophy. But since they were so close together, every night and morning, she was subjected to the full force of both. She could not fail to compare herself to Rosalind. She could not fail to be aware that Rosalind had a far more amusing and exciting life than she did, and she could not fail to be aware of the reasons.

Probably she had been preached at a little too much. Probably she had been fed too overwhelmingly serious a view of life.

She hoped her parents would not be in England during term-time, or if they were that they would not come to visit her. She had never felt ashamed of them before, but now she looked at them, in her mind's eye, through Rosalind's eyes. The kind of father who wanted her to get a place at Birmingham University. The kind of mother who bought bloomers like Colette's bloomers. That was what they were like and what they looked like.

Colette heard a cock crow thrice, but when Rosalind pulled a lacy nightdress over her head the cock-crows ceased to reverberate.

It wasn't only that Rosalind's mother gave her night-dresses which shamed Colette's flannel pyjamas. It was also that Rosalind's father gave her the biggest allowance Colette had ever heard of. If it wasn't the biggest in the school, then whoever had a bigger one kept very quiet about it. Rosalind kept fairly quiet about hers, though she told her best friends. She didn't boast about having so much money; she didn't throw it about; she was generous to her friends, but she didn't try to buy popularity. She had no need to. She was a natural leader. Colette didn't mind being led, not by Rosalind. She had a sense of being led into a new world which was more glamorous and more exciting and in every way absolutely better than the world where she had been living, the world mapped out and inhabited by her parents and the Malham House teachers.

All the same, Colette was a little aghast at what they had done this evening. Of course she and Amanda had gone along with Rosalind's plan. They always did; Colette was sure they always would. That was how it was, in their set. Rosalind said they might be suspected, at least by The Moaner, but there was no way they could be truly found out, no way anything could be proved. All they had to do was deny it, and tell exactly the same story about where they had been at the time. Then nobody could do anything to them. The Moaner on her own couldn't do anything to them anyway, except report them, because she was only in charge of babies, which was all she was fit for.

Colette did not laugh away her own fears. She let Rosalind laugh them away. She did not silence the voice of her own conscience. Rosalind did that too.

Malham House might have worked better as a school if it had been designed and built as a school, even in 1905, when neither the comfort of the pupils nor the convenience of the domestic staff was much considered. But it had been built for a man who had made a fortune in the Argentine railways, who had bought an estate in a flat and featureless part of East Anglia, and who unwisely overruled his architect on a number of points. He and his family had been used to slaves indoors and peons out of doors; they accommodated English ousemaids as they had accommodated the illiterate mestizos of Buenos Aires. They did not care

21

how far the dining room was from the kitchen, or up how many stairs coals and hot water had to be carried.

The principal rooms, downstairs and up, were large, cold and characterless. The little rooms higher up were a warren of medieval complexity.

The house changed hands rather often after the death of its builder. The estate was steadily reduced.

In 1935 a new owner built on a four-roomed wing for his widowed mother. It was the most comfortable part of the establishment – the only convenient, well-lit, easily heated part.

In 1939 the house was requisitioned. It became successively a training-school for Signals officers, a naval cadet station, and a military hospital. Derequisitioned, and a good deal knocked about, it was bought cheaply with a few acres by Colonel and Mrs Hapgood, who collected a Board of Governors out of *Debrett's Peerage*, a kind of teaching staff out of the women's services, and a minimum of finance. The Malham House School opened in 1948. It survived precariously, always undercapitalised for proper conversion and maintenance, always unable to attract good teachers with decent salaries, always scraping through in the reports of the Inspectors of Schools from the Ministry of Education, never able to boast of honours and scholarships.

The Hapgoods made a pretty nice living out of it. They were comfortable and warm in the new wing, their bills paid for them. Colonel Hapgood liked his glass of whisky before dinner and his glass of brandy after it.

Headship and subsequently ownership were inherited by the Hapgoods' daughter Gwyneth. She moved with her husband, Lt. Commander Edwin Barrow (R.N.R., retd.), into her parents' quarters, which they immediately redecorated. As the wing was part of the school complex, the work was of course paid for by the school, which had the effect of postponing the redecoration of dining-hall and dormitories. The bursar's objections were stillborn. The Board of Governors never knew about it. Everyone on the staff knew about it. Nobody said anything; if they lost the jobs they had they would be hard pressed to find others.

Commander Barrow eyed the older girls on the playing-fields. He poured sherry for visiting bishops. He was not otherwise involved with the life of the school, being too closely involved with the life of the golf-club to have much time to spare. His life-style closely resembled that of his father-in-law, except that he preferred whisky to brandy after dinner.

At the moment when the Commander was splashing soda into his glass, Ramona Charnley, his wife's youngest employee, was dragging herself up the fourth of the flights of stairs to the attic passage where her bedroom was. The passage was unheated. There were other bedrooms nearby, which had housed under-servants when the house was a house and when it was first a school. But all except one of the maids now came in daily, fetched in a minibus by Norman the odd-job man. Ramona was alone on her floor. This gave her exclusive use of one tiny and arctic lavatory; for a bath she had to go down a floor, and the bathroom was used by five others.

Ramona had hoped, when she started at Malham, that she would get used to the stairs. But the years had made them more and steeper. She had thought she would get used to her little beige box of a bedroom, with an iron bedstead brought up from a dormitory, her shelf of paper-backs, and a single-bar electric fire. There she was more successful. She no longer noticed the room. She had had ideas, right at the beginning, of making it pretty and welcoming and her own, inspired by memories of her father's house. But the difference between those two lives was so gigantic that it was hopeless and ludicrous to try to imitate the past in the present. Nothing could be done to the room, and she had no money to spare.

That night something had been done to the room. The bed had been partly stripped, and a bucket of water poured on it. There was a dark patch a yard across, sopping wet to the touch. The water had soaked the underblanket and the mattress. In the middle of the saturated patch was a

23

screwed up ball of torn purple paper, the lurid cover of a paperback.

Rosalind Tuck. Ramona felt sick. Revenge for her defeat in the library. And this was vicious. The bed could not be slept in. It might be days before the mattress was properly dry. This was deliberate, nasty-minded cruelty. This was not something for lines or being kept in a few afternoons or even scrubbing the kitchen floor. This came close to a case for expulsion.

Ramona's hands, stilled by her own effort of will and by Marigold Kent's friendliness and kindness, were shaking again with rage and shock.

Nobody would have seen Rosalind, on this empty attic floor. Nobody would have seen her on the stairs, if she took the minimum of trouble not to be seen. She would say she had not touched the book-cover after she had put it in the bin. Amanda Loring and Colette Davies would confirm that Rosalind had left the library without again touching the bit of purple waste-paper. Rosalind would deny having been anywhere near Ramona's room. Amanda and Colette would swear that Rosalind had been with them all the time until bedtime, in the library or some other part of the building.

It was blindingly obvious, absolutely certain, who had done this thing; and it was not going to be possible to prove it.

Rosalind would deny that there had been any unpleasantness in the library. Backed up by Amanda and Colette, she would say she had dropped a bit of paper, by mistake, into the fireplace. Miss Charnley had pointed it out to her. Immediately she had picked it up and thrown it at the bin. She had missed the bin, and therefore picked the paper up again and put it in the bin. That was because she was a bad shot, unable to throw straight. She had exactly obeyed Miss Charnley's orders. She had not in the least minded doing so, because she knew Miss Charnley was right – it was a pity to spoil the appearance of the fireplace with a lot of rubbish. Rosalind had said nothing the faintest bit impertinent. In fact she had hardly said anything at all.

That last part was true. Ramona could not lift a finger against Rosalind.

Presumably, Rosalind would say with a compassionate and diffident air, somebody had a grudge against Miss Charnley. Somebody she had reported, perhaps? Somebody who had been punished? What else was there to believe?

There was this that could be believed – that Ramona had wet her own bed in the night, and then blamed it on someone else.

Ramona sat down on the bed, involuntarily, not thinking. Immediately she felt the wetness soaking through the stuff of her skirt. She stood up, her hands shaking, wondering where to spend the night.

CHAPTER TWO

There was no chair in Ramona's room that she could sleep in – only a rickety cane-seated upright chair which was for hanging clothes over rather than for sitting on. Ramona tried rolling herself up in the unsaturated bedclothes on the floor; but without a pillow it was going to be impossible to sleep, and the pillow was soaking wet. A sweater rolled up should have served as a pillow, but a trial of a few seconds made it clear that it would not. It was unpleasant to be on the floor; there was a howling draught under the door, and a smell of ancient dust. It was intolerable to be forced by a vicious, vindictive child to try to sleep on the floor. There were empty bedrooms nearby, but they had no beds in them. There was no such thing as a spare bedroom anywhere in the building, except in the Headmistress's wing; that bedroom might have been in Australia for all the use Ramona could make of it. There were sickrooms; there were sick girls in them. No member of the staff was away, leaving an empty bed.

Ramona turned on the single bar of her electric fire, and draped the wet sheet and underblanket over the little chair in front of it. There was nothing she could do about the mattress and pillow. There was a big drying-room next to the boilers, but it was in the basement. Five flights downstairs, with a mattress, single-handed, was impossible.

She perched miserably on the dry end of the bed, and waited, and waited. She was bottomlessly tired. Her class

26

had been fractious and destructive, and two other teachers had complained about the noise they were making. Supervising the Evening Study Period was an ordeal, an emotional strain. Rows were exhausting, if her brush with Rosalind Tuck could be called a row. Shocks were exhausting, and so was rage.

When at long last she was sure that all her colleagues would be in bed, she put on her dressing-gown over her clothes, and tiptoed downstairs to the Common Room. A few dim bulbs were left burning on the stairs, in case there was a fire and a panic. She was in no danger of falling downstairs, and not in much danger of meeting anybody. She had a story ready, in case she was seen – sleeplessness, need for a book. There had in the old days been a night-watchman, so they said, but he had been judged an avoidable extravagance. The only real danger was that she would fall asleep before she reached the haven of the Common Room.

She made it to the room, and to the chair with the fewest broken springs. She realised at once that she should have brought a rug with her, one of the dry blankets off her bed. She had been too tired to think clearly. Now she was too tired to go all the way upstairs again.

Then, as so often, the sleep that she needed so urgently and wanted so desperately withdrew, mocking, and ran away from her when she pursued it.

Hopelessly wakeful, she remembered the last time she had spent the whole night in an armchair. It was during her mother's final illness. That chair had a broken spring, too. The night was full of moaning and bubbling and retching, and the air of the stuffy little room was full of the sweet stench of disease and incontinence.

Ramona hauled her mind away from that miserable memory, and sought another.

Yes.

By the swimming-pool at Garston. On certain breathless nights, when she was small, she was allowed to sleep on one of the long wicker chairs on the verandah of what they called the hut. Hut! It had two big changing-rooms,

27

showers, bar and refrigerator, telephone. It was built of brick, plastered and painted white, with a green-tiled roof curved upwards to look like a pagoda. It was in excellent taste – everyone admired it. From the first it fitted into the lovely garden as though it had always been there.

They knew she was perfectly safe to sleep there on her own. She was a good and obedient child, anxious to please her beautiful, loving parents. If by any chance she went sleep-walking and fell into the pool, she could swim like a fish.

Ramona remembered with aching clarity the magic of those midsummer nights. Every time she slept by the pool she resolved to stay awake all night. She never did. But the birds woke her when the sky began to pale – birds within yards of her, unfrightened birds, as she lay still, almost within inches of her. She shared the empty world with a million songbirds. As the light strengthened, the formal rose-garden took shape, with the statue and fountain in the middle, the great lawn with its great, placid trees under which, all summer, visitors friendly or frightening came and went, playing croquet, or having tea, or drinking champagne cocktails . . . And then, beyond, just visible through trees, Garston Hall itself, the perfect William and Mary house which was the only home Ramona had ever known or ever wanted.

As soon as the sun peeped over the roof of the house – never before, by a rule she made for herself – Ramona pulled off her pyjamas and jumped into the pool. There was a special joy in shattering the flawless mirror of the water, not yet agitated by the clock-controlled pump and filter and heater. There was a special, sensuous delight in swimming naked, not allowed later when people were about. She would climb out, tingling and triumphant, and run about in the horizontal rays of the sun until she was dry. Then, and only then, she would put on her glasses.

Then indoors, to patter upstairs to her sunny bedroom, to brush her teeth and drag a comb through her hair (better than letting Nanny do it – Nanny tugged too hard at the tangles, and nearly pulled Ramona's hair out) and pull on

28

a cotton frock and a pair of sandals, and downstairs to breakfast with a gigantic appetite.

Breakfast. It symbolised life at Garston. There were none of the usual post-war improvisations and economies. The sideboard – only a few years younger than the house – had chafing-dishes, over low flames, of kidneys and kippers. Ramona's father liked the look of the flames, in preference to a humdrum, modern electric hotplate. There was coffee, fresh roasted and ground, Indian and China tea, brown toast and white, Cooper's Oxford marmalade and Tiptree strawberry jam, honey in the comb and home-made butter. The morning sunshine winked on the George II silver and the George III decanters on the sideboard, and on the gilt frames of the pictures, the racehorses and foxhounds . . .

Ramona's older sister Persephone never spent a night by the pool. She never wanted to. Nor did Patrick, her younger brother. He was in any case too young, in the days when Ramona did it. It was Ramona's private adventure, unspoiled by anyone else. They would have spoiled it, too, complaining about the midges and the birds waking them at dawn.

After breakfast there were always five million things to do, so many it was often a real puzzle to know which one to choose. There was her pony, Brock, who would charge at her across the paddock when she went to catch him, and stop just in time, and scratch his chin on her head. If she went riding on a weekday it was usually with a groom. On Saturdays her parents were almost always at the races, even at the other end of England. But on Sunday, just occasionally, she trotted along the headlands behind their gleaming hunters, and that was the best of all.

Percy and Patrick had ponies too, but Percy only wanted to ride when it was a competition with prizes, and Patrick was still on a leading-rein.

Then there was the boat on the lake, a proper sailing dinghy. Ramona and Nanny would strap on life-jackets and tack to and fro across the lake. Nanny was no use with horses, but her brother was in the navy and she knew all about boats. Ramona learned to sail the dinghy almost as soon as she learned to swim, which was almost as soon as she learned to ride, which was almost as soon as she learned to walk.

Even when she was very small, Ramona was aware – proudly but somehow guiltily aware – that she was her father's favourite. It was riding and sailing that made her so, and swimming and diving, and being interested in the pictures and in the horses in the pictures, and all sorts of other things that made her special. She did not want to be special, but she just was and she had to accept it.

Of course there were ways in which Percy was special. She was six years older than Ramona, and very beautiful and grown-up and interested in clothes and playing the piano brilliantly. And of course there were ways in which Patrick was special, because he was the son their parents had longed for, and he was the future of everything. Ramona was honestly glad that there were enough things special about Percy and Patrick to make up a bit for all the things that were special about herself.

If she was not riding or sailing, there were still three million things to do. Sometimes she helped her mother pick flowers, and arrange them in the Majolica jars or silver buckets or Waterford vases in the flower-room by the pantry. Sometimes she helped Harry groom the horses and clean the tack, loving the smell of saddle-soap and the slow, methodical tempo of the life of the stables. Sometimes she helped old Emily in the dairy with the butter-churns and the clotted cream. Sometimes she practised the piano, the upright in the nursery, not the grand in the hall, though it was depressing Percy being so brilliant. Sometimes she drew pictures of the house and garden and horses and dogs, with the superior French crayons Lord Horndean had given her, in the superior sketch-book Lady Voakes had given her.

Lord Horndean and Lady Voakes were specially nice, giving presents to Percy and Patrick as well as Ramona, but in other ways they were just like nearly all the people who came to Garston for lunch or dinner or for weekends.

30

The point about them was that they were racing people, all racing people, a few trainers of a special sort who had been cavalry officers, but nearly all owners and breeders. Ramona's father was a bloodstock agent. Ramona knew that this was what he was called long before she knew what it meant. He found horses for people who wanted them, and sold them for people who wanted to make a profit out of them. He went to the sales at Newmarket and Doncaster and Deauville and Dublin and Saratoga and Lexington, buying horses for people. He sent horses to Australia and Japan and South Africa. He managed horses for people who liked racing them in England but lived in Barbados. He managed stallions for people, finding enough mares for them and the right mares for them. All this Ramona gradually understood, listening to grown-up conversations over the years; some of it her father or more usually her mother told her about, when they had time, answering her silly questions as patiently as they could. She understood that her father had to know everybody who was anything to do with racing, and it seemed to Ramona that every single one came to Garston. The parties there were fashionable and fun, and people drank a lot and laughed a lot, and sometimes even played hide-and-seek with Ramona and Patrick, but really it was all business. Ramona understood that business could be fun, and that though her father worked very hard, in his London office and on all the racecourses and at home, he enjoyed every moment.

When he went stalking and salmon-fishing in Scotland, and grouse-shooting in Yorkshire, and pheasant-shooting in Suffolk, and trout-fishing in Hampshire, it was all what he loved and it was business. He was buying and selling and managing. He came back and told Ramona's mother about it, or spent a long time on the telephone talking about it.

Ramona was glad her father was a bloodstock agent, because he loved it and it meant they could afford to live at Garston.

There was one person who came often to Garston who had nothing whatever to do with racing, and hated horses

31

and everything about them, and yet, in spite of this dangerous madness, was Ramona's favourite person in the world after her father and mother. She was another Ramona. She was Aunt Ramona. She was not actually Ramona's aunt, but her great-aunt; she was Ramona's father's mother's much younger sister. She was really called Mildred, but she changed her name to Ramona when she was about eighteen, because she thought it suited her better. Everybody else seemed to think so too, because nobody ever called her anything but Ramona. And when her second great-niece was born, and named after her, the child was christened not Mildred but Ramona, which was lucky.

Great Aunt Ramona was also Ramona's godmother. She had been very pleased to be asked, she told Ramona, and she liked being a godmother and she liked her godchild. She was generous, which was nice, but she was also friendly and interesting and funny, which was even nicer.

There was something a bit funny, something special, about Ramona and Great Aunt Ramona, which Ramona was a long time understanding. Great Aunt Ramona always arrived at Garston in a huge black Rolls Royce, with a chauffeur and a maid. Other people arrived in Rolls Royces, some with chauffeurs, but none with maids, not in 1965. She always seemed to Ramona to be swathed in chinchilla and dripping with jewels. She let Ramona play with the jewels on her dressing-table when she was having breakfast in bed. So that was one thing that was special about Great Aunt Ramona – she was terrifically rich. She was much richer than her older sister, Ramona's grandmother, especially because Granny seemed to spend all her time gambling in all the casinos in the South of France, where she lived. Great Aunt Ramona had married a man called Sir Gregory Plante, who had a fortune from something or other. They had no children. He came to Garston sometimes. He was fat and bald and quite nice. Ramona's father was always trying to get him interested in buying racehorses, but he never was interested.

What was special about all this, as far as Ramona was

32

concerned, was that when Sir Gregory Plante died he would leave everything he had to Great Aunt Ramona, and when she died she would leave everything to Ramona.

Ramona overheard her father say, as Great Aunt Ramona was leaving after a three-day visit, 'It's lucky the child's fortune is her fortune, because her face never will be.'

'It's only those glasses,' said Ramona's mother. 'We'll get her lenses as soon as she's old enough.'

'It's not only those glasses. Never mind. She'll have a ball. She'll probably breed thoroughbreds. Shall I be my own daughter's stud manager?'

'Yes,' said her mother, laughing. 'She'll be able to pay you more than you make at the moment.'

Yet, thought Ramona, that must have been a lot. It was obvious to Ramona, even at that age, that her father earned more than anybody else who lived nearby, whose houses and families they knew. It was obvious to everybody. For some reason it was most obvious at breakfast-time.

A man once came into the dining-room at breakfast time, a man who had not been to Garston before. Ramona saw him look round slowly, and sniff the fresh-roasted, fresh-ground coffee, and see all the things on the sideboard and all the things on the table, and see Lucy the parlour-maid coming in with a fresh pot of Lapsang Souchong; and the man said, 'I tell you what you've managed, Chuffy. You manage to live a pre-war life post-war. Nobody else I know can do it. Not the millionaire dukes, nobody.'

'Well, thank you,' said Ramona's father. 'We do our best. But things are slipping, just the same. A lot of things you can't get nowadays. The biscuits we used to put on people's bedside tables before the war. Where can you get a boiled shirt properly starched? Where can we get our painted Venetian furniture restored by somebody who knows what he's doing? Where can you find Polish vodka, or fresh Périgord truffles, or a box of matches that fits into these Edwardian holders?'

33

'You know what I mean. That's fine detail. I'm talking about the essentials.'

'The essential consists of an accumulation of fine detail,' said another man, who was eating a poached egg and reading the *Sporting Life*. 'You're right about the matchboxes, Chuffy, but in general I agree with Sam.'

Ramona knew that her father really agreed with Sam, too. She could tell when he was pleased, and he was very pleased.

Dermot Charnley – 'Chuffy' since his private school, because he was mad about trains, and always being an express or a shunting-engine – was pleased. Sam Drummond had quoted, with supreme if unintentional tact, the exact words he himself had used to himself when he moved into Garston. People would step over the threshold and go back thirty years – without, to be sure, losing any of the modern comforts. They were very lucky, he and Margot, that it was possible. It was possible because of the job he did, the life he had led and led still, the person he was.

Probably none of it would have been possible without the war, in which he had also been lucky. And none of it would have been possible without his mother's sister and her money.

Chuffy was born in 1920, and entered at birth for Eton. His father would have sent him there, at whatever financial sacrifice; but his father died when Chuffy was four years old, leaving his mother pretty poor. Her sister Mildred – Ramona, as she called herself – had just married old Gregory Plante and his Far-Eastern millions. Very sportingly, the Plantes paid for Chuffy's education. They also gave his mother a moderate allowance. It would have been folly to give her a big one – however much she had, she would lose it at roulette. In the holidays, when his friends were off to Scotland, Chuffy went shamefacedly by train to Menton, where his mother had an economical flat some way back from the sea-front. These visits were a kind of agony for him, and he was thankful to get back to school. He loved his mother dearly, but she had become embarrassing; she wore little-girl clothes and heavy make-up, and pretended to know the whole aristocracy.

A great friend at Eton had a father with a string of racehorses. The horses were trained at Newmarket by one of the 'society trainers', Etonians and cavalry officers who had to work but could do a job they liked. Some of these were pretty bad trainers, but Chuffy's friend's father's trainer was a pretty good one. Chuffy talked to his friend; the friend talked to his father; the father talked to his trainer; and Chuffy went straight from Eton to a job as the trainer's assistant.

He was there for a year, and discovered two things about himself. One was that he hated getting up very early in the morning to watch the 'first lot' work on Newmarket Heath. The other was that he had a good natural eye for a horse, which developed remarkably during that year, and which he was confident he could refine to a point that would make him a really good judge of horseflesh.

He was at a crossroads in his life when Hitler walked into Poland.

He joined up immediately, his contacts made over the previous year pitching him straight into a first-class cavalry regiment. He had a good war and he was unscathed. He commanded a tank in North Africa and a squadron in Italy. He finished the war with the rank of Major, an MC and bar, and contacts in the regiment worth much fine gold.

He was demobilised in 1945, still only twenty-five, with no money and unlimited faith in himself. The Plantes, Gregory and Ramona, offered to set him up in any business that had nothing to do with horses. He trusted his star, his contacts, and his eye for a horse, and announced himself as the Beeswing Bloodstock Agency. He picked the name because it was beautifully distinctive – once heard, he thought, always remembered; because Beeswing had been a great race-mare, winning race after race, year after year, as he himself expected to do; and because he had a print of her, bought off a stall in the Portobello Road.

He needed some working capital. He raised it not by asking for loans, but by selling slices of the infant business. He communicated his confidence to his richer friends; he convinced them their money would grow and grow.

He had to take the first real gamble of his life. With every penny he could raise, he bought some yearlings at Doncaster. He did not pay much, even by the standards of the Doncaster sales in 1946; he did not buy fashionable pedigrees; he trusted his eye. He managed to sell them all on, some at a loss, with an odd but not unheard-of provision written into the bill of sale: if the horses won races, their value was to be reckoned to have escalated according to an agreed scale, and he was to be paid accordingly. Six of the eight horses won as two-year-olds, and a seventh won as a three-year-old. This had the effect of giving Chuffy a welcome injection of capital. It had a far, far more important effect: it immediately made him well known as a personality and well respected, young as he was, as a judge of yearlings.

By the time Chuffy married, in 1948, the Beeswing Agency was much talked about, much admired, much resented, and pulling in clients almost daily. It was still a one-man show, though now there were secretaries and telephones and a London office.

Chuffy's bride was called Margot Warren. She was really Marjorie, but like Ramona Plante she had improved her name. She was very pretty, very young, and very poor. She had spent her childhood in the tropics, her father having been an educational administrator in one of the West African countries which were then colonies. They came home at the beginning of the war, when Margot was thirteen. She was sent to a better school than her parents could afford. Mrs Warren died in 1943, her system after all those tropical years unable to stand up to an English winter in wartime. Margot was just old enough to spend a few months in the Wrens at the very end of the war. She enjoyed the companionship and she learned a lot. After her demob she went to live with her father, whose health was also broken by the diet and the draughts of the war. They lived economically in Hove, on the Sussex coast. Margot got a job in a bookshop in Brighton, coming in daily on a second-hand autocycle.

Chuffy was in Brighton for the races. He passed the bookshop and glanced at the window. He went in not to buy a book but because he had seen Margot. It was Wednesday, early closing; she was free all afternoon; he took her to the races.

At first he thought her lovely, sweet, innocent and ignorant. By the end of that afternoon he still thought her lovely and sweet and pretty innocent, but not ignorant, not after nine months in the Wrens. He gave her dinner at Wheeler's, and drove her home with the autocycle in the back of the car. He said he would come to the bookshop in the morning, and take her out to lunch. He kissed her goodnight, gently, already nine-tenths in love.

She went to bed ten-tenths in love. He looked magnificent, with shiny fair hair and a weatherbeaten face and a deep dimple in his chin. He was modest about his war but he was evidently a hero. He was modest about his job, his career, but he was evidently brilliantly successful. Margot had never been on a racecourse before; she was enchanted by it. She was enchanted by Chuffy's evident popularity, by the friendship and esteem in which everybody seemed to hold him. His expression when he looked at her in the candlelight at dinner made her heart jump in her breast as had the trout they were eating. After he had dropped her at home, she carefully avoided washing the place where he had kissed her.

Chuffy came back and back, and she took him to see her father. The old man – not so very old, but aged by illness and ill-temper – was querulous. Who would look after him? He needed her. Chuffy consulted friends, and found a nursing-home the Beeswing Agency could afford. Mr Warren went onto the payroll of the agency, and his bills became an operating expense.

By this time, having taken the very best advice, Chuffy

had a very good accountant, who looked after both the agency's books and his private affairs. Nobody could accurately discern the frontier between the two, least of all the Inspector of Taxes.

The way was clear for the marriage, which took place in October at Caxton Hall. The Beeswing Agency gave a party afterwards. Most of the guests, Chuffy's friends, were naturally racing folk, so the whole thing was tax-deductable. The exceptions were swamped – Gregory and Ramona Plante, who by now knew Margot well and liked her very much, and a few friends of Margot's from school and the services. She had no close relatives except her father.

Calling yet again on his contacts, Chuffy found them a decent small house for rent on the edge of Lambourn, a place swarming with racehorses and racing people. The agency paid rent, rates, heat and light. Meanwhile, the Plantes were closing one of their houses; even they were drawing in their horns a little, in the bleak winds of socialism. Suddenly they had a lot of furniture to spare, and they gave it to Chuffy and Margot. Chuffy had it valued for insurance. Some of it was good. The valuer told him what made it good, and got him interested in the subject. He began dropping into antique shops, learning all the time. He absorbed both knowledge and taste, developing an eye for objects like his eye for horseflesh.

After six years the first child was born, a girl they called Persephone. They assembled resplendent godparents. The rented house was really too small for a baby as well as the treasures they were gradually and skilfully collecting. Their accountant told them to buy, because property values were going to go up dramatically. A friend produced news of Garston Hall, even before the owner had quite made up his mind to sell. Negotiations began, and the house was never put on the open market. Never had the boundary between the Charnleys' private affairs and the agency's commercial affairs been more deeply shrouded in fog.

Working harder than ever, Chuffy set himself to provide a background for Margot and himself and for their

38

beautiful, miraculous daughter. The background was how their life was lived, as well as the objects it was lived among. There was a change of government, and an immediate end of all rationing. That helped. It helped that you could still buy really good antiques pretty cheaply, if your contacts and your taste were good enough. It helped that heat and light, carpets and redecoration and new bathrooms, were operating expenses of the Beeswing Agency.

When Persephone was five and another baby was on the way, it became obvious that the agency could no longer function without a swimming pool. To build a little unheated pool, with a little wooden hut beside it, would be a false economy. Shrewd investment added to the value of the property. Groom, Nanny, cook, maids, gardeners were all on the payroll of the agency.

In the middle of this world that Chuffy had recreated, Margot shone like a sun. She had begun to grow into this role from that very first afternoon when he took her to Brighton races. Her narrow, respectable background dropped away from her, as forgotten and invisible as the butterfly's abandoned chrysalis. She became an accomplished horsewoman and an expert on gardens by being well taught and working hard; she became a wonderful hostess by the purest instinct. Usually together, they appeared often in the pages of the *Tatler* and *Queen*. It would have been hard to say which was prouder of the other. Persephone was not at all neglected. They badly wanted a boy.

The second girl was born in 1960; the name Ramona was almost inevitable. They hid their disappointment and struggled to play fair. Another Persephone would have consoled them for the child's sex, but another Persephone was too much to hope for. The little thing tried, all right; she was dogged; she was dull. Persephone had always done everything gracefully without visible effort; Ramona battled on, bumping into things. One reason for this was a natural awkwardness, a graceless clumsiness; another was that she had very bad eyesight. Thick glasses did not improve her, but they did not detract from her as much as they would have from a prettier child.

When the son finally arrived, the celebrations went on for weeks.

People said that Gregory Plante never really recovered from that party. He did begin to look different. He still came occasionally to Garston, but looking more and more different. The rest of his hair fell out, he put on a lot of weight, and he was a great worry to Ramona, his wife. He took to his bed in the summer of 1965, and died quietly a year later. The Charnleys genuinely mourned him – he had been a good friend to them, in spite of his blindness to the magnificence of thoroughbred racing as a sport and as a business.

The effect on his widow was curious. It came in two contradictory stages, an immediate effect and a delayed effect. The immediate effect was most warmly welcomed by the Charnleys – she came often to Garston, where she found comfort. There was a particular value in her visits – she took her little namesake off everybody else's hands. Perhaps she was sorry for her clumsy, half-blind god-daughter; perhaps she saw in her merits which nobody else could see. At any rate, they were very close. It was all a very good thing, an excellent thing, and it boded well for the future.

When she arrived for her third or fourth visit after she was widowed, in the autumn of 1966, she brought a present for her god-daughter different from any she had brought before, and, from her, surprising. She brought a dog for little Ramona, a four-month-old Tibetan spaniel puppy, a pretty little dog almost entirely white, with a tan face and a tan patch over his quarters. The child adored him immediately and extravagantly, and was actually surprisingly good with him. She called him Hector, a good name, a hero's name and an easy word to shout. As far as possible, they made Hector into Ramona's personal dog. They encouraged her to be responsible for him. She fed him and exercised him, and she tried to house-train him, and to teach him not to chew the furniture. He was universally

40

affectionate, even to a fault, but there was no doubt that Ramona was the centre of his universe. When she lay on her back on the lawn, he climbed on her chest, and licked her face until her spectacles were entirely opaque with saliva. Everybody laughed to see this. It was very good for the child. It had been very kind and clever of the old lady.

That was her last visit to Garston. As the weather got colder, she said she could not face another winter in England; and every corner she turned, everywhere she went, she came face to face with memories of Gregory. She went out to Menton to join her sister. In the short term, it was a great loss to her little namesake. In the long term, it would make no difference at all.

There were two tragedies the following year, within weeks of one another, one large but far away, the other small but in their midst. The large tragedy was the death from pneumonia of Chuffy's mother. She was only seventy-three, but she had been living for many years as unhealthy a life as her small income afforded. The Charnleys worked hard at feeling solemn, but all their memories of her made it difficult. The sufferer was her sister, who was determined to stay in France, but who was now really lonely. The other tragedy, much smaller, hit much harder. Ramona's beloved Hector was run over by a tractor in the farmyard. If the tractor-driver was to blame, he was only a very little to blame. The dog was an exuberant little creature; he had been running after some hens with the object of making friends with them.

It was probably unfortunate that Ramona should have been there, witness of the whole thing. One might have expected her – any young child – to scream hysterically, at least to burst into tears. But she went into a kind of trance. She stared and stared at the tractor-driver, who was trying to say how sorry he was; and afterwards she would never talk about Hector at all. She buried him, all on her own; nobody knew where, and she never said.

Two years later, at the age of ten, Ramona went to her first boarding school. She had not said one word about Hector; she had refused her father's offer of another dog.

That was the year Ramona Plante married her French-man. She was just seventy, he, by all accounts, a little younger. If it ended her loneliness, and if he was a decent fellow, it was something to be welcomed. The letter with the news that arrived at Garston gave them a *fait accompli*. By the time they got the letter, the new Madame Meurice and her husband had set off on a trip round the world.

Ramona got the news during her first term at school. She had got over the first and worst agonies of homesickness. The teachers were kind and the girls mostly friendly, and there were almost as many things to do as there were at Garston. 'You'll *never* guess what's happened,' wrote her mother. Indeed Ramona would never have guessed. She found the whole thing blankly incredible. Her great-aunt, her godmother, a widow, who had seemed immemorially old ever since Ramona's first memories of her . . . that was not the sort of person who got *married*. In all the stories she had ever read, it was young girls who got married.

Full of her astonishing news, she told the other girls about it. They were sympathetic but depressing.

'My Ma's cousin has a friend whose mother did exactly the same thing,' said one girl. 'They were hoping for a dollop when she died, but they didn't get a bean. French law says that when a wife dies her husband gets everything. Even if she's got a family. He can give them something if he wants to, but he hasn't got to.'

'Poor Ramona,' said another girl. 'I expect your great-aunt's married some beastly little hairdresser.'

'A lifeguard on the beach,' said another girl.

'There aren't any lifeguards on the beach at Menton.'

'Yes, there are.'

'I've been there. I was there last summer.'

'I've been there too. The summer before last. Lifeguards all over the beach. More lifeguards than people swimming.'

'Not one single, solitary trace of a lifeguard.'

The disputants began fighting. It was not a serious fight. They fell apart, giggling. Ramona's great-aunt's indiscretion was forgotten, except by Ramona. She thought the girl who said she knew about French law had probably got it wrong.

Young as she was, Ramona was at about this time introduced, by a perceptive English teacher, to those parts of the greatest literature which she was capable of understanding. The teacher tried her on *The Pickwick Papers*. Ramona understood a good deal of it. She read it in bits all the rest of that term, and at the end of term she took it home with her. It opened doors into places she had not known existed. Her mother read books, but Ramona thought they were not like this book. Her father was too busy or too tired to read about anything except racing. She began to wonder, for the very first time, if there might be important things in the world that her parents knew nothing about.

It was just as well, even at that kindly little school, that she had the consolation of literature. She was hopeless at games, all games, because of her eyesight and her way of bumping into things and falling over her feet.

These things were touched on in Ramona's school reports, which were much unlike Persephone's school reports. Persephone left school with no academic distinctions and no need of them. She was beautiful, the predictable daughter of her parents. She sometimes went racing with her father, who showed her off proudly. She spent a generous dress allowance with a daring which sometimes startled her mother. She spent a year between Lausanne and Florence, during which she hardly spoke a word of French or Italian. She came back to 'come out'.

The merry-go-round of debutante dances and the London season was supposed to be dead. Nobody would have known it who saw Persephone's dance, at Garston, in the Goodwood week of 1972. Ramona, of course, was not there. She heard a lot about it later, and saw a lot of photographs. That was the year she went on to her new school, her main school, following Persephone there. The staff hid their surprise that she was Persephone's sister.

Her season finished, Persephone went on the payroll of the Beeswing Bloodstock Agency. She had a roving commission. She travelled everywhere. It was supposed that she looked at horses and reported to headquarters; that was what the Inspector of Taxes was invited to believe.

A shocking thing happened the following year, during the Christmas holidays. Ramona, now fourteen, had just come home from school, a depressing sight, blinking through pebble-spectacles, dumpy in her winter clothes. She was up at the farm, seeing somebody about something. The home farm tractor-driver was backing a load of firewood, on its way to the big house, across the farmyard. Ramona was nearby, but not right on the spot. She did not see what happened. The tractor-driver's cottage was hard by the farmyard. His wife was out of the house, hanging washing on a line between apple-trees on the far side. They had a baby daughter, not yet walking but a vigorous crawler. The baby somehow clambered out of her play-pen in the cottage kitchen, and crawled out of the cottage and into the farmyard. She crawled under the wheels of the reversing trailer. The driver saw nothing, because of the load of firewood in the trailer behind him. He felt nothing, because tractor and trailer were bouncing anyway on the pot-holed surface of the farmyard. The first he knew about it was Ramona's scream. She had come round the corner and seen not the accident but its aftermath. It was hard to recognise the baby as a baby, after the loaded trailer had been over her first backwards and then forwards.

It was hard to blame anybody, but the tractor-driver and his wife in agony blamed themselves.

There was another death, in February. Great-Aunt Ramona, Mme Meurice, died in her husband's arms in Tahiti, where they lived for three months of the year.

Her godchild's schoolfriend was right about French law. Every effort was made to contact M. Meurice, but as soon as he had buried his wife he disappeared from Tahiti and from his old haunts in Menton. He took with him the number of the bank-account in Zurich and the keys of the safe-deposit boxes. He was never heard of again, and nor was any of the money or the jewellery.

44

It was not clear to her parents if Ramona quite took in how savage a blow this was. To spell it out for her would have been unnecessary cruelty. They contented themselves with cursing the vanished M. Meurice; it was all they could do.

Life had to go on. The following spring, when she was twenty-two, Persephone brought home a tall young man called Harold Stagg. Chuffy's enquiries were immediate and the results satisfactory. Harry Stagg had been at Winchester and Christ Church, he had won a half-blue for squash, he was a member of Boodle's, and he was a merchant banker with a golden future. The engagement was announced in *The Times*, and nobody was the slightest bit surprised.

Ramona picked up one of the extension telephones, intending to ring up a school-friend to ask her to stay. The telephone was in use – somebody was talking on one of the other extensions. Ramona heard Persephone's voice. Persephone was talking about bridesmaids.

'Your little sister, I suppose?' said the voice that was not Persephone's.

'You must be dotty,' said Persephone. 'Absolutely raving bananas.'

Ramona hung up as quietly as she could.

The wedding matched the dance of four years before. There were a lot of bridesmaids, ravishing girls in filmy, romantic dresses designed by Persephone. Harry was posted to Hong Kong that winter, by which time Persephone had started a baby.

Patrick had in the meantime started at Eton, though some people who knew him were surprised that he got in.

In the meantime, also, Ramona had sat her O-Levels, and had done as well as anybody expected. She did well in the English Literature paper. But there was hardly time for anybody to talk about it, that summer at Garston, with the excitement of Persephone's wedding and of Patrick going off to Eton.

Margot had another preoccupation, that year and the next: her husband's health. He was still working like a

45

demon. It was still a one-man band – his junior partner, as everybody knew, was simply a messenger-boy. People wondered how flesh and blood could have stood thirty years of such self-driving, such demoniac energy. Brandy was one answer, much more of it than a few years previously, too much of it.

Ramona was about to sit her A-Levels when she was called into a teacher's study to be given the news.

Her father had just come home from Newbury races, a long and tiring drive after a long and tiring day. He was going upstairs, carrying a glass of brandy. He was running upstairs because he wanted a bath so badly. He collapsed on the top step, and rolled all the way down to the bottom. He was dead when he came to rest at the foot of the stairs.

Ramona was sent home at once, feeling herself surrounded by a fog of earnest kindness. She found Patrick already there, silent, his face pinched. Their mother was being brave and competent, with the doctor and with the telephone. Ramona saw what it was costing her to speak calmly and behave rationally.

The cremation was private – the three of them, and the longest-serving servants. The casket of ashes was buried in the churchyard on the most beautiful day of the year. There would be a memorial service later, to be announced, in one of the big London churches.

At this time of shock and numbness, of incredulity and despair, Garston ministered to their spirits. To Ramona's, to her mother's, even to Patrick's.

The accountant came, grave faced. He had only recently taken over the clients of his retired senior partner, which included the Charnley family and the Beeswing Agency. He had not had time to make himself familiar with their affairs, until this crisis obliged him to read a great many papers very quickly.

He spelled it all out, because it had to be spelled out. He did it as gently as he could. He tried to hide his anger that a successful man could have been so supremely improvident, so incredibly selfish and thoughtless.

The first thing to get clear was that neither Garston nor

anything in it was the personal property of the deceased. It was owned by the agency. House, garden, pool, farm, stable were the property of the agency. Furniture, pictures, curtains and carpets, silver and glass, clothes and jewels were the property of the agency.

The second thing to be clear about was that, in the certain knowledge of everybody, there was no Beeswing Bloodstock Agency without Major Dermot Charnley. He had breathed all its life into it; with his death it ceased to exist.

The third thing to be clear about was that from its inception he had not owned the agency. Having no capital, he had sought and found investment. The people who had started him in business in 1946, or their heirs, were owners of the agency. They were owners of Garston and its contents, and Mrs Charnley's furs and jewels, and Ramona's dinghy on the lake, and all the cars. Major Charnley had lived, in effect, in his country office which was paid for as such. He had given himself such salary as he needed for small change.

And the fourth thing to be clear about was that he had no life insurance. Time and time again he had meant to get around to it. Margot knew that, because he had talked about it. The accountant knew, because his partner had talked about it. And then, when he started to do something about it, the telephone would ring from Newmarket, or somebody would have news of stallion nominations for sale privately, or a man from Lexington would come in . . .

The implications of all this seemed to fall on all their heads like sandbags stuffed with lead.

CHAPTER THREE

Persephone's letter arrived the day after the accountant's visit. Her husband's head office in London had sent the news to Hong Kong by Telex. Persephone would have telephoned immediately, but the company would not have paid for the call. She thought none of them would want to be bothered with telephone calls, when they must have been so shattered and there must have been so much to do.

Persephone's letter was very long, which was unlike her. Her mother gave much of the morning to it. There were a thousand things to do, but what she did was read the letter.

Persephone wrote about her own feelings, and what she knew must be her mother's and brother's and sister's feelings. She sent all kinds of messages from her husband, expressing condolence in acceptable terms.

She said that the last thing she wanted to seem, at such a moment, was grabby, but that it was rather important that they knew how they stood. She had remained after her marriage on the payroll of the Beeswing Bloodstock Agency, and had been for the previous eighteen months, as she supposed her mother knew, its Hong Kong representative. Her retainer in this capacity was hardly more than a retainer – which was something she had been intending to write to her father about – but it was rather important to them. ('Rather important' was a phrase much used by

Persephone in her letter, the 'rather' sometimes underlined and sometimes not.) Of course she might have earned commission additionally, but she had not, in the event, bought or sold or imported any horses. With a young child she had hardly had time for business, and it was necessary for her to entertain and to be seen in public. In any case the established bloodstock agents, British and Chinese, local and international, had secured a stranglehold on horse-dealing which was monstrous and unfair and restrictive and unethical and achieved by bribery, and a newcomer to the business, however brilliantly connected, hadn't a hope. The point was, that it was rather important to them that the agency continued to pay her the retainer, and it ought to be a rather larger retainer.

The cost of living in Hong Kong was terribly high, and she had to dress well and entertain. She had to have a Nanny for the child. She thought another baby had started, although it was too early to be certain. This was unexpected and thoroughly unwelcome, especially as all kinds of medical attention was terribly expensive and the company didn't help as much as they had been led to understand it would.

Another thing was that Harry had been expecting the promotion he so richly deserved, but somebody in London had been intriguing behind everybody's back and it was the Night of the Long Knives and typical of some of the people at Head Office and it would be at least another year.

So, though not wishing to sound grabby, they were a bit anxious to know how much to expect from the will, not that there was any screaming hurry, really, but it was rather important that they should start planning how to invest it, because they wanted capital growth as well as income, although Persephone had to say that the income was rather important to them too.

It was a difficult letter to reply to. Margot postponed replying to it.

*

The deceased's Executors were Lord Horndean and a lawyer called Spence. They had expected a complicated task, unravelling the personal estate from the affairs and property of the Beeswing Agency. But their task was simple. There was no personal estate. After the announcements in the papers, the cremation, and other expenses, the estate was a few hundred pounds in debt.

The accountant, who was titularly Company Secretary of the agency, faced the business of tracing the original investors in the firm. That task was simple, too – they traced him. A few had been succeeded as part proprietors of the agency by their heirs; most were alive, vigorous, and fully in possession of their faculties. None had had the least idea that the business – their business – had so entirely financed the splendours of Garston, and the lavish hospitality which they had all so much enjoyed. They would not have enjoyed it nearly so much if they had known they were paying for it. They would not have permitted Chuffy to take them for such a very long and very expensive ride. They blamed themselves for gullibility, for having trusted the manifestly untrustworthy, for assuming that because a fellow dressed and spoke like a gentleman, he managed his affairs like a gentleman.

There were a good many angry conversations on racecourses and in London clubs. They stoked one another's anger. There was a revulsion of feeling against Major Dermot Charnley. The position taken, almost unanimously, was that there must be an immediate sale and distribution of all the agency's assets.

The situation of widow and children was sometimes mentioned. What about them? They had been living for years and years off the fat of somebody else's land. It was perfectly certain that Margot had salted something away. It was certain that Chuffy had diverted some of the agency's turnover into provision for them all. The boy would have to leave Eton? He should never have gone to Eton if his father wasn't prepared to pay his own bills. One of the girls was married to a merchant banker. She was all right. The other was – what? – eighteen? Then she could go out

50

and get a job. They'd all been paying for her to have the most expensive education in the country. Now she could put it to some use.

Somebody, even so, suggested a whip-round. The idea was not popular.

Ramona and Patrick could both finish their terms at school, since the fees had been paid in advance. Ramona could sit her A-Levels. It was pointless her doing so. The crucial period of the run-up to the examinations had been too hopelessly disrupted. She was too shocked to revise properly, to concentrate, to do herself justice. And her mother needed her at home. Surveyors were prodding at the fabric of the house and sniffing at the drains, and men from the auctioneers were listing everything that had a value, down to kitchen spoons and stacks of firewood.

Patrick refused to go back to school. This was not because he felt any duty to help his mother, whom, in the absence of his father, he blamed for the mess they were in. It was because most of his particular friends were the sons of racehorse owners, and all of them would know all about everything. They would feel, and show, pity and contempt. Patrick wanted pity. He deserved more pity than anybody else in the entire world. But if the pity was going to be mixed with contempt, he was not going to subject himself to it. He went and sat in a boat on the lake, until the boat was taken away to be sold.

For a time they lived among ever-increasing gaps, in the rooms and on the walls. The gaps were horribly noticeable; there were patches pale or stained, where pictures and sofas had been. The house was having its teeth drawn. It looked shabby, as a toothless face falls in on itself. A lot of people came and were taken round. Many said how much would need to be done. Ramona had thought that nothing had needed to be done, but as the rooms grew barer more and more warts showed.

51

Latterly they were camping, restricted to servants' bedrooms and part of the kitchen.

Some money was scraped together from somewhere. Ramona did not know how much it was, or where it came from, and her mother was reluctant to talk about it. Perhaps some of the original investors had after all relented; perhaps there had been a whip-round; perhaps some personal savings had crept out onto the surface from somewhere. At any rate, it was just enough money to make sense of house-hunting, provided they set their sights low enough in the house they hunted. Margot sometimes took Ramona. They travelled almost entirely by bus – the cars had gone, and trains were expensive. Unfortunately, the sensational rise in property values had already happened – a cottage which would have cost £5,000 in 1960 was already £40,000 or £50,000 in 1978, as more and more executives had second homes in the country, and as more and more of England was served by motorways. Humbly, realistically as she thought, Margot had visualised some-thing like her father's cottage on the outskirts of Hove. The wheel would have come full circle. After the blazing years, a return to the dim fringe. Well, it had been toler-able then; it could be tolerable again. It was a shock to find that a cottage like her father's was now far out of reach.

Any country cottage of which they could afford the purchase price needed money spending on it which they did not have. They were committed to a suburb, to the working-class fringe of a provincial town, to a four-roomed semi-detached or terrace house in a street near a gasworks or a railway station.

It was weary work, going up and down the cramped stairs of all those dark little mid-Victorian houses. There was hardly one without damp patches on the walls of the bedrooms. There was hardly one in which electric light would not be needed, in the kitchen, at noon in midsummer.

Patrick never came on these expeditions. He seemed not to believe in anything that was going on round him. When Ramona and his mother came back, from Reading or Watford or Swindon, he listened incredulous, uncomprehending, to their accounts of the houses they had looked at. It was not possible that what they described should be his home. It was not in the order of things. Something had gone temporarily wrong; God would put it right again. The family was rich and popular; his mother and sister were gibbering.

Ramona thought her mother was showing amazing courage. She herself began to get backache from the angle of the seats of all those buses.

Time was running out. They had the roof of Garston over their heads only until it was sold. An American electronics company was the front-runner among the prospective purchasers; it would use the house for sales-training courses; they were pleased with the pool, the tennis-court and the lake, which they called a pond; they said to one another, in Margot's hearing, that a lot would have to be done to the place.

The place the Charnleys finally found was a lot less terrible than most of the places they had seen. The town was called Bilborough, forty miles from London. There was a Bilborough Industrial Estate and a main-line station. There was some long-established local industry – glass, leather, canned food. There was a lot of new building, both commercial and residential. The new houses were little yellow boxes set in handkerchief gardens, and they were far too expensive for the Charnleys. There were old houses, too, not altogether charmless, on the London Road and the Oxford Road. A lot of them were for sale. The one they picked was in Brewster Terrace, a steep little street which joined the London Road at a roundabout. There was a big garage on the roundabout. The nearest shops were only half a mile away, a grocer and a newsagent, little places like village shops. Buses went along the London Road to the middle of the town where the supermarkets were.

The house was Number 53, third of a row of seven of which the middle one, their neighbour, had a carved stone let into the brick over the front door reading 1882. The seven formed a terrace which climbed the hill, each house a couple of feet higher than the one next below. They were built of dark red brick, with slate roofs. Number 53 was the only one of the seven for sale, which constituted a kind of advertisement.

The kitchen was dark and the stairs were narrow. Those were things you had to accept, in their price-range. The previous owner had died within a day or two of Chuffy's death. He had been a retired bus-conductor. Margot and Ramona heard about his life and character at greater length than one would have supposed a retired bus-conductor could have afforded. He had been a great handyman. Though money had been short, effort had not, nor skill. The house was accordingly painted and papered to a pretty high standard, though the colours and patterns would not have been everybody's choice. There was a little paved front yard, and twenty feet of spick-and-span garden behind. The bus-conductor's widow was sorry to leave the garden, which was full of memories for her; but she was off to live with her married daughter in Southsea.

They had not been on close terms with any of their near neighbours. Some were too stuck up to know them, and some were too rough for them to know. Here were the names of the doctor and a plumber and an electrician, but you were lucky if you got them round within six weeks. You might be drowning or electrocuted. The Co-op dairy came along. There wasn't a butcher, fishmonger or green-grocer nearer than the middle of the town, Market Street, nice shops there, everything you wanted.

'I wonder what Patrick will make of it,' said Ramona.

'There's bound to be a school for him in a town this size,' said her Mother. 'I expect he'll learn just as much, as soon as he gets used to it.'

They got a bus in the London Road, back to the bus-station in the centre. With two changes they got back, late and exhausted, to what had been home. To Patrick they were cheerful about the little house. Solid. Well-built. Clean. Convenient. Not ugly, really. A garden. They were lucky to have found it. It was worth all the trailing about they had done, to have found a house that would suit them so well.

Patrick was hardly listening. He was not taking any of it in. He did not believe he was going to live in a four-roomed terraced cottage on the edge of Bilborough.

The major contents of Garston had all gone to the London auction houses, to be included in important sales of English eighteenth-century furniture, silver, sporting pictures, and the other categories. The bits and pieces came under the local auctioneer's hammer, on the premises. Some dealers had come to view, and, having viewed, had not bothered to attend the auction. A curious crowd of locals came. There was spirited bidding for power mowers, garden tools, electric mixers, sets of saucepans. People filled the boots of their cars with incongruous fragments of the Charnleys' lives. A fair amount of junk was unsold. A junior Chartered Surveyor was present, with a watching brief on behalf of the owners of what had been the Beeswing Bloodstock Agency. He looked with gloom at the furniture from the servants' bedrooms, unsold, which was piled higgledy-piggledy in the stable yard.

He said, 'It'll have to be a bonfire, I suppose. What would be the best place?'

Margot said, 'We'll take it.'

That solved the immediate problem of furnishing Number 53 Brewster Terrace.

Persephone's reply arrived, to her mother's reply to her own original letter. Allowing for the bitterness of her disappointment, it was wrong of her to write so savagely of betrayal, selfishness, fraud. It was clear that she did not believe what her mother had told her. Mother, brother and sister had cheated her because they were on the spot

55

and she was the other side of the world. They expected to be double-crossed by sharks in Head Office in London, but Persephone had supposed that she could trust her own family. If they thought she was going to sit down under that they were very much mistaken. She was going to take legal advice, and write some other letters, and they could expect big trouble.

On top of the auction on the premises, Persephone's letter was more than Margot could bear. She broke down, for the very first time. She sobbed, noisily, helplessly, a dry, ugly, heartrending sound. Ramona tried to comfort her. She did not want Ramona's comfort. She wanted the clock turned back. She railed, for the very first time, against Chuffy's unbelievable selfishness. She was all right in the morning. They pretended it had not happened.

The furniture went in an open lorry, since neither the size nor the facilities of a pantechnicon were in the least needed. The lorry was cheap; it belonged to an obliging local builder, who was picking up something from somewhere. He owed the Charnleys a large part of his present prosperity; he even considered, for a moment, letting them have the use of the lorry free.

The Charnleys went by bus. On the way to the first of the buses which accomplished the journey, Patrick turned in the lodge gates and had a long last look at Garston. He did not say a word then, or any word throughout the journey. He walked with them up Brewster Terrace, up the hill to Number 53, carrying his suitcase.

'Here we are, darling,' said Margot brightly. 'We'll be as snug as bugs in rugs.'

'Not me,' said Patrick. 'I'm not living here.'

'Darling, what can you mean?'

'I am not living here.'

'It's not what any of us would have chosen. It's what we've got, and we're very lucky to have it. It's your home. It's the only home you've got.'

'It's not a home I've got.'

'Patrick, you have no choice!'

'Of course I have a choice. I don't choose this.'

'Where else can you go?'

'I might hitch to London. I'll get hold of some money. I might go abroad. I don't care where I go, as long as it's not here.'

He turned, and started back down the hill with his suitcase.

Margot raised both her arms towards his receding back. She opened her mouth to call out to him. She closed it again.

'Keep in touch with us!' she screamed after him. 'For pity's sake keep in touch!'

Patrick paused and turned. 'How can I?' he said. 'I don't know the address.'

Ramona woke up with a jerk, as some movement in her sleep caused a spring to jab her in the backside. She was sprawled in an armchair; she was fully dressed, with a dressing-gown over her clothes. For a moment she was completely puzzled. She remembered. She was full of remembered anger, and of a new anger because she was stiff and cold. She groped on the floor beside the chair for her spectacles – she was frightened to cross the room in the dark to turn on the light in case she stepped on them. She had a moment of panic. Normally they would have been safe on her bedside table. Rage drove out panic – it was intolerable, obscene, that she should be reduced to groping in the dark for her glasses on the threadbare carpet of the Common Room.

Her hands trembled with rage at her humiliation and her helplessness. She could do nothing until she found her spectacles. Trembling, her fingers brushed the wire frame. Even in the dark, with her spectacles on her nose she felt better able to deal with things. She got stiffly up out of the chair, and groped her way across the room to the writing-table. Her back was hurting from sleeping in the armchair. She bumped into the table. Groping, she knocked over the reading-lamp. In the absolute silence the noise was shocking. She stood, aghast, listening for shouts and running feet.

She righted the lamp and switched it on. She looked at her watch; it was just after six. She could safely stay in the Common Room for another hour: but if she did that she must on no account fall asleep again. She might easily do so, because she had not had nearly enough sleep. If she sat down again, even in that awful chair, she would probably drift off. She ought to have brought down her alarm-clock as well as a blanket. The thought of her attic bedroom, with the saturated pillow and mattress, was intolerable. But she thought she had better go there.

She was half way in the weary climb to her room, when an idea came to her so obvious that only extreme fatigue could have stopped it coming before. She went back to the door of the Common Room and to the small lobby beside it where the teaching staff hung their coats. She could lie on her raincoat as though it were a rubber sheet.

Rubber sheets were a hateful memory. The stairs were steeper than ever before.

The electric fire had not fully dried the bottom sheet and under-blanket, and the mattress and pillow felt as wet as ever. The raincoat was not comfortable to lie on – it felt as hard as a sheet of metal, and buttons seemed to be everywhere. Rolled up clothes made an uncomfortable pillow. The wonderful idea was not much good – she had been better in the Common Room chair. She dozed a little, lightly, constantly woken by discomfort. She was thankful to hear, far away and below, the electric bell that roused the school.

During breakfast in the dining hall she was aware of giggling. Rosalind Tuck and Amanda Loring were giggling. There was no teacher at their table. Hilda Joy should have been there, but she often missed breakfast. All the girls at the table turned to look at Ramona, including some that

58

Ramona thought of as nice girls. Many of the girls giggled. Perhaps the nice ones were not so nice, after all.

Marigold Kent was the only person Ramona dared confide in, thc only person whose advice she wanted. She told her in a whisper, in a corner of the Common Room, as they drank instant coffee in the eleven-o'clock break.

'You can't be completely sure it was her,' said Marigold.

'Oh Marigold, haven't you been listening? Of course I'm sure.'

'Not so as to satisfy dear Gwyneth. Not so as to satisfy Hilda.'

'Are you suggesting that I let that little toad get away with it completely?'

'Do you want the whole school to know that your bed was wet?'

'Oh.'

'That really will let you in for some persecution.'

'Oh my God,' said Ramona.

Hilda Joy glanced up, shocked.

Supper, two days later. The smallest children, Ramona's children, were already in bed. Eight-year-olds and upwards were eating something brownish. The noise was tremendous, ninety girls between eight and eighteen jabbering at one another and clattering their forks on their plates. Ramona was in charge, obedient to the duty roster pinned up on the notice-board in the Common Room. As it happened, it was her first spell of supervising the bigger girls since the Evening Study Period of three days previously.

Most of the maids had already gone away in the minibus with Norman the odd-job-man. A skeleton staff remained, assisted with shrieks and breakages by the girls whose turn it was. (It was part of the philosophy of the Malham House School, as spelled out in the prospectus and as explained by the Headmistress to prospective parents, that the girls

59

looked after themselves and one another, as far as was possible without prejudice to their academic achievement. It encouraged self-reliance; it taught them to be useful and caring members of a community; it saved the school several thousand pounds a year.) One of the domestics remaining was a slow-moving, muddy-skinned girl called Maureen Maynard; she was infinitely willing and educationally subnormal. She might have been picked on, in the way of sport, by some of the very nastiest pupils; Ramona could imagine a scene like the bear-baiting she had read about. This had not in fact happened, or only to an extent so minor that Maureen had not noticed. It remained a possibility, even a probability.

Maureen, trudging backwards and forwards between the dining-hall and the kitchen, found a parcel which somebody had put down somewhere. She brought it into the dining-hall. It was about the size of a shoe-box, neatly wrapped in brown paper and with a label stuck to the top. Maureen stared uncomprehending at the typewritten words on the label. A girl helped her. The label was addressed to Miss Ramona Charnley, Malham House School. There was no stamp or postmark; the parcel had been delivered by hand; it was impossible to guess how it had found its way to the kitchen passage.

Maureen delivered the package to Ramona, as though she herself had bought the contents and they were the crown jewels.

In her three years at Malham, Ramona had received five letters. The most recent of these had been eighteen months before. She had never received any parcel.

She took the parcel from Maureen, thanking her. She stared at it in perplexity. She became aware that silence had fallen in the dining-hall. The jabbering was stilled; no forks were clattering on plates. Everyone was sitting quietly; everyone was looking at her, waiting for her to open her parcel.

It was not so very extraordinary. Other people got parcels. Some of the girls seemed to get parcels by practically every post. Nobody was coy about opening parcels,

60

unless it was a girl who knew somebody was sending her some packets of cigarettes. Perhaps all the girls were so interested in Ramona's parcel because it had been mysteriously delivered by hand: perhaps because she had never before received a parcel.

She tore away the brown paper wrapping, and then some inner wrapping. She uncovered, amidst the torn paper, something that meant nothing to her. She could not understand what it was, what it could possibly be for, why she had been sent it. It was whitish, rubbery, folded. She shook it out and held it up.

It was a pair of pants, knickers, bloomers, voluminous, elasticised at the waist and legs, made of rubber.

The dining-hall exploded into a sudden, howling inferno of laughter.

In the midst of the howls of laughter, cutting through them or shrieked over them, words could be made out.

'The Moaner wets her bed. The Moaner's a bed-wetter.'

Ramona got up and stumbled out of the dining-hall. She wanted to stalk, but she stumbled. She was not at once blinded by tears. She stopped herself crying until she was almost at the door. The tears came just before she reached the door; they came in time to be seen by quite a lot of girls.

Ramona, her face puddled with tears, came face to face in the hall with the Headmistress.

'Whatever's the matter?' said Mrs Barrow. 'What on earth have you got there?'

Ramona realised that she was holding the rubber bloomers.

Rubber. That came later. There was nothing like that at first, at Number 53 Brewster Terrace.

Patrick went on down the hill. His mother and sister watched him in silence, until he disappeared round the corner at the bottom.

61

Soon the lorry came, with the unsaleable pile of junk which was their furniture. The driver, who was alone, needed their help to unload it. They piled it in the little yard in front of the house. It looked derelict, shameful, abject. Net curtains twitched in windows across the street. Their worldly goods were being scrutinised. Ramona wanted to stare arrogantly back – 'Yes, these are our belongings, what are you going to do about it?' – but she was too shy and too embarrassed.

The lorry-driver said he would have helped them get the stuff into the house, but he had to get on to pick up his load by tea-time.

It was not difficult carrying the gimcrack servants' furniture into the house, but it was very difficult getting beds and chests-of-drawers up the stairs. By the time they were done, Ramona's mother was speechless with fatigue.

Food. There was no food in the house. They had finished the sandwiches Ramona had made for the journey. Patrick had eaten his mother's. She had said she was not hungry. She was hungry now. Ramona went out, and along the London Road to the bus-stop. She took a bus into the middle of the town, where the nice shops were. It was early closing. All the shops were shut.

Margot had celebrated her fiftieth birthday in May of that year. She had seen no need to make any secret of reaching this awesome milestone – all their friends knew she was a grandmother, and she was a pretty good fifty in face and figure. She was often told so, and she knew it was true. She explained it by saying she had been spoiled rotten since her wedding-day, and that was also true. The very best in hairdressers, beauticians and health-farms was at her disposal, and she made full use of them all. (It was a necessary operating expense of the Beeswing Bloodstock Agency.)

She had kept house for her father, modestly but well above the poverty level. She had worked for two years in a Brighton bookshop, having nothing to do with ordering, stock-control or accounts. She had run Garston with a full complement of servants and a massive housekeeping allowance. She had chosen menus for dinner-parties, shrubs for herbacious borders, and clothes for her back. Beyond these things she had no qualifications at all. There was no job she could do. She was supremely unemployable. There was not the slightest point in her making the slightest effort to get any job. She would do the housework at Number 53, and try to remember how to cook. All this was as obvious to Ramona as it was to her mother.

Ramona was young, and she had some O-Levels. She was well read, and she knew something about some branches of painting and some of the more familiar parts of the classical music repertoire. There ought to be a job, in a place like Bilborough, that fitted these qualifications. There had better be. They needed the money, and they needed it at once.

The woman in the Labour Exchange was pessimistic. Typing and shorthand, double-entry book-keeping, basic computer programming, a Cordon Bleu cookery diploma, these things were passports to employment. It was very nice, no doubt, to know the names of the characters in *Vanity Fair*, to recognise the 'Pastoral' Symphony, to know a Herring from a Sartorius, but nobody paid you money for anything like that.

Typing and shorthand were taught at the Bilborough Polytechnic. It was too late to enrol there. She would have to wait another year, and then spend a year. There was no time. There was no way, in time, that she could learn any of the other things that might have made her employable. Immediate courses in anything, that she could have started next day, had to be paid for. There was no way she could pay to have herself taught anything.

Her mother had worked in a shop, a fact which Ramona only now discovered.

None of the shops in Bilborough were interested in a girl with thick spectacles and a lah-di-dah voice which would irritate the customers.

They were not starving. They desperately needed one

63

or two pieces of solid furniture. They needed more sauce-pans, and a vacuum cleaner. Since they could not afford the laundry, and the laundrette was too far to walk, they needed a washing machine. They could have none of these things until Ramona got a job.

Her mother had expected to shoulder the housekeeping part of their lives. But it was beyond her. She tried to scrub bath-towels on a washboard, and sweep the stairs on her knees with a dustpan and brush; she tried to shop sensibly, with a list, and bring everything back safely on the bus; she tried to remember how to cook cabbage, and heat milk without boiling it over, and choose the most economical cuts in the butcher's. But those Garston years had unfitted her for scrubbing, and cabbage, and buying ox-cheek. Exhausted from trailing about the town in search of a job, Ramona came back and did the housework.

She tried not to feel too thankful, too often, that Patrick had walked away down the hill.

Justin and Janey Bryan had taken over the Bilborough Bookshop in the spring. Janey's father had bought the lease and the goodwill, because he was fed up with having the two of them hanging about the house. Justin had had a bit of capital, with which he had started something called Polyp, a specialised publishing house which had stopped being able to pay the printers after three months of trading. Books were what Justin liked, which was fair enough. Justin was what Janey liked, which was simply extraordi-nary. There you were. A few thou was well spent, getting them off his back to the other end of England.

The Bilborough Bookshop, when they first went to suss it out, was full of what they had learned to call 'non-books'. Cookery spin-offs from TV series. Show-jumping for children. Indoor plants. The Princess of Wales in pictures. Paperback fiction could be ordered. Hardcover fiction unheard of. A local author might have been stocked, but there were no local authors. It was the only bookshop in Bilborough, except the newsagent on the station, and that only had Mills and Boon. It was not only a commercial opening, the Bryans agreed, it was also a kind of cultural duty, a quiet crusade, the filling of a need which people would find they were feeling the moment it was pointed out to them. Under this vibrant new management, an entirely different sort of stock was ordered from the publishers' reps.

Within two months, Janey asked for a bit more help from her father.

Within four months, cookery, show-jumping and indoor plants were back on the shelves, and the Princess of Wales filled the window.

Janey started her first baby, and they told her to keep her feet up. Justin hired a girl to take her place in the shop. She was a pretty little thing, willing and quite well-spoken. She was called Carol. Coming home to the flat in the evening, Justin reported that she seemed to be learning the ropes. Then he started coming home late, once or twice a week. He talked about stocktaking. Janey smelled a rat. She went round one evening. Justin and Carol were in the storeroom at the back, with a bottle of supermarket plonk, and Carol's sweater was round her neck. That was the end of Miss Carol, and it was nearly the end of Justin.

Janey said she'd choose the next assistant, and that it would be a man. This was not, in the event, practicable. No man would work for as little as a pound an hour, and they couldn't afford as much as a pound an hour. They reached an impasse. Janey, defying doctor's orders, spent an hour or two a day in the shop.

It was while she was there, one day in late September, that a funny little creature came in. Janey thought at first she wanted to buy a book. But she didn't. She wanted a job. She was small, about five foot two, her figure lumpy but not terrible, her clothes – a linen coat and skirt – surprisingly classy, well chosen and expensive. Her voice was classy, too. Janey had worked hard on her own voice, but she knew from kind friends that the Geordie twang was ineradicable. The girl wore thick spectacles, behind which gentle, pale-blue eyes swam like fish in twin bowls.

The girl was shy. She seemed frightened. Janey was not used to people being frightened of her, except Justin, and he was only frightened of her because he needed her father's money.

Janey hired Ramona Charnley to work full time in the Bilborough Bookshop for sixty pence an hour. She presented Justin with a *fait accompli*, and Justin was dutifully effusive.

Even Justin wouldn't be rolling that girl's sweater up to her neck.

'Your father first saw me in my bookshop,' said Margot. 'Perhaps history will repeat itself.'

'I bought some chops to celebrate,' said Ramona. 'They cost exactly three hours' work.'

CHAPTER FOUR

Sara Corderey the little new-girl, shy, frightened, miserably homesick, thought she was the only person in the dining-hall not screaming with laughter at the sight of those rubber knickers.

She had heard about the joke. It was impossible not to have heard about the joke. She did not understand why it was funny to say that someone wet their bed. It was not funny if they didn't, and it was even less funny if they did. Sara's little brother Thomas had been a bed-wetter, not often, when he was sleeping exceptionally deeply, when he was away from home or unhappy. He had almost died of shame and embarrassment, even though he was told that it was not really his fault, that it was something wrong with him that could be put right. It was just possible, Sara thought, that being in a new place, among strangers, being in the parson's family in Dorset, might upset poor little Thomas enough to start him off again. They might not understand. They might be disgusted, and punish him, which would be cruel and pointless.

Miss Charnley, The Moaner, was being punished, although she had not done anything, and it was cruel and pointless, and not funny in the least.

Sara had to pretend to laugh. She had to wear that much protective coloration, conform to that extent. To sit among all the others, not laughing, would have been begging for trouble. It did Miss Charnley no extra harm, Sara pretending to laugh. It was something she dared not not do, to be normal, to be like the others. She was enough of a freak as it was, being younger than the rest of the form, but ahead of all but Colette Davies in most subjects, being physically a late developer, being still a little girl when they were almost grown-up as far as their bodies were concerned. There was no sign, after more than three weeks of the term, that the form was beginning to accept her. There was no sign of anybody wanting to be her friend. Everybody else had somebody they whispered to and went for walks with. Some people had gangs of whisperers and walkers. Rosalind Tuck, who was so beautiful, had been in the school exactly the same length of time as Sara had, and she was always surrounded. When she said anything, everybody listened and laughed. Nobody listened to anything Sara said, so she never said anything.

They spoke about her, when they could be bothered to, as the White Mouse. They did not address her by this name, saying 'White Mouse', because none of them ever talked to her at all. She would not have cared what they called her, if only somebody had sometimes said something to her.

Sara thought it was just possible for somebody to be more miserable than she was. She thought Miss Charnley, The Moaner, was more miserable than she was.

Ramona told her story to the Headmistress, there in the corridor outside the dining-hall. The gales of laughter from the dining-hall subsided slowly, slowly. The Headmistress would go in there to restore the full rigour of discipline after she had heard Ramona's account.

Ramona had contrived to stop crying. It was ridiculous to cry because somebody had played a stupid practical joke. Rubber pants were nothing to cry about. Ramona told her story in a flat voice, telling the exact truth, making sure that the Headmistress understood that Rosalind Tuck had felt herself defeated, humiliated in front of her friends.

Ramona finished. She forced herself to look up, to look

68

the Headmistress in the eye. She wished very much that she was not still holding the rubber pants, but, since she had hold of them, there was for the moment nothing else she could do with them.

The Headmistress looked down at Ramona. Her face was kind and sympathetic. She nodded her head many times very quickly. It was evident to Ramona that the Headmistress understood exactly what had happened, and would do something about it.

'Tell me, dear,' said the Headmistress, in a gentler voice than any Ramona had ever heard her use. 'Has this happened before? Is there a history of it?'

'Of what?'

'Of bed-wetting.'

They settled into a routine, Ramona and her mother, at Number 53 Brewster Terrace. On weekdays, of course, they were only together first thing in the morning and in the evening. Neither was a talker in the morning. They would both have preferred coffee, but they had tea for breakfast because it was cheaper. In the evening, every evening, they were both numb with fatigue. Ramona was exhausted by hours in the bookshop, on her feet nearly all the time – there was nowhere to sit properly; you could only perch; and Janey Bryan was against anybody sitting down even to write out a bill. She was exhausted by doing the shopping in her lunch-hour, which usually meant that she missed her lunch which she could in any case not afford. She looked forward to eating a sandwich in the little park behind the bus-station, six months on when the weather was warmer. It was not possible to sit in the park that November. Ramona's mother was exhausted by trying to do things which she was no longer capable of doing. Her failure to get the dust out of the stair-carpet was as exhausting as her efforts to do so.

Ramona greeted such neighbours as she saw, morning and evening. She got monosyllables or nods or nothing. She and her mother might have seemed stuck-up, because

69

of their voices, or too rough to talk to, because of the shameful furniture the whole street had seen. The effect was the same. Ramona persisted, thinking it might be simply a question of time before they were accepted as residents of the street, thinking that the day might come when friendly neighbours would be important. She persisted out of a certain defiance, which she was surprised to find in herself. Her mother did better, or said she did. She reported long chats with Mrs This and old Mrs That. In these chats, as retailed over supper to Ramona, there was no content whatever. Nothing was actually said on either side – no information or opinion was communicated. Dogs of doubtful temper sniffed at one another for a long time – that was what Ramona's mother's pavement conferences came to.

Most weekends, all that winter, Ramona devoted to the house. The bus-conductor's wilder extravagances of orange and turquoise were covered. As the house was so dark, it seemed sensible to paint most of it white. The cost of gloss paint was a shock.

Ramona usually grossed a little more or a little less than £30 a week, depending how much overtime she worked. Stamp and tax came out of that. What she took home fed them. She tried to save, for all the things she needed in the house, for the clothes they would need when the few they had wore out. It was just about impossible. Going anywhere was impossible. An evening out, a meal, television and telephone were impossible. Ramona found she could perfectly well do without any of these things. When she cried for the moon it was Garston she cried for, and a day trip to Oxford, a curry at the New Assam in the London Road, held no charm.

Occasionally she wondered if Persephone was having that second baby. Persephone had not written again, although Ramona had sent her their new address. It was quite likely, knowing Persephone, that she couldn't bring herself to write to such a dreadful address. It was likely that, since her family were no longer any use to her, she stopped bothering about them. Absence made the heart grow fonder if punctuated by regular remittances. Persephone had a hard streak.

Occasionally Ramona wondered about Patrick too, and her mother wondered out loud what had become of the boy. They both spoke of him, it seemed to Ramona, as though he were an acquaintance who had shared their lives for a time, and moved on unregretful and unregretted. It surprised Ramona how little it surprised her that her mother should talk like that. Feeling so little might be a defence against feeling too much, but Ramona thought not. She thought her mother was apathetic about Patrick. She was apathetic about the world news, the racing results, the stories Ramona brought home about comical customers in the book-shop. She was in a fair way to anaesthetising herself. Ramona wished it was a trick she could learn.

Sara Corderey's Aunt Jennifer wrote suggesting that she took Sara out for a day, any Sunday, if Sara would like that and the school rules permitted it.

Sara would indeed like it, although the prospect was slightly alarming. Jennifer Corderey was Sara's father's much older sister. She had been a teacher all her life, in China before the war and then in Barbados and Kenya. She had hardly seen her family in those years; she hardly knew Sara, and would probably not recognise her. She had just retired. She was at present house-sitting for a friend, who had gone to stay with her daughter in New Zealand leaving two Pekes and a canary. The house was only twenty miles from Malham, and she had the use of her friend's little car.

Sara would without hesitation recognise her aunt, although it was four years since she had seen her. Tall, with the leathery skin of years in the tropics, hair in an old-fashioned bun, tight and hard as a walnut on the back of her head, large feet in sensible shoes, and a huge invariable bag made of the skin of some Chinese animal. In the bag would be books, new and old, which formed Aunt Jennifer's principal and favourite topic of conversation. She wanted anyone she was with to have read them, or to be about to read them immediately – history, travel, biography, critical essays, and fiction if it was at least 120 years old. Sara at the age of ten had not, of course, been able to sustain a conversation on such lines. Aunt Jennifer had not expected her to; she had talked instead about her travels, the yellow and black and brown children she had introduced to the English classics, and Sara's own ambitions for her life. Now it would be different. Sara at fourteen might be expected to have read pretty widely, coming as she did from a literate family, being serious and precocious. Sara would be grilled about the reading she had done and the reading she planned to do. The prospect was a bit daunting.

It was much, much better than the other prospect, the dragging lonely hours of a boarding-school Sunday when nobody wanted to talk to you, or cared if you lived or died. Aunt Jennifer's lunch would probably be better, too.

Sara was by all means to bring a friend, if she wanted to, said Aunt Jennifer in her letter. That would have been nice, to have a bit of a buffer against the interrogation of Aunt Jennifer, to have someone else to be stared at by those beady old eyes. But it was impossible. Nobody would go out with Sara. Nobody would be prepared to admit to having done so.

Sara wrote at once, politely and correctly as she had been taught, on the crested school writing-paper, in her tidy and well-formed handwriting. She would very much like to come out for the day with Aunt Jennifer, and would be allowed to do so the Sunday after next. She could be collected at eleven, after Chapel. She did not have to be back until the seven o'clock Roll Call. She thought she would not bring a friend, because everybody already seemed to be doing something that day.

Ramona found a huge bunch of forgotten keys, on a nail in what had been the housekeeper's room beside the kitchen. She dragged it all the way up the stairs, and found to her gigantic relief that one of the keys fitted the lock of her bedroom door.

It made no difference that the maids would not be able to get in. The maids never went in anyway. The principles of self-help applied at Malham to the junior teaching staff as well as to the girls.

She bought herself a little peace, for the moment, in her bedroom.

She was still known throughout the school, most of the time, as The Moaner. She was also referred to as The Bedwetter, a nickname subject to variations, more or less disgusting. The girls knew she knew it.

Peace would not last. She was a target. The girls knew she knew that, too.

Her mattress and pillow seemed at last quite dry.

Except in the very worst weather, every girl in the school was supposed to be out of doors between two-thirty and four. There were organised games three times a week (there were even teams which went away in buses to play hockey and lacrosse against other schools); there were supervised walks for the younger girls; there were bird-spotting and botanising expeditions to a nearby marsh, a disused quarry, and other places of scientific interest. The older girls were allowed to wander pretty freely. It was well known in the Common Room, though apparently not to the Headmistress, that what some of the older girls did was find some shelter and smoke cigarettes. From time to time the shelter they found was discovered, and they were flushed out of it – an old stable-block some distance from the house, older cow-sheds, a deconsecrated chapel built by some ancient, pious owner of the estate. They found a new place, and smoked their cigarettes there. They were well used to it. None of them was ever sick.

It was not known for certain if, at that period, any or many of the girls had assignations with local youths. It was not known what happened between them if they did. There had been one pregnancy, long before Ramona's time, still spoken of with dismay. Somebody had come for the girl, who had gone off with an attempt at swagger. Nowadays, as Marigold Kent said, they were all too sophisticated to get into trouble. Probably they were on the pill, with or without the knowledge of their mothers. Boys came sometimes in the middle of the night, gangs on motorcycles, who gunned their machines and went round or over the circular lawn in the gravel in front of the house. Once or twice the police had had to come out. It was not thought that many of the girls consorted with the motorcycle gangs.

Any local youth who saw Rosalind Tuck would be round on his motorcycle in no time.

Ramona was not in the ordinary way sent to snoop round the stables, cowsheds or chapel to surprise the smokers in their den. What she did sometimes have to do was to go round the school, top to bottom, to eject any girl who was staying indoors when she should have been healthfully out. There were nearly always one or two lurking somewhere, lazy girls, girls who hated fresh air and exercise, the sort of girls who would have slept with their windows shut if they'd been allowed to.

It was a surprise to Ramona to find Sara Corderey breaking the rule about being out of doors. She was in the library, standing on a chair to look at the books on an upper shelf.

'I've been told to stay indoors, Miss Charnley,' said Sara. 'I've got a bit of a cold. I get bronchitis if I have a bad cold. Our doctor wrote to Matron about it.'

Sara was giving more of an explanation than was really needed. She just had to say she'd been told to stay indoors. But she was nervous, anxious to be convincing, anxious to be believed.

Of course Ramona believed her. The child did seem to have a sniffle. It was bad luck to get bronchitis at that age. Even a much less biddable, less conscientious child than Sara would have told the exact truth in such a situation, because it would be so extremely easy to check up.

Ramona said, 'I'm afraid the books up there are no more interesting than the ones down here. In fact they're even less interesting. They're the ones nobody uses any more.'

'Oh.'

Sara gave a little smile, relieved that she was in no kind of trouble.

Ramona did not think she had seen Sara smile, ever before. She generally had a tense, almost a hunted look. Ramona recognised it as an expression she thought she herself probably often wore. Sara's smile was quick, nervous, tentative, but it transformed her face. Ramona realised something that had not occurred to her before – when Sara grew and filled out, when her childish features were formed, she was going to be very pretty. If not strictly pretty, certainly very attractive. She had a lovely skin, nice eyes, a little turned-up nose, and that sweet smile. Ramona thought that when they were both grown up, Sara would attract a much higher class of man than Rosalind Tuck would. Rosalind's beauty was and would remain undeniable, but there was a film-star obviousness about it. The moment you saw her, you saw all there was of her. Rosalind would never surprise you. Sara, Ramona thought, would one day surprise a lot of people.

Ramona said, 'What we need is a millionaire benefactor, to stock up this library with some proper books.'

'What books would you have, Miss Charnley?' asked Sara, seeming interested, seeming to want to know the answer.

Ramona started with Jane Austen, and went through the major nineteenth-century novelists. She added Addison and Swift, Defoe and Carlyle, Sir Thomas Browne and Oscar Wilde, pulling names out of her memory and out of the centuries.

'No poetry?' said Sara.

'Good gracious yes. But no anthologies. Complete works. Milton, Dryden, Pope, Keats, Wordsworth . . .'

She had once known them all, well taught in a good school, brought up with a good library at home, even

75

though her father had bought his books by the yard as part of the proper interior decoration of a gentleman's house. It seemed years since she had so much as seen the outside of a volume of Milton.

A bell rang. A flood of girls would in a moment pour all over the building.

'Um,' said Sara, looking as though she wanted to say more but did not know how to say it. She was evidently anxious to run away. She did not want to be seen deep in conversation with The Moaner. Her standing was insecure as it was. But she was nervous about running away without being dismissed – nervous about seeming rude, nervous about doing anything for which she might be ticked off or punished. Ramona understood, because at Sara's age she had often been in the same predicament.

Two days later Ramona was coming back from an afternoon walk with some of the youngest children, the babies, her charges. Getting them to recognise birds or trees was uphill work. They wanted to be sitting in front of the television. They hated the cold, the boggy fields, the bare trees and the slate-grey sky. They seemed to hate Ramona. She thought they did not really hate her, but only what she was made to make them do.

To Ramona's surprise, the dismal little procession was intercepted by Sara Corderey, muffled up in a woolly scarf and with a woolly hat pulled down over her ears. Sara's nose was pink from the wind and her cheeks had a high colour.

'Hullo, Sara,' said Ramona. 'Is your cold better?'

'Yes, thank you,' said Sara.

'Are you heading for home?'

'I think I will.'

'I think we shall, too. I can't get my class much interested in fieldfares or redwings or the different sorts of oak-trees.'

'Are there different sorts of oak-trees?'

'Hundreds, I believe. Anyway dozens. And lots of different sorts of lime-trees, and lots of different willows.'

76

'What a lot there is I don't know.'

'Knowing that is the first step to putting it right.'

Ramona was surprised to hear this remark in her own voice. She did not think she had ever before said anything quite so school-marmy. She was oppressed by a sense of a future fuller and fuller of such remarks, of herself becoming more and more exactly the sort of person who made such remarks.

'Of course,' she added, 'reverting to what we were saying two days ago, it's difficult to do much without books.'

'There *are* books in the library.'

'What you need for O-Levels. Not what you need for your soul.'

There she went again. She wondered if it was the effect of solemn little Sara.

'My aunt would agree with you, Miss Charnley,' said Sara. 'She was a teacher. My father says she eats books for breakfast.'

'She's lucky to come by them.'

'She'd die without them. I'm going out with her the Sunday after next. It's a bit frightening.'

'Why frightening? Is your aunt frightening?'

'Not exactly. But she'll want to know what I've been reading.'

'Tell her.'

'But I haven't really been reading anything. I haven't found anything to read. I've read a bit of Jane Austen and a bit of Dickens, but that was before I came here. I haven't read any of the others. And I don't see how I'm going to.'

'Perhaps your aunt will lend you some books.'

'Yes. Yes, she might. But . . .'

'It's no disgrace to be seen with books.'

Sara looked as though she thought it would be a disgrace to be seen with books. She said, 'Where would I keep them? Keep them safe, I mean, where they wouldn't get torn up or scribbled on.'

'Is that what your friends do? Tear up books and scribble on them?'

77

'Friends?' said Sara, as though the word was strange to her.

It was only afterwards that Ramona realised that Sara had not met them by chance. She had joined Ramona's group because she wanted to talk to Ramona. Did she have no one else to talk to? Was that because the others wouldn't talk to her or she wouldn't talk to the others? The question reminded Ramona of their relationships with their neighbours, hers and her mother's, in Brewster Terrace. They were isolated in a sea of apathetic hostility. It shouldn't happen to a fourteen-year-old. But it was not something that Ramona could do anything about.

'Sara, that problem of yours. About where you'd keep books safe if your aunt lent you some. I've had an idea. I don't know why I didn't think of it before. I could keep them for you. They'd be perfectly safe in my room. Nobody goes in there.'

'Somebody did.'

'Yes, but now I keep it locked.'

'Oh,' said Sarah. 'Oh. Would you really do that?'

'On condition I'm allowed to read the books too.'

Sara smiled. It was the third or fourth smile of Sara's that Ramona had seen. It was the broadest she had seen, and lasted the longest. Sara was coming to trust Ramona, perhaps to like her.

If a friendship was what they were beginning to have, it would not do to let it be obvious.

'Miss Charnley – '

'Yes, Sara?'

'Um. This is going to sound like awful cheek . . .'

She was embarrassed. She was blushing, and almost wriggling.

She said in a rush, 'I wondered if you were doing

78

anything next Sunday? I mean, going out to lunch or anything?'

Ramona shook her head. The only person who had ever taken her out to lunch, in her three years at Malham House, was Marigold Kent. Those outings were very welcome but very rare, because whenever Marigold had an off-duty weekend she tried to keep it free for her own school-age children.

Sara stared at her feet, and said, 'I was just wondering whether by any chance you'd like to come out to lunch with my aunt. You'd be able to talk about books and things. I'm sure she'd like that. She asked me to bring someone.'

Bring someone. Yes. It was usual. When parents came to take their daughters out, one or half a dozen special friends normally went out too. Sara's aunt would be expecting a friend. She would not at all be expecting Ramona. She would think it odd of Sara to have asked Ramona, and odd of Ramona to have accepted.

'Thank you very much, Sara,' said Ramona. 'And we'll work on your aunt to lend you some books.'

'Um, Miss Charnley,' said Sara, as embarrassed as before. 'I've done something you may not quite approve of.'

Ramona was startled. She could not imagine Sara doing anything seriously wrong. She wondered what was coming.

'I've told them that somebody in your family knows somebody in my family. As a reason for your coming out to lunch.'

'I see,' said Ramona.

She saw. Sara would otherwise be ashamed of her choice of guest. Now it was an adult arrangement, made over her head. Sara's aunt, if she knew about it, would be more surprised than ever.

Sara could pretend to her classmates that she was horrified to be trailing The Moaner along. She might not do that, but she had given herself the option. It was ingenious. A bit devious, but probably sensible.

79

They were in the corridor outside the dining-hall. Ramona became aware that Rosalind Tuck was watching them. Sara became aware of it, too.

She said, 'I'd better go,' and sped off to be lonely in another part of the building.

Miss Jennifer Corderey knew more or less why her niece had been sent to Malham House. It was one of those decisions that should have taken years to arrive at, but which in the event had to be reached in hours rather than days. The drought victims in Central Africa couldn't wait. The child's father was already there, trying almost single-handed to save thousands of lives in refugee camps with polluted water. The mother was packed and ready to go. The mother was a good soul, but not in her sister-in-law's view a fit person for making a decision that so gigantically affected an important young life. She was too trusting. She would believe what she read in a prospectus about creative arts and home-grown vegetables; she would believe what a glib headmistress said about discipline and the quality of the teaching.

Jennifer Corderey had never heard of Malham House. This was not so very surprising, as nearly all her working life had been spent abroad. She asked about among her contacts in the educational world; she was increasingly surprised to find that nobody else had heard of it either. It was not, it seemed, one of those schools that regularly secured top scholarships, or provided members of the European Youth Orchestra. The child's mother had been told about it by some Oxfam or Action Aid colleague; and then time was too short to pay it more than a flying visit.

Jennifer was highly curious to see her niece again. She had been a delightful ten-year-old, painfully shy at first, but thawing into a real companion with exceptionally good communication. She was someone who could be infected by Jennifer's lifelong love of literature. Jennifer promised herself the keen pleasure – undiminished after all those

80

years of teaching – of introducing the child to some of the works that had given her so much joy.

She was bringing a friend. Like-minded? It was to be supposed so. Unless Sara had changed more than Jennifer thought possible, a vapid teenager thinking about nothing but pop music would not be her chosen companion.

It would be interesting to get a cross-bearing on the school, another opinion to set against Sara's impressions; it might be rewarding to get something of a cross-bearing on Sara herself, how she fitted into that community, how the others regarded her.

Jennifer put the roast into the oven, and herself into her friend's small Renault. She was highly pleased with the luxury, previously unknown to her, of a casette player in the car. The stereo reproduction was excellent. She picked through the stack of her friend's tapes that lived in the car's glove compartment, and chose a Beethoven piano sonata recorded by Emil Gilels. It was not a work she had ever been advanced enough to play; and in many of the places where she had worked pianos were hard to come by, and usually ruined by the climate.

There were compensations to retirement. Beethoven on tape was one; the chance to feed her niece's mind with literature and all art was another.

She arrived at Malham on the dot of eleven. This was typical of her. A lifetime of starting classes punctually, in places where there were no electric bells, had given her something like an obsession about time. She did not want to keep the children waiting. She did not want to be kept waiting. She did not want to overcook the roast.

She pulled up among other cars on the gravel sweep in front of the building. The other cars were mostly Japanese. Several were quite small, but none was as small as the Renault Four she was driving. She did not find the house prepossessing. It could not have been lived in as a house, in the 1980s; it was the sort of building for which some other use had to be found. Probably a school was as good a use as any. You could not judge the quality of a school by the colour of its bricks.

81

Girls were coming out of the front door. They looked like girls; they were pretty well-dressed. The parents collecting them seemed all to be deeply tanned. They seemed modern. The fathers tended to longish hair, leather coats and turtlenecks, the mothers to much longer hair, Angora sweaters, and trousers with high heels. No valid judgements could be made on that evidence; but they all looked greatly unlike Jennifer Corderey, greatly unlike Sara's parents.

Sara appeared. Her aunt recognised her immediately. She had not changed between ten and fourteen as much as girls usually did. That was neither a bad thing nor a good thing. She would be adult soon enough. With her – not merely coming out of the door at the same time, but somehow evidently her companion – was a young woman. She was somehow evidently a member of the staff, a teacher. She was simply dressed, rather dumpy in figure, with thick spectacles. Jennifer supposed she was in her middle twenties. She was not a beauty, but she was not hideous. Her face had a soft, unformed quality, as though it had not kept pace with the rest of her when she grew up. She looked nervous and self-conscious, not at all like a teacher. Jennifer Corderey, who had no illusions about the way she herself looked or the effect she had on people, could imagine no person more different from herself than this shy little creature in spectacles.

And this was Sara's chosen friend? Could neither of them do better?

Jennifer would have liked a quick tour of the school, out of professional curiosity. She would like to have seen classrooms, design of desks, teaching aids, library, art studio, chapel, evidence of drama and of a school orchestra. But that would not have been fair to the others, who presumably wanted to get away from the place. And the roast would be overcooked.

She got out of the car, calling among the many calls which volleyed over the gravel. Sara heard, saw, waved, and ran towards her. The little teacher, if she was a teacher, followed more slowly, as though bashfully.

*

'It must have been interesting, working in a bookshop.'

'Oh yes,' said Ramona.

Interesting? There were worse jobs. The job she had now was worse. It was tiring, and grossly underpaid. The job she had now was more tiring and, considering what she had to do, worse paid.

Interesting? Only one really interesting thing had happened, all the time she worked in the bookshop.

It was her second Christmas. She had worked there for fourteen grinding months. She had twice, greatly daring, asked for a raise. Janey Bryan said they couldn't afford another penny, and Ramona knew it was true. Ramona had not got close to Janey, who was in and out of the shop unpredictably but less and less often. She had not got very close to Justin, either, although they were together for hours of every day. They got on all right. In quiet moments Justin used to ask her about herself. She kept quiet about Garston Hall. He asked her, in quite a friendly and tactful way, about boys, her social life, her sex life. She clammed up, not because she had secrets but because she had no secrets. She was twenty. It would have been unutterably humiliating to admit that nothing shameful or wicked had ever happened to her.

And then that Christmas Eve. Justin had come back from lunch slightly unsteady, and smelling of something peculiar. He was carrying a long parcel. He unwrapped it with an air of giggling triumph. It was a litre bottle of Italian red wine.

At Garston, very good wine had been drunk in very great quantity. It was a necessary operating expense of the Beeswing Bloodstock Agency. From an early age Ramona, like her sister and later her brother, had been given a little wine in a lot of water. By the time she was in her teens, she was allowed it half-in-half. On her fifteenth birthday she had her first full glass of undiluted wine. Thereafter her father often gave her a glass of wine, and tried to make sure that she appreciated what she was drinking. She had a good memory, and they said she had a good palate. They said she had a lifetime of enjoyment ahead of her,

83

especially with Great Aunt Ramona to finance the laying down of a cellar. When Great Aunt Ramona's money vanished with Antoine Meurice, wine still appeared at Garston, two lunches out of three, three dinners out of three. Since her father's death, Ramona had not drunk one drop of alcohol of any kind.

A litre of Italian red. Not what her father would have given even to the servants. It had not a cork but a plastic stopper. Justin produced two paper cups. He spilled a little wine when he poured it.

'Merry Christmas,' said Justin. 'Janey's in a tizz about tomorrow's dinner. No chance she'll be in.'

'What a pity,' said Ramona politely.

'Balls to that. I'm going to shut up the shop.'

'It's half an hour early.'

'Balls to that too. It's my shop, and you're my slave. Aren't you my slave, darling?'

'I – ' Ramona began, much startled.

'Knock that back and have some more. You've been growing on me, you know. What started as respect has become affection. Desire. You know I desire you, don't you? Of course you do. Do you desire me, even a little bit? Knock that back and have some more, before you answer.'

Soon they had drunk three quarters of the bottle. Justin's arm was round Ramona's shoulder. Part of her mind was surprised at this; part woozily accepted it. Part of her mind knew that her head must have been weakened by more than eighteen months of total abstinence. Part was soothed and uplifted by the unfamiliar clouds of alcohol in her brain, which banished the aching of her back and the grimy vision of Number 53 Brewster Terrace.

Justin tried to clink his paper cup against Ramona's. The contact between the paper cups was soundless. Justin laughed. Ramona began to laugh. She heard a sort of whinnying giggle, which she was surprised was the sound of her laughter. Justin drained his cup, and dropped it. There was a trickle of wine on his chin. Very carefully, using both hands, he took off Ramona's glasses. She could

84

still see him pretty clearly, with the dribble of wine on his chin, but the shop in the background was a blur. It looked better as a blur. He put his arms round her waist, and pulled her towards him. She came awkwardly, unfamiliar with this routine. He began to kiss her, gentle little mumblings on her cheeks and forehead. He kissed her lips. It all became very wet and puzzling. She felt hands on her breasts. She tried to move her mouth away from his kisses and her breasts away from his hands. The effort seemed too great, and after a moment it seemed silly. Everybody else did this sort of thing. Everybody spoke well of it. Ramona began to think well of it.

They were knocking coffee-table books by the dozen onto the floor when Ramona felt his hands under her sweater.

Justin was sick. He had had far too much to drink at lunchtime, and then most of the litre bottle of red. The smell was acrid and the sight disgusting. The sound was disgusting. He was sick over his own feet and Ramona's feet and the floor.

Sobered but not sober, Ramona went out to the back and put her shoes under the tap. She thought of trying to do something about everything, but there was too much. There were too many heavy books on the floor, and too much vomit, and Justin himself was huddled in a corner with his face in his hands. Guiltily, thankfully, Ramona walked away from the whole situation.

She felt better with every stride in the cold, clean air. She turned the corner and started up the hill. Suddenly she stopped. What would have happened if Justin had not been sick? Would she have let herself be seduced by a married man? Was that what she wanted? Could she have stopped him, stopped herself?

The memory of his tongue on her tongue and his hands on her breasts made her knees tremble so that she clung to a lamp-post.

She tried to compose her face, and to discipline the twitching of her hands, when she let herself into the house.

Her mother looked up, incurious. 'The shopping, Ramona? Our food?'

Ramona had left their supper, their Christmas dinner, all their food for Boxing Day, in the shop.

She walked back to the shop, of which she had a key. Justin had gone from his corner, but books and vomit were still all over the floor.

On her way home again, with heavy armfuls of shopping, she realised she was in love with Justin. It was not an emotion which she could recognise from experience, but love was what she knew she was feeling. Anybody could be sick. You did not not love somebody because they were sometimes sick. She had been sick herself, with gastric 'flu, or after too many little sausages at a children's party. Probably she had been in love with him for a year, without realising it.

That changed everything. They would come together. Janey was all wrong for him. She, Ramona, was his, every bit of her was his. The hell with prudery. She was twenty years old. Life came once. His respect had grown into affection, affection into desire. Desire. That was what she felt. Lust. Call it lust. Suddenly she was grown-up and she could do what she liked with her own body, and that was what she chose to do.

'You are a silly,' said her mother. 'Having to go all the way back. What has come over you?'

'What sort of thing?'

'You look as though you'd won the pools.'

'It's the cold air.'

In most of the house, it was almost as cold as in the street. The lights were dim, to save money. There were no Christmas cards. Not a single Christmas card had come for them, that year or the year before. Perhaps a few cards would have come, from friends of the old days, but Ramona's mother had not told anybody their new address. Nobody knew where they had gone to, and they were not in any telephone book.

*

86

Justin treated her with a certain grumpiness when the shop reopened three days after Christmas. He treated everybody with grumpiness. He had eaten and drunk far too much; he was feeling bilious and queasy.

His grumpy treatment of her was camouflage.

As soon as they found themselves alone she said, 'Are you going to get any more of that red wine?'

'Never as long as I live,' he said. 'Filthy stuff. I suppose it's full of anti-freeze. Don't tell me you had some?'

'Don't you remember?'

'Remember what? I had some rum with those boys from the estate agency. Then what? Wine, yes. That was an error. Janey made the most frightful fuss. She came in here yesterday to check up on things. Somebody had been sick all over the floor. Was that you?'

'It was you.'

'Oh. I told Janey it was you. I couldn't remember myself.'

He couldn't remember anything.

'Oh yes, Miss Corderey,' said Ramona. 'Sometimes it was quite interesting working in the shop.'

CHAPTER FIVE

Miss Jennifer Corderey sniffed something odd about the Malham House School. It was difficult to pin down. It was an accumulation of details, rather than the revelation of a single large awfulness.

Those trendy parents, tanned and hung with chains. It would be ludicrous to judge moral or cultural standards on such flimsy evidence, but to her those youngish parents, mostly rather boisterous in manner, were creatures from Mars – they were more foreign to her than black pupil-teachers, Mission School children, the Chinese Christians among whom she had worked. She knew she was gravely out of touch with the Britain of the middle eighties, having only recently returned to it: but the people she had seen when shopping locally, the women she had met at coffee mornings, were like people, like the people she remembered, not in the ordinary way at all like the Malham House parents.

It would be quite wrong to jump to premature conclusions which might be grossly unfair.

Her immediate trouble was, that present circumstances made it difficult, well-nigh impossible, to arrive at a reasoned conclusion. Obviously, neither Sara nor the little schoolmistress would be frank in the presence of the other. Sara would not risk derogatory remarks about the school, supposing she was inclined to make them, in front of a member of the staff. Equally, this Ramona Charnley would not say anything frank, supposing she had anything frank to say, in front of a pupil. It would be possible to get one of them alone for a little – Sara over the washing-up, for example, Miss Charnley taken upstairs to powder her nose – but it was in the last degree doubtful if either would open up even in private. Anything they said might be quoted, especially by an old busybody like herself.

Their very silence about the school – pupil and teacher both – was one of the details that contributed to Jennifer Corderey's uneasiness.

Report – to put it more exactly, absence of report – seemed to be right. Malham House was not a school that shone academically or artistically. Games? They played games. Neither of Jennifer Corderey's guests seemed much aware of victories and defeats. Miss Corderey herself deplored an excessive emphasis on athletic prowess, but she recognised the educational value of discipline, team-work, the unselfish subordination of the individual to the group. She received the impression that at Malham there were a few girls who were keen on hockey, and who therefore played hockey, and that nobody else was much interested. It was not what she was used to, even in China.

Miss Corderey was impressed when she heard where Ramona Charnley had been at school. That was a place which, unlike Malham House, everybody had heard of. It shone academically, artistically, athletically, and above all socially. The social aspect was not one which interested Jennifer Corderey, but she could not be unaware of it. Ramona Charnley had not, it seemed, even sat her A-Levels. It was odd that a product of that school should be teaching at Malham House. It was odder that a product of any school should be teaching at any school, without even A-Levels, let alone a degree or a Dip. Ed.

Then the subject of books coming up. Sara's nervous suggestion, prompted by Ramona Charnley. The books would be safe from vandalism. The books were *necessary*.

Books? Necessary? At a school? The problem for children at school was too many books, not too few. The Malham House library – what of that?

They were still careful, both of them, in what they said about the school. But in order to explain why Sara wanted – needed – the loan of books, they had to explain about the Malham library.

Hearing this, fighting down the outraged comment which was bursting to spring to her lips, Jennifer Corderey considered sending an immediate cable to the child's father, urging him to take her away from so grossly inadequate an institution, begging him to make other arrangements, offering to make enquiries, herself, which, with her contacts, she could easily do . . . But Sara's father was waist deep in human misery. He would have no facilities for sending cables, and no time for writing letters. The mother was probably equally hard to reach, and certainly useless if reached. Miss Corderey could do nothing on her own initiative – had no shadow of legal right to move the child from a school in which her mother had placed her.

But something would have to be done. In the short term, Sara's suggestion was all that could be done.

She began to pull books out of shelves, discussing with the others what Sara would like, what would suit her.

At the sight of cascades of books – good books, real books – both Sara and the teacher became more animated than at any previous moment. They were picking them up and leafing through them. Sara squeaked with excitement at something she found. They were children with their stockings on Christmas morning. Jennifer Corderey had never seen anything like it. In all her years of teaching, she had never seen a child or an adult make such a fuss about books. Really it was too much fuss. Important as books were to herself, she thought her young guests were over-reacting.

She thought she had better ration them. Too much serious reading, done too quickly, would lead to mental constipation. The object would be defeated. They could come again, for another armful.

In her neat, spiky writing, with her old-fashioned fountain pen, Jennifer Corderey listed the books she was lending them. She made sure that her name was in each.

On two, which showed signs of fragility, she put brown-paper wrappers secured with sticky tape.

They had tea with little biscuits, the darkening sky shut out by chintz curtains.

They had chosen a chintz, Ramona and her mother, from an oddments shop on the London road. Fortunately the windows of Number 53 Brewster Terrace were small. Margot had made curtains in the days when she kept house for her father; she was sure she could do it again. She was quite wrong. She did not understand the new generation of plastic hooks and runners. It was almost immediately obvious that if she took responsibility for the curtains, there would be no curtains.

It was hard on Ramona's myopic eyes, stitching away by artificial light after a day in the bookshop. A sewing-machine was an unattainable luxury. The curtains were a long time in the making, and Ramona's mother became querulous about them. She began to nag. Ramona struggled to make allowances.

It was just as the curtains were finished that Ramona's mother began to be restless in the night. At three and four and five in the morning Ramona would be woken by a crash. Sometimes, appallingly, it was the evident explosion of glass or china; sometimes it was only a chair being upended. Groggy with sleep, Ramona struggled down the little stairs, buckling her spectacles onto her nose, knotting her dressing-gown cord round her waist. Her mother would have an air more often purposeful than puzzled. She had a perfectly good reason for being downstairs at four in the morning. She had smelled burning. She had heard someone moving about. She wanted to admire, once more, the fine new curtains.

By midsummer it was impossible to keep her in bed at night; and to replace the broken glasses Ramona bought indestructible plastic beakers. Her mother began to lose weight. She began to look like an old woman. She was still only fifty-five years old.

Ramona tried to get the doctor to come. The man they were registered with was one of a panel in a raw new building on the edge of the town; it had pink tiles and a huge carpark. The doctor's receptionist refused to bother the doctor with the Charnleys' unimportant problems. A middle-aged woman was sometimes downstairs in the small hours? There were cases of cancer, leukaemia, acute asthma on Doctor's list; there were horrifying industrial accidents, teenagers coming off their motorcycles and cracking their skulls, babies choking. Try a hot drink at bedtime; try locking the door; use a little initiative, a little commonsense, and don't come running to have your hand held.

The goings-on in the small hours became more confusing and louder, and they went on longer. Ramona's mother clamoured for her tea at four in the morning, for her supper at five. She demanded daylight, and accused Ramona of cruel perversity when the sky remained dark.

The doctor was contacted by a social worker, to whom a neighbour had reported strange noises from Number 53. The neighbour said nothing to the Charnleys; nobody said anything to them. The doctor confirmed, via the social worker, that Mrs Charnley was capable of getting on and off a bus. He told Ramona to bring her mother to the Surgery.

Ramona took an hour off from the bookshop, to Janey Bryan's displeasure. She got home to find her mother in bed. She had decided it was bedtime. Of course she was tired, having been up much of the night. Ramona felt drunk with fatigue, also having been up most of the night. Ramona's mother utterly refused to do something so idiotic as to get up out of bed, put all her clothes on again, and go down to the bus-stop in the middle of the night, all to see a doctor for whom she had not the slightest need. Nothing Ramona said would budge her. Ramona tried to heave her out of bed, appalled at using physical force on her own mother. Her mother went limp. She did not actively resist Ramona, but simply flopped. It was impossible to dress her.

Ramona helped her back to bed, and walked downhill to the bookshop.

With the first frosts came the incontinence. Even with a rubber sheet it meant a lot of extra washing. It was difficult to dry sheets and blankets without a proper airing-cupboard, without proper heating.

Lack of sleep caused Ramona to make mistakes in the bookshop. She undercharged one customer by five pounds. Janey docked the five pounds from Ramona's pay-packet.

A social worker came, a girl no older than Ramona. She said the house needed airing.

In early December the doctor came, a fussy little man who looked as though he, too, was short of sleep.

He examined Ramona's mother pretty thoroughly. He said that she was under-weight – that Ramona must feed her more and better food, and keep her warmer. He said that she had suffered one or more of what he called 'mini-strokes', which, without at once impairing physical capacity, would have done minor but irreversable brain damage. Such strokes were often the result of acute loneliness. Ramona was at fault in not having made friends with the neighbours, in not having arranged company for her mother. If things went on as they were going, Mrs Charnley would need full-time care. She could not be trusted not to fall downstairs and break her hip, perhaps just after Ramona had left the house in the morning; not to upset a saucepan of boiling jam over herself, or electrocute herself on a heater. It was not a suitable case for the public ward of a hospital – the other patients would be disturbed, and the beds had to be kept available for cases of real physical disability or injury, or in which treatment had to be given in a disciplined environment. There was no serious physical disability here, and there was no treatment, properly speaking, either. Sedatives, sleeping-pills, a tonic. Those were the only things that would help, and Ramona could give them to her mother as well as a trained nurse could.

It would still be possible, though risky, for Ramona to leave her mother alone for a few hours at a time. In a

93

month, or six months, or six hours, that would no longer be possible.

Each day at the bookshop now threatened to be the last day.

There was no word from any of their old friends, none of whom knew where they were. There was no word from Persephone or Patrick.

Miss Jennifer Corderey drove them back to the school, through the clammy November darkness. The books were in a plastic carrier-bag from a supermarket. They arrived comfortably before Sara's seven-o'clock deadline. Ramona and Sara made all the proper noises of thanks, for the two lifts, for lunch, for tea, and above all for the books.

Of course the books were to be returned, and other books borrowed. The only means by which this exchange could take place was for Jennifer Corderey to come again to Malham House. If she did that, she would of course take Sara out to lunch again; and if she did that, she might perhaps take Ramona Charnley out too.

Ramona did not hide her eagerness to be asked again.

Sara was allowed out on alternate Sundays. The occasion could be repeated in a fortnight, even though Sara would not have read all the books by then. Ramona might have done so, perhaps; she had read most of them already, but a long, long time before.

Jennifer Corderey drove home, with her usual extreme caution. Though she was concentrating on the road, she thought about her niece and the school the child's mother had placed her in. A library with nothing but school text-books. Music lessons, but no emphasis on music; an art class, but no emphasis on that, either. On what, then? On getting through the term. That and hardly anything more. The moment she got home Jennifer would write a careful and tactful letter to her brother. She did not want to fill him with horror – his life was full enough of horror already, in those appalling camps – and she did not want to seem too interfering. But she did want the child moved to another school.

At least those books were one small step in a good direction. Presumably Ramona Charnley could be trusted to look after them. She would do a little more than that, Jennifer thought. To a limited extent, and more or less in secret, she would take Sara under her wing. It was not much of a wing to be taken under, but it was the only one available. She would be, in a sense, Jennifer's representative in Sara's life, an agent for literacy.

Thinking about Sara, Jennifer found herself thinking about Ramona. That first-class, very expensive education suddenly interrupted. Those years – was it years? – in a provincial bookshop, with an invalid mother to look after. There seemed to have been a sudden and savage reversal of fortune, but Jennifer's kindly questions had not elicited many answers. It was a pity she had no qualifications. It was a pity her eyesight was so poor. Sara seemed to like and trust her, and probably she was right to do so.

Jennifer had the sense of having a friend in what she thought of as the enemy's camp. She wished the friend were older, tougher, more qualified, more influential. Anyway, nothing dreadful could happen.

She got back to her borrowed cottage, tired from the strain of driving in the dark, tired from making conversation all day. The letter to her brother was urgent, but not top on her list of priorities. First she tidied up the very small amount of confusion left by her guests. Then she laid the little table in the kitchen, and put the remains of lunch to heat up. Then she addressed herself to an exercise in forceful tact.

It was a good thing the books were in the opaque plastic bag from Waitrose. It should not have been, but it was. They should have been coals to Newcastle. In fact they were hostages to fortune; they were frail invaders of hostile territory, contraband, fifth columnists. Sara could not let herself be seen associated with a lot of stodgy, square, highbrow, wrinklies' books. Ramona understood that. She herself was better not seen with them.

As they crossed the gravel towards the light over the front door, Sara began to skitter, or hop, as though she badly wanted to go to the lavatory. Ramona began to thank her. Sara looked up. Her face had a stricken look. Once again Ramona understood.

'On you go,' she said, herself stopping.

Sara nodded, her face full of relief. She trotted away into the building. Probably no one had seen her coming back from her Sunday out with The Moaner.

The books, mostly paperbacks, were not so very heavy; but they felt terribly heavy to Ramona when she carried them all the way upstairs to her room. It was only when she got there that she realised that she had not given Sara any of the books. Perhaps it was as well. She would not get much chance for solitary reading on a Sunday evening at Malham.

Ramona herself debated between instant coffee in the Staff Common Room and one of Miss Corderey's books. A little guiltily, she decided that the coffee would not wait but the books would. She went downstairs empty-handed.

Books, books, books. Ramona began to hate the kind of books she had to sell in the Bilborough Bookshop. They were not really books at all – they were imitations, expensive frauds, bright photographic jackets concealing an absence of content as total as her mother's conversations – real or imagined – with the people of Brewster Terrace.

There was no other job she could do. There was no other job to be got. She had no time, between the bookshop and the shopping and her mother, to go looking for a job. Janey gave her a small raise, which made up for about half of the rise in the price of food.

One evening just before Christmas she came home to find that her mother had decided to start spring cleaning; and had then decided to stop. The little house was in greater chaos than would have been thought possible, considering how few things they owned. Many of their few plates and all their remaining proper glasses were broken. A bucket of soapy water had been poured over the rug in the sitting-room. Ramona's mother called from upstairs that she wanted her lunch.

That was the worst yet. It was one o'clock before Ramona got to bed. At two o'clock her mother decided to start again on the spring cleaning. When Ramona tried to get her upstairs, she sprawled limp as overcooked spaghetti.

Ramona telephoned in the morning from the garage by the roundabout, the call-box at the top of the hill having been vandalised. She waited in all day for the social worker, who came two days later. A decision had already been made by the Head of Department, on the basis of the social worker's previous report. There were vacancies in two Council-run old people's homes, but Mrs Charnley was too young to be admitted. She was too confused. 'Confused', Ramona found, was the accepted euphemism for roaring craziness. The doctor had reported that Mrs Charnley was not and would probably not become certifiable, so that there was no question of her being put in a mental home. There was in any case an acute shortage of beds in the local mental homes. The situation was quite unfortunate, but there was a bright side. The bright side was that there was an able-bodied daughter living at home and capable of looking after her mother. This factor would of itself debar the institutionalisation, at public expense, of Mrs Charnley. Ramona could apply for Supplementary Benefit and Home Nursing Allowance, to make up for the wages she would be losing. Well, perhaps not quite make up, and it was true that there would be a delay while the applications were processed.

Leaving, the social worker sniffed and said that the house needed airing.

The new regime started two days before Christmas.

Some benevolent authority caused a telephone to be installed. The theory was that help could be summoned in

97

a moment of crisis, and food could be ordered from shops. Practice fell short of theory. There was on Christmas Eve what Ramona thought quite enough of a crisis to justify calling for help – her mother locked herself in the bathroom, ran a bath which overflowed and began to drip through the sitting-room ceiling, and then forgot, or said she had forgotten, how to unlock the door. After two hours of an exhausting shouting-match through the locked door, Ramona went to the telephone. The matter was not deemed a crisis, at least on Christmas Eve. All she had to do was reason with her mother, or, failing that, break the door down. She broke the door down. It was astonishingly tough – a solid, authentic slab of Victorian woodwork; she had none of the proper tools; she shrank from trying to borrow hammer and chisel from a neighbour; she managed it in the end by using the handle of a frying-pan as a lever. She cut her hand on a splinter, and bled over the shattered wood of the door. She found her mother curled up in a puddle on the bathmat.

The little local shops did not deliver. The supermarkets did not deliver. There were a few superior shops in the middle of the town which delivered, but none of their vans had ever been seen in Brewster Terrace. In any case, they charged extra for delivering.

A third reality was that, if Ramona turned her back for a moment, her mother jumped to the telephone and began dialling numbers. Any numbers. She might have been calling Peru or Penang.

The telephone was removed.

Shyly, Ramona knocked on doors up and down Brewster Terrace, trying to recruit mother-sitters so that she could go shopping. Some said they had enough problems of their own; hearing the howls of young children, Ramona saw that it was true. She would come only if there was a TV. Some wanted a pound an hour. Ramona struck lucky at last with a little old woman like a wren called Mrs Thurston. She was genuinely sorry for Ramona and her mother; all the reward she wanted was a cup of tea. She came twice a week, for two hours at a time. She was competent, confident and soothing. She restored Ramona's faith in humanity. The arrangement lasted until nearly the end of January. Then Mrs Thurston's niece came to visit her, heard about it, and forbade it. She came and told Ramona so, perfectly polite, adamant.

The Social Services sent a woman who arrived twenty minutes late. Ramona scuttled thankfully out, for the first time in ten days. She came back after an hour to find her mother alone in the house. She was asleep in the sitting room, in front of the electric fire. The fire was on its face on the floor; it had burned a foot-square hole in the carpet.

Ramona thought she could not go on. She had run out of strength and courage.

But despair did not solve current problems. The room was full of a thin green pall of smoke, not immediately visible, and of an acrid, chemical smell from the smouldering carpet. Ramona righted the electric fire; the handle at the back burned her fingers. She scrubbed out the glowing tufts of synthetic fabric with the sole of her shoe. She opened the window. She considered waking her mother, but decided to let her sleep. She got a blanket from upstairs and draped it over her mother, because of the bitter air from the open window. She sat down at last herself; she wanted a cup of tea, but she despaired of finding the strength to get it.

They got through the rest of the winter, and the spring. Ramona acquired the ability, which she had never previously had, of cat-napping whenever her mother dozed off. She roused herself as immediately and totally as a dog when her mother woke up and started moving about. Social workers came and went, seldom the same face twice, making notes on pads; occasionally the doctor and the District Nurse came.

In the mounting wad of reports in the Social Services file, there was no hint of panic. There was no battered wife here, no child whose safety was threatened. There was a confused middle-aged woman, underweight and in indifferent health but not in danger; there was a strapping unmarried daughter, in her early twenties, living at home and looking after her mother. They were in receipt of their full entitlement of allowances. Attention could be directed to where it was needed, in the black ghetto behind the railway station.

Life was easier in the summer, because the bedclothes could sometimes be dried in open windows.

Ramona found it more and more difficult to get any food into her mother. She could grip some things – she could grip Ramona's arm, painfully hard – but not a spoon. When she did take hold of her spoon, she was apt to drop or throw its contents in any direction except that of her mouth. The mess and the waste were awful. With a sort of shame, Ramona tried feeding her. This enraged her mother, which Ramona understood. She became thinner and thinner, birdlike and then sticklike.

The autumn cold came early. There were hard frosts before the end of October. It was more than ever necessary to keep the house warm, and more than ever difficult to do so. Ramona was helped with the electricity bill. This enabled them to go on living there, and obviated, in the official view, any need for Mrs Charnley to be placed in an institution.

Even with more heating, it was more difficult to dry the things that had to be washed, because there were more of them. It was more difficult to get away to the shops, and more difficult to make the money spread. They were not in danger of starving or freezing to death. Ramona knew that there were people in the world – people in Britain, even – much worse off than they were.

She tried never to think of Garston. When she wept, it was either from fatigue or from memories of Garston. She found herself weeping more often, as the iron winter took hold of Brewster Terrace.

Huge open fires at Garston, sometimes as many as six when the house was full – fires in the drawing room, the hall, the library, her mother's pretty little sitting room, her father's study . . . Coming in to tea from the park or one of the farms, coming in to buttered crumpets, toast and Gentleman's Relish, a boiled egg after hunting, tea in the

100

nursery or the great flagged kitchen, tea as she grew older in front of the drawing room fire with the grown-ups . . .

The end of January. The anniversary of the visit of Mrs Thurston's implacable niece. Ramona had occasionally seen Mrs Thurston, in the distance, when she was out shopping. She had not spoken to her. Mrs Thurston was avoiding her.

The weather was bitter. To go shopping, Ramona wanted a big sheepskin coat of the kind everybody had worn in the winter at Garston. She could not afford any kind of warm new winter coat. Her old one, smart and expensive, was a shabby disgrace. She bought a stained tweed coat in the Oxfam shop.

Her mother continued to shrink. It ought to have been easy to carry her up and down stairs, but it was impossible. The stairs were too steep and narrow, and though her mother was now too weak to resist actively, she had developed her technique of flopping into an unmanageable rag doll. After months of silence on both subjects, she began to talk about Persephone and Patrick. She remembered them inaccurately. She remembered Persephone as an angel of beauty, gaiety and kindness, and Patrick as a gallant, courageous and generous little gentleman. She compared them with Ramona, when she recognised Ramona. Ramona had sent them away, out of jealousy. Ramona became the object of bitterness, of seeming hatred. That was in the lucid moments.

The weather continued iron into February. The northeast wind carried flurries of gritty snow down Brewster Terrace. Going out was like hell. Staying in was like hell. It became more than ever difficult to do the washing, to dry what had been washed; it became more than ever a constant necessity. A home help came once, and stole some sugar.

Ramona's mother took to lurid swearing, which was totally out of what had once been her character. She swore not at any particular object – not at Ramona, as a rule – not in any particular rage. It was just that when she opened her mouth there were sometimes yearningly nostalgic

101

memories of Persephone or Patrick, and sometimes obscenities which Ramona had only ever heard before when one of the Garston workmen hit his thumb with a hammer, or her father found that a housemaid had broken a piece of the Waterford.

There was an evening in the middle of February when Ramona found herself sitting alone at the kitchen table in absolute despair. Life could not go on. Her life, as it was, was unlivable. She was always cold and always exhausted. Dripping washing hung everywhere, always. Even with all the scrubbing Ramona did, the house reeked. Her back hurt, from the necessary scrubbing of bedclothes and floors. Her shoes had holes in them. Upstairs her mother, warm in bed under a mountain of covers, was calling for Persephone. There was practically no food in the house. She would have to go shopping in the morning; she might be able to slip out, having locked her mother in her room. She was too tired to make the effort to remember her mother as she had been; she was too tired to make the effort to love her mother as she now was. She lived with the reality of somebody who had turned not merely crazy but also nasty, horrible to see, to hear, to touch.

The clichés of despair rolled round Ramona's numbed mind. She had come to the end of her tether. She had shot her bolt. She was at the end of the line. There was no light at the end of the tunnel. The last straw had broken the camel's back.

That night the impossible happened.

Ramona's mother was covered, when Ramona went to bed, with a pile of blankets and an elderly eiderdown. It was essential that, in her weakened and emaciated state, she should be warm, especially in the small hours of the morning when the temperature was at its lowest and human resistance also at its lowest. Ramona made sure that everything was tucked in securely. There was no chance that her mother could find the strength to lift the weight of her bedclothes off herself, especially as they were so firmly anchored under the mattress. But when Ramona went into the room in the early morning, she saw that the covers were off the bed, pulled to the foot and to the floor. Her mother lay on her back uncovered except for the elderly flannel of her nightdress, itself once warm but now thinned by almost daily washing.

Of course she was dead. Of course it was hypothermia. She had died of cold. Ramona noted with a kind of frozen objectivity – as frozen as her mother's poor little shrivelled body – that hypothermia was what the doctor would put on the death certificate.

Ramona wrapped up as warm as she could, and walked down the street to the call-box at the roundabout. She called the doctor; the receptionist said she did not know what time he would be round. Ramona must wait for him. Foodless, Ramona waited in the house with her mother's fragile corpse.

She occupied some of the time in writing to Persephone. She said in her letter that if, by any extraordinary chance, Persephone knew where Patrick was, she might give him the miserable news. She could not go out at once to post the letter, because she had to stay in to wait for the doctor.

It was the longest day of her life, even though part of it was occupied by her letter to Persephone.

The doctor came in the early evening. He was very tired. He looked as tired as Ramona felt. He inspected the deceased, and listened to Ramona's account of the previous night.

He did not quite come out and say that her mother's death was Ramona's fault for not keeping her tucked up warm in bed.

Victims of hypothermia were old people who lived alone, not those who had active and well-educated daughters living with them and looking after them.

Ramona was made to feel like a murderess.

There was no will. The estate consisted of the house and its contents. Ramona continued to live there, for the time being.

She went alone to the cremation. There was no service.

Her flowers were the only flowers. It was a small wreath, expensive because flowers are expensive in February. The Department of Health and Social Security contributed a small grant towards the cost of the cremation. There was still a considerable bill to pay, which would be paid out of the estate as soon as the house was sold.

A reply to Ramona's letter came from Persephone, her first letter since the one in which she had accused them of cheating her.

She was in touch with Patrick, who had somehow got himself to Hong Kong and had stayed for several weeks with Persephone and at her expense. He was now in Australia, selling reproductions of the Mona Lisa in the suburbs of Sydney. Ramona would, of course, be selling the house and its contents immediately, and would send a third of the proceeds to Persephone and a third to Patrick. The sale should be immediate and the price high. Persephone and her husband required copies of all correspondence with the lawyers and house-agents.

A letter came from Patrick, to whom, it could be assumed, Persephone had given the Brewster Terrace address. He also required copies of all relevant correspondence.

Ramona went back to the Bilborough Bookshop, for the first time since she stopped working there. There was no such place. Where it had been there was a restaurant called the Taj Mahal. The owner was courteous but busy. He did not know what had become of Justin and Janey Bryan. He had not bought the premises from them, but from some other short-lived enterprise.

Probably that job would not have been going anyway. Probably no job was going.

The house-agent's board went up in the tiny front yard of

Number 53. It was advertised, with two dozen others, in the local paper, described as a 'Character period residence suitable for modernisation'. The house-agent, in the person of a very young man with a long red nose, put an asking price of £35,000 on it. He said that it should be scrubbed throughout, and very thoroughly aired, before any prospective purchaser was allowed to view it.

It seemed to Ramona that the smell lingered, that it hung in the woodwork and the brickwork, that it would be there for ever.

She began showing people round in late March. She was embarrassed to show them the furniture and carpets. All the furniture and all the carpets were for sale with the house. This seemed a resistable selling-point. The people who came thought £35,000 was a joke.

Another letter came from Persephone. It was quite brief. She wanted the names and addresses of the lawyer and house-agent, so that she could instruct them directly.

The house went for £18,000, to a Bangladeshi family, at the end of July. They did not want any of the furniture or carpets, but they liked the chintz curtains Ramona had made.

Ramona bought some new clothes, to assist in job-hunting. She moved into a furnished bed-sitter nearer the middle of the town. She paid the rent partly out of capital; on the lawyer's advice, she had put her share of the price of the house into a building society, but she could not live on the income.

Letters came from both Persephone and Patrick. They were furious at the miserable price fetched by the house. Their letters were so similar that they might have consulted, but this seemed unlikely to Ramona. She was not much hurt by the letters because she had expected them.

Nobody wanted to give her a job.

Mrs Gwyneth Barrow, in her tenth year in charge of the school founded by her mother, had a sudden and vexing problem in the autumn of 1983. It was only a problem because of the time element – the new school year was to start in under a week. What happened was Caroline Hodder's sudden marriage. Caroline had, for two years, had charge of the very youngest children. Her job was really to keep them quiet, not to teach them anything. She could not have taught them anything, because she was totally unqualified. This enabled Gwyneth Barrow to pay her an extremely small salary. Nobody could object, and Caroline was not, of course, a member of any union.

Caroline had got herself engaged at the beginning of the summer holidays. There was no way, she said, they could get married until the following summer. This gave Gwyneth Barrow a full year to find a replacement. Then the wretched young man was offered a job in America. He wanted to take it, and he wanted to take Caroline, and she wanted to go. Both families were reported to be delighted, but Gwyneth Barrow was not delighted.

She used the word 'treachery', to her husband and others, more frequently than she had ever had occasion to use it before.

None of the other existing staff could add responsibility for the youngest children to the duties they already had. If the school was not precisely understaffed, there was certainly no margin of error. There couldn't be, if the operation was to show a reasonable profit to Lt. Commander and Mrs Barrow. Another keeper had to be found for the babies, and within three or four days.

There was no time to advertise, to invite written applications and C.V.s. Mrs Barrow spent hours on the telephone, ringing up people who might know people who might do. There were only two qualifications, really. The successful candidate must be available immediately, and she must be prepared to accept the salary Mrs Barrow was offering.

Either one of these two requirements could have been met, the first easily, the second with more difficulty. The two together began to seem to pose an impossible problem.

Mrs Barrow began telephoning Labour Exchanges, in

London and places near London. Bilborough was high on her list because of its initial letter.

Somebody called Ramona Charnley was desperate for a job, had a small income of her own, was available immediately, and had a few O-Levels. Mrs Barrow spoke to Miss Charnley on the telephone. She had an educated voice, calculated to please those among her pupils' parents who took account of such things; and she was impressed by the school the girl had been to.

They met in the foyer of the Charing Cross Hotel, which was a good deal more convenient for Mrs Barrow than it was for her interviewee.

Mrs Barrow was dubious. She was not sure about taking on somebody who looked so young, who acted so diffident and vulnerable, whose eyesight was so bad. She found that the girl was surprisingly well read, and that she would have sat her A-Levels but for the sudden death of her father. Beggars couldn't be choosers. The term was practically beginning. The creature would do as a stop-gap. If she was called a probationary teacher, her salary could be even lower.

She seemed to fit in all right, perhaps because nobody much noticed her.

Ramona gave Sara Corderey *Our Mutual Friend* from the small store of treasures locked in her bedroom. There should not have been the least reason why the handing over of the book should not have been public. A teacher handing a book to a pupil – what could be a more normal part of school life? It was not a part of Malham House School life. Sara could not let herself be seen accepting a book from The Moaner. She would not have been safe and the book would not have been safe.

'I wonder where I can read it?' said Sara.

'It's a pity it's not midsummer,' said Ramona. 'You can't sit under a tree with it in this weather.'

Somebody went by the door of the music-room where they were, singing in an attempted American accent a piece which would not have been at home in the music-room. With an expression of embarrassment, even of guilt, Sara thrust the bulky old book up inside the waist of her sweater, over her hip, so that she could hold it there with her elbow. Ramona supposed that Sara imagined that she looked like a girl who was not carrying a book. In fact she looked like a girl who was ashamed to be carrying a book.

Sara slipped away out of the music-room, seeming to move lopsidedly because of the weight and bulk of the book under her elbow. Ramona envied her, coming to *Our Mutual Friend* for the first time. Ramona knew that she herself should be feeding her soul on some of the other books upstairs in her room. It was high time she read those she had never read, high time she reread the ones she had read long ago. There was very little time during the day; at night she was exhausted. The very thought of embarking on a big, long book was tiring. Perhaps Sara's aunt could be persuaded to lend Ramona books during the holidays. That was it – the holidays, when there was so very little to do, would be the time for her to catch up with her reading and rereading. She was able to feel virtuous that she had made this resolution. She was able to go for coffee in the Staff Common Room without feeling that she was letting herself and Sara down.

Ten days passed without excitement or outrage. The school was in the grip of mid-term apathy. The freedom of summer was a distant memory. The freedom of Christmas was far in the future.

It was cold. Norman the odd-job man crooned busily over the antiquated boilers. Tepid water thrummed and gurgled in its labyrinth of pipes. Some of the girls wore fur coats to class. Rosalind Tuck looked stunning in hers. Sara Corderey's nose was red.

Ramona asked Sara, during one of their few and oddly furtive meetings, how she was getting on with the Dickens. Sara was getting on better with the low-life Thames-side characters than with the Podsnap strands of the story.

108

Ramona thought she remembered finding the same; but she had difficulty remembering anything about the book, or about any other book.

It was understood that Ramona was to join Sara for another Sunday with Miss Jennifer Corderey. It was understood that neither of them would say anything about this arrangement. It was understood that, if Sara was directly tackled about it by anybody, she would say that The Moaner's family knew some of her aunt's family, and that her joining the party was all the aunt's idea.

Friday evening was very mild for November. Ramona's duties, such as they were, had kept her cooped up indoors all day, and although it was already almost full dark she strolled out to get some fresh air. Her feet crunched on the gravel in front of the house. A brown owl hooted a long way away. There was no other sound at all. Unusually, the whole school was quiet. Ramona found herself revelling in the luxury of solitude and silence, after a day beset by shrieking small girls and by the yapping voices in the Staff Common Room.

The silence was broken by the sound of a distant engine. The snarl grew louder. It was a motorcycle, Ramona thought. It got much nearer very quickly. It was being driven fast, too fast. It was coming up the Malham House drive. There was only one. This was not the skinhead gang who sometimes made a frightening nuisance of themselves. Ramona wondered whatever a solitary motorcyclist could be doing, roaring up the drive in the dark.

Ramona wondered what to do. There was nothing she could do. She wondered what was going to happen. Probably nothing would happen. The youth would be contented with the disturbance he had made, the joyride he had had; he would turn round and go away again.

The motorcycle slowed right down, about fifty yards away, just round the corner of the drive, just out of Ramona's sight. She could see the glow of its headlight on the drive and on the spindly shrubs bordering the drive.

She heard a voice, a girl's voice, raised over the muted puttering of the engine.

'Stop! Stop here!'

It was just a shrill girl's voice, screeching at the driver to stop. Ramona had no idea whose voice it was.

A man's voice answered, saying something which Ramona did not distinctly hear, which she did not understand. She thought the tone was dismissive, contemptuous, jeering, but that might have been the man's normal tone of voice. The motorcycle, which had stopped, now started again. The glare of its headlight preceded it round the corner, clear of the clump of shrubs on the corner. It was almost completely invisible behind the beam of the headlight. Ramona thought she saw the gleam of two crash-helmets, gigantic spherical visored plastic heads like those of visitors from outer space.

'For Christ's sake stop!' shouted the girl.

'Bugger that,' said the man.

At this moment the headlight swung as the motorcycle turned towards the house. The beam raced along the gravel, impaled Ramona, raced on again. There was a wordless scream from the girl on the pillion. The motorcycle swerved away. It skidded to a halt, just visible in the light from the windows of the house. The passenger climbed off. She tugged off her crash-helmet and gave it to the driver. She ran away into the darkness. Ramona saw a gleam of hair in the light from the windows, long, impossibly blond hair, absolutely distinctive hair.

The motorcycle gunned and turned. The beam swung and again caught Ramona. It came slowly straight towards her, keeping her full in the headlight. It stopped a yard from her.

'You one of the teachers here?'

'Yes,' said Ramona, loudly so as to be heard over the noise of the engine.

'You want to take better care of these birds,' said the man. 'That one's a right tart.'

He hooked the spare crash-helmet over something

behind his saddle, gunned his engine, and roared away down the drive, scattering gravel.

Ramona hurried indoors, her duty being to try to catch Rosalind Tuck coming in.

She did not catch her coming in. She found her in the library with Amanda Loring and Colette Davies, the slave she had brought to life and the slave she was bringing to death. Rosalind Tuck was panting. Her colour was high and her hair wild. A heavy outdoor coat was thrown over the back of a chair, with a scarf and a pair of sheepskin gloves.

All three girls turned and stared as Ramona came into the library. There was fright, guilt in Colette Davies's face. There was neither fright nor guilt in Rosalind Tuck's face.

'We've all been here for the last hour, Miss Charnley,' said Amanda Loring.

Ramona had not spoken, and was not looking at Amanda.

She turned to her now. 'You may think it's brave to tell lies to save your friend from punishment, Amanda. But it's not sensible and it won't work. What about you, Colette? Are you going to lie to save Rosalind too?'

Colette glanced at Rosalind, who looked back at her steadily.

In a high voice Colette said, 'We've all been here for an hour.'

'You stupid children,' said Ramona.

She turned and went out of the library. She was proud of herself. She had been dignified and authoritative and grown-up. Her hands had not trembled and she had not blushed.

As she went away along the corridor she heard Rosalind Tuck's derisive laughter.

CHAPTER SIX

As soon as the Headmistress was available in the morning – as soon as she had finished breakfast in her warm and sunny annexe – Ramona presented herself to her. She reported Rosalind Tuck's misdemeanours. The girl had broken a number of major rules. She had broken bounds. She had been out after dark unsupervised. She had been in company with an unknown man. She had been riding on the back of a motorcycle. She had apparently been engaged in some activity sufficiently immoral for her to be described as a tart. A little reluctantly, Ramona was also obliged to report Amanda Loring and Colette Davies for lying.

The other girls would probably be punished, but probably not severely. To lie as they had done was naughty but not evil, and it must, Ramona thought, be evident even to the Headmistress that they were terribly under Rosalind Tuck's influence. For Rosalind herself it was altogether another matter. Her crimes, taken together, came close to meriting expulsion.

'I couldn't expel her, even if I wanted to,' said the Headmistress. 'Her parents are abroad and she has absolutely nowhere to go. I don't suppose anything so very terrible happened yesterday evening. A yob like that calls a girl a tart if she's pretty and wears nice clothes. It wouldn't be fair to jump to conclusions on that evidence. The child's only been here a few weeks. I daresay she's vague about some of the rules. She hasn't been used to boarding-school discipline – she hasn't really taken in that we mean what we say. I think our job is to bring her to a sense of what's right, not to destroy her life for her. She'll be gated for the rest of the term, and she'll do a lot of extra homework. That will be a good thing, incidentally – I understand she's rather behind. I'll see all three of them, separately, later this morning. You were right to tell me about this, Ramona.'

As Ramona came away, her mind's ear heard Rosalind's mocking laughter from the library.

Miss Jennifer Corderey found that both her young guests were more relaxed, more outspoken, than on their first visit. They were good for one another, perhaps, and she herself was good for both of them.

All the same, the situation was a little odd.

Jennifer Corderey remembered her own schooldays as a sort of marathon of grim cheerfulness, with nearly everyone working hard and playing hard. The worst thing about her school, as Jennifer Corderey remembered it, was the food; the best thing was the companionship. She had remained in touch with some of her friends (fewer and fewer each year) in spite of the remote places where she had spent most of her life. She had greatly admired, greatly liked, some of the teachers of her youth; but the point was that she would never have asked one of them out to lunch with her family. You just didn't do it. It was unthinkable. You asked your friends. Was that not the case at this Malham House place?

Chatting at lunch (chatting ever more freely) Sara revealed that other girls did go out with one another's families – uncles and aunts, very often, because so many of the parents were abroad. Girls asked their friends, then, exactly as in Jennifer Corderey's day.

Had Sara no friends in the school? Not one that she could ask out, or wanted to ask out? Only this funny little teacher of infants? Had Ramona Charnley herself no

113

family, no close friends among the staff? Had she made no friends locally?

These were not questions it was easy to ask, but Jennifer Corderey set herself very delicately to ask them.

Ramona Charnley reported, hesitantly and in confidence, that to her Sara seemed unusually shy and probably exceptionally homesick, the latter because, no doubt, her family was exceptionally close and affectionate.

Jennifer Corderey confirmed that this was so.

Ramona said that the authorities had put Sara into a class with girls all older than herself, because she was at that academic level.

'But if she'd been put in with her contemporaries,' said Jennifer, 'by your account she would have lost a year, even two years.'

'Yes, but she would have been with kids of her own age. She would have found it much easier to make friends.'

'Which is more important?'

'I don't know. She's got a lifetime ahead of her for catching up with her education.'

'She's got a lifetime ahead of her for making friends.'

'I think she's going to be very attractive.'

'So do I. Her mother was. None of us was surprised when my brother produced her. A very gentle character, infinitely kind, trusting to a fault, believing the best of everybody. No wonder she rushes about the world digging wells and feeding the starving and getting herself absolutely adored.'

'She makes friends, then.'

'Yes, but I can well believe she was just as shy as a schoolgirl as Sara is.'

To Sara, Jennifer Corderey put the same questions in different terms. Sara did not admit that there was no schoolmate that she could or would ask out. What Sara said was that Miss Charnley had no family and practically never went out, and liked talking about books more than anybody did at school, and so . . .

And so Sara, by her own account, was taking pity on Ramona Charnley as much as the other way about. Two lame ducks, whispering in a corner and supporting one another. Jennifer Corderey longed to inject some vim, spine, defiance into the pair of them. She had these things, in abundance, always had had. They had made her independent, free-spirited, sometimes crusading, sometimes rebelling. They had made her respected and – sometimes a shade cautiously – liked. Driving them back in time for the evening roll-call, she wished there was some sort of transfusion by which the vehemence and steel of her own character could be implanted in Sara's and Ramona's.

She lent them no more books. They had more than enough to be going on with.

She stopped the car among many other cars on the gravel in front of the school. Ramona got out of the front seat and Sara out of the back. They thanked her conventionally and, she thought, sincerely. She wanted to back out of her parking-place and start home immediately, but a stupid woman was making a muddle of turning a Jaguar. Waiting for the creature to sort herself out, Jennifer Corderey watched the girls walking together towards the building. She saw them only in silhouette against the light over the door. She supposed they would go into the building together, discussing, no doubt, the lunch or the cottage or herself. She was surprised to see the slighter silhouette suddenly detach itself from the other, and sprint on its own into the full glare of the light, up the steps and into the building.

The Main Hall was full of chattering and shrieking girls, as it always was on Sunday evenings. The ones who had been taken out for the day were boasting to the ones who had not, shouting passionately about the ice-creams they had eaten, the films they had seen. There was a tendency for groups who had been out together to stay together, as though some special loyalty bound them together in defiance of the rest of the world.

They were assembling for the seven o'clock roll-call, to be held in this place in a few minutes.

Ramona was well used to this scene, but tonight there was something unfamiliar about it. There was an unusual sense of focus. The crowd of girls was not milling about all over the hall, but densely packed in one part of it. Dozens of girls, scores, were crowded round the notice-board. This was a large piece of cork, into which notices were stuck with tacks – the rosters for waiting in the dining-hall, times of hockey practice, music lessons. It normally attracted only the most cursory interest. It had never before been scrutinised so avidly by so many eyes at once.

And the shrieks were not about ice-cream or films or the silly thing somebody had said. They were shrieks of astonished laughter. All the girls were laughing at something pinned up on the notice-board.

A girl turned round, and saw Ramona standing puzzled in the middle of the hall. The girl nudged and whispered. Nudging and whispering spread at high speed through the crowd. More and more faces swivelled to face Ramona. The laughter continued, but it was muffled. Some of it was only just muffled. Howls came from behind hands. Faces were scarlet with the effort to control laughter.

At the very fringe of the crowd, perhaps not really a part of the crowd, stood Sara Corderey. There was something in her face, but Ramona did not know what it was.

Most of the girls drew back from the notice-board. Many turned their faces away from Ramona, either to hide their laughter or to make it more difficult for her to remember that they had been there. A few stayed in front of the notice-board, as though to hide from Ramona what had been amusing them all so very much.

Ramona approached the notice-board. The girls who were still there drew back with the rest.

Ramona did not at first understand what she was looking at. Then she understood exactly what she was looking at.

It was an illustration from a book, roughly torn out and pinned to the board. Ramona remembered the picture well, although it was a long time since she had seen it. It was one of the 'Phiz' illustrations to *Our Mutual Friend*. It was the one of Bella and her father, late at night in their little house. The father was dressed, but Bella was in her nightgown. Ramona thought she remembered that the picture illustrated a very touching, very Dickensian scene between these two, who loved one another very much.

Two pieces of paper – cut out gummed labels, perhaps, for re-using envelopes – were stuck to the illustration. They were cut into oval shapes, not accurately, with arrows extending towards the heads of the figures depicted. They were speech-balloons. Ramona was familiar with this kind of joke. Marigold Kent sometimes brought copies of *Private Eye*, which somebody had given her, into the Staff Common Room. *Private Eye* had this kind of joke, speech-balloons superimposed on press photographs of the Queen or the Prime Minister, with ridiculous remarks in the balloons. Ramona did not always understand the jokes in *Private Eye*, but she understood this joke.

The captions were typed. Someone had used the type-writer in the school secretary's office. No doubt they had found there also the sticky labels and the scissors to cut them with.

The father was saying, 'Ramona! Why are you up at this time of night?'

The daughter replied, 'I've wet my bed.'

And obviously the page had been torn out of Miss Jennifer Corderey's copy of *Our Mutual Friend*.

The book, missing that one illustration but not otherwise mutilated, was found on a shelf in the library.

There was, of course, the page of text missing which backed the illustration.

Ramona managed to steam off the pieces of sticky label, using the electric kettle in the Staff Common Room. The steam had the effect of making the paper buckle and crinkle. The page could be returned to its proper place in the book, but it would be unlikely to stay there if anybody read the book.

*

'It was in my locker, Miss Charnley,' said Sara Corderey. 'It was hidden under my files. It really was hidden.'

There was a rule, generally obeyed, that the girls did not invade one anothers' lockers. Even very new girls would have been made aware of this rule. It was a rule of which, unlike most of the rules, the girls themselves thoroughly approved.

Ramona did not remember a case of any girl ever being punished for messing about in another girl's locker, because no case of this crime had ever been reported.

If the offence could be proved against any girl or girls, the punishment would probably be severe.

The point was entirely academic.

Rosalind Tuck had not been out on Sunday, with her own family or anybody else's family. Her special friends Colette Davies and Amanda Loring had also been in or about the school all day. So had sixty other girls.

Nobody admitted having been anywhere near Sara Corderey's locker. Nobody admitted having been in the office, having used the typewriter, having taken and cut out the gummed labels.

If taxed directly, Rosalind Tuck would be given an unshakeable alibi by her friends. There was no point in taxing her directly. There was no point in doing anything. There was nothing that could be done.

It was obviously now necessary to keep all the borrowed books, all the time, in Ramona's locked attic bedroom. This was in fairness to Sara's aunt and to the books themselves. The new arrangement made it much more difficult and complicated for Sara to get any reading done. She had to come and get her book from Ramona when Ramona was in her room, and she had to return it.

It was infuriating, because any number of books should have been safe in the child's locker.

Sara exclaimed at Ramona's room the first time she saw

118

it. She avoided explaining why she squeaked with surprise, but Ramona understood. She had expected a mistress to be living somewhere altogether grander and more comfortable.

The room had a bed and a chair. It became obvious that Sara could lie on the bed or sit in the chair, and read her book without fear of assault on herself or the book. She could be there for quite a long time without being missed, because the other girls didn't notice whether she was there or not. This was because she was shy and a late developer and much the youngest in her class.

Usually Ramona left her alone, with her book and the one-bar electric fire. Sometimes she stayed, when she was off duty and there was nobody she wanted to talk to in the Staff Common Room. On those occasions Sara's book was apt to flop into her lap, and Ramona's also, and they talked. Ramona found herself talking more freely to Sara than to anyone since her mother's mind began to go – more freely than to Justin and Janey Bryan in the bookshop, more freely even than to Marigold Kent.

Life as it had been lived at Garston in the great days was totally outside Sara's experience. She had hardly even read about such grandeur, glitter and luxury, except in children's stories set in mythical kingdoms. Even when not labouring on the Equator, her own parents lived very simply. She could hardly believe in a dairymaid making, on the premises, all the butter they ever ate, in a stable full of horses with a full-time groom, in a sideboard with spirit-lamps under the breakfast kidneys, in a lake with a sailing-boat on it. She could not associate these things with Ramona.

Ramona could hardly associate them with herself.

Ramona stemmed the stream of Sara's questions with questions of her own. Gaining confidence, gaining trust, Sara spoke more and more freely about her family and herself. In those closing weeks of the winter term, Ramona got to know Sara better than any other girl of her age in all her time at Malham. Of course she had got to know some of the tots, her own charges, inside out; but a fourteen-year-old had a great deal more to say for herself. Ramona found that Sara was in most ways what she seemed – very much a product of her high-minded, self-sacrificing family – but that she was saved from priggishness by an unexpected sense of humour. Growing in confidence, she became really good company. She had a very sweet smile. Ramona was sure she saw far more of Sara's smile than anybody else in the school. Sara saw more of Ramona's, too. They did manage to get quite a lot of reading done.

Rosalind Tuck was asked out to lunch on Sunday by a girl called Mary McPhee. Mary was being given lunch by her brother, who was nineteen years old and an officer cadet at Sandhurst. He was on a forty-eight hour pass, and he was driving up in his vintage sports-car. Lunch was to be in a smashing restaurant which had been established in a country house. Mary's brother had told her to bring along the most beautiful girl in the school.

Mary had a photograph of her brother, which she showed to Rosalind. He was six foot tall and he looked like a hawk.

Rosalind asked permission of her tutor, Miss Hilda Joy, as the rule was. It was only a matter of form. Miss Joy reminded Rosalind that she had been gated for the rest of the term. Rosalind knew this, of course, but she had not taken it seriously. At first she found it impossible to believe that she was actually forbidden to go out to lunch, in a smashing restaurant, with an officer cadet from Sandhurst, who looked like a hawk and drove a vintage sports-car. Miss Joy was almost apologetic. She did not actually say that she thought the punishment harsh and dispro-portionate, owing to her loyalty to the Headmistress; but she communicated something of the sort.

Mary McPhee said her brother would be very disappointed.

There was an unwritten law that 'shop' was not talked in

the Staff Common Room. It was broken whenever any member of the staff opened her mouth. This was inevitable, not only because necessary conversations would not otherwise have been held, but also because without the affairs of the school and the personalities and problems of the girls the staff would have nothing to say to one another. At the very beginning of term they could talk about what they had done during the holidays; at the very end of term they could talk about what they were going to do during the holidays; in between they talked about the school and the girls.

Hilda Joy frequently interrupted the conversations of others by restating the rule against 'shop'; as frequently she broke the rule herself. She was doing so when Ramona came into the Common Room for the mid-morning coffee-break. She was talking about Rosalind Tuck not being allowed out to lunch the following Sunday. She was saying how surly Rosalind's manner had been, when she understood that the punishment was being made to stick. Hilda Joy would not have allowed anyone else to say that Rosalind Tuck was surly; but she was herself, by her own rules, allowed to say it.

The story was new to Ramona. There was no reason she should have heard about Mary McPhee's invitation, and she had not done so. Rosalind Tuck's resentment might reasonably have been against the Headmistress, who gave the punishment, and her tutor, who enforced it. But even Rosalind Tuck would not dare to commit atrocities against those formidable creatures. Her resentment would be directed at Ramona, who had simply done her duty by reporting her. Probably she would commit an atrocity, another one. Ramona felt frightened and a little sick.

If there was any other job she could have done, any other place she could have lived, she would have done the other job and lived in the other place. She had tried and failed and she was stuck.

She began to feel the despair that had pressed on her head in Brewster Terrace.

*

121

To Sara Corderey, Rosalind Tuck was a creature from another planet. There was no one like her in Sara's family, among the children of her parents' friends, or anywhere in her other schools. It was impossible not to envy her – her beauty, her precocity, her popularity, her apparently unlimited spending money. She didn't care twopence about learning anything. She said she didn't need to, and she was right. She didn't say this to Sara, because she didn't say anything to Sara, but Sara heard her saying it to other people.

A girl like Amanda Loring became a kind of somebody, a kind of public figure that people talked to and listened to, just because Rosalind had chosen her for a friend. It didn't make Amanda any different, but it made her completely different.

And then suddenly, one morning, in the five-minute break between the second and third lessons, Rosalind waved to Sara, across the whole width of the main hall. Sara took it that there was somebody behind her, somebody like Amanda Loring, that Rosalind was waving at. She glanced round. There was nobody behind her. It was herself Rosalind was waving at. She was so surprised that she almost didn't wave back. But she did wave, just in time. Several people saw the two of them waving at one another, as though they were friends.

That day in the dining-hall, three girls spoke to Sara who had never spoken to her before.

There had been a faint hope that one or other of Sara Corderey's parents might make it home for Christmas. The hope disappeared. Sara expected to be sent to the Dorset parsonage where her younger brother was. Then her aunt asked her, in a note. The note said that Sara would be doing her old aunt a favour, by preventing her from having the first solitary Christmas of her whole life.

Sara reported this to Ramona, looking up from the closing chapter of *Our Mutual Friend*.

'That's very forgiving of your aunt,' said Ramona, 'considering what happened to that book.'

'She knows it wasn't our fault. Where will you go, Miss Charnley?'

'Nowhere. I've nowhere to go.'

'No family?'

'Not here. My sister's in Hong Kong and my brother seems to be in Australia. I haven't got any cousins or uncles or anything. I did have a great-aunt, but that was a long time ago.'

'You'll be *here?*'

'Where else?'

'But all alone?'

'Oh no. Norman will be here.'

'Norman? Oh – the odd-job man.'

'And probably Maureen Maynard. We'll have Christmas lunch together, in the kitchen. It's what we've done for the last three years. It's not so bad.'

'But what about the Headmistress?'

'They always go away. There's a hotel they always go to, in Jersey.'

'I think I should hate Christmas in a hotel.'

'So would I. I'd rather be here.'

'I should hate to be here. I wonder if . . .'

They looked at one another, with a wild surmise.

Colette Davies, for so long the great white academic hope of Malham House, did unaccountably badly in the end-of-term examinations. Opinion in the Staff Common Room, where the matter was discussed in the absence of other matters to discuss, was that the influence of Rosalind Tuck was responsible. Colette had taken her eye off the ball.

Hilda Joy, possessive as always of 'her' girls, would not have this – forbade, as far as she could, the view being expressed.

'She's a menace, that Tuck girl,' said Marigold Kent softly to Ramona. 'But, by God, I wish my daughter was a bit more like her.'

123

Ramona knew and liked Marigold's daughter Debbie, a stocky, uncomplicated child with a passion for frogs. She thought that Marigold, who was not mad in any way at all, was quite mad.

Sara Corderey slipped into the classroom unobserved, as she hoped. She was carrying, hidden in a fold of file-paper, her aunt's copy of *Vanity Fair*. It was a paperback, easier to hide under the books in her locker than the massive hardcover Dickens, unillustrated and so less liable to vandalism; Miss Charnley and Sara had agreed that they could take the risk, so that Sara could make best use of the greater amount of free time that went with the approaching end of term.

But the classroom was not empty. Rosalind Tuck was there, sitting at a desk, looking blankly at a book.

Rosalind smiled at Sara. Sara smiled nervously back. She did not *know* that Rosalind had torn the picture out of *Our Mutual Friend*.

Rosalind switched her smile off. She said, 'Bloody extra homework, because The Moaner reported me for doing what anyone normal does all the time, if anybody asks them, which I bet nobody ever has her.'

'I don't think you can really blame her,' said Sara.

'Oh no. She has to keep her nose clean with the boss. She'd never get another job. I'd be a tart rather than have a job like that.'

Sara giggled nervously. Rosalind laughed.

Rosalind said, 'I think I'd be a smashing tart, actually, but I won't have to be one. I'm going to be a model.'

Sara saw that this was true. It was inescapably obvious. Rosalind's lovely face would pout from the pages of every glossy magazine; she would be jetted to Martinique and Haiti and Bali, to be photographed among exotic flowers whose beauty she would outshine; and the gorgeous birds would drop off their perches in mortified envy.

'That's one of the reasons I don't need to understand

French,' said Rosalind. 'And I bloody well don't understand this French. What do you make of this muck?'

Sara made of it a perfectly straightforward passage from
André Maurois, without a single word which she had to
look up. Rosalind wrote at Sara's dictation, in her big,
round, unformed handwriting with circles instead of dots
over the 'i's.

'Bless you, bless you, bless you,' said Rosalind when
they had finished. 'You're a better friend than any of my
friends.'

The following afternoon Sara helped Rosalind with some
extra arithmetic.

Sara was not suddenly bewitched by Rosalind Tuck. She
was young and ignorant and inexperienced in human
relationships, but she was not a complete fool. She did not
try to convince herself that Rosalind's conversation was
interesting. On the contrary, it was often boring and sometimes shocking. She talked about boys a little and herself
a great deal. Of her two greatest friends, Amanda Loring
was still a lump, and Colette Davies seemed to Sara a sort
of battlefield. Of course Sara knew about Colette's exam
results, and the reason given for them. In a small, closed
community like that sort of boarding school, nearly everybody knew nearly everything about everybody. It was
Colette's business, and if she wanted to be one sort of
person rather than another sort of person, it was not Sara's
business to try to stop her.

None of the three, nor any of their other near-intimates,
were the friends Sara would really have chosen. Simply, it
was so nice to feel yourself belonging to something.
Simply, it was so nice not to be so lonely.

Sara acquired a nickname. She was called 'Mouse'.
Perhaps it was not the most flattering nickname in the
world, but it was something to have a nickname at all. It
was a sign of something. Sara had never had a nickname
before, at other schools or in her family.

People said, 'Hullo, Mouse' who would not have said

125

'Hullo' otherwise, who would not have said anything at all.

Probably Rosalind Tuck invented the nickname and started people using it.

In asking Ramona Charnley to join Sara and herself for part of the Christmas holidays, Miss Jennifer Corderey felt a little like her sister-in-law – tricked into a greater benevolence than she had intended. But Sara's arguments had been impossible to resist. It was terrible to think of that girl sitting down to her Christmas dinner with an odd-job man and a mentally retarded maidservant – terrible to think of her never going away from her place of work because she had nowhere else to go.

Sara quoted to her aunt an account of the home where Ramona Charnley had been brought up. She made the place sound like Vita Sackville-West's 'Chevron', in *The Edwardians*. Jennifer Corderey was getting the facts at two removes, and she dismissed much of what Sara told her as gross exaggeration. She simply didn't believe in a dairy-maid making butter on the home farm, just for the use of the household, in the 1970s, in the England of the Wilson and Callaghan governments.

But she did accept that Ramona had been sent to one of the most expensive schools in the country.

The end of term was not quite like that of any ordinary boarding-school. Many of the girls' families came home on leave for Christmas, to short lets in furnished houses, so that those girls had no idea where they were going or what they would find when they got there. They were used to it, if their fathers had been working abroad for any length of time. Other girls flew out to join their families. A few were planted on families not their own, as would have been invariable in the days before everybody flew everywhere.

Rosalind Tuck was joining her parents in the Gulf. Quite a large group of them were going to Saudi Arabia and

126

Bahrain. It was all discussed with envy in the Staff Common Room. Holiday tasks were discussed. Rosalind Tuck was taking a lot of books, listed for her by Hilda Joy; by getting plenty of reading done she would help herself to catch up with her class.

'Catch up with the class?' murmured Marigold Kent to Ramona. 'She's already left the class behind. She doesn't need to be bothered with reading. All she needs is a good agent.'

Ramona kept quiet about her own plans, even to Marigold Kent.

Sara Corderey, being now a person that other people spoke to, answered questions about her Christmas. She said she was going to her aunt. There would be just the two of them. Probably it would be pretty quiet.

'No parties?' said Rosalind Tuck. 'Poor Mouse. I shall start going to a party the minute I arrive, and I shan't stop till I leave.'

'What about all those books?'

'I'm not even going to take them.'

'But – '

'I don't need to read them, do I? Because I've got you to tell me what they're about.'

It seemed to Sara that Rosalind had her life well planned. It was not a plan that would have suited Sara, but it suited Rosalind beautifully.

Mary McPhee said, for the hundredth time, what a shame it was that Rosalind had not been allowed out to have lunch with her brother. It was as though she was reminding Rosalind that she had invited her, that she had done her bit, that she thereby qualified to be one of Rosalind's special friends.

'I haven't done anything about that, have I?' said Rosalind. 'I must be slipping.'

*

127

The last full day of term was given over almost entirely to packing. Ramona supervised the packing of her own small charges, which meant in effect that she did all their packing for them. In the dormitories where the smallest girls slept, the belongings of all of them had been distributed among the belongings of all the rest of them. Some items – Cashmere sweaters, nice shoes – were fiercely claimed as their own by two or more children. Items like woolly underwear, or blouses considered childish, were disclaimed by their actual owners as well as by everybody else. All the clothes of all the children were supposed to be clearly marked with name-tapes or with indelible ink, but some of the children's mothers were not conscientious about this. A lot of things had been lost, by their owners or their borrowers. Some of the children were leaving their heavy winter clothes behind, in trunks under their beds, because they were travelling by air to hot places. The things to be left behind had to be sorted out from the things to be taken. The noise of the excited, squabbling little girls was piercing and unceasing. Ramona was unable to control them. She did not really want to try – they were entitled to be excited, to chant the traditional anthems of escape which had not changed by a syllable since Ramona's schooldays, or, probably, her mother's. She would not have been able even to try to control the children, because she was up to her neck in odd socks and single games-shoes, in sweaters claimed by three girls and underpants claimed by none.

A few older girls, whose own packing was simpler, were told off to help Ramona. They were not much help. Amanda Loring was one of the helpers, quite good humoured about it but not helpful at all.

When the packing was at last done, except for the overnight things that would go in last, Ramona felt battered from the screaming. Her back was aching from a day of crouching and squatting and carrying. She made, exhausted, the exhausting climb to her room.

She felt in her pocket for the key. The key was not there. If she had lost it she had locked herself out of her room. Norman the odd-job man would have to come up with tools. But the first and last days were the busiest of the term for Norman, pulling trunks about on trolleys and stacking them in the hall. It would be hours before Norman would be free to do a bit of carpentry on Ramona's door, and he would be quite as tired as she was.

Ramona stopped, frowned, tried to remember. She had taken her coat off early in the day, and hung it on a hook on one of the dormitory doors. Certainly at that point the key had been in the pocket. She had been in that room about a third of the time, until the packing was finished and she put her coat on again. She had not worried about the coat – it was no use to the little girls, and of no interest to the bigger ones. It was a practical, durable schoolmarm's tweed coat. There was nothing else in the pockets except a handkerchief and a pencil. They were both there.

It was possible that one of the children had knocked or nudged the coat off its peg, and that when it fell the key fell out of the pocket. In the excitement and the confusion and the yelling, this might have gone unnoticed by anyone. The key might now be under one of the beds in that dormitory. It might have got bundled up in somebody's dressing-gown, and be at the bottom of a trunk. That was more likely – if the key had fallen onto something soft it would have made no sound – would be less likely to be noticed. But it might be lying around, or one of the children might have picked it up, not knowing what it was, what door it opened.

As a matter of form, knowing it was useless, Ramona tried the door of her room. It opened.

Somebody had stolen the key from her pocket, knowing what key it was. Amanda had stolen it and given it to her adored Rosalind Tuck.

Ramona was appalled at the thought of Miss Jennifer Corderey's books, which should have been safe under lock and key in this room.

The books had hardly been touched – only a little, and incidentally. All Ramona's clothes, every item of her small and meticulously looked-after wardrobe, had been taken out of drawers and off hangers, and spread about over the floor. A five-litre can of yellow paint had been emptied over them. Paint was everywhere. There was a lot of paint on the bedclothes and on the electric fire. There was paint on Ramona's hairbrush and on her toothbrush. It was a strong mustard yellow. There was a penetrating smell of wet paint.

The paint was for the showers in the basement, which the girls used after playing games. Norman was going to do the painting over Christmas. It was a good colour for those basement showers. The bursar had chosen it, and Ramona, though not consulted, had agreed with his choice.

Several cans of paint were already in a corner of the showers, waiting for Norman to get at the job.

Anybody seen carrying something in a cardboard box, this day of all days of the term, would excite no comment at all. Everybody in the school was running up and down with things in bags and boxes. Rosalind Tuck's packing would have been simple and quickly finished.

None of the children would particularly remember Amanda Loring being anywhere near Ramona's coat, hanging on the door of the dormitory. They were all rushing about and shouting. Nobody would have seen her take the key, because she would have done it when nobody was looking. Nobody would have seen her give the key to Rosalind Tuck. Nobody would have seen Rosalind going into the showers with a light cardboard box and coming out with a heavy one. Nobody would have paid any attention to anything she was doing, because they were all busy and preoccupied.

The can was there, upside down and empty on a pile of Ramona's underwear. Its lid was there, glued by paint to Ramona's one evening dress.

The cardboard box was there. It had held packets of detergent. There were dribbles of paint inside it but not outside. Rosalind had used it to keep paint off herself. No doubt she had been very careful. No doubt she had locked herself in, and then poured the paint so that not a drop of it got on herself or her clothes or shoes.

There would be people who would say that Rosalind

was with them, every minute of the day. There were always people anxious to ingratiate themselves with the Rosalinds of this world, the natural leaders, the dangerous enemies.

Ramona stared at the paint, incapable of thought or movement.

CHAPTER SEVEN

Ramona sank to the floor, in the doorway of her little bedroom. She sank to her knees, not in order to pray for strength or deliverance, but because she seemed to herself too tired to stand. She would have sat, but paint spattered the bed and the single chair. The clothes she was wearing were free from paint. They were the only things she had that were free from paint, and it seemed important to keep them that way.

The smell of paint filled the room. It was one of the things that made Ramona feel sick, on her knees in the door of the room.

Number 53 Brewster Terrace had been full of the smell of paint. Ramona's mother had complained about the smell. The paint there was only on the walls and wood-work. The windows could be opened. Ramona could not get to her window to open it, without treading in splashes of paint, without tracking more paint over the floor.

It would take gallons of white spirit or gasoline, hundreds of pieces of rag, to get all the paint off the floor and furniture. Probably it would be impossible to get all the paint off her clothes. Some of her things – tights, bedroom slippers, a woolly shawl – were obviously ruined, fit only for the incinerator stocked daily by Norman the odd-job man. Some of the other things might one day be usable, but most of them would bear indelible traces of mustard-yellow paint.

Ramona could not sleep in the room. She could not have done so even if the bed had not been splashed with paint. She could not have done so even without the sickening reek of the paint. She was sickened less by the smell than by the vicious, vindictive cruelty of that horrible child.

Some of the things which Rosalind Tuck had ruined had come from Garston. Ramona had had those bedroom slippers at Garston. She had pattered along the upstairs passage, between her bedroom and the nursery bathroom, in those slippers. They had lasted well. They had been very expensive, and she had looked after them carefully. They were among the very, very few surviving physical links with Garston. She had treasured them for that reason, and because she knew that she would never again be able to afford such beautiful and comfortable slippers. Now they would go to Norman and his incinerator.

Far away, far below, there were shouts and bumps. It would have been impossible to impose normal discipline on the last night of term, and nobody tried. The distant shrieks of excitement were the only sounds in the top-floor passage of servants' bedrooms. Then there was another sound, which Ramona tried in vain to stifle – her own hard helpless sobs.

Idiotically, she felt she was weeping in mourning for her bedroom slippers, fluffy sky-blue slippers which had been among her Christmas presents when she was seventeen. Slippers which had been alive and were dead, throttled and fouled by gobs of mustard paint. The whole unthinkable outrage was represented, to Ramona, by the destruction of her slippers, as to a newspaper reader the horrors of an earthquake or a bombardment are represented by a photograph of a single grieving child. Ramona wept over the paint-daubed corpses of her slippers.

Norman would help clean up the mess, with rags and scrubbing-brushes and turpentine, but not for several days. He worked long hours, day after day, at the end of every term, cleaning up the girls' accumulated mess, scrubbing or painting out graffiti, cording great bales of blankets and taking them to the steam-laundry in the town. Norman

133

would expect some kind of tip or bonus, for the extra work of cleaning up all this paint. He would have earned it – certainly he would deserve it. But it made a problem. Even as she knelt weeping, Ramona faced the problem. She lived free during the term-time, but in the holidays she was expected to contribute to the cost of her meals and to that of heating whatever rooms she used. That was more or less fair – obviously the rest of the staff had to pay to eat and to live when they were not at school. But tipping Norman, at the scale he would expect and deserve, would leave very little over for replacing the things Rosalind Tuck had ruined, and almost nothing for Christmas presents for the Cordereys, aunt and niece. They would expect books. Hardcover books, of the kind you would give people like them, cost £10 and more.

She could perhaps explain to the Cordereys about the paint. She could not explain to Norman about the Cordereys.

She decided to do as much of the cleaning up as possible herself, leaving Norman as little as possible. She was too tired to start immediately. She had none of the necessary equipment for cleaning up wet paint. She had reports to write; they had to be done carefully, even for such young children, because reports were one of the things the parents thought they were paying for. Then order had to be brought back to her classroom cupboards after the havoc caused by end-of-term excitement; and then an inventory had to be made of crayons and paper and alphabet blocks, and given to the bursar so that he could order replacements (he wanted as much time as possible, so that he could shop around). There were a dozen other things that had to be done. The first few days of the holidays were almost as tiring as the term. They were not as frightening.

All the rest of the staff would presently be in their beds. All the girls would ultimately be in their beds. There would be no empty beds in the building. It was another night in the Staff Common Room. On subsequent nights, if the smell and the sense of horror lingered, she could use one of the beds in one of the dormitories.

134

Ramona managed to stop crying, and to struggle to her feet. She tried not to look at the obscenity of her room, but it was impossible not to look at it. She knew exactly what had happened and why, and there was nothing in the world she could do about it. It was not even worth reporting the fact of the outrage, if she had not and would never have a shred of proof as to the identity of the culprit.

It would be better not to report it – to say nothing to anyone except Norman. If the Headmistress got the idea that Ramona laid herself open to persecution . . . a weak teacher, vulnerable where she should have been stern, was a menace to discipline throughout the school. If the Headmistress took that view, then Ramona's job was under threat.

She would not say anything even to Marigold Kent.

Wiser after her first experience, she would take a couple of blankets down to the Common Room, if she could find two blankets free of paint. She couldn't go down for a long time yet. She couldn't let herself be seen, trailing about the building with a couple of blankets. The girls were up till all hours, running about the passages, on the last night of term. The prefects were supposed to restrain them, but the prefect system was not reliable at the Malham House School. The prefects were probably smoking in the boiler-room.

Ramona wondered where to spend the hours – three hours, perhaps – before she could put herself to bed in the Common Room.

She spent them staring at the paint on her clothes and bedclothes and bedroom slippers.

It was no easier to sleep, in the best armchair in the Common Room. Rage had the same effect as a jug of strong coffee. Ramona had had strong coffee, proper coffee, just twice since they left Garston. Both times in little cups. Both times after lunch with Miss Jennifer Corderey. Tea at Brewster Terrace. An anonymous khaki fluid in the Malham House dining hall. Instant in the Staff

Common Room. But she remembered Garston coffee, and the wonderful smell of fresh-roasted, fresh-ground beans . . . Some of the people who came to Garston never had coffee after dinner, because it kept them awake. Rage would have kept them awake, but there was nothing at Garston to get angry about.

Hatred kept Ramona awake. She had only felt it before once in her life. That was with the tractor-driver who ran over her dog. There had been nothing, immediately, that she could do about that. There was nothing, immediately, that she could do about this, either.

She was better for having two blankets off her bed, in the armchair in the Common Room. One had a little paint on it. She was careful not to let it smudge onto anything. She could not, this time, wear her dressing-gown over her clothes, because her dressing-gown was covered in paint.

She climbed upstairs in the dawn, carrying blankets and alarm-clock. She thought she was early enough, but she was hardly early enough. Some of the girls were so excited they were already up and running about. She thought none of them saw her. She thought that, if they did see her, they would think she had some reason for walking about fully dressed carrying blankets.

A thought struck her which made her feel as sick as the stench of paint of the night before. They would say she was walking about, dressed and with blankets, because she had wet her bed again.

She thought her room would look less horrible by daylight. It looked neither more nor less horrible, but exactly the same, and the smell was exactly the same.

Cars began to arrive soon after breakfast, and the bus which was taking a lot of girls by the Dartford Tunnel to Gatwick Airport. It was taking Rosalind Tuck. She had resumed high heels and skin-tight jeans. As soon as she was on board the bus, she could regard herself as immune from school discipline, as though she had crossed the three-mile limit at sea. It was evident that she did so regard

136

herself. Sitting by a window on the side of the bus nearer to the school, she took out a compact and a lipstick. She painted her luscious mouth a vivid scarlet, and then painted her eyelids, upper and lower, with heavy black mascara. She looked stunning. She looked twenty-three years old; she looked like jailbait.

When she had finished putting on her make-up, she lit a cigarette. That was a gesture of defiance that should not have been overlooked. But the staff were busy saying hello to mothers and aunts, and goodbye to girls, and nobody wanted to spoil the happy running-up-to-Christmas atmosphere. Other girls began smoking as soon as they were sitting in the cars that were taking them away. Nobody could do anything about that. If in a car, why not in the bus? Rosalind Tuck got away with it.

Miss Jennifer Corderey came for her niece. Sara struggled out to the car with her suitcase, passing the window of the bus where Rosalind sat painted like a whore and puffing at her King-Size. Rosalind waved and smiled. She called, 'Happy Christmas, Mouse!' but through the heavy glass of the window her voice was inaudible. Sara grinned and waved back.

Sara was followed to her aunt's car by several voices which called, 'Have a good hols, Mouse! Happy Christmas!' Sara turned and waved, smiling, to the people who had called to her.

To Miss Jennifer Corderey, waiting by the car, the bus was head on. The only person inside it that she could see was the driver. She saw her niece smile and wave at a passenger in the bus, but she could not see the passenger. She did see other girls waving and calling their farewells to Sara, and Sara's replies.

Evidently the child was settling in and making friends, in spite of being a baby and a bookworm. That was good, very good indeed. The school might have a better, a more loving atmosphere than Sara's earlier loneliness had suggested. It might not be such a bad place, after all. Its academic and artistic life might be there, but somewhat hidden to a new arrival. After all, arriving in a new boarding school was pretty like arriving in a new country, which she herself had so often done. You discovered things about it slowly, after living in the midst of them for weeks and months; some of the most excellent and exciting things about a new country kept themselves longest hidden from a newcomer. So it must of course be with a school. By finding friends, young Sara was feeling new pulses, walking new roads.

Knowing so well, after a lifetime of teaching, the reticence of youth about the matters most important to it, Jennifer Corderey resolved to do no prying. Anything Sara said, Jennifer would listen to with the closest interest; anything she left unsaid would be something she chose not to say. That was something to be respected.

In the car, Jennifer detected small but unmistakable changes in Sara, even since the last time they had seen one another. She seemed to have grown, developed physically, which was scarcely possible; certainly she had grown in confidence, in social ease. She had smiled more often and more broadly on her second visit than on her first; now she smiled more still, as though she at last found it possible to be happy.

Little Ramona Charnley was right. That broad smile was very sweet, and lit up the solemn little face, and gave a promise of a most attractive and interesting adult.

Jennifer Corderey found herself looking forward to a Christmas which she had, she admitted to herself, been slightly dreading.

By lunchtime nearly all the girls had gone. The staff could start doing all the things they had to do.

In the wakeful patches of the small hours, in the armchair in the Staff Common Room, Ramona had decided that her first priority was Miss Jennifer Corderey's books. There was not much paint on them, but any was too much. Spots of mustard-yellow showed up like the effects of a calamitous disease on one or two which had blackish old bindings – a copy of *Hard Times*, a copy of *Pendennis*.

All she needed was turps. She needed rags: scraps of her ruined underclothes provided dozens of rags. She went to find Norman, the odd-job man, for a bottle of turps. Norman was having his nap. Nobody knew where he was. The door of his store-shed was locked. Getting the paint off Miss Corderey's books became a project for another day.

The reports had to be written. Perhaps they were the priority.

At the end of her first term at Malham, Ramona had been astonished to be asked to write reports on five-year-olds. There was nothing to report. The children were moderately good or moderately naughty – the same child, on different days, was good or naughty – and that was all that could be truthfully said about them. The Headmistress had patiently explained to Ramona about the need for reports. She was so elusive, so oblique, in her explanation, that Ramona was no nearer understanding what she was supposed to say or why she was supposed to say it.

Marigold Kent, as so often, made the whole thing clear.

'It's an exercise in public relations,' she said. 'Customer relations. They want these kids to come back, right? They don't want to lose a single one, even if the parents are posted back to the U.K. It doesn't matter if the child's a moron, a delinquent, a genius or whatever. The function of your report is to subtly convey that the child's future happiness, success, personal fulfilment and social advancement depends on her staying at the dear old Malham House School.'

'To subtly convey,' Ramona's mind priggishly and ungratefully echoed. She did not think she would ever, in the most informal conversation, have so gratuitously split an infinitive. She was for a moment distracted from what kind Marigold was telling her.

The message got through, though. She was to suck up to the parents about their child – to suck up, in effect, to

139

the child – without telling too many blatantly obvious lies, with the object of maintaining the income of Lt. Commander and Mrs Edwin Barrow.

Ramona remembered the language of house-agents, which she and her mother had learned during the long, long search for Number 53 Brewster Terrace. 'Suitable for modernisation' meant that £20,000 would have to be spent before the place was habitable. '3/5 bedrooms' meant three bedrooms and two broom-cupboards. 'Compact, manageable garden' meant six square feet of asphalt. She adopted this semantic philosophy when compiling the reports of her pupils. It began to amuse her – a little, a very little – to contrive euphemisms like those of the house-agents. 'Full of vivacity' meant a spoiled, uncontrollable, tearaway brat. 'Amenable and co-operative' meant an apathetic dumpling. 'A little behind' meant subnormal. 'Reacts with enthusiasm' meant hysterical. The Headmistress approved the reports without seeing the jokes. Of course, she saw very little of the children.

Compiling her reports, for the thirteenth time, Ramona was able to forget, quite often, and for as long as five seconds, what awaited her upstairs in her bedroom.

Rubbing with turpentine, and with the corner of a pair of ruined knickers, did not obliterate the nail-head sized spot of mustard paint on the binding of *Hard Times*. It spread it into a dung-coloured cloud no larger that a girl's hand.

'Christ A'mighty, Miss', said Norman the odd-job man, 'whyever did you bring a tin o' my paint all the way up here? You woulda done better, *if* I may suggest, to of informed me of your wish to of redecorated your room. Now I hardly knows where to commence. Was these by way of being your bedroom slippers, Miss? More like a pair of cuttlefish, ol' paint bin an' dried that hard. Pity, really.'

Ramona was sleeping on a bed in one of the small

dormitories used by the older girls. She carried her own blankets to the dormitory late at night, and carried them back again in the dawn, because every stitch of the girls' bedclothes had gone off to the steam laundry in the town.

Five days after the end of term, when her reports were complete and her classroom cupboards reorganised, she took a lift into town with Norman in the minibus. She drew a small amount from the small amount of her savings. She bought a box of chocolates for Maureen Maynard, a carton of cigarettes for Norman, and books for Jennifer and Sara Corderey. These last were difficult, because the bookshop, into which she had never been before, carried a stock just like that of the Bilborough Bookshop. There were no books, properly so called. The covers were resplendent, but the contents could not have commanded the attention of any literate person for more than fifty seconds.

Ramona knew that, in spite of the life she had been living, she was a kind of intellectual snob. She thought that, on the whole, it was a good thing to be.

She found a second-hand bookshop, near the station. Blowing away the dust, she found an early edition of John Clare's poems for Jennifer Corderey, and a selection of Guy de Maupassant, in French, for Sara. The saving was considerable. It enabled her to buy two extra pairs of tights and some very cheap bedroom slippers, and leave enough over for Norman's bonus for the paint-removal.

The staff dribbled away, a few in their own cars but most in other people's. Marigold Kent went back to her own children, and to the cottage she had salvaged from the wreck of her marriage. Hilda Joy went off to the married sister who had once again, and barely, overruled the objections of her family. Lt. Commander and Mrs Edwin Barrow went off to their hotel in Jersey, to the bridge tables, the muffled conversations, the resentful suspicion of persons spending Christmas there for the first time, the terribly knowledgeable scrutinies of the wine list. Ramona knew where all the others were going, because it had made something to talk about, over the previous fortnight, in the Staff Common Room. They knew that she was to stay with friends of her family. This fiction had now fossilised into the semblance of truth, the respectability of permanence, in the Common Room as in the classroom. It was easier for everybody.

Ramona was alone in the school for three days with Norman and Maureen Maynard, neither of whom had anywhere else to go. They had their meals in the kitchen, and Norman went out to the pub.

Ramona made herself sleep in her own room again, although it felt like a place haunted by the memory of a brutal rape.

On a freezing afternoon, four days before Christmas, Miss Jennifer Corderey came in the little Renault. Sara was not with her because she had one of those colds that tended to go to her chest. Ramona had less luggage even than she would have had before the end of term. She had Miss Corderey's books. She began to explain about the books and to apologise for them before she was properly in the car. Her explanation could be said to have contained an element of truth.

Sara seemed really pleased to see Ramona. Her smile was wide and sweet and welcoming. Her cold was hardly more than a sniffle.

They had tea and toast and Bovril in front of an open fire. One of the Pekes – a major reason for Miss Corderey's occupation of the house – snapped insincerely at Ramona when she stroked it. They were old dogs, gustily asleep most of the time.

At very long intervals, Ramona allowed herself to remember her adored and adoring Hector, white with a tan patch on his face and one on his rump, prancing and plumy-tailed, brave and affectionate and comical . . .

After tea, Miss Corderey showed her to the bigger of the two spare bedrooms. If it was really the bigger, the other, Sara's room, was very small indeed. Ramona's room was under the eaves, so that almost the whole of the outside wall was at forty-five degrees. It was spotlessly clean and immaculately tidy, without being antiseptic and unwelcoming. There was no smell of paint; there were no splashes of mustard paint on the scrubbed pine floorboards or on the flowered eiderdown. There were a shelf of books, three watercolours of Eastern markets, a wardrobe and a small armchair. The bathroom was next door.

'For me this is like heaven,' said Ramona.

'As we are, in a manner of speaking, professional colleagues,' said Miss Corderey, 'and as you have, so to say, been recruited as a member of this family for Christmas, I think, don't you, that we might venture Christian names?'

Ramona was calling her 'Jennifer', almost without self-consciousness, almost at once.

Ramona's father had always had a bath before dinner, even if it made dinner half an hour late. It was an absolute rule; it was something he commanded; if circumstances somehow conspired to prevent his bath before dinner, his evening was grumpy and ruined. Ramona, for various reasons, had never in her life had a bath before dinner. She had only just started coming down to dinner, when they left Garston, and then not always. Baths before dinner were impossible at Number 53 Brewster Terrace, because she had to cook the dinner, however tired she was after a day in the bookshop. At Malham House, there were senior mistresses who laid claim to the bathroom before dinner; and in the holidays she and Norman and Maureen had high tea at six-thirty so that Norman could get out to the pub. Ramona's first evening in Jennifer's house was her first ever bath before dinner: and she understood exactly how her father had felt.

Jennifer wore a long skirt for dinner. Ramona's one long skirt would never be wearable again.

Ramona and Sara washed up after dinner. The three of them would share all the chores.

'While we're here,' said Ramona over the suds, 'I wish you'd call me Ramona, if you can bear it, and if you remember not to do it at school.'

143

'I was hoping you'd ask me to,' said Sara, 'but I couldn't do it until you asked me to, and I didn't think I could ask you. Ramona. It's a strange name, if that's not rude. It's exotic. It's sort of haunting – it's somebody in a poem by Edgar Allan Poe.'

'I was given it for very mundane reasons,' said Ramona. 'I was named for a great aunt who'd married a millionaire. She was going to leave me everything.'

'Well, I'm glad she didn't,' said Sara, 'because if she had you wouldn't be here. I know that's rather a selfish point of view.'

Ramona laughed, wiping the steam from her spectacles with a dish-cloth. She was touched. She was not sure she had inspired anyone with affection since the tractor-driver murdered Hector.

Sara began calling her 'Ramona' immediately, with less apparent self-consciousness than she herself felt in saying 'Jennifer'.

The sheets were scented with lavender. Ramona dreamed of the boat on the lake at Garston.

In a sense, Sara had correctly predicted to Rosalind Tuck how Christmas would be with her aunt. They were quiet. There were no parties. They went for long walks in the bright cold weather, over crackling fields and through woods with ice-coated twigs, each time trying to persuade the dogs to come and each time failing. (The dogs' refusal to go further than the end of the garden became one of their standing jokes.) They talked at great length, about everything under the sun. Jennifer, obviously, did most of the talking, because she had most to talk about. She kept stopping herself, in her accounts of far places, in case she was boring her young guests, but they always pressed for more. They all did a lot of reading. Mostly, all three spent most of the evening reading (there was no television in the cottage).

144

But in a deeper sense it *was* a party – a happy party every minute of every day. The three of them got on extraordinarily well, considering all the differences – perhaps, in part, because of the differences.

Ramona was sometimes struck into wondering speechlessness, by the extraordinary, the utterly unfamiliar, sensation of feeling happy.

'Of course, having been a teacher all my adult life,' said Jennifer one evening, out of the blue but as though continuing a conversation, 'I've always been surrounded by children, young people. Often almost overwhelmed by them, engulfed. Equally obviously, being an old maid I've never had a family of my own. All those thousands of children, all the years I was working, made me forget the fact. Made me not mind what I was missing, not realise what I was missing. But now, do you know, I feel for the first time in my life that I have got a family of my own. This is the happiest Christmas I think I've had since my childhood. I really am grateful to you two.'

Sara caught Ramona's eye, and they smiled at one another.

They went to church on Christmas morning; Matins; the ugly little church was packed. The cadaverous middle-aged man who read the second lesson had a heavy head-cold, so that the lovely words came out as though bubbling through a tube of mud.

Ramona's father had always read the lesson on Christmas morning in Garston Church. He loved doing it, and he did it very well. He was perhaps a little on the theatrical side as a reader of Holy Scripture; he was especially fond of long dramatic pauses. Ramona heard his strong, soothing voice, in her mind's ear, through the rheum-bleared tones of the reader.

They lit the fire in the sitting room as soon as they got back from church. They opened their presents. It was the

145

Corderey family custom to open presents in front of the fire after church.

At Garston, there was always a gigantic Christmas tree in the hall. When Ramona was a child, it was always decorated after she had gone to bed on Christmas Eve. As in so many areas of life at Garston, strict tradition controlled the placing of the decorations on the tree. It was as though Ramona's parents, successfully striving to live their pre-war life in the post-war world, had manufactured traditions in order to have traditions to maintain. It would have been a shock to Ramona, coming down to breakfast on Christmas morning as soon as she had opened her stocking, to find the Christmas angel out of her usual position, or the big red glass balls hanging anywhere except at the very ends of the branches.

There was a little, token plastic Christmas tree at Number 53 Brewster Terrace. There was hardly room for a real tree, and £5 for a Christmas tree would have been a ludicrous extravagance. Their presents to one another were token presents. They did not go to church. Ramona's mother seemed to feel that if she could not have a proper Christmas, a Garston Christmas, then a token Christmas was all she could be bothered with.

There was nothing token about Christmas with the Cordereys. Ramona saw what Jennifer Corderey meant. It felt like a family Christmas. It felt full of love.

Ramona had to go back to Malham a week before the beginning of term. This was not because there was anything to do, but because the Headmistress might need a messenger, or someone to do odd jobs of a kind different from Norman's.

Just before she got into the car beside Jennifer, Ramona stood talking to Sara, saying goodbye, au revoir, goodbye for the moment. Each was wondering whether they were supposed to kiss one another, which they had not previously done. It was not awkward in the context of the Christmas they had been spending together, but it was

146

awkward as between teacher and pupil, even though that teacher did not teach that pupil. The conversation was absurdly prolonged, each hoping that the other would make the forward move that would herald a normal female peck.

Although she was grown up – could be said to have been grown up for years – Ramona was as uncertain in this silly situation as Sara. She and her best friends at school had kissed one another with shrieks of joy at the beginning of terms and shrieks of misery at the end of terms; since then she had kissed nobody of any age, except her mother. Even her mother had latterly recoiled from kisses, and Ramona had guiltily recoiled from them too. (Justin Bryan's drunken kiss did not count.)

'Come on, children,' said Jennifer Corderey from the driver's seat. 'Kiss goodbye and let's be off.'

It was a comfort to be given a command in the matter. Sara giggled with what seemed to be relief. Their pecks at one anothers' cheeks were, nevertheless, so tentative that they almost missed.

Sara waved furiously as the car crunched away.

Ramona reported for duty the moment she got back, because she was a little late getting back. There was nothing particular for her to do. There was no reason for her to be there.

The Barrows seemed dyspeptic after three weeks of hotel meals.

Ramona lugged her case up to her room, carrying the new books and some of the old books that Jennifer Corderey had lent them. She wondered as she climbed about getting a new lock for her door, about getting Norman to put it in. It was not a thing she knew how to do, or had tools to do. She wondered if the bursar would pay for the lock and for Norman's time; she thought not.

When she opened the door the smell of paint struck like a sharp instrument. The window had not been opened since she went away. As far as visible paint went, Norman

147

had done his best. There were lines of paint, as though drawn by an unsteady pen, in the grain of the floorboards at the edge of the room. There was not much on the carpet where the carpet still had a nap, but on the threadbare patches, where the web of the backing was exposed, paint had soaked between the strands of fibre to create an effect of mustard-yellow check.

Ramona's mother had had a yellow checked tweed coat, for racing at Sandown in the winter. The threadbare patches where paint had struck looked a little like Ramona's mother's tweed coat. The coat had been owned by the Beeswing Bloodstock Agency. Its purchase price had been a necessary operating expense. It had gone off in a packing-case, to be sold for what it would fetch.

None of the other members of the teaching staff had returned. None were expected for two or three days. There was no reason for them to come sooner: the dormitory and study allocations, and the timetables of classes, would be exactly as during the previous term. Ramona had high tea with Norman and Maureen Maynard in the kitchen, early so that Norman could get out to the pub.

Norman had got it firmly into his head that Ramona had herself carried the pot of paint up from the showers to her room, meaning to smarten up the dingy little room. She had overturned the pot, probably while opening it, because no woman could be trusted not to overturn a pot of paint. He would entertain no other explanation of the presence of the paint in the room – the thing was obvious, argument was silly. Maureen Maynard listened closely to his monologue on the subject, her eyes wide with wonder.

Ramona gave Norman money to buy a new lock for her room, and money to put it in. She had to take his word for it that the lock cost what he said. He had not thought to get a receipt, he said, because he had not dreamed that she wouldn't trust him. She did more or less trust him, but she was a long time persuading him of this.

She was deeply thankful to have a new lock with a new key. She hung the new key on a string round her neck, and hid the spare where nobody would find it. Nobody would see the string, under the clothes she would be wearing until the warmer weather. But in the summer, when she would be constantly wearing one or other of her open-necked blouses? That problem could surely be left to solve itself when the time came. But it bothered her. She tried to dismiss it from her mind, but it buzzed round in her skull like a fly in a bottle. The front part of her mind told the back part that she was getting obsessive, that it was ridiculous to be worrying in early January about where a piece of string could be worn invisibly in July. The back part of her mind replied that she had something to be obsessive about, something to be frightened about. She was faced with vicious and ingenious vindictiveness. Front part said: it is crazy to be obsessed by fright of an ignorant teenage girl over whom she was set in authority. Back part said: it would be crazy not to be.

The time crawled and raced until the moment when the school was flooded with its pupils. Ramona wondered whether the time passed fast or slowly, in a condemned cell, the night before execution.

Those in-between days, that lost and purposeless little slice of her life, made it even more difficult to believe than in the termtime that she was the same person who had lived at Garston. At least during the term there was action, distraction, a great deal to do. It was horrible, but it had the merit of giving you very little time to think. Now there was unlimited time to think. Jennifer Corderey's books, try to concentrate on them as she might, did not stop her thinking.

She could hardly believe she had lived at Garston. She could hardly believe she had spent Christmas with Jennifer and Sara Corderey. Homesickness for Garston had been a permanent part of herself, from the moment they left it – from weeks before they left it, when their home was being destroyed around them. It ebbed and flowed, like a chronic disease, sometimes even now giving a pain so sharp that she almost cried out, never less than a little dark ever-present twinge. And now she was homesick for the little house which Jennifer Corderey had borrowed for the winter. She was homesick for the family which she had found and lost.

The rest of the staff came back, bringing a sort of exuberance into the Common Room, a sort of boisterousness which showed that these disappointed women were jolly and sophisticated souls at home in the outside world.

There was always that atmosphere, just before the beginning of term. It would only last a day or two.

Those who had had an interesting time talked about it at length. Those who had had a boring time talked about it as little as possible. Ramona said she had had a delightful time, very quiet, with old friends of her family recently returned from abroad.

The girls returned. The noise was terrific. The gravel sweep in front of the building reminded Ramona of a racecourse car-park. A bus arrived from Gatwick – the flight from Bahrain was on time. The other bus came much later, because the flight from Riyadh had been delayed. It was eleven at night before that group spilled out of their bus into the hall. Most of them looked tired and dishevelled. Not Rosalind Tuck. She had incompletely wiped the lipstick from her mouth and the mascara from her eyes. She had a new coat and very tight new leather trousers. She had a tan. None of the others had tans, but she was an astonishing gold.

'Sauna and sunlamp,' murmured Marigold Kent. 'But I'd sell my soul to look like that.'

Rosalind said, 'I was groping my way last term. I didn't really know my way around. I do now. I'm going to have some fun.'

It seemed to Ramona that Rosalind pretended not to see that Ramona was standing within earshot; that Rosalind spoke loudly enough to be quite sure that Ramona heard.

CHAPTER EIGHT

For Sara Corderey, the beginning of her second term was as different as could be from the beginning of her first. The moment she got out of Aunt Jennifer's car, people were saying, 'Hullo, Mouse. Have a good Christmas?'

She was part of it all.

Of course they had got used to seeing her about. Then they had got used to her being top or nearly top of the form, week after week. A lot of them didn't resent that, although she was younger, because they didn't want to be top of the form. But Sara's acceptance by the others had one single cause which was far more important than all the other causes put together. It was being made a friend by Rosalind Tuck. Not as great a friend as if they were in the same dormitory; not as great a friend as Amanda Loring or Colette Davies; not one of the ones she whispered to, the subjects of the whispers being made pretty obvious by the shrieks of delighted horror which greeted them. But still a friend, greeted, smiled to, waved at, joked with, complained to. They said Rosalind's plane was late – she might be hours. Sara was sorry that she would probably not see Rosalind until the following day. She was glad that she would see her then.

She saw Ramona in the distance, with lists on a clip-board. She now liked Ramona very much indeed, but she was not going to risk everything by letting it show. It was not really hypocrisy, it was just self-preservation.

Neither Ramona nor anybody else actually knew who had played that practical joke last term with the rubber knickers, or torn the page out of *Our Mutual Friend*.

Sara was 'Mouse'. She had a nickname. The name was used not in derision but in affection.

All sorts of people said, 'Hullo, Mouse,' who would probably not have said anything at all, even at the end of last term. It was as though the holidays had made her one of them, had made her a person to say 'Hullo' to. It was as though Rosalind's influence had gone on working during the holidays, beaming friendship for Sara over desert and ocean all the way from Saudi Arabia.

The lights were turned on in the dormitory, for Rosalind Tuck and two others to go to bed. It became evident that Rosalind was the same colour all over – every bit of her was the same golden-brown as her face. She was the Scandinavian type of blonde, tanning as readily as a Latin. There were no bikini lines on her breasts or buttocks. If she had put on any weight, it was where she wanted it. Her Christmas had, as she expected, been one long party. Some of the party had been while she was tanning, and some in other places.

Ramona went to bed very late and very tired. She had had to wait up for the late arrivals, and help sort them out.

There was hardly any smell of paint in her bedroom, as she had been airing it for a week.

In bed, Ramona made a New Term's Resolution. Some of Jennifer Corderey's stories had included difficult, rebellious children who had not been interested in education and had resisted it being thrust upon them. Something or other, in the stories, had changed those children's hearts – some accident, some stroke of luck, some seeming miracle. It was obvious to Ramona that what had changed

152

the children was the force of Jennifer's personality. She herself, if tackled, might not have denied that she had helped, but she would certainly have disclaimed sole credit. Ramona did not resolve to change Rosalind Tuck's heart; she knew it was beyond her, and she was not really interested in Rosalind's heart. What she resolved was to stand no nonsense from the girl. She would not attempt to be Jennifer Corderey, but she would attempt to be Marigold Kent. She had the authority, the backing of the system. The power was available if she had the guts to use it. She could not stop herself blushing, but she would be red with rage, not with embarrassment or misery.

A slight whiff of paint rekindled her rage. She went to sleep feeling very brave.

The school settled into apathy more quickly than usual, it seemed. Perhaps it was because the weather was so cold. Norman stoked the boilers with extra fury, increasing the fumes that hung about the corridors. The spring term was the shortest of the three. Nothing else good could be said about it. Everybody agreed about this.

Something else good could be said about it, Ramona thought. It brought nearer, day by dragging day, the end of the school year. Half term would also be half year. The end of term would wrap up almost two-thirds of the year. Then there were the long summer holidays. After them, of course . . .

The classrooms were full of chilblains and sniffles. One of the dormitories had to be turned into an extra sickroom, its normal occupants redistributed among the beds of the suffering. Maureen Maynard ran up and down with trays. Lt. Commander and Mrs Barrow were glad of the open fire in their drawing room, which they kept in twenty-four hours a day.

'Hullo, Mouse,' said Rosalind. 'I hoped they'd move you in here. What fun.'

153

Sara went to sleep to the sound of Rosalind telling Colette Davies about the airline pilot who had kissed her on New Year's Eve.

There was a smell of winter schoolgirl, in the library, in Evening Study Period – Vick, peppermint coughdrops, wool, shampoo, here and there tobacco. Rosalind Tuck smelled, not overpoweringly, of a scent unknown to Ramona – not one, she thought that Persephone had ever used, not one that her mother would ever have used. There was no rule against using scent, perhaps because there was no point in using it.

Ramona had been too young to wear scent at the moment when it became impossible for her ever to be able to afford scent.

Ramona was at the desk on the dais, reading, with the half eye she could spare, Jennifer Corderey's copy of *Barrie Lyndon*. Rosalind Tuck was sitting with her back to the dais. Amanda Loring was one side of her, Colette Davies the other. Sara was three places away, at the same table. She was reading and taking notes. Rosalind might have been doing these things, for all Ramona could see, but Ramona thought not.

The stage was set for history to repeat itself.

Rosalind Tuck's hair gleamed almost silver under the harsh overhead lighting. There had been an argument in the Staff Common Room, two days before, about how much Rosalind's hair was touched up. It was not a subject you would have supposed would have exercised several middle-aged women, but it was what they were arguing about. Marigold Kent wanted to bet anybody any amount that a bottle was involved in producing that colour. They could settle the bet by asking the girl. Hilda Joy forbade any such thing. When Lady Pellinger came for the weekend to Garston, which she did two or three times a year, there were bets in the family about what colour her hair would be. Patrick always lost but he always refused to pay.

154

Memories of Garston had no business visiting Ramona during Evening Study Period.

Memories of Christmas, of Jennifer Corderey's cottage, had no business visiting her either. Sara, bent over her book and making notes on her pad, was wearing a sweater which she had often worn during the day over Christmas. It was blue, with a crisscross pattern knitted into the wool. It was not very glamorous, but the colour suited her. She wore it to help with the washing-up and to bring in armfuls of firewood. A little of the total sensation of Christmas was recreated by the colour of Sara's sweater.

Under her own blouse and sweater Ramona was aware of the tiny itchiness of the piece of string on which her new key was hung. It was not an unpleasant feeling, but, on the contrary, deeply reassuring. There was a long road ahead of her, to the end of spring term, to the end of the summer term, and it was mined and booby-trapped every inch of the way. There were hazards of ruptured discipline, of suddenly exploding situations, of ill-will and cruelty; there were the hazards of her own lack of personal authority, her short sight, her ready blushes. But at least nobody could get into her bedroom.

There were ten minutes of Evening Study Period to go. Ramona felt like a rider in a steeplechase with only the final jump to negotiate before the run-in and the winning-post.

Rosalind Tuck scraped back her chair. It was not certain that she made more noise doing so than she need have made. She stood, turned, and walked slowly to the raised desk where Ramona sat. It was not certain that she was exaggerating a voluptuous walk, that she was committing deliberate insolence by the way that she walked.

Amanda Loring and Colette Davies looked up, and followed Rosalind with their eyes. Sara looked up from her book and note-pad.

'Can I be excused?' said Rosalind.

Her voice was not gratuitously loud, but the room was completely quiet, and probably everyone in the room could hear what she said.

155

'Can't it wait ten minutes?' said Ramona. She was tense, because what was happening was one of the things she had expected to happen. She had control of her voice and she did not blush.

'Not without disaster,' said Rosalind.

There were giggles, not effectively muffled. Rosalind, standing in front of Ramona, hid most of the room from her.

'I've got the blessing,' said Rosalind.

Ramona looked at her blankly. There were more giggles, less restrained.

'You probably call it the curse,' said Rosalind.

'Very well,' said Ramona. 'Come straight back.'

'Thank you, Miss Charnley,' said Rosalind, in a tiny little-girl voice.

All over the library there was giggling. It was impossible to say which girls were giggling and which not. Ramona tried to search the faces of the girls that she could see past Rosalind's intervening body. Many had their hands half over their faces, and their noses deep in their books, so that they might have been stifling giggles or they might have been studying particularly hard.

Rosalind turned and swayed towards the door. She was imitating Marilyn Monroe with fair success. Giggles from behind hands carried her to the door, as though they were waves and she a surf-board.

Only after Rosalind had closed the door, very softly, behind her, did the penny drop in Ramona's mind.

The 'blessing', which she herself would have called the 'curse'. She was saying that menstruation was a relief. She was effectively admitting to, or boasting of, sexual experience which had not resulted in pregnancy. Presumably every girl in the room had understood immediately what it had taken Ramona ten seconds to understand. Even Sara Corderey? Yes, certainly, even Sara, because although she was young and innocent she was neither stupid nor deaf, and she must have been exposed to all the same conversations that all the rest were exposed to.

Sara had been moved into the dormitory where Rosalind

156

Tuck slept, because her own had been turned into an extra sickroom.

Ramona fought not to blush. A lot of girls were looking at her. Sara had her face resting on her left hand, so that her expression was invisible.

Rosalind Tuck might have been telling the truth, or she might simply have been bored in the library, or she might have left in order to commit an atrocity. There would be no members of the staff patrolling the corridors and stairs of the building. Ramona wanted to know what Rosalind was up to, but she could not leave the library unsupervised. There was no girl capable of keeping order if she left the room, and none that could be trusted even to try to do so. Evening Study Period had five minutes to run.

The 'blessing'. Yes, it was a public boast. She could not really have been afraid of pregnancy, if she had actually been to bed with one or a dozen men over the holidays. As Marigold Kent said, they were probably all on the pill, and none more certainly than Rosalind. Even if the doctor had told the girl's mother, the mother would have been browbeaten into giving her consent, even if she had wanted to refuse it.

The boy on the motorbike had called Rosalind a tart.

Probably she was not a tart, in the way of getting money or presents by means of her body. She did not need money or presents. She wanted to live, to be grown up, to be wicked, to feel and use power over men. Perhaps she actually enjoyed the act of sex. Perhaps she loved it.

Ramona felt, like a corkscrew in the stomach, the sexless aridity of her own life. It was all passing her by. It had all, already, passed her by. Rosalind knew it. Every girl in the room knew it. Sara knew it. They despised her for it. Some of them might pity her. They were right.

She looked up and down the rows of faces of teen-aged girls, some spotty, some soft and half-formed, some with delinquent pig-eyes, some sucking at pencils as though they wished they were cigarettes, some who gave every appearance of being decent, ignorant middle-class children. She liked many of them quite well, as individuals.

157

They had bayed with laughter at her, on the occasion of the rubber knickers, because they had become a pack, a hunting pack, a many-headed monster which ceased to be composed of separate and reasonably kindly individuals. She remembered episodes from her own schooldays, which seemed an unimaginably long time ago. There had been times, even in that cultured and tolerant environment, when there was collective cruelty among girls who would never have been cruel as individual to individual.

All it took was somebody thoroughly nasty, with a strong character.

What was Rosalind really doing? Had she really been frightened that she might be pregnant? How many of these fifteen- and sixteen-year-olds had run the same risk, or taken precautions not to run it? When? Where? With adult men or boys of their own age? With enjoyment or horror? How much would it have hurt?

Few of the girls now showed any signs of giggling. Few made any pretence that they were still working, with the bell on the point of ringing. They were far too young for it, emotionally if not physically, but that didn't seem to stop anybody. Mental images, all unbidden invaded Ramona's mind. She pushed them away, feeling disgust and envy. She felt disgusted at her own prurient curiosity and at her envy.

The bell rang. The room exploded. Ramona had passed the winning-post, still in command, safe. There was no sign of Rosalind. Ramona saw Amanda Loring pick up Rosalind's books.

Ramona saw, rather than heard, Amanda and Colette Davies call to Sara Corderey. Ramona could not hear, in the hubbub, what they said to Sara or what Sara called out in reply. Sara smiled and nodded. She picked up her books and went to the door with Amanda and Colette. They formed a compact little group within the crowd. A compact little group, or part of a slightly larger one whose leader was somewhere else.

Sara did not look at Ramona when she went out of the library with her friends.

Probably it was Ramona's duty to go and find Rosalind, to make sure she was all right. You were supposed to do that, when a girl asked to be excused urgently. She might have collapsed, or be vomiting wretchedly in some corner. It had happened. The school was responsible for the health and safety of its pupils. Ramona, being on duty in the library, was personally responsible for Rosalind's health and safety. Rosalind could look after herself far better than Ramona could look after anybody, herself included. She was a survivor. She was a predator. She didn't need protection from other people, other people needed protection from her. Colette Davies most obviously needed protection from Rosalind, but she was not going to get it from anybody at the Malham House School.

Surely Sara didn't need protection from Rosalind? Surely Sara had too much sense, too much discrimination, to fall under the spell of a vain, vulgar little exhibitionist like Rosalind?

They found Rosalind where they had expected to, sitting on a desk in their classroom. She greeted them languidly. She had left the library because she had got bored with being in the library.

Sara gave them a resumé of the chapter in the French book which they should all have been reading. They listened attentively, so that they would be able to answer questions about the chapter the following day, so that Sara was made to feel clever and important.

'Mouse, you're a marvel,' said Rosalind. 'The Mighty Mouse. How lucky you are to be so clever. How lucky we are to have such a clever friend.'

Rosalind began calling Sara 'Mighty Mouse'. The new nickname caught on at once in the dormitory. By lights-out, Sara was 'Mightymouse'.

'No hassles?' said Marigold Kent, switching on the electric kettle in the Common Room.

'None at all,' said Ramona.

'You've got the measure of the little toads,' said Marigold. 'The iron fist inside the iron glove.'

Ramona laughed, aware that she had been building up nothings into monsters, aware that the things that had been done to her were tiresome rather than dreadful, aware that she would not let anything else be done to her.

And it was important to remember that nothing that happened at Malham House could be as horrible as many of the things that happened at Number 53 Brewster Terrace.

Rosalind Tuck and Colette Davies, in side-by-side beds four feet apart, were whispering after lights-out. Sara Corderey, at the other end of the dormitory, could hear only that they were whispering. You always whispered after lights-out, in case Matron or one of the teachers was prowling along the corridors. Also perhaps because other people wanted to go to sleep. Also perhaps because you didn't want anybody else to hear what you were talking about. Rosalind and Colette had been together much of the day, as usual. Amanda normally with them, Sara herself sometimes with them and sometimes not. It was a good thing to be seen with them, but it was boring to be with them all the time.

Sara saw quite clearly that Rosalind was using her, to save herself trouble, to keep herself out of trouble, to get reasonable marks without doing any work. She saw that Rosalind's friendship was for sale, and that she was buying it by doing her work for her. She did not think that Rosalind saw that the opposite was equally the case – that she was using Rosalind. She was accepted, admitted, nicknamed, after nearly a term of being an outcast, and that was what she bought by buying Rosalind's friendship. Sara thought she might have been used before, but she had never used anybody before. It made her feel a little bit guilty and a little bit triumphant. She went to sleep to the sound of Rosalind's whispers.

*

Ramona in the Staff Common Room tried to get through a few more pages of *Barrie Lyndon*; she tried to feel the enjoyment she knew the book ought to be giving her. It was impossible. She was too tired. She was distracted by a bickering, interminable exchange between Hilda Joy and the matron. The matron was complaining that no single item belonging to a particular girl was marked with either name-tapes or ink. The girl was one of Hilda Joy's pupils. Hilda was not so much defending the girl or her mother, as complaining about the matron's complaints. It was not an unusual sort of conversation in the Common Room. Both women had books open on their laps. The matron's book was a paper-back called *World War III Stories*; Hilda Joy's was a biography, borrowed from the Headmistress to whom it had been given for Christmas, of Princess Michael of Kent.

Ramona got up to go to bed, earlier than usual, depressed to be a member of a community in which one girl's name-tapes gave rise to an hour's acrimonious argument. Marigold Kent winked at her as she went out of the door.

People at Garston sometimes went to bed before the evening was over, so Ramona understood from breakfast-time conversations. Some people went to bed early because they were simply exhausted, especially after shooting. Some people were driven to bed by their wives, because they were getting drunk. The conversations about such people, at breakfast and in front of the children, were apt to be conducted in a sort of fractured French which Ramona could perfectly well understand. Nobody at Garston ever went to bed because they were bored and irritated by a pointless and distasteful argument. Nobody could ever have been bored at Garston, Ramona thought, any more than she could ever have been bored there. The only person who was ever irritated was her father, and that was only because of some failure in the arrangements, some shortcoming in his own hospitality.

Ramona almost laughed out loud, as she undressed in front of the single bar of her electric fire, to think of her

161

father's reaction to the conversation between Hilda Joy
and the matron. He would have listened politely for a little
while, gone away with some polite excuse, and then made
a good story out of it. He made good stories out of almost
anything. Ramona often failed to understand them, but all
the grown-ups always laughed. Garston was full of
laughter, chuckles and shrieks and whinnying like that
which came from the stables when the horses were excited
before hunting.

There was no laughter, not once, not from either of
them, all the time they were at Number 53 Brewster
Terrace.

In the Staff Common Room of the Malham House
School, Marigold Kent sometimes laughed.

Ramona giggled inwardly at the absurd thought of her
father in the Staff Common Room, among members of a
species not possibly to be confused with the one to which
he and his friends belonged. Presently she lay warm and
comfortable in bed, not because she was very warm or
very comfortable but because Evening Study Period had
passed without a hitch, without any challenge to her authority, without her once blushing.

Iron fist? Not that, perhaps, not yet, not ever. But she
thought she might at last be growing up.

Sara came as furtively as ever – even, perhaps, more
furtively than ever – to take or return books. She no longer
stayed reading, in hiding, in Ramona's bedroom. She no
longer left books with Ramona while she was in the middle
of them.

'They're quite safe now,' she said. 'Nobody will touch
them in my locker.'

'Are you sure, Sara?'

'Oh yes. Even if I'm not there, my friends will see that
nobody touches them.'

'And it's all right for you to be seen reading them?'

'Yes, of course, why not?'

'You don't need me, then, except as a lending-library.'

Sara smiled. Her smile, which for so long had been seen only by Ramona, was now a familiar sight in the school.

She did not stay long. She went away with *David Copperfield*. She went away to read it somewhere in public, unashamed, unafraid, her eccentric preference tolerated, her small person and her large book under the protection of powerful friends.

Was it possible to believe that she was having a civilising influence on her contemporaries? That through that vessel messages were seeping into the school, from Jennifer Corderey and her love of literature, from Ramona herself? Was it possible to believe in the operation of the Holy Spirit, implanting loving-kindness and love of beauty?

Was it possible that Ramona was safe from Rosalind Tuck?

It continued very cold. Emanations from Norman's boilers penetrated to corners where no heat followed. The girls were made to go only for very short walks. If they smoked, they must have done so with their gloves on.

Of course Sara reverted to calling Ramona 'Miss Charnley' in public. What was she to call her in private? They were in school, but they were insulated from the school. At those moments in Ramona's room they were in no-man's-land, not part of the school but not in Jennifer Corderey's cottage either – a long way from the routine of term-time, but an equally long way from the Christmas holidays.

Sara called Ramona 'You' when she came to return or collect a book.

On the third Sunday of term, the girls were allowed out for the day. The theory was that if they were allowed out sooner, they would become unsettled. Three weeks were deemed to have settled them. They were resigned to durance and to discipline, and to smoking only in secret.

163

Jennifer Corderey, aware of and understanding this rule, asked Sara out for the day. She was to bring Ramona or, if she preferred, one of her friends of her own age. Jennifer knew that her niece now had friends of her own age, or a little older.

Sara considered the matter. She *did* have friends of her own age, or a little older. She was not precisely ashamed of showing her aunt to her friends, or of showing her friends to her aunt; she asked Ramona.

Jennifer picked Sara up on the gravel sweep in front of the school. They picked Ramona up half way down the drive. This arrangement had been come to between Sara and Ramona, both completely understanding the reasons for it, but neither coming out and expressing them. It did not seem as odd to Jennifer as it would have done during the autumn.

They had a good day, a marvellous day, as good as any day they had ever had, even at Christmas. Sara called Ramona 'Ramona', and all was as it had been.

Coming back in time for roll-call, they dropped Ramona on the drive.

Rosalind Tuck was also out for the day, with a family in leather coats who arrived in a Jaguar. She was seen to return with a large rectangular package, something she had bought, although it was Sunday, or something she had been given.

'It's not a luxury. It's a necessity,' she said to people who asked her about it.

She unwrapped it in the dormitory. It was a radio, a heavyweight ghetto-blaster, gleaming with chrome and complex with sophisticated knobs.

There were a lot of electronic noise-makers in the school, varying widely in type and cost; there were strict rules about when, where and at what volume these devices could be played. The rules in this area were more stringently enforced than most of the rules, owing to the dislike on the part of many of the teachers of the kind of music played.

The radio was a present from Rosalind's father, delivered by way of the family she had been out with. It was the largest and the loudest radio in the school.

It was unfair that Rosalind should have not only the best figure but also the best radio in the school.

Sara had *David Copperfield*, instead of a radio, and she had no figure at all.

Patrolling the school in the mid-afternoon when the girls were supposed to be out – only briefly out – Ramona heard a *thump-thump-thump* which she took at first to be mechanical. The sound was coming from the basement. Ramona steered towards it, wondering whether to try to find Norman. The boiler room. The thumps resolved themselves into rock music. Norman had a radio. To Ramona, Norman was an ally. The school was supposed to be empty. There was no reason Norman should not have music, so to call it, while he stoked.

There was a scream over the thumping, a girlish scream from the boiler room. In a moment of cowardice, Ramona pretended to herself that Norman had screamed, or his shovel, or somebody in the radio studio. She could not lie to herself on these lines for more than two seconds. She threw open the door of the boiler room.

It was a scene of pagan worship in a low-budget movie. A single unshaded overhead bulb glared down on a huddled congregation. Boilers, pipes and people cast dramatic shadows. Concrete slabs rose like monoliths in semi-darkness. The radio sat in the middle, raised, gleaming, as though on an altar, object of adoration. There were fifteen or so worshippers, squatting or grovelling about the shrine. Rosalind Tuck, priestess, stood by the altar, by the god on the altar, adjusting the volume of the radio. The volume was terrific. Another scream, half human, was cut off abruptly when Ramona opened the door.

165

In the deep, dramatic shadows it was impossible to distinguish the faces of the other girls. Ramona's eyesight was least good under these testing conditions. Probably several girls turned their faces away from the door. It was impossible not to see Rosalind. She stood in the middle of the group, full in the glare of the light, facing the door defiantly. She looked beautiful. It seemed to Ramona that she turned up the volume of the radio.

Ramona was angry not at the breaking of the rules – she herself would have been reluctant to go for a walk on such an afternoon, and she knew that to teenaged girls such music spoke with mysterious power – but at the insolent defiance in Rosalind's face, at the way in which she gratuitously increased the already horrendous volume.

Ramona shouted to Rosalind to turn the radio off. Rosalind did not hear, or pretended she did not hear. Ramona's anger was under control. She felt a cold and effective anger. She knew what to do and how to do it. She went to the kind of concrete plinth on which the radio rested. Girls with averted faces got out of her way. She was aware that some girls were already scuttling, unrecognised, out of the door.

Ramona peered at the big radio. It might have been the instrument-panel of a jet. She had no idea which knob did what. She risked making a fool of herself if she fiddled with the controls. She screamed at Rosalind, 'Turn that thing off.'

Rosalind could not pretend not to hear, not to understand. She twiddled a knob. On purpose, perhaps by mistake, she turned the volume up instead of down. The noise of the rock-group, percussion and synthesisers, was for a long moment loud beyond the possibility of endurance for more than a moment. Rosalind turned the radio off. There was a sudden silence, which seemed a complete silence. It was not complete; there was a gentle burbling in the pipes that led from the boilers, temporarily inaudible after the insensate howling of the radio.

'Thank you,' said Ramona.

Rosalind gave a little bow.

166

'You know very well,' said Ramona, 'that you're all supposed to be out.'

'We were out, Miss Charnley,' said a voice near Ramona's knee. 'We were sent in.'

'Who by?'

'Miss Joy.'

It was possible. Hilda Joy, in the passenger seat of somebody's car, might have taken pity on a group of girls miserably tacking against the north-east wind.

'I'll ask her,' said Ramona.

'Do,' said Rosalind Tuck, with an air of cordiality.

There was no doubt that the girl who had spoken from the level of Ramona's knee, together with an unknown number of other girls, had indeed been out and had been mercifully sent in by Hilda Joy. There was no certainty that every one of these girls had been out, that Rosalind Tuck had been out. At least the radio was silenced. There was no rule against being in the boiler room, although Norman chased girls out when he was stoking.

Most of Ramona's anger had subsided, because she had won. She turned and went out of the boiler room. Somebody shut the door of the room behind her. She had only gone a few paces when the pounding, wailing jungle noises of the radio welled once again through the door and along the basement passage.

This was too much. Ramona's anger returned, still under control.

The whole scene repeated itself, Rosalind looked at Ramona, as though unable to hear her over the noise of the radio, with an appearance of polite interest. She turned the radio louder before she turned it off. After she had turned it off, she waited with an air of courteous enquiry for Ramona to speak.

'Are you mad,' said Ramona, 'or just very, very stupid?'

'Both, I expect,' said Rosalind.

'If you turn that on again, it will be confiscated.'

'Oh dear. We can't have that.'

'You're lucky you haven't already had that.'

'But, Miss Charnley, I turned it off when you told me

167

to. I thought you just wanted it off so you could ask us why we weren't out. I turned it off the moment I knew that's what you wanted. You didn't say anything about not turning it on again.'

The burbling in the hot-water pipes was again the only sound. The girls were waiting for Ramona's reply. She felt like a duellist. She felt coldly angry. She sought inspiration, and found it.

'If I had been talking to a retarded three-year-old,' she said, very loudly and clearly and slowly, with hardly any nervous wobble in her voice, 'I would have expected it to understand me. But I'm afraid I overrated your intelligence.'

Ramona knew, even as she spoke, that this slanging-match was not dignified – that it was not good discipline, not good educational practice, to score easy points off a pupil in a verbal battle of wits. But she felt a little flush of triumph. The horrible child could put that in her pipe and smoke it.

And there was a little ripple of laughter, of sycophantic tittering. The Moaner had scored.

It was possible that some of these girls were jealous of Rosalind – of her beauty, her popularity, her immediate and instinctive leadership, her lavish allowance – and they were not so very sorry to see her put down.

Put down Rosalind certainly was. She made no reply. There was no reply. The corners of her mouth drooped. There was no denying it was a lovely mouth.

Ramona turned and left the boiler room for the second time. Nobody shut the door after her.

Half term came, a three-day exeat. About half the girls went away for the break. Rosalind went off with Mary McPhee and her family, to meet at last the brother who was a Sandhurst cadet, who had a vintage sports-car. Sara went off with her aunt. Ramona would have gone with them too, but she was one of the staff detailed to stay behind to look after things. There was not much to look after. She spent the time quietly, with Jennifer Corderey's books.

The shrieks when the school reassembled were a muted version of the beginning of term. It was difficult to get them all quiet and into bed.

Rosalind had bought some things. She showed them to Amanda Loring and Colette Davies, but not to Sara or to anybody else. She hid some things that she had bought. Amanda and Colette whispered and giggled, but Rosalind went about with a kind of grim resolution. Sara had no idea what was going through her mind. She had heard various versions, more or less conflicting, of the episode in the boiler room.

Sara had missed Ramona, over the three days of half-term. Aunt Jennifer missed her, too – she said so more than once. Ramona was part of the party there, part of the temporary family, slipping into the routine that had established itself, a necessary third of the threesome. The house seemed incomplete without her. Aunt Jennifer said the same.

Meanwhile Rosalind, Amanda and Colette were busy about something, something that excluded herself. It was not for her, they said, not even for their Mighty Mouse. They managed to reaffirm their undying friendship, admiration and gratitude, while not seeing very much of her. Sara was not altogether sorry to be deprived, mostly, of their company, of which she had had rather a lot. Rosalind was important to her in some ways, and Dickens was important to her in other ways, and less of Rosalind meant more of Dickens, and of the company of other girls who now seemed to like her.

A tool was found, inexplicably, in the late afternoon, in a classroom. It was a brace and bit, an effective, old-fashioned hand-tool for drilling holes in wood. The bit was three-eighths of an inch. The tool was presumed to belong to Norman the odd-job man. Indeed it did. He crooned over it, when they were reunited, as he crooned over all the

169

tools in his shed. He was outraged. Found in a classroom? Somebody had pinched it without asking, somebody had used it, dumped it in a classroom, probably bent it and blunted it . . . He had not himself used it for two or three weeks. There had been no call for any holes to be bored in any wood. Not needing it, he had not missed it. There was no knowing how long it had been out of his care and keeping. Sometimes he locked his shed and sometimes not, but from now on locked it would be day and night if he wasn't in there.

Norman's rumbles about his brace and bit became quite tedious. The few people who could be bothered to think about the matter at all assumed that Norman himself had, absent-mindedly, left the tool in the classroom.

As often as she could – three and sometimes four times a week – Ramona had a bath in the middle of the afternoon. It was a queer time to have a bath, but for her it was the best time. The bathroom was hers, and for as long as she wanted it. At all the ordinary times there were other claimants, with superior claims. She had tried the crack of dawn, but early as Norman stoked the boilers, it was not early enough for hot water at six o'clock. By the time the water was hot, the bath was reserved according to an unalterable rota.

Released from nature-walk or netball, and if not on duty to supervise tea, Ramona would slip upstairs, undress, and in her dressing-gown go down the narrow stairs from her attic floor to the floor below where the bathroom was. She seldom saw anybody. Any of the staff who saw her knew very well why she had her bath at tea-time. It was no secret. Marigold Kent had laughed about it, in the Staff Common Room, when Ramona came in damp-haired and late for tea.

Ten days after half term, four days after the discovery of Norman's brace and bit, Ramona was having her tea-time bath. She lay luxuriously back in water that was probably at its hottest. She used her own soap (they all

170

did) but her bath-towel belonged to the school. She stared up at the ceiling, feeling the general benevolence brought by hot water. It was a very high ceiling, because the bathroom had not long been a bathroom. It was the end of the passage on this floor of upper-servants' bedrooms, plumbed and partitioned off when Malham House was turned awkwardly into a school. Directly above was one of the empty little bedrooms neighbouring Ramona's. It seemed a waste, having those empty rooms when so many people were homeless, but it would be complicated to have lodgers on top of a girls' boarding school, and if the top floor was full of people there would have to be another bathroom . . . Ramona thought she had better get out of the bath soon, or the water would get cold and she would get cold. Not for the moment. She lay for a moment, pink, relaxed, content. She stared up at the ceiling, unable to see it clearly in the steam, unable to see any detail without her glasses. Her glasses were nearby, safe, on the cork-covered bathroom stool. They would need a wipe before she could see through them.

Even without her glasses, she thought she could see something odd in the ceiling, something unfamiliar. There was something black on the ceiling, a blob or stain or nailhead, perhaps a beetle. To her it was a blur, but it was certainly there. It was not anything in her eye. She had stared at that ceiling, from that position, three and more times a week for nearly three years, and she was nearly sure the black blob had never been there. All the times she had stared at the ceiling, in the steam and without her glasses, she had seen neither better nor worse than she saw at this moment.

Had Norman been fixing something? *Could* it be a beetle?

She tried to wipe her glasses on the corner of the bath-towel, without getting out of the bath. She put them on, imperfectly wiped. She could see a little better, but only a little. She thought the blob was not a beetle, but she was no nearer guessing what it was. It was directly over the bath, over the middle of the bath, over her own middle.

171

It seemed to change as she stared at it, as she blinked through the steamy smears on her lenses. It was growing. It was growing downwards, a pale tubular stem. It was a fungus, growing downwards at an impossible speed. She thought it grew an inch, two inches, and stopped. The black circular blob was not a blob but a hole. Something was coming down through the hole. She stared at it fascinated, utterly puzzled, obscurely frightened. It was something out of *Doctor Who*, the antenna of a bug-eyed monster. It was something out of Conan Doyle, a tube through which poison gas would be pumped . . .

Yes, it was a tube, a narrow plastic tube being pushed through a hole in the ceiling. Ramona was suddenly aware of her nakedness, her defencelessness. She struggled to a sitting position in the bath so that she could climb out of the bath.

At that moment something began to fall from the tube. A jet of fluid fell from the tube into the bath. It looked black as it fell. It splashed into the bathwater and onto Ramona's skin. It turned the bathwater a brilliant purple, more intense with every second as more fluid fell. Ramona scrambled out of the bath, spilling purple water over the floor and over her bath towel.

Ink? It was the colour of purple ink. She wiped the steamy mirror over the washbasin, and saw that her face was plentifully splashed with the purple water. No more of the fluid was now pouring from the ceiling. She ran the tap in the basin, to wash the stuff off her face and the rest of her.

Some washed off, but much stayed. She scrubbed her face and her breast with soap and a stiff nail-brush, and there were still sploshes of purple dye over much of her face and body. She was an obscene sight, piebald pink-and-purple, as though diseased, as though disgusting and untouchable.

It was indelible dye, and it would be there until time flaked away the present outer layer of her skin and grew a new one.

She lowered herself slowly so that she sat on the edge

172

of the purpled bath. For the second time in her life she felt absolute despair.

CHAPTER NINE

Sitting naked on the edge of the purple bath, her face and hands and most of her body blotched with indelible purple dye, Ramona, in utter despair, remembered utter despair.

It was not after all true that nothing that happened at Malham House could be as bad as things that had happened in Brewster Terrace. This was exactly as bad as the worst, in a different way. It was exactly the same in the one important way. Life as it was could not go on. Life as it was was not bearable. Nobody could be asked to bear it. Something would have to be done. As before, as that other time, it was one thing or the other.

It was death, either way. The only question was whose. It was a straight choice.

Ramona began slowly to dry herself, purple towel on purple flesh. She was supposed to be on duty in a couple of hours, supervising supper. It was something that had to happen, her supervising supper, and could not happen. It was necessary and impossible. Life as it was was impossible but not necessary.

In despair she remembered despair. The blank impossibility of going on was a ticket that carried her back to the blank impossibility of going on.

Drying absently between her toes, Ramona remembered that other February evening almost exactly three years before. Herself sitting alone at the kitchen table, bottomlessly tired, almost too tired to think, not too tired to know, with absolute certainty, that she could not get through another day like that day.

Then, as now, her own disappearance was one of the options, one of the two options. It was perfectly feasible and had many advantages. Then, as now, Ramona considered, sanely and objectively, the advantages of that solution.

Then as now, she felt herself rebelling. She expressed herself, to herself, with unusual strength. Why the hell should she be forced into such a step? Why should she let herself be destroyed? The situation was not of her making. None of it was her fault. She could honestly say that she had done her very best, all that anybody could have done. She had suffered beyond endurance, and it was time the worm turned.

She was the worm, sitting then at the kitchen table, now on the edge of the bath. The worm had had a right to turn then; it had a right to turn now.

Her mother had been tucked up warm in bed, the only place either of them could ever be warm in that house. Tucked up so firmly, and under so many bedclothes, that in her emaciated frailty she could not have lifted the bed-clothes off herself.

She did not lift the bedclothes off herself.

Ramona hauled herself to her feet from the kitchen chair. In the numbness of her fatigue she knocked over the chair. As though sleepwalking, she went upstairs and into her mother's room. The room was very cold, because Ramona's mother could not be trusted with an electric fire, still less with a paraffin heater. The window was open a crack. This was entirely necessary, or the house would have become uninhabitable. Cold air like a knife-blade came in through the crack.

Ramona felt nothing as she pulled back the bedclothes. She was too tired for any feelings. It was something that had to be done, so she did it, just as she did the washing up when she was too tired for that.

The doctor next day had not really meant it when he

175

hinted that Ramona was responsible for her mother's death. He was overtired himself. Several old people had died in the extreme cold. The house could at last be properly aired, which was necessary before it was put up for sale.

That was the situation, that February night three years before. Perfectly simple. Two possible courses of action, one chosen. This was the same situation. In essence perfectly simple, the same two possible courses of action, one already chosen. In detail it was much more complicated. It was an interesting intellectual problem, like the crossword puzzles some of the people who came to Garston started in the Sunday papers. They never finished them, either because the puzzles were too difficult or because there was so much else to do.

There were prizes for winning those crossword puzzles. You got a £10 book token if yours was the first correct solution opened. People at Garston joked about winning the book token, about what book they would buy. They would buy the *Timeform Annual*, in order to read about their own racehorses, except that they already had it.

There was a prize for solving Ramona's problem, too. She would think about it, hard and long; she would think about it another time, because she was getting cold sitting naked on the edge of the bath in the unheated bathroom.

Ramona got herself upstairs to her room without anybody seeing her. She dressed quickly. She was able to hide the dye on her legs with coloured woollen stockings, that on her hands with woollen gloves, that on her neck with a woollen scarf. There was nothing she could do about the dye on her face. She examined herself, with a sick feeling, in the mirror over her dressing table. Most of the right hand side of her face was purple, with a white patch round the eye like a panda in a photographic negative. The left side was streaked and spotted with dye. The left side looked like an accident with a pot of dye; the right side looked like a monstrous birthmark.

She tried to cover the dye with make-up. She had little make-up, none new and none expensive. At her own expensive and faraway school, they had been taught to put on make-up, though they were not allowed to wear it except during those particular lessons. All the girls, including Ramona, had expensive make-up. They were taught to put on lipstick – just a very little – and eye-shadow, and to emphasise their cheekbones if they had those sort of faces. Those lessons were a long time ago. Ramona had had neither need nor opportunity to profit from them, ever since. They had not been taught to cover splashes of purple dye.

The Malham House girls had no need of lessons in make-up. It was grotesque to think of any of the teaching staff – the Headmistress herself – giving Rosalind Tuck lessons in putting on eye-shadow.

The make-up made her look worse. It made her look like someone trying to cover splashes of purple dye with cheap make-up applied inexpertly. She wiped off the make-up with cold cream. Parts of her face shone white, childish, meticulously clean.

In an hour's time she would be supervising supper.

She went to the empty bedroom, three doors down the passage from her room, which she knew to be over the bathroom. It was completely bare. There was no trace of anything, of anybody having been there. A yard from the wall, two holes had been drilled. Why two? Ramona prodded with a pencil, and the answer was immediately obvious. The first attempt had struck a joist, one of the small beams between larger beams which were holding up the floorboards. The driller had tried again, two inches nearer the wall of the room. That time there was no mistake. The hole was narrow, but wide enough to accept a piece of tubing.

The course of events was perfectly clear. Rosalind, publicly humiliated by Ramona to a very small and forgettable extent, had devised a new revenge, a new torment.

She had made her purchases over the long half-term weekend: a half-litre, perhaps, of dye, presumably intended for marking laundry or lambs or muggers; tubing; a little plastic funnel. Probably a pair of rubber gloves. She would have covered her tracks, directing to that task an intelligence which was not in evidence in schoolwork.

Could those tracks be uncovered? Ramona squatted back on her heels, and had a brief dream of exposing Rosalind's guilt. In theory it would be possible to discover where she had been, and with whom, throughout the half-term weekend. Somebody, on her behalf – possibly at two or three removes – had made these purchases. Theoretically, some chemist could be identified, in some town, who had sold these items on the Saturday or the Monday of half term. To whom? To any of seventy million people.

She slipped into Norman's tool-shed, when Norman was stoking the boilers. Maybe she tried several times, and found the door locked. She tried at a time when the door was not locked. One of her friends stood guard while she searched for and found a drill that would go through pine floorboards.

She had to find out about Ramona's bath. That would not have been difficult – it was simply a question of inconspicuously watching and waiting. One or other of her slaves probably did the watching and waiting. That would have been easier in the bitter weather, because the girls were only made to go out of doors for a short time.

Probably it happened the other way about. Somebody remarked on the number of teachers who used the same bathroom. Somebody, in conversation with a teacher, heard about Ramona's mid-afternoon baths, which were not shameful nor any sort of secret. This was reported to or overheard by Rosalind, which gave her the whole idea.

She drilled the hole when Ramona was busy, far away, with the kindergarten. The brace and bit would have made a fair amount of noise. No doubt there was somebody standing guard at the top of the stairs, and probably somebody on the floor below, at the top of those stairs. It would have been a time when there was nobody about. If anybody

178

had come anywhere near, it was easy to hide in that warren of attic bedrooms.

The polythene bottle of dye, the tubing, the funnel, the rubber gloves, were no doubt already at the bottom of a skip full of kitchen waste – perhaps already in the incinerator and burning. It would be no help if they were found intact. The drill had simply been dumped in a classroom. That was intact and that was no help.

In three quarters of an hour Ramona was to supervise supper.

Ramona went downstairs with a furtiveness that must have looked like furtiveness to anybody who saw her. The older girls had classes in the late afternoon in the winter, which kept them and most of the teaching staff out of the corridors. Ramona pulled her woolly scarf up over her face, as though she had toothache or neuralgia. It was a good idea to do so, pending decisions which she could not yet predict.

The connecting door between the main building and the Barrows' annexe was, as usual, locked. Ramona went out. It was almost full dark, although the days were perceptibly lengthening. She swallowed drily, and pressed the bell by the Headmistress's front door.

The Headmistress came to the door. The Barrows went pretty far, but not so far as to have living-in servants on the payroll of the school.

The Headmistress turned on the outside light over the front door as she opened the door. She stared with astonishment and visible annoyance at the figure on her doorstep, muffled like an Eskimo and calling at a thoroughly inconvenient time.

Ramona unwrapped the scarf from her mouth, so that she could speak. Her face was full in the glare of the light over the door.

'Good God,' said the Headmistress, and then began to laugh.

Laughing, she gestured Ramona to follow her indoors. It was immediately warm when she shut the door. The

179

narrow hallway was lit by three candle-bulbs, mounted on a piece of wrought iron and shining through pink glass shades. Ramona thought that her purple face would not be bathed in a rosy glow.

Through the open door of the sitting room Ramona saw Commander Barrow and the Bursar standing in front of the open fire with glasses in their hands. They were both looking at the fire, but they turned to see what was happening.

'Good God,' said the Bursar, as though this had been established as the correct response to Ramona's appearance.

Commander Barrow simply stared. Neither of the men laughed. Their manners were not very good, but they were better than the Headmistress's.

The Headmistress was controlling her laughter. She stared at Ramona with fascinated horror rather than derision. She led Ramona into her own little private sitting room without which, she sometimes said, she would go demented.

'What *have* you been doing to yourself, Ramona?'

'Somebody did it to me. I think I know who, and why, but I don't see how I can prove it.'

'It's not a very good idea to make accusations you can't substantiate.'

'I know. That's why I'm not making any accusations.'

The accused was convicted and sentenced, in a secret and implacable court; in the fulness of time the sentence would be carried out.

'Tell me exactly what happened.'

Ramona began to do so.

'But why on earth,' the Headmistress interrupted, 'were you having a bath in the middle of the afternoon?'

'A lot of us share that one bathroom, Mrs Barrow. I'm much the most junior. I have to use it when I can.'

'Good gracious.'

Ramona went on with the story. There was not much of it which was undeniable fact. She was aware of speaking ploddingly, her voice unemotional. She felt unemotional.

There might be times for emotion – times for cringing embarrassment, sick anger, hatred, a time, now inevitable, for secret triumph and gigantic, permanent relief – but this was a time for soldiering on and doing whatever the Headmistress required of her.

Once upon a time, very long ago, she had had occasion to feel the surge of secret triumph. It was revenge and punishment, and it was sweet. She remembered what it felt like, and it would happen again.

'It may be a bit of time fading,' said Ramona. 'I scrubbed and scrubbed, and it made no difference at all.'

'It doesn't actually hurt, does it?' said the Headmistress. 'It doesn't smart or burn or itch or anything?'

'Oh no. You can't feel anything.'

'That's all right, then.'

'Yes, but I wondered what the girls . . .'

'Ramona, it may be weeks before your face is back to its normal colour. Are you suggesting you go on holiday, just after half term? For the rest of the term? For the rest of the school year?'

'No, but perhaps it will fade faster than that – '

'When it fades they will stop laughing, if they have been laughing. It may take a little moral courage, just at first.'

'Yes, it may.'

'You're not asked to supervise a pack of wild beasts.'

No?

'Normal girls, from decent families. They may giggle a bit. You have the authority – if it gets out of hand, stamp on it.'

'Yes, Mrs Barrow.'

'If you find that beyond you, then I am obliged to suggest that you're in the wrong job.'

'Yes, Mrs Barrow.'

'After all, although your lack of qualifications only permit us to employ you to look after the very youngest children, it must be part of your duties to supervise the others. Other people in your position have done so. Your immediate predecessor, although she acted latterly in a treacherous and ungrateful way, had no difficulty, as far

181

as I know, in supervising the older girls. If you hide yourself away, it will put a dreadful burden on the rest of the
staff. They really can't be asked to bear it. I can't ask them
to bear it.'

'No, Mrs Barrow.'

'How long do you go into hiding? A week? A month?
The dye will not have faded, by your own account, not
completely. The girls would react in exactly the same way
in a month's time as I suppose they're liable to react in a
few minutes' time. If they laugh, Ramona, they'll have
more to laugh at. They'll laugh at your having been in
hiding. They won't just be laughing at a bit of purple,
they'll be laughing at cowardice.'

Very easy to say, sitting in your warm little sitting room
in your private annexe. Very easy to say when you haven't
got purple dye all over your face.

'Yes, Mrs Barrow,' said Ramona.

'I think you said you're down to supervise supper. If you
leave now you'll be in pretty good time. I hate to seem
inhospitable, but . . .'

'Yes, Mrs Barrow,' said Ramona, these words having
become her only possible contribution to the conversation.

The sample was small, but Ramona thought she had
amassed enough experience to enable her to predict reactions to her face. Everybody stared. A majority said,
'Good God.' A minority laughed. The majority of the girls
would not say 'Good God' out loud; Ramona was sure –
having heard hundreds of *sotto voce* conversations – that
many of the girls would use far coarser language, obscene
or blasphemous or both, but quietly. It was too much to
hope that only a minority would laugh.

Ramona walked towards the dining hall, trying to force
herself not to drag her footsteps, to postpone a moment
that had to come. She thought with a sort of exhausted
rage about Mrs Barrow's remarks. The most infuriating
thing was that she was right. If they giggled and it got out
of hand, she was to stamp on it. Quite right, no arguing

182

with that. If she couldn't do it, she was in the wrong job.
No arguing with that either. If she went away and hid for
a fortnight, emerging still largely purple, the girls would
laugh more and have more to laugh at. If she went away
and hid until the purple completely disappeared, she would
be replaced. The school would have no choice. She'd be
on the dole and with nowhere to live.

Very well, she was to put a brave face on it, a brave
purple face on it. To questions she would reply, 'Somebody
here has a very childish sense of humour. You don't want
to be sorry for me, you want to be sorry for anybody so
feeble-minded that they think this sort of thing is funny.'

She rehearsed this reply. It sounded pretty good, grown-
up and dignified but not without wry humour. It should
be said with a slight smile, a pitying smile that would invite
the listener to share Ramona's own tolerant contempt for
the prankster.

Ramona tried to rehearse the smile as well as the words,
but even alone in the dark she thought it was a failure.

It was quite important not to burst into tears. It was not
so important not to blush, because a blush would hardly
show under the purple.

She reached the door of the dining hall. There was a
fair amount of noise, a normal amount, the rhubarb buzz
of scores of conversations, laughter, the rattle of forks on
plates. She was only a little late. At least two other teachers
were there.

Ramona opened the door and went in. Eyes swivelled.
A hush started near her, and spread away from her, as
though a stone had been dropped into a pool, creating
silence. She found herself ducking her head, turning her
face away. That was no good. She raised her chin. She
tried to walk to her place with easy arrogance.

There was laughter, of course there was. There was only
a little laughter. It was muffled and at the far end of the
dining hall. If there were murmured blasphemies, they
were very softly murmured. There were stares, plenty of
stares, staring which may have been rude but was entirely

183

understandable. Ramona read no derision or cruelty in the stares, but astonishment and even pity.

'If it's not a rude question, Miss Charnley,' said a girl called Fiona Clay, 'whatever . . . ?'

' . . . Have I done to my face? Of course it's not a rude question. If you were covered in purple dye, I'd ask you how it got there. I feel like a sheep that's just fallen into the sheep-dip. I'm afraid you'll have to get used to it – it's going to be there for weeks.'

'It's not medicine or anything?'

'No, just dye. Somebody's infantile sense of humour.'

'I call it a lousy joke,' said Fiona Clay.

There was general clucking of agreement, among the girls at the table where Ramona had sat down. There was nothing special about those girls – they were just girls, like most of the rest of the school. There was nothing specially nice or nasty, perceptive or thick-skinned, about Fiona Clay. They were all reacting exactly as Ramona was pretending to react – treating dye on the face as unimportant, feeling contempt for so childish a practical joke.

Rosalind's bomb had backfired.

Ramona felt almost drunk with relief and with courage. She heard herself becoming chatty about the feelings of a sheep in a sheep-dip. She made the girls laugh. They were laughing with her, not at her. She enjoyed the stodgy school supper, and the conversation of the girls at her table.

It all came as a very great surprise.

Euphoria survived going to bed. More or less intact, it survived her contemplation of herself in the mirror when she brushed her teeth.

It was not to be expected that she should go to sleep at once, and she did not.

Euphoria did not survive wakeful small hours of the morning. Her mind active, indocile, as with too much black coffee, as with hatred, Ramona heard the church clock strike one. If you heard the church clock from Malham

184

House, it meant that the wind was exactly in the east. Euphoria did not survive that one-o'clock-in-the-morning east wind.

Because it came to Ramona, with the wind, with the chilly distant bong of the church clock, that Rosalind would try again. She had had allies. The whole saga of the purple dye argued allies outside the school, who might not matter, and allies inside it. At least two allies, their identities supremely obvious. Rosalind's triumph had fizzled, in the sight of those allies. It was almost inconceivable that nobody else at all knew anything about the plot. There must have been whispers – 'Wait till you see The Moaner at supper.' Rosalind would have been preening herself for the predicted, blazing audacity. And what did she get? Contempt for herself, chuckles of good-natured sympathy for the plucky victim.

What a lot of face Rosalind must have lost. What a rage she would be in. What a very different attack she would now mount.

Ramona heard the clock strike two as she tried to insert herself into Rosalind's mind, as she tried to predict the new stratagem.

It struck three before she realised that she was approaching the problem in a negative and defeatist way. The despair of the side of the bath, the resolve that despair generated, those were the things to hang onto. The point that had become clear was that it was all a question of time. It was a race. Rosalind could do nothing to Ramona or to anybody else, if the ultimate solution was found.

It had better be found quickly. Rosalind didn't hang about.

It was a question of time, and ways and means, and being perfectly certain it worked, and being perfectly safe. It was one of the crossword puzzles that people did at Garston, with a prize at the end.

The younger children reacted more basically than the older ones. Ramona's tinies shrieked and clutched one another,

185

in pretended terror or real terror. Ramona had difficulty quietening them; there were complaints from nearby classrooms. Nothing useful was accomplished in the junior class that morning. The point was without importance. Nothing useful was accomplished in that class on any morning.

Reactions in the Staff Common Room varied between the extremes of the Headmistress on the one hand, and Fiona Clay on the other. Hilda Joy voiced the view of a minority (Ramona hoped it was a minority) that Ramona had brought it on herself, by dint of her evident vulnerability, her lack of authority. Hilda Joy almost, but not quite, said that it was letting all of them down, letting discipline and the system down.

Ramona was inevitably asked, over the instant coffee, whether she had grounds for suspecting any individual.

'I can only guess,' said Ramona, 'and I'm not going to do that out loud.'

'I bet it's something,' Marigold Kent murmured aside to Ramona, 'to do with your silencing that monster tranny.'

Ramona shrugged. She could not stop her colleagues seeing the obvious, although only Marigold Kent seemed to do so.

'How *can* you, Mouse?' said Rosalind Tuck.

'I only asked,' said Sara, 'because somebody told me it was you.'

'Who? I'll kill them very slowly with a blunt corkscrew.'

'In that case I'd better not tell you.'

'Listen carefully, Mouselet. Listen closely to auntie. I freely admit that I'm lazy and stupid, and I'd rather have a good time than a good brain, and an awful lot of people disapprove of me, and an awful lot more people are going to disapprove of me before I've finished. But I truly believe that if you had to think of something good to say about me, you'd say I was kind. You'd say I wasn't cruel.

186

Wouldn't you? You know me well enough. You know me as well as anybody does. Better, because you're brainier. Do you honestly think I could do something like that to somebody?'

'No,' said Sara.

Their heads were close together as they came back from a walk. Just the two of them, the difference in their real ages and the greater difference in their apparent ages obscured by thick winter coats. Rosalind talking, talking, earnest, gesturing vehemently; Sara listening, nodding, solemn as an owl, as a disciple.

Ramona watched them from the library window.

Sara had been moved into the dormitory where Rosalind was, and she was still there. The 'flu epidemic would probably keep her there until the end of term.

Sara took not one book but four from Ramona's room. She said there was no need for her to keep bothering Ramona, now that she had friends, now that her property and privacy were respected.

Ramona was not saving only her own life. It was a thing not to forget. It was another reason to solve the crossword quickly.

Sara said nothing about the dye on Ramona's face. She glanced at it and quickly away from it, not obviously. Many of the girls forbore to stare at the dye, and many made no remark about it, pretending it was not there. This was an effort at good manners, although Ramona thought Fiona Clay's manners were better.

Was Sara's silence an effort at good manners, or did she know something she was frightened of giving away if she spoke?

Ramona wanted to take hold of Sara's shoulders and shake her till her teeth rattled. She wanted to say, 'How can you be so stupid and gullible and vulgar, to attach yourself to something like that, to be sucked into the web

187

of that horrible, delinquent spider, to lower yourself and cheapen yourself?'

This was another speech which Ramona rehearsed. It was not needed yet, but it might be needed later.

Nobody doubted that Maureen Maynard had a thoroughly good heart. She was infinitely willing and good-humoured. She was slow, at the best of times. If you let yourself get impatient with her, she was slower still, because she got in a muddle. The thing to do was to give her one job at a time, and let her get on with it at her own speed. You knew that the minute she'd finished one job, she'd come asking what she was to do next. It was no good, while she was doing one thing, telling her what to do afterwards. That was just the sort of thing that got her in a muddle.

Probably she had never had the mental capacity to understand anything that was not immediately obvious. She had never had the mental energy to make the effort to understand anything. Marigold Kent, who was the last person in the world to be unkind to, or about, somebody like Maureen, said the girl had been deprived of oxygen when she was in the womb. Marigold said this was a recognized scientific phenomenon. She even used the word 'phenomenon'. Ramona did not know how scientific this really was, but it seemed pretty convincing. The mechanism of Maureen's mind moved as though lubricated not by oil but by syrup. Nothing audibly creaked, but very little visibly happened. Anything beyond her she ignored, as though it were a chance-heard conversation between two strangers in a foreign language. Her passivity was an inbuilt defence against a hostile world, which had the result that the world was not hostile.

Ramona was thankful, for everybody's sake, that Maureen had never been employed at Garston. Ramona's father did not suffer fools gladly.

The other servants mostly ignored her. Nobody was cruel to her. Norman the odd-job man constituted himself her protector, but there was really very little she needed protection against.

To the girls, as far as Ramona knew, Maureen was part of the landscape of the Malham House School, like the dreadful marble fireplace in the library, like the winter smell of the fumes from Norman's boilers.

Maureen never did anything ridiculous, because she never ventured to do anything she had not been told to do. She would never have been a bull in a china shop, but only a sleepy cow, unlikely to do much damage.

It was for this reason that the episode was at first so completely surprising. Of course it was all quite soon explained, but at first it seemed so very out of character. When it was explained, there was a good deal of tolerant amusement. That was, as it were, the permitted and proper public response. If there was intolerant amusement, it was kept secret.

Hilda Joy found her at it. It was the middle of a weekday afternoon, and the building was almost empty. Maureen was on her hands and knees in the main hall, by the wall. She was passing her hands backwards and forwards through the air, about an inch from the floor. After a little she shuffled, on her knees, a yard to her right, and repeated the strange movements of her hands. It was as though she were a blind person searching for something she had dropped, as Hilda Joy afterwards reported, or somebody in pitch darkness groping for a box of matches. On her face, said Hilda Joy, there was that dogged expression which she wore when she was scrubbing.

Maureen could explain what she was doing, and did so readily and rationally. That Rosalind Summat had a pot of face-cream, ever so expensive. It had disappeared, into thin air. It was meant to disappear, and that was just what it had done. If you put it down, you couldn't find it. That's what Rosamund Summat had done – dropped the pot somewheres and now she couldn't lay her hands on it. Asked Maureen to prod about the place in the hopes she came on it. Maureen never heard of such a thing as a pot

189

of face-cream that vanished, but seemingly it was something you bought very special.

'The penny dropped,' said Hilda Joy afterwards.

She sent for Rosalind Tuck, who was the obvious candidate for 'Rosalind/Rosamund Summat', and who was as likely as any girl in the school to have a pot of expensive face-cream. Rosalind showed nothing but dismay at the way Maureen had misunderstood her, at the way she had grabbed the wrong end of the stick and put herself to so much trouble. She had indeed mislaid a pot of rather super vanishing-cream. She knew she was not allowed to wear cosmetics at school, but this was not make-up but a sort of medicine. It was necessary to a skin like hers because of the very hot sun of the Middle East. The doctor said so. Well, not exactly a doctor, but a skin-care consultant. She was supposed to rub the cream in twice a day. It all got absorbed, it didn't show at all. That was why it was called vanishing-cream.

Hilda Joy nodded. She had never herself possessed or used any vanishing-cream, but the concept was familiar to her. Meanwhile the events of the morning were explained. Rosalind had missed her pot of expensive cream, without which, even at her age, her skin would rapidly deteriorate after the fierce ultra-violet of Saudi Arabia. She had mentioned the loss to Maureen. She had not asked Maureen to look for the cream – she knew very well that Maureen was not paid to go searching for things the girls lost – but simply to return it to her, Rosalind, if she should happen to stumble on it.

Yes, she had mentioned 'vanishing-cream', because that was what was on the label of the jar.

Oh, the jar had turned up. Somebody had found it somewhere.

Rosalind said she did not think it was funny, but on the contrary rather sad, that poor Maureen should have been scrabbling about on her hands and knees trying to find a vanished pot of face-cream.

Hilda Joy said in the Staff Common Room, 'I couldn't make the child see the funny side. I suppose she must have a soft heart under all that glamour. One does feel for Maureen. Of course she's one of the people who wouldn't have a job at all, if they didn't have the job they've got here.'

'Thanks,' said Ramona inaudibly.

Of course the ridiculous little saga was all over the school by suppertime, there being so few other things to talk about. It was too much to expect that the wits would let the thing drop – the licenced buffoons who vied with one another to be jesters of their groups. Maureen was asked to find the vanishing mustard. The owners of blindly groping hands said they were searching for the vanishing gravy. One girl slid under the table and hid there, and the others said she was the vanishing girl.

For the very first time, Ramona saw that Maureen was actively unhappy. She did not understand the jokes about vanishing mustard, but she knew she was being got at. Probably it had happened to her as a child, and she had never forgotten that or got over it.

It was obscene. Behind the fading and half-forgotten purple dye on her face, Ramona felt a flush of disgusted anger. That horrible little bit of work with golden hair might at least take on someone her own size. It was contemptible to make a butt of someone as defenceless as Maureen. It was not to be permitted.

Of course so easy a success would have her baiting Maureen again. And everybody had always been kind to Maureen. In that very imperfect community, you could put on the credit side that people recognised the truly good and valuable qualities that Maureen had. There was a notion running through all history of the saintly fool, somebody so simple as to be without any craft or artifice, any wish or capacity for evil.

Ramona thought of bear-baiting, and of the terrible poem by Edith Sitwell.

Would others follow where Rosalind had shown the disgusting way? Certainly yes, if she was there to lead them. And then Maureen would be in the bear-pit indeed, pinpricked from all sides, not understanding who was

191

hurting her or why, bellowing with uncomprehending pain
and rage, losing faith in people and in herself and in the
livability of life . . .

The trapper needed a tethered goat. The tethered goat
was to hand. The trapper would be her own tethered goat.
The beast of prey, the ruthless predator, the dangerous
vermin would stalk the goat, belly to the ground, silent
and secret, alert. But the tiger's alertness would be a little
dulled by greed, by arrogance, by overconfidence. The
tiger despised the goat, and that contempt would be the
death of the tiger.

Ramona switched her metaphors, finding one equally
satisfying. She remembered the bottom-fishermen in the
ponds and canals near Garston, men with stools and
umbrellas and packets of sandwiches, with porcupine-quills
and lead shot, with endless patience. They caught perch
and roach and such, spiky inedible fish which they kept
alive in a keep-net, and put back at the end of the day.
Her father let the local club fish the lake at Garston,
provided they picked up their litter and kept their radios
quiet. He himself was not interested in that sort of fishing.
For him only salmon and trout. Only salmon, really,
because his temperament was too dashing for the subtleties
of dry-fly fishing on a chalk-stream. But on the Scottish
salmon rivers of his racehorse-owning clients, he did great
execution among the salmon. His sport provided no useful
precedent for Ramona. The humble bottom-fishermen did.
She remembered them, hours before or days before they
fished, casting bread upon the waters. Perhaps not bread.
Something or other they threw into the lake, just where
they were planning to sit, so that fish would be attracted
to that spot. It was called ground-baiting.
  Ramona planned her ground-bait.

*

192

Once, when Ramona was small, her parents had been on a three-week hunting safari in East Africa, guests of one of the racehorse owners who had salmon rivers, or perhaps one of the other racehorse owners. They had come back very brown, with floppy hats of greenish khaki which were given to Ramona, and with stirring stories of stalking this or that. Most of their hunting was in fact done with a camera, as Ramona was glad to learn; the sort of licences they had did not allow them to shoot lions or leopards or elephants. You might not have been aware of this, all at once, from the way they talked about it.

The great thing was to study the ground. Ramona's father had stalked a great many stags in Scotland, on the deer-forests of racehorse owners, and he understood about studying the ground. He explained it all to people who came to Garston, mentioning, in a self-deprecating way, how surprised the professional hunter had been, that a newcomer to Africa should understand so thoroughly about forward slopes and dead ground and wind direction. Ramona heard quite often about studying the ground and about the professional hunter's surprise.

Ramona studied the ground.

The killing-ground. That was not a safari expression but an army one, also used by her father. It meant a bit of ground where you hoped the enemy would go, or where you could make him go or lure him to go, and where, when he got there, you killed him. You were hidden, but in a position of strength. The enemy had no idea you were there, because you had cleverly got there in secret, because you had cleverly convinced him you had gone somewhere else. Studying the ground was even more important in battle than in hunting. If you were hunting something and you missed, nothing was lost except a bullet and a bit of time. In battle more was at stake, including yourself. To an extent, Ramona was bound to take a risk. But by studying the ground she could reduce the risk to a minimum, and increase the chance of success to the maximum.

Ramona wanted a floppy hat, like the one her father

193

had worn on safari. Or a steel helmet, like the one he had worn commanding tanks in Italy.

Or a judge's wig. Of all the metaphorical hats she could put on, that was the closest. The big white wig; and on top of that the little black cap. In the Old Bailey, the accused saw the cap, when they brought him back to hear the verdict. It was a pity the accused in this case would never know what had happened to her.

CHAPTER TEN

The architect of Malham House had introduced, more or less ineptly, a few nods towards the Palladian style, alongside ill-digested gobbets of renaissance and baroque. The most obtrusive item of neo-classicism was, to be sure, the marble fireplace in the library. But there was another and more meritorious Palladian touch. From the middle of the stone floor of the main hall, you could look right up to the very top of the house, to the slightly domed ceiling of the attic corridor. It was a tall house; that ceiling was a long way up; you had to crane your neck to see it; this was a thing very few people bothered to do. The effect was not so very Palladian, because successive landings overhung the hall, obscuring all but a strip of the distant topmost ceiling.

It followed that, looking down from the attic landing, you could see all the way to the floor of the main hall. Ramona had an excellent head for heights, and had, as a child, climbed many tall trees, but even she found it vertiginous to lean over the rail and look all the way down. It was, in any case, a thing to do carefully. The architect's Palladian notions had not extended to the balustrade of the attic landing. There was a wooden rail a little less than a yard above the floor, running through three uprights about five feet apart. Between these upright posts there were vertical slats, hardly more than laths, four inches apart. The rail was not a single, continuous piece of timber, but separate five-foot lengths slotted into shallow sockets in the uprights. The uprights themselves were slotted into sockets in the joists which supported the floorboards. All this work had been scamped originally, and ill-maintained ever since. Norman could not be blamed – he had plenty on his plate already. When the house was built, only servants had ever climbed so high in the building.

Without great physical effort, the central upright of the three could be wobbled in its socket – pushed outwards from the vertical an inch at the top, and after a little more wobbling two and three inches outwards. The effect was that the ends of the two sections of rail which met at that upright very nearly slipped out of their sockets. It was all most unsafe. If any of the girls in the school had ever gone up to the attics, the parents would have had a legitimate cause for concern and grievance.

The door of Ramona's bedroom was almost opposite the most unsatisfactory of the three uprights of the railing.

She might not look it – she did not look it – but for most of her life Ramona had been physically extremely fit. Her childhood and teens had been full of riding, swimming, sailing, running about, jumping over things, climbing trees. Both at home and at school she had been given an excellent, balanced diet. She had not eaten so well in Brewster Terrace, but she had still taken plenty of exercise. She walked to and from the bookshop – and coming back entailed climbing a stiff hill – and she swept the stair-carpet on her hands and knees, and scrubbed the kitchen floor. The food at Malham was better – it was said in the prospectus to be supervised by a qualified dietician – and Ramona still took a lot of exercise. She had to. Apart from taking the children for walks, there were all those stairs to her bedroom.

She was a lot stronger than she looked.

Rosalind Tuck never took any exercise at all that she was not, under threat of punishment, obliged to take. When she was made to go for a walk, it was as short and as slow a walk as she could get away with. Her figure was naturally excellent, but it could be assumed that her muscles were flabby. Disco dancing might possibly have strengthened her legs. Strong legs would not be much help to her.

Ramona confirmed that the spare Yale key to her bedroom door was hidden in the place where she had hidden it. It was necessary that it should be there and not elsewhere, throughout what followed.

The key she used was still on its string round her neck, where nobody had seen it.

She let it be seen. She left undone the second button of her woolly blouse, over which she was wearing a V-necked sweater. If she leaned forward, the key winked into momentary visibility. It did not have to be done often, or to a large audience. It would be remarked, in form-room or dining hall or dormitory, that The Moaner had a Yale key on a string round her neck. It would be completely obvious what lock that key opened.

Nobody had realised that The Moaner kept a diary. Even to Marigold Kent, the nearest thing she had to a close friend in the Staff Common Room, it came as a complete surprise. Obviously she had intended to keep her secret secret, but absent-mindedness, or something, gave her away. It was a great big book, about the size of a late Victorian single-volume edition of a Dickens novel. It was wrapped in brown paper, as obscene books are sent 'in plain wrapper' according to the terms of mail-order advertisements.

Nobody could remember when, where, or by whom the word 'Diary' was first suggested. The rightness of this notion – a rightness deriving from its very absurdity – was immediately and almost universally accepted.

Sara Corderey could have said, 'I think it's one of my Aunt Jennifer's books, which she lent to Miss Charnley for me to read.' Perhaps she should have done so. But that would have been asking a degree of moral courage from a child who was not particularly brave.

It made no difference. It seemed that The Moaner herself confirmed, to somebody or other, that the big mysterious book was a diary.

'What in God's name does The Moaner have to write in a diary about?' said Rosalind Tuck. 'Do you suppose she's having a secret affair with Norman? No – Norman's having it off with Vanishing Maureen. Oh, I know. She's a dyke, and she fancies somebody. I bet she's got hotpants for our Mightymouse. It's full of steamy dreams about you, Mouse.'

'I doubt it,' said Sara, blushing and giggling.

It was true that nobody – not even Marigold Kent – could imagine what went on in Ramona's life to give her anything to write about in her diary.

'I wouldn't half mind a look at that,' said Rosalind.

'You can't read people's diaries,' said Colette Davies, who was still only ninety-eight percent under Rosalind's influence.

'There's a lot of things they say I can't do,' said Rosalind. 'And I'm going to do nearly all of them.'

Amanda Loring thought this was exactly how life should be lived – at least, how Rosalind's life should be lived by Rosalind. If they said you couldn't do a thing, it was because they were scared of trying to do it themselves, or because it was too much fun.

Sara continued, privately, to be doubtful about this diary of The Moaner's. From the description of the book people had seen, it sounded exactly like one of her aunt's copies of Dickens, even to the brown-paper wrapper. And if there was really a diary, surely there would have been some sight of it at Christmas? Some talk of it, since they were all three so close, so relaxed, so much like a family? But everybody was determined it was a diary, and she, Sara, didn't know for certain that it wasn't one.

*

198

Of course it became obvious, after painstaking and analytical examination of the problem (as undertaken by guests at Garston trying to do the crossword puzzles in the Sunday papers), that the kingpin of the whole operation was Maureen Maynard. Backward, overweight, sweet-natured, trusting – Maureen was the key to the whole operation.

Item: Maureen liked and trusted Ramona perhaps more than anybody else in the world. Her instinct was to like and trust everybody, but this instinct had been given a jab, by Rosalind Tuck and her sycophants, from which it might never recover. She trusted Norman and the cook and the bursar, and the Headmistress and Marigold Kent and a few others, but nobody more than Ramona. Ramona did not spiritually pat herself on the back for this, but it was a factor in the situation which it was important to appreciate.

Item: Maureen's simpleness made her trusting – completely trusting of the people she trusted. The number of these might have been reduced by ninety per cent, owing to Rosalind Tuck's idea of a joke, but that meant that the people she did trust she trusted the more implicitly. She would believe anything Ramona told her.

Item: it was not least on Maureen's own account that the action had to be taken. There was justice in Maureen being an instrument, however unwitting, in the mechanics of the action.

What Ramona needed was one of Maureen's free afternoons, coinciding with an afternoon when she herself was off duty. It would not be long to wait. It had better not be. Time was still of the essence. Rosalind would not wait until the summer term.

The thing was to find a place – a function, a project, a chore – to which Ramona could feasibly take Maureen, feasibly, visibly, credibly, on Maureen's afternoon off which was also a free afternoon for Ramona.

The problem was technical, almost mechanical. It took thought and a bit of leg-work, no more. Some of the decrepit outbuildings of Malham House, long disused, were not so very decrepit – were usable, at least in the summer. There was an erstwhile tackroom at the end of the tumbledown stable-block which was well-lit and structurally sound. It had once had a pot-bellied stove with a metal chimney going through a hole in the roof, but of that there now remained only the hole in the roof. It was not a place to use in the winter, but it was a place which, scrubbed out and refurbished, could well be made use of in the summer.

Ramona put it to the Headmistress – having knocked almost inaudibly on the study door – that modelling in clay was considered by educational theorists as particularly creative, therapeutic, diverting and absorbing for the youngest pupils. Bored, and oddly embarrassed, the Headmistress assented to this proposition, put to her with such earnestness by her least important employee, in charge of her least interesting charges, and whose face was still largely covered in purple dye.

Clay modelling could not be done in silence. Ramona's children's classroom was adjoined to other classrooms. There were already regular complaints about the noise made by the tinies when they were busy with paper cutouts and building blocks. The clay modelling had better be done somewhere else. The old tackroom at the end of the stables would be a fine place, in the summer, once it was given a scrub-out and the hole in the roof was plugged.

The Headmistress understood that an hour of Norman's time, to fill the hole in the ceiling, was all it would cost the school. She agreed with the bursar, over a glass of Peter Dominic sherry, that modelling in clay could be an optional extra for the youngest children, the charge for which would cover, with a bit over, the cost of modelling clay.

The project was mentioned in the Staff Common Room. It was mentioned among the girls in their classrooms and dormitories. It was not discussed in depth or in detail. It was not of the slightest interest to anyone.

Ramona was seen once more – two and perhaps three

times more – carrying the portentous book in the brown-paper wrapper. She was seen carrying it upstairs to her bedroom. It was now part of the folk-wisdom of the community that the book was Ramona's diary.

Ramona approached Maureen, very casually, very tactfully, one evening in the corner of the kitchen where Maureen was polishing off some left-overs.

Maureen had heard about doings in the old tackroom at the end of the stable-block. It had been mentioned in the kitchen. Opinion there was neutral about the project. Nobody gave a damn. Maureen had absorbed this view, until Ramona began talking to her about it. Ramona was her friend, her well wisher. Ramona was keen on the notion of the smallest children mucking about with fancy clay. That made it a good idea, something to be on the side of. Maureen readily agreed to give Ramona her next afternoon off to helping clean out the old tackroom.

There was one further piece of reconnaissance of the highest importance. Ramona had done it briskly. She did it again, minutely. It was quite all right, that she should be seen hanging about in and near the old tackroom – everybody knew she was turning it into a place where the babies would make pigs of themselves with modelling clay.

The tackroom was oblong, about twenty feet by twelve. Half way across, the narrower dimension was divided by a wooden barrier seven feet high, ending in a doorway from which the door had disappeared. The barrier effectively cut the room in half. Nobody could understand why the tackroom had been so divided. Ramona, who had been brought up with horses and grooms and stables, thought she understood quite well. The inner half of the tackroom served as a bedroom for a groom who would be on twenty-four hour call if a mare was foaling in one of the boxes. This inner half had a window, a yard square, its sill a yard from the brick floor. After much labour, performed quite publicly, Ramona induced the window to open. Not at all publicly, she established that she could get through the window when it was open. She established that she could shut it from outside, and open it again from outside.

Ramona showed the window to Maureen, who was pleased that Ramona was pleased about it. Maureen accepted what Ramona told her – that the window could only be opened two inches.

The door of the tackroom was in full view of the house, if you chose any one of three or four of the dozens of windows on that side of the house, and if you had any reason for looking at so dismal a view. The window of the tackroom was not visible from the house: it was not visible from anywhere. If a small animal popped out of that window, it did so unseen, and remained unseen in a tangle of shrubbery. You could then go behind the stables, invisible from the house, and reach a point very near the little side door of the house at which, when the house was built, such people as the fish-seller called.

Between the end of the stables and the tradesmen's door there were a few yards of open ground, passing the back of Norman's tool-shed. A few windows gave onto that piece of ground. Ramona did not expect any eyes to be at any of those windows. Eyes that would be following her would follow her to the tackroom door; then they would be otherwise employed.

It was one of the elements of risk. There were plenty of others. Ramona weighed the whole lot of them against what she stood to gain, against what Sara and Maureen and the civilised world stood to gain. It was no contest.

Anyway, a life in which your face was purpled and your bedroom fouled was not worth living.

To other glimpses of the big book in its brown paper wrapper, Ramona added other glimpses of the key on its string round her neck. Not often; as though by the merest accident. Not so much a glimpse of a Yale key as a hint of a small, machine-made metallic object, the kind of indication of a key that a Flemish painter might have given by a flick of bright paint on the sombre background of a tavern interior.

Ramona wondered if she were not overdoing it. Might not the chub, or whatever those patient anglers were after, have been alerted by too obvious a descent of goodies into a particular corner of their lake? On reflection, she thought not. She let herself be seen again in the old tackroom at the end of the stables; she let herself be heard again planning the modelling in clay that her pupils would make so much noise at in the summer; she let the big book be seen again, and the key.

She made very sure that the key was safe on its string round her neck. The moment of its removal to another place was H-hour minus a very few minutes.

Ramona had qualms.

She saw Rosalind Tuck in the distance, from above, one of a group. Rosalind was not obviously dominating the group, she was simply a member of it. They all looked very young. From above, Rosalind looked very young. She had not really started living. She thought she had, but all the important experiences of life were still ahead of her. Triumph was probably ahead of her; suffering certainly was. Suffering was ahead of everybody. It taught you things. It taught you different lessons, according to what sort of suffering it was, according to what sort of person you were. Would Rosalind suffer physical disability, pain, rejection, heartbreak? What would these things do to her? What would she become? What would she do to the world, for the world?

Was Ramona to play God, to rewrite a human history by chopping it off almost before it had begun?

Was Ramona to take, herself, so fearful a personal risk?

She looked at herself, at the distorted reflection of her face in the looking-glass over the washstand in her bedroom. The purple dye was fading, but still vehemently visible. It filled her less with remembered rage and hatred, but with an opposite memory – the goodwill she had met, the active kindness, the hint of admiration, even, for the courage and good humour with which it was supposed she had taken the episode.

But you could not forget the hole drilled in the ceiling, the elaborate planning, the malice, the deliberate and unthinkable cruelty. When your thoughts started in that direction, you remembered Maureen on her hands and knees, groping for vanished vanishing-cream . . .

Ramona felt like a pendulum. The extremes of the swing were a long way apart.

How much of her tolerance was cowardice? How much of her new courage was actually abject funk?

They began the 'bedwetter' business again.

It had almost been forgotten, but now it would never be forgotten. Rosalind Tuck would make sure that it was not forgotten.

There would be no end to it.

It was as though the girl had decided to proceed not with bombs but with pinpricks. Bombs could blow up in your own face. Pinpricks were safer. Pinpricks were more fun, because it all went on longer. It went on for ever.

There was nothing like the horrible rubber pants unwrapped in the dining hall – nothing like the page torn out of Jennifer Corderey's book. Probably there would be. Certainly there would be. For the moment there were only laughing, half-heard murmurs down passages, round corners, through doorways. Enough to bring the joke back to life, to keep it alive for ever. Presumably the rest of the teaching staff knew about the joke. Presumably they ignored it, as being only one example among many of dirty-minded teenage humour.

All the girls knew about it, all right, every single girl in the school. Did they actually believe Ramona was a bedwetter? Perhaps some of the very smallest did, those who had themselves had accidents owing to fright and home-sickness . . .

'Bedwetter. The Moaner's a bedwetter.'

The whispers were louder, more blatant, more frequent. They followed Ramona along all the corridors of the building, up and down all the stairs. When she was out of doors, they came to her on the wind, from clumps and shrubbery, from behind trees and outbuildings.

There were women who packed up all the school's laundry every week, women among those fetched by Norman in the minibus. The staff's linen was kept separate from the girls' linen. Ramona found that her sheets were kept separate from those of the rest of the staff, packed away on their own in a polythene bag. Those women knew what to believe. The whispers followed Ramona into the kitchen and the back premises and down into the basements.

'See you later, Alligator' was a catchphrase already old-fashioned when Ramona was a young schoolgirl. It had never quite died. It was occasionally called out by one girl to another at Malham House. But a new version became current.

'See you later, Urinator', was what girls called to one another. Some of the very smallest children, Ramona's own class, cheerfully called out this newly-in form of farewell, innocently, in front of her, not knowing what they were saying, not knowing what the word meant. The ones who did know crimsoned and cracked up with giggles.

The term still had three weeks to run.

Ramona had pictured Maureen Maynard as a bear being baited in a pit by the rabble of a town. She was that bear.

The bear in the pit was chained. It was unfairly hampered in its fight for survival. It could not turn and rend its tormentors, because of the chains that bound it.

The only chains that bound Ramona were those of conventional morality and of personal cowardice. It was obvious to her, supremely self-evident, that conventional morality had not been framed with situations like hers in mind. As well be righteous about the bear's attempts to

205

get at the dogs. As to the other, it diminished as a factor with each half-heard whisper of 'Bedwetter', with each farewell called by one girl to another.

The pendulum swung to one extreme, and stuck. It was pushed there and stuck there by the whispers and the farewells, and by the three remaining weeks of the term, and by the fact that the summer term followed the spring term.

From somewhere Ramona remembered the phrase 'conjuction of the planets'. It meant that Mars, Venus, Mercury and the rest, in the course of their elliptical journeys round the sun, all came somehow together. Ramona supposed that it happened very seldom. Perhaps not all the planets were involved, but only those nearest, those that mattered most. What followed were signs and portents, wars and rumours of wars, floods, bumper harvests, babies born with deformities or with genius, high tides, low tides, destruction, salvation – Ramona had forgotten what marvels or miseries, if any, the conjunction of the planets was supposed to bring. She had to wait for her own conjunction of the planets, and it would not be a long wait.

The central, critical conjunction was that Maureen Maynard should have a free afternoon when Ramona had a free afternoon. The other conjunctions would follow, or could be devised.

It was the Tuesday of the last week but two before the end of term.

Ramona had a word with Maureen, in the kitchen, just after breakfast. Maureen had had an idea of going off somewhere with somebody on her free afternoon, but, under gentle prompting, she remembered of course that she had promised to help Romana turn the old tackroom into a place for clay modelling; under still gentler prompting, she remembered the debt that she owed Ramona for nearly three years of kindness and understanding.

They agreed to meet at two o'clock, in the back passage. They would both be wearing clothes suitable for mucking out an old tackroom.

Girls who were helping to clear away the breakfast (in accordance with the school's philosophy that service to the community was an essential part of the educational process) might not have been in the least interested in the fact that The Moaner was having a deep discussion with Vanishing Maureen; but they could not possibly have been unaware of the fact. Some words of the conversation were inevitably overheard. It was probably unnecessary for Ramona to make sure that the crucial parts of the conversation were overheard – that the two of them would be off to the tackroom at two o'clock, with appropriate cleaning implements, and that they would probably be there for at least an hour and a half.

The point of the two-o'clock rendezvous was that two-fifteen was the moment by which, hurried on by the electric bell, all the girls were supposed to be out of the building. Games were still impossible, in the bitter weather. Fresh air was just possible and was enforced. No girl went out a moment before two-fifteen. Ramona and Maureen would be seen, by anybody who took the trouble to stand by an appropriate window, disappearing into the tackroom at about twelve minutes past two.

Rosalind Tuck would leave the building at or after the last possible moment. She would be in the company of the cronies she most completely dominated – of Amanda Loring and Colette Davies. Her alibi for the next hour, if she needed one, was thus secured. Obviously Ramona was guessing at this stage; but the possibility that she was guessing wrong was very small indeed.

In the mid-morning break, Ramona went not to the Staff Common Room but all the way up to her bedroom. She scraped, with nail scissors, at the piece of string by which she hung her door-key round her neck. She scraped until only a few strands of the string remained. She made sure that the fraying looked like fraying – like the gradual deterioration of any piece of thin string in constant use.

She made sure that enough of the string remained so that it would not break until she broke it; but that, with one sharp tug, she could break it without anybody seeing her do so.

She regretted not having used string of a strong, distinctive colour. She had used ordinary, buff-coloured string, the string that came to hand. She had not foreseen any of this, when she chose the string for her key. The point was probably unimportant. Everybody in the school would know what key it was, a Yale key on a bit of frayed string.

She left Jennifer Corderey's copy of *Bleak House*, brown-paper-wrapped, on a corner of her bed. On the book she left a ball-point pen. This touch pleased her; it would suggest that the 'diary' had a brand-new entry – something written, perhaps, as recently as that very morning. It lent, as it were, a touch of spice to the bait.

Ramona pushed in the lock of the door and depressed the catch. The door was unlocked, and for the time being would remain so. This represented a risk so tiny that it could be ignored. Nobody was going to come all the way up here in the middle of the morning on a weekday. No girl was going to come up here, until the one girl came who was going to come, at the time of Ramona's choosing. If one of the cleaning women came up, for any strange and unprecedented reason, nothing was lost. It was less odd that Ramona's room should be unlocked than that it should be locked.

Ramona pondered for a moment on the landing, making ticks on a mental check-list. She was glad she had done so. She went back into her bedroom, and drew the curtains over the single window. They were not very good curtains, elderly unlined cotton, and she drew them incompletely, so as to leave an inch between them. She studied the effect, and saw that it was exactly right. Coming into the room from the landing, you would take it to be empty, especially if you knew its occupant was far away in the tackroom. You would see the big book lying on the bed, with the ball-point pen across it. You would not see another person hiding behind the door, a person in dark clothes and with dark hair, a person with purple dye on her face.

The rails of the balustrade on the landing outside Ramona's bedroom door were only just contained in their sockets in the upright. The upright wobbled freely. It could be pushed with little effort far out into emptiness. It was really shockingly bad workmanship.

When the house was first built, a yard-square skylight had lit that topmost landing. No way had ever been found to stop the skylight leaking. The glass had been removed, and replaced with sensible slates. This made the landing dark, even at midday. An electric light had been put on a bracket on the wall, with switches at each end of the landing. By straining upwards, Ramona could just reach the bulb. She took it out. She knocked it against the wall, gently and then with gradually increasing force. She contrived to break the element inside the bulb without breaking the glass. She replaced the bulb. It was not likely that Rosalind would commit her burglary in the glare of electric light, but the light was an avoidable risk of the kind Ramona was determined not to take.

She got through the rest of the morning with difficulty. She could not stop her hands shaking. The whispers roared in her head, like high winds in a confined space. She was very frightened and very excited. She was strange to the children, breaking all her own rules, over-indulgent and then disproportionately harsh. They showed they thought she was being odd. They were moderately pleased at the prospect, next term, of sloshing about with wet clay in the tackroom.

Ramona broke the string round her neck at that moment of noisy confusion when the girls flooded into the dining-hall. Of course the trick was to drop it where any of a dozen particular pairs of eyes would see it. It would not matter if other eyes saw it too, as long as those eyes saw it. Rosalind Tuck's eyes, or the eyes of any of the dozen girls who most sedulously sucked up to Rosalind. There were girls who, finding and recognising the key, would immediately return it to Ramona. Even at the Malham

209

House School, there were many more girls who would do that than would get the key to Rosalind. It was a question of choosing the moment, of waiting for the moment and using it.

In the event it was easy. Ramona dropped the key in front of Amanda Loring. Amanda immediately dropped her handkerchief. In picking up the handkerchief, she picked up the key too. She did it pretty neatly. Ramona thought that very few girls saw the episode. A lot of girls saw Amanda crouch down to pick up her dropped handkerchief, but few of them took in that she also picked up The Moaner's key.

It was possible that a decent girl would have seen what actually happened – would now either tell Amanda to return the key at once to its owner, or tell Ramona what had become of her key. That would make no difference at all, the key now being in Amanda's possession. Amanda would deny having the key, having seen or touched any key. She would be telling the truth about not having the key, because she would already have slipped it to Rosalind under cover of all the pushing and shouting that went on at such a moment, of girls getting to their places and sitting down and starting to gobble pieces of bread.

Ramona had an orderly mind. Her brain did not have other outstanding merits, never had had, but she was methodical. This was noticed during her childhood, at school and at home. She was not as quick as other children, but when she really went at something she did it thoroughly. Her father could appreciate this in her, although it was not the cast of mind that he personally admired, that he felt sympathy with, that he had himself. But since it was what she had, he said he was glad she had it. He was glad she had something on the credit side.

Ramona had been since early childhood aware of this quality in herself. It remained baffling how she had inherited it. Her father was dashing and instinctual in his intellectual processes, so to call them. Meticulous, painstaking, he was not: the sorry shambles of his personal finances, as revealed by his death, were evidence of that, if the daily evidence of the previous years were not proof enough. Her mother had been, as far as Ramona knew, an effective manager of Garston, but with the coolly efficient support of first class servants. Thrown onto her own resources, in Brewster Terrace, she had simply crumpled.

Some grandparent, some remoter ancestor, had bequeathed to Ramona genes which made her take trouble, plan carefully, anticipate eventualities; which had made her advance by inches, sure of her ground, rather than dash with impetuous heroism into the midst of the minefield.

So it was, so it had been, that Tuesday afternoon of the last week but two of the spring term. Ramona set out with Maureen, from the door at the end of the back passage, at nine minutes past two in the afternoon, carrying brooms and buckets and scrubbing brushes, making for the old tackroom at the end of the stable block. They were both well wrapped up against the bitter east wind. They went slowly, leaning into the wind. They were burdened. There was no hurry. To try to bustle Maureen along was to get her confused – to reduce her usefulness, even as a scrubber, for half an hour.

Anybody who was watching for them had plenty of time to see them.

Ramona had time to consider, in that short and visible walk, the things that might happen or not happen during the next hour, that were a little different or a lot different from what she had planned, from the train of almost inevitable events which she had set in motion and steered. There was one glaring and enormous possibility – that Rosalind Tuck might simply come nowhere near Ramona's bedroom. The effect of that was not to change anything, but simply to postpone it. Deeply annoying but not fatal. The pendulum, stuck at one end of its swing, was not now going to move, not ever again. It was not very likely. Ramona had contrived a conjunction of the planets as

211

providential for Rosalind as it was for Ramona herself. That child would not let that chance pass.

They reached the door of the tackroom a little after two-eleven. Ramona kept an eye, not obviously, on her watch. She would have been glad to listen for the two-fifteen electric bell, but in a strong contrary wind there was small chance of her hearing it. A moment would come when there would be no eyes at the windows that gave to the tackroom door. At that moment, speed would become as essential as, until that moment, lingering was essential. Ramona felt her heart thudding under the layers of wool that protected it from the east wind. She had felt like this before, but not often and not for a long time. She did not think she was enjoying any of this.

Ramona explained carefully to Maureen, one eye all the time on her watch. They were to divide the work, at least to start with, at least till they saw how they got on. Maureen was to start in the outer part of the tackroom, the part by the door. Rubbish was to go in that bin which had once been a corn-bin. The thing was to get the place more or less clean. They could decide later about paint. Ramona herself would be doing just the same job, but in the inner half of the tackroom. There was another old corn-bin there, for the rubbish she collected up. It would take them an hour, maybe an hour and a half, to get rid of the worst of the ancient dirt.

Maureen nodded, understanding perfectly, agreeing with Ramona's ideas about doing the job. It was all well within her powers. Show her a job that needed doing, give her the tools for doing it, and she was as good as anybody else. Better. She didn't waste time talking. She was not one for talking much, or for listening in the ordinary way. Doing things was more in her line, and sweeping and scrubbing and dusting were exactly in her line. Perhaps it was a funny way to spend your afternoon off.

Two-sixteen.

Maureen, with a great clatter, was starting with a long-handled broom on the cobwebs of the ceiling. She would neither need nor want any further instructions, any interruptions at all, for an hour at least. Ramona was already out of her sight, behind the partition, in the inner half of the tackroom. She made a token clatter like Maureen's clatter. She opened the window, and slid awkwardly through it into the wintry tangle of shrubs. Her clothes were the clothes for the job she said she was doing, dingy, inconspicuous.

The next stage was make-or-break – one of the half dozen make-or-breaks in the whole process. If anybody saw her, clearly enough and closely enough to identify her positively, then the whole thing was off.

Postponed.

Nobody did. The domestic staff would not be peering out of those windows. The teaching staff would certainly not be peering out of any windows. There were supposed to be no girls in the building at all.

The inconvenient complexities of the building suited Ramona perfectly. They would be suiting Rosalind too, as they had suited her before. Back stairs, back passages, areas of darkness even at midday – no-go areas not because they contained any threat but because there was no reason to go to them.

It was barely possible that Rosalind would have beaten Ramona to it. If so, she would find herself in possession of a volume of *Bleak House* inscribed as being the property of Miss Jennifer Corderey. It was in the last degree unlikely; Rosalind would take herself and her slaves obtrusively away from the building, well away from it, before creeping back. Once inside the building, she would move as stealthily as Ramona had moved. She would not be in a hurry, because she knew where Ramona was and how long she was likely to stay there. She would not get to Ramona's room for at least ten minutes, and possibly not for as much as half an hour.

In spite of this logic, Ramona went up to her room as fast as she could. She ran when she dared. She had never climbed the stairs so fast. She was panting harshly when she reached her landing. She clicked the switch of the landing light. Nobody had replaced the broken bulb. She

213

opened the door of her room. Nobody was there. Nobody had been there. It was all as she had left it – curtains, book, ball-point.

She shut the door, and stood behind it to wait. Slowly her breathing was getting back to normal, but her heart thudded and her hands shook. She could not wait for more than three-quarters of an hour. If by three o'clock nothing had happened, she would have to get back to the tackroom and to Maureen.

Waiting was terrible.

Ramona had faced the necessity of waiting for twenty minutes, thirty minutes, but she had not expected the second-hand of her watch to slow to virtual immobility; she had not expected to feel physically sick with suspense, excitement, fright.

Slowly as the time was running, the time was running out. It was ten minutes to three. It was difficult for Ramona to see the face of her watch in the dim light – like many myopic people, her sight was comparatively worse in a bad light, and in near darkness she was almost blind – but by squinting and tilting her wrist she was able to see that it was ten minutes to three. In ten minutes, not a moment longer than ten minutes, she would have to get back to Maureen Maynard. It was not likely that in less than forty-five minutes Maureen would have finished cleaning the outer half of the tackroom, that she would come to Ramona for further instructions, but it was a possibility; it was one of the risks that could be avoided and must not be taken.

Time that had been going unbelievably slowly began to go unbelievably fast.

Rosalind Tuck and her disciples had been joined by other girls who might not give her an alibi. She was not with her disciples but with a boy from the town. She was not interested in the diary, a chub indifferent to the ground-bait. She had sniffed the ground-bait and found it dangerous – she suspected a trap. She had fallen down a

214

rabbit-hole and sprained her ankle. She had been spotted sneaking back into the building, and sent out into the healthy fresh air. There were a thousand things that could have happened to prevent anything happening.

The time was seven minutes to three.

The thought occurred to Ramona, unbidden and ludicrous, that she was now committed to the messy boredom of the clay-modelling project. The prospect filled her with exhaustion.

The time was six minutes to three.

Ramona heard a tiny grating noise, metal on metal. It was coming from the door, from the lock a yard from where she stood. It was the key sliding needlessly into the lock. Perhaps she should have locked the door after she re-entered the room. She could not see that it made any difference.

She took off her glasses, and put them on the shelf by the door. If there was to be any kind of struggle, she would be better without them. In the near-darkness it made little difference whether she wore glasses or not.

The key would be turned, encountering no resistance. Would that make any noise? It seemed to Ramona that it made a tiny noise. It seemed to her that her heart was thudding so loudly that it was amazing that she could hear anything at all, amazing that Rosalind outside on the landing could not hear the bang-bang-bang of Ramona's suffocating heartbeats.

The door-handle turned, slowly, almost inaudibly, making a minute noise which could only be described as the noise of a door-handle turning. There was a small juddering sound. The door was being pushed open, slowly, slowly. The door stuck slightly in the frame. It did not stick enough so that it suddenly burst open, or that it emitted a high give-away screech; it stuck enough so that, without being able to see it except as a blur among dark blurs, Ramona could be certain the door was being opened.

It was opened six inches, a foot. Rosalind would see

that the room was in semi-darkness. Rosalind would know that Ramona was far away in the old tackroom.

The door was opened eighteen inches, two feet, enough to admit a person. It admitted a person. Rosalind stood in the doorway. Ramona sensed rather than saw that Rosalind looked round, slowly, thoroughly, seeing that the room was empty, seeing that the diary was on the corner of the bed. Rosalind looked bulky – she had not taken off the huge fun-fur coat she wore when she went out of doors in this weather. That was sensible – if she had left it anywhere downstairs it might have been spotted and recognised by one of the staff. She had covered her head with something dark, a scarf, a shawl. That was sensible, too, for anyone with hair like Rosalind's.

Rosalind moved, delicately, the few paces to the end of the bed. She picked up the big book. She did not open it. She would not have been able to read it without drawing the curtains. She was not fool enough to draw the curtains.

When she picked up the book, the ball-point pen fell on the floor. It fell on the bit of carpet, making a noise that was hardly a noise. Rosalind ignored it. She started back towards the door, moving a little more quickly, making the floorboards creak a little more loudly. Ramona stood like a stone, sure that she was herself virtually invisible. The door had swung almost shut of its own weight, as it always did when it was left open, because of the slight unevenness of the frame. Rosalind transferred the book from her right arm to her left, and with her right hand pulled the door open. There was another tiny clink of metal on metal as her right hand grasped the door-handle. Ramona realised that she was still holding the Yale key in her right hand. Rosalind stood for a moment in the open doorway, as anybody would in such a situation, looking, listening, making sure she was safe.

Ramona went at her like a bull, a bulldozer, a tank. She caught Rosalind in the small of the back. Utterly unprepared, taken utterly by surprise, Rosalind almost fell to her knees in the middle of the landing, where without the light it was almost as dark as in Ramona's room. She tried to turn, to struggle. Ramona bore her forward with the strength of fury, despair, hatred, with greater physical strength than Rosalind's, with all the advantage of having chosen the place and time, with all the advantage of surprise. Rosalind clawed at the balustrade, hampered by the book which she still carried. She clawed at the rail which ran into the unsafe upright.

She nearly took Ramona with her.

There was a slight splintering noise, an unimportant noise for so important a moment. The balustrade sagged out over the void. Ramona, on the very brink, pulled clear of Rosalind's clutching hand. Rosalind went over the edge.

The noise Rosalind made as she fell was not like any noise Ramona had ever heard. It was not a scream but a drone, a mechanical noise, a siren. The noise she made when she hit came from a long way below. It was another noise unlike any Ramona had ever heard.

Ramona paused for a moment, looking and listening exactly as Rosalind had done. Nobody came running because nobody was about. It might be many seconds before anybody realised what had happened; it could hardly be more than that.

Ramona recovered her spectacles. She clicked the lever on the lock of her door, and locked herself out of her room. She went downstairs as fast and as cautiously as she had come up. She was hardly panting, after a struggle which had hardly happened. It had been ridicously easy, but there were still difficulties. She got to the little trades-men's door without being seen. Still there were no screams, no sounds of running. She bolted across the one small stretch of open ground, ninety-nine percent certain of not being seen, virtually anonymous from behind in the sort of clothes she was wearing. She trotted the length of the stable-block, certain now of being unseen. She opened the tackroom window and crawled in over the sill. She stood for a moment, then staggered, dizzy, hit by reaction, appalled and triumphant in almost equal parts.

She recovered enough to put on a face for Maureen, and walked with elaborate care into the other half of the

217

tackroom. Maureen did not need a face put on for her. She was on her hands and knees in a corner, with a brush and dustpan.

'Great work, Maureen,' said Ramona. She tried to speak in a normal voice, but her voice was far from normal.

Maureen looked round, over her shoulder. There was no particular expression on her face. There seldom was any particular expression on Maureen's face.

Ramona went, casual as could be, to the door of the tackroom. As she did so there was a lull in the wind, and in the lull they heard the first screams.

Followed by Maureen, Ramona ran into the house. There were more screams, louder.

'Where are thcy?' said Ramona. 'What can have happened?'

'Hall,' said Maureen.

They ran to the hall. Hilda Joy and Marigold Kent were trying to shepherd screaming girls away from something on the floor in the middle of the hall. Near the body lay the brown-paper-covered copy of Miss Jennifer Corderey's book. Inches from one of the body's hands was a Yale key on a piece of frayed string.

Weeping silently over the body, and suffered by the teachers to do so, was Rosalind Tuck. Smashed almost to porridge as it was by the fall, there was no mistaking the body of Amanda Loring.

CHAPTER ELEVEN

Ramona was kept on the fringes of what immediately happened. All sorts of action had to be taken, but the fewer people taking it the better.

Police came quite quickly, with a doctor. Various procedures went on which Ramona saw only from a distance, heard about only from report. Boots clumped upstairs, and the broken balustrade was examined. Covered with a blanket, the body remained where it was for what seemed an intolerably long time.

Ramona had got the whole thing absolutely right and absolutely wrong.

Amanda had not given the key to Rosalind; or, if she had, Rosalind had given it back. Amanda would have an alibi for the burglary of Ramona's room, provided by Rosalind and probably Colette Davies. Amanda was running Rosalind's errands for her.

It was possible that Rosalind had known nothing about it – that Amanda had taken it on herself to get the 'Diary' for Rosalind to snigger over. It would be a proof of her love and loyalty.

The key found by the body was tentatively identified as Ramona's, and the identification was made certain when it was tried in the lock of Ramona's bedroom door. The book was identified by Sara Corderey as one which her aunt had lent to Miss Charnley.

It became evident that everybody thought that the copy of *Bleak House* was a diary.

Rosalind Tuck had lent Amanda Loring her warm coat; Rosalind had other coats, and Amanda felt the cold. Several girls had seen Amanda wearing Rosalind's coat.

Ramona was at last questioned.

Why a lock on her bedroom door? Because even though she herself owned nothing of any value, she had in the room valuable books borrowed from a friend, which it was her clear duty to safeguard.

Why the key on a string? Where kept? On a string round her neck, because that was the only way she could be sure of not losing it. She had in fact lost it, because evidently the string had broken, but she did not know when or where. She had the key, for certain, in the middle of the morning, because she went upstairs to her room to get an extra sweater. She had imagined that she still had it, until it was shown to her by a policeman.

She had left the bedroom curtains open. She had left the copy of *Bleak House* on her bed, because she was about to reread it.

She had no idea how the notion had got about that the book was a diary. She did not keep a diary, and had not done so since childhood. She had not told anybody that it was a diary; if anybody had understood her to say that it was, then that person had misunderstood whatever she had actually said.

She had not been aware of the weakness of the balustrade on the landing outside her bedroom. She had never leaned over it to look down; there had never been a reason for doing so, and she would have been frightened of doing so because she had a bad head for heights.

The electric light on the top landing had been functioning normally in the middle of the morning.

She had known Amanda Loring, obviously, but not well. She did not teach girls of Amanda's age. She had had contact with her, when supervising meals and study periods. Amanda had never given her the slightest trouble.

220

As far as Ramona knew, Amanda had never given anybody any trouble.

Yes, it was impossible to doubt that Amanda had somehow acquired Ramona's key, that she knew what key it was, that she had come stealthily back into the building at a time when she was supposed to be out of it, that she had let herself into Ramona's room, that she had taken the book – almost certainly in the belief that it was Ramona's diary – and locked the door behind her. It was impossible to doubt any of this, and it was impossible for Ramona to explain any of it. There were teachers who knew Amanda far better than she did, and girls who knew her far better still. They might have some idea of Amanda's motives; Ramona herself had none.

There was no single member of the school or the staff who could not prove that she was a long way away from the top landing at the moment when Amanda went through the balustrade. Foul play might have been suspected, but it ruled itself out as flatly impossible.

The life of the school carried on, more or less, for the remaining two and a half weeks of the term – it had to, since a large proportion of it had nowhere else to go. Everybody seemed to move in a kind of miserable dream. It seemed impossible to teach and be taught, to set books to read and be set them to read, as though nothing had happened.

Amanda's parents were with difficulty located, and presently flown home by her father's company. They came to Malham House, but it seemed they were to see nobody except the Headmistress and her husband. In the event they saw also Rosalind Tuck, whose name had been often mentioned in Amanda's letters. Nobody witnessed this interview, from which both Rosalind and Amanda's mother emerged in tears.

There was a Service of Thanksgiving for Amanda's life,

221

in the main hall where she had died, conducted partly by the Headmistress and partly by the local parson who was also part-time Chaplain of the school. The hymns included Blake's *Jerusalem* and the metrical version of the 23rd Psalm. It was inevitable that some of the girls stood, and knelt, on the area where Amanda's body had hit the flagstones.

Rosalind Tuck wore a black veil for the service. Nobody had guessed that she owned such a thing. She did not. It emerged that she had borrowed it from one of the daily cleaning-women, who had herself inherited it from a grandmother.

'What sickens me,' said Rosalind Tuck, 'is the awful bloody waste. The poor old thing ending like that, and for what? For a rotten great book by somebody called Dixon.'

The Coroner's Inquest, mandatory in such a case, was an ordeal for everybody. The verdict had to be 'Accidental death', but the Coroner was clearly dissatisfied. Norman the odd-job-man, in evidence which he gave in great distress, admitted that he had never even examined the balustrade of the top landing. The Headmistress was driven onto the defensive by the Coroner's questions, the tendency of which seemed to her to blame her personally for the tragedy. There was something approaching a clash, which reduced the dignity of the proceedings. Of course the Coroner had the last word. He concluded the proceedings with a highly critical comment on the school authorities, for their negligence in allowing such a potential death-trap when their duty, their very first duty, was to ensure so far as in them lay the safety of the young people entrusted to their charge. He corrected himself: it was no longer a potential death-trap but a trap which had caused a tragically untimely death.

Legal action against the school by the dead child's family – something almost inevitable in America and not at all unlikely in Britain – was contemplated but not seriously considered. Punitive damages would have bankrupted the school, leaving nothing for the litigants and very little for the lawyers. There was a surge of relief in the Staff Common Room when Hilda Joy, privy to secrets, let fall this piece of news. Ramona was not the only one who would have had difficulty finding any other job.

Jokes seemed to have died with Amanda Loring. Whispers of 'Bedwetter' no longer followed Ramona down the corridors, and when girls called goodbye to one another they said 'Goodbye'.

Ramona did not suppose this meant that Amanda had been the one responsible for the pin-pricks, the bear-baiting. She had never had the initiative to be responsible for anything. It meant only that Rosalind Tuck was stunned, punch-drunk, shocked by something that hit her personally probably for the first time in her life.

April in Saudi Arabia would heal those wounds. She would come back for the summer term like a giantess refreshed. She might have notions of revenge, blaming – all illogically, from the evidence she had – Ramona for her friend's death. *Term of Trial*. Hadn't that been the name of a film, made some time after the war, some time before Ramona's birth? The summer would be a term of trial, and there might be two judges and two defendants, and each judge was the other's defendant and each defendant was the other's judge . . .

Some of the things Rosalind had tried had partly succeeded, and some had more or less abjectly failed. The one thing Ramona had tried had completely succeeded in all but a single regard. Ramona was just as determined as Rosalind, and cleverer, and tougher, and on the side of right.

Miss Jennifer Corderey's friend, owner of the cottage, was obliged to stay abroad for another three months. Sara

223

Corderey's parents remained committed to trying to save the lives of the doomed. Jennifer Corderey would stay in the cottage, and Sara would be there for the Easter holidays. Ramona would join them for a week and a half of the three weeks of the holidays.

Ramona had seen less of Sara, since the precious books were now deemed safe in her locker, since she had begun to make friends of her own age, since she had become, improbably enough, a kind of probationary friend of Rosalind Tuck. But there was still, invisible to anybody except themselves, a special relationship between them. There was certain to be, after that unforgettably happy Christmas. Eyes met. Unspoken messages passed. That which might have died, of simple needlessness, had survived. Their kind of cousinship had been born, for sure, of the child's loneliness, but it had strengthened into a mutual respect and affection which no armies of Rosalind Tucks could destroy.

At least, Ramona now thought so, after mid-term doubts which she now put behind her. In time, Sara's intelligence would make her immune to the Rosalinds of the world, as her own popularity, her being liked for what she actually was, would make anybody like Rosalind unnecessary to her. Time was an enemy and a friend. It was almost the end of term. Soon, and for ten days, the three of them would be reunited in the cottage.

The indulged indiscipline of the end of term – almost ritual – was inevitably muted. There were no pillow-fights and few shrieks. It would be a relief to everybody to get away from the place.

The topmost landing was put out of bounds for all girls under any circumstances, a rule which made no difference to almost anybody because almost no girl had ever been up there.

Builders were brought in to make a new and reliable balustrade, the only logical object of which was to save Ramona's life. Norman the odd-job man refused to fraternise with the builders. The noise the builders made, even from so far above, distracted classes already inattentive because of the end of term.

It was rumoured in the Staff Common Room that several girls were being taken away from the school because of the accident. Even Hilda Joy did not know how many, or which girls. The Headmistress – haggard since the accident, more haggard since the Coroner's strictures at the Inquest – went about with an expression which lent colour to the rumour.

Ramona stole what time she could to make rapid stabs at cleaning out the back half of the tackroom, to do the work which Maureen Maynard and everybody else supposed she had done. There was not time enough; she was not tall enough; she got cobwebs all over her spectacles.

Buses to Gatwick, Heathrow, Luton. Fleets of Japanese cars. Hugs and hurrahs – muted hurrahs. Sara Corderey away in the little car with her aunt. The staff settling down to write reports. The staff away one by one. The Headmistress and her husband away to a country-house hotel in Wales with a golf course and trout fishing. Ramona alone with Norman and Maureen, early supper so that Norman could get out to the pub. Ramona and Maureen clearing away the supper, Maureen saying neither more nor less than usual. The tragedy had not affected her. She knew that it had happened, but it touched her personally no more than an accident to a black man in a far country reported in small print in the newspaper. Ramona was surprised. To someone with horizons as narrow as Maureen's, even small events within those horizons would seem large. So you would suppose. So it had been – when someone broke a plate in the dining-hall, it was a cataclysm to Maureen. Perhaps the death of Amanda Loring was not even a small event to Maureen. Perhaps plates and the breakage of plates were within her horizons, the life or death of the girls outside them.

*

The wind began to swivel between east and west, the clouds being flung first one way and then the other. Westerly and southwesterly winds brought the promise of spring, of the rebirth of green things and the shedding of awful stiff tweeds.

As though by some celestial arrangement, the first really good day of the year was the one on which Jennifer Corderey came for Ramona in the little Renault. Spring could be seen, smelled, felt. Ramona felt a surge of happiness at the sight of the sun and of buds on branches, and at the thought of the next ten days.

During the drive to the cottage, on the roadside, they saw the first primroses. By some mysterious process of psychic association, the frail yellow flowers made Ramona think of Amanda Loring.

The links were perhaps youth, innocence, inexperience, helplessness. Men from the Council would come with machines to cut the verges of the roads, and the uncaring machines and their uncaring drivers would mow the primroses as efficiently as the grass. Amanda had been mown. Ramona felt truly sorry for her, killed doing something naughty but not vile, doing something entirely for somebody else. Rosalind had been the cause of Amanda's death. Ramona was so seized by the sudden grasping of this undeniable certainty that Jennifer Corderey had to repeat her question – did not Ramona think, honestly, that some of Thackeray's heroines were downright boring?

In one respect, it was as though no time had passed between that Christmas holiday and this Easter holiday – as though the intervening term had been snipped out, and the edges of the two holidays had been invisibly stitched together. Sara ran out of the cottage as the car drew up; Sara and Ramona kissed one another as though continuing their parting kiss after Christmas, as though there had been in their lives no electric bells, awkward little meetings in Ramona's bedroom, taunting of retarded maidservants, or sudden deaths.

226

But in another respect, the cottage and its occupants had been magically transported into a different world. It was a simple matter of the thermometer. Windows could stand open; the little dogs lay on the lawn; the garden could be strolled in.

Warmth and the opening of petals happened inside the cottage as well as outside it: in the three of them as well as with the celandines and primroses. There was a stronger sense of family. There was no caution, restraint, embarrassment. Of course Ramona knew, after the week of Christmas, where the teacups were kept and where the milk-bottles were put out, which made it easier for the machinery to restart as though it had never stopped.

They were extraordinarily lucky with the weather. The 'uncertain glories' became certain. They were out of doors as much during the hours of daylight as they were in. The garden was a well-loved half acre which included a lawn, an herbacious border, a small formal rose-garden, fruit trees, and many ornamental shrubs. Obviously it was a condition of Jennifer Corderey's rent-free occupation of the place that she left the garden as tidy as she found it. Her life in exotic places had left her with almost no knowledge of the management of an ordinary English garden, but it was obvious that things were suddenly beginning to grow at great speed, including weeds, and that a lot had to be done. Sara knew nothing about gardening. The large and lovely garden of Ramona's childhood had been looked after by professionals (on the payroll of the Beeswing Bloodstock Agency). Jennifer bought a couple of how-to-do-it books, and books in hand they mulched, weeded and pruned. These were activities that often brought two of the three together, less often all three. They talked endlessly. It was perhaps paradoxical, but it was unmistakable, that intimate confidences came more easily when you were squatting among the plants in the border than sitting in front of the fire with books in your laps.

There was no mention of Rosalind Tuck, and not much of Amanda Loring, alive or dead. Neither Ramona nor Sara had so much as seen Amanda's family, during their

227

brief and miserable visit, and neither knew much about her background. Neither speculated to the other about Amanda's visit to Ramona's room, her taking the book, her unexplained dive through the balustrade. Even among the emerging shoots of delphiniums and paeonies, even among all the confidences about the past and the future, there were large and nearby subjects left unmentioned.

Jennifer Corderey was able to give Ramona valuable advice about teaching young children to make things with modelling clay. It was something she had herself much enjoyed.

It became the custom that they kissed one another, all three, when they said goodnight and good morning.

They went to early service on Easter Sunday – eight o'clock Communion in the dank Victorian church in the village. They took the day off from gardening. Ramona and Sara sat for two hours after lunch, talking, on the rustic bench on the lawn. There was almost nothing, by now, that each did not know about the other.

On the Tuesday after Easter they went into the town in the car. They shopped for a few things that could not be bought in the village, spending carefully because they all had to spend carefully. They passed, but did not enter, the hotel where the girls of the Malham House School were normally taken out to lunch by the adults who visited them. They went to the art gallery, a surprisingly good one for an obscure provincial town, owing to somebody's generosity a century before. This visit provided surprises all round. The pictures were fairly predictable – nearly all English, nearly all between 1750 and 1850 – landscapes, portraits, sporting scenes, still-lifes of flowers and fruit. The formidable Jennifer Corderey, whom nobody could stump in the whole area of English literature, knew nothing about painting at all. Sara's life had hardly exposed her to any serious art. Ramona's had. Her father's pictures (the Beeswing Agency's pictures) were not major masterpieces, but they were authentic and meritorious – he had three Henry Alkens, a Ben Marshall, and a reputed Wright of Derby; and at her school she had been taught art appreci-

228

ation by a woman who really cared about pictures, and taken to many galleries and exhibitions. She knew about these pictures; she was at home among them; she could spot the best without hesitation or self-doubt, and explain to the others why they were the best and what was good about them. It happened that the curator of the gallery overheard her. He joined the conversation; it became a conversation between Ramona and the curator, with the others listening and occasionally putting in questions.

'You've kept all that under a bushel, dear,' said Jennifer, later, in the car.

'Not purposely,' said Ramona. 'I suppose it's never come up.'

'I feel as if a door had opened in front of me,' said Sara.

Many of the books in the cottage were Jennifer Corderey's property – beloved, battered volumes that had gone with her into deserts and banana-groves, and others she had collected since her retirement, picked up in the remoter shelves of second-hand bookshops. There were some books belonging to the cottage's owner – she would hardly have been a friend of Jennifer Corderey if she had been completely bookless – tending to biography, wildlife, dogs. There were three books, all guessably presents, of the coffee-table kind, large and lavish, placed flat on a topmost bookshelf by Jennifer Corderey, just in case somebody spilled a cup of something over them. They were in any case not, or had not been, of high immediate interest to her. One dealt with the treasures of Venice, one with French painting of the eighteenth century, and the third with Flemish painting.

Sara brought all three down as soon as they got home. They chanced to open first the Venice book – hundreds of individual masterpieces, beautifully reproduced, interiors and exteriors of churches, the horses and the lion of St Mark's . . . Ramona knew the book. Somebody had given it to her mother, their last Christmas at Garston. Ramona thought she was the only person who had thoroughly

229

looked at it, certainly the only person who had read any of the text. She was on familiar ground again, though she had never been nearer Venice than Dover.

Ramona heard herself explaining, to aunt and niece, why Titian was a greater painter than Tiepolo, why it was a pity that Byzantine churches had been filled up with renaissance and baroque decoration, why it was a pity that some of Palladio's patrons had run out of money before he had realised his grand designs. She had forgotten that there was so much that she knew; she surprised herself as much as her hearers by the certainty of her retrieval system. It was the more astonishing because she had not looked at a book of this kind since her parents' library (property of the Beeswing Bloodstock Agency) was packed into tea-boxes and taken away for sale; because, until that day, she had not looked at a picture of any merit since the last of her father's sporting paintings (property of the Beeswing Agency) was lifted down from the wall.

There was a moment which, to Jennifer Corderey, was unexpected and unsettling. Turning the pages of the Venetian book, Ramona came to a photograph of an elaborate sculptured group at the top of a column. The caption said that the carving was Florentine, not Venetian. It was fifteenth-century, and it was placed on the north-west corner of the Ducal Palace, near the Porta Della Carta. The carving was in high relief, and the material Istrian limestone. They read these details with solemn attention; none of them remembered having heard of Istrian limestone.

The subject of the sculpture was the Judgement of Solomon. Two very beautiful young women stood either side of a taller figure, a man, armoured, apparently wigged, with a naked infant boy at his mailed knee. Some sort of lady-in-waiting stood behind, and a fig-tree arched overhead. One of the young women looked heavenward, with a hand in her lap, as though her mind were elsewhere. The other stared downwards, at the child, a hand to her throat. It was to be presumed that the latter was either the real mother or the better actress. The face of the central figure, of Solomon, was tender and concerned, perhaps with a hint of sternness.

'I wonder why they got a man from Florence, when they had such talent at home?' said Jennifer Corderey.

Ramona was not listening. She was staring at the photograph with a look of passionate intensity. Something about it meant something terribly important to her. Jennifer was struck more by the furious intentness of Ramona's face than by the miraculous stonework. Either Ramona was remembering, with a stab of nostalgia, the time and place of her first sight of the picture; or something in the sculpture or the subject was touching her very heart. Her face looked pinched, shrunken. It looked as hard as the limestone of the carving.

'What is it, dear?' said Jennifer Corderey. 'Turn the page if it upsets you so.'

'Judgement,' said Ramona, not as though needlessly explaining the subject of the picture, but as though talking in her sleep. 'Sometimes you have to judge. And then you have to carry out the sentence. Solomon would have.'

'Cut the baby in half?' said Sara, half smiling, incredulous.

'Yes,' said Ramona flatly. 'I did it once.'

Jennifer and Sara glanced at one another, behind the back of Ramona's head. It was not possible to believe what Ramona had just said.

Ramona seemed to wake up, but slowly. She turned the page at last, exposing a colour reproduction of a painting of the Coronation of the Virgin in Paradise. The moment passed, but it was not easy to forget it, and Jennifer Corderey did not forget it.

They turned, early in the evening, from the vehement magnificence of Venetian art to the delicate frivolities of Watteau, Fragonard, Boucher, Lancret, and Ramona felt, of herself, what Sara had said about herself – a door had opened in front of her.

231

When, on Sundays during the summer term, Ramona came out to the cottage for lunch with Jennifer and Sara, they would take the books out into the garden, and place them carefully on a table with a clean top; they would lie back in deck chairs, and imagine themselves in a gondola on the Grand Canal, or by a fountain in a garden at Versailles, or among canals and windmills. Ramona passionately hoped that the cottage's owner did not come back before the end of the summer term; and she was startled when Sara voiced the identical hope, and for the identical reason.

Two days later, Ramona had to get back to Malham House, to perform needless tasks in a detestable place. They drank wine. Except on Christmas day in this cottage and in this company, it was the first wine Ramona had drunk since that Christmas Eve in the Bilborough Bookshop, when Justin Bryan had been sick; and that was the first wine she had drunk since just before her father's death, soon after her seventeenth birthday at Garston. Sara drank a little wine in a lot of mineral water. They only had half a bottle between the three of them. The wine was not one Ramona's father would have endorsed – he would not have used it in a wine-cup with lemonade for a teen-age tennis party – but for the little party in the cottage it celebrated the voyages of discovery they had been making.

It celebrated the extent to which, all three, they had come to love one another.

Going back to Malham House was not as bad as Ramona had expected. Nothing there was changed, so it should have been as depressing, as frightening, as boring as it had always been. The building was no less ugly, Ramona's attic bedroom no less bleak, Maureen Maynard no more stimulating a companion, the other returning teachers no more congenial. Everything was the same, but everything

232

was different. The change was not in Malham House but in Ramona.

Only once before in her life had she experienced that most remarkable of all experiences – that most literally and specifically divine of all experiences – being truly and generously loved by another living creature. Of course her parents had loved her, but it was biologically probable that they would do so – it was, so to speak, their duty to love her, and they deserved no great credit for doing so. But Hector, the little Tibetan spaniel given her by dearest Great Aunt Ramona, Hector had loved her for no reason, he had loved her for what she was, because she was Ramona Charnley and no other, he had loved her with that devotion which is its own reason. When Hector was killed by the tractor driver, Ramona thought she would never get over it. She would never lose the sense of pain and loss. She would never again feel, night and day, the glow of being so loved. She never had felt it – not from her family, not from anybody who came to Garston, not from even her closest friends at school – not, God knew, from anyone in Bilborough, from anyone at the Malham House School. She would have liked, but did not expect, the romantic devotion of a man. She would not at all have liked the romantic devotion of a woman, but she did not at all expect that either. The sort of love she had known from Hector was God-given and unrepeatable.

Not having it had blackened the edges of Ramona's life, and drained the colour from the middle. It had made her cowardly, uncertain, weak. It had made her vulnerable, and threatened her health and her livelihood. To be loved was armour outside, and warmth and strength inside. Threats could be ignored if they were trivial, squarely faced if they were serious. You became the Pilgrim in Bunyan's hymn. You became Galahad. A once rocking world stabilised onto an immutable axis. Shadows fled. It was a rebirth.

One of Ramona's colleagues, a grey spinster called Dorothy Venables who taught A-level French, was interested in Spiritualism, had read many books on the subject,

233

and would expound its discoveries to anybody who would listen. By Dorothy's account, death was passing through a door into a place called the Summerlands. Hector was waiting for Ramona in the Summerlands. Ramona herself, without benefit of death, had passed through a door into the Summerlands.

Nobody noticed the difference. They noticed that the purple dye was now almost invisible.

Marigold Kent came back only just before the beginning of term, having had to take her own children to their schools.

'So how was your Easter?' she asked Ramona. 'Family friends, wasn't it?'

'Sort of,' said Ramona. 'It was very nice, really. Quiet, but nice.'

'Mine was bloody awful,' said Marigold. 'Miss Deborah Kent and I disagree on every single issue. God, how I hate teenagers. I thought I'd like my own, but I don't. I'd rather stay at home in term-time, and come here for the holidays.'

Ramona laughed. Perhaps Marigold's daughter was becoming rather a pain. Marigold did not notice the huge and lovely difference in Ramona. She noticed that the purple dye had continued to fade.

The girls came back, wave after wave, car after car, coach after coach from the airports, some of the youngest crying.

They seemed to have got over the previous term's tragic accident. The sense of shock, the muted quality of life, the habit of talking in hushed voices, had all been left behind, purged away by the holiday, by the sun of Saudi Arabia or the gusting winds of the English seaside. This was not obviously callousness. Life had to go on. For some, examinations approached which had to be sat, even though, for many girls, the results were perfectly irrelevant.

One girl still seemed numbed by Amanda Loring's death. It was Rosalind Tuck, a Rosalind Tuck of lower

234

candlepower, silent and unsmiling, often choosing to be alone. It was remarked on in the Staff Common Room. Hilda Joy was worried for the girl, though morally impressed by her loyalty. Ramona found this ironic, since Rosalind had been morally responsible for Amanda's death. It was not an irony in which she took any pleasure.

Everything was easier for Ramona, from the first minute of the first girl's arrival, than it had ever been before. She had a new authority, a new strength, a new cheerfulness. She was untroubled by supervising meals or by Evening Study Period. No whispers followed her.

The response to the clay-modelling project, by the parents of the youngest children, had not been enthusiastic. They did not want extras on their bills. Not enough interest was shown to justify the fitting out of a studio, even though the room was available and had been cleaned out. The Bursar was mildly disappointed – he had costed the operation so that it was self-financing and a bit over. Ramona was relieved. Nobody else gave a damn.

Ramona had hardly any contact with Sara Corderey, public or secret. It made no difference. She heard regular reports of Sara in the Staff Common Room – Sara was discussed because she had become the great white hope for bringing academic credit to the school. In this capacity she had replaced Colette Davies, who had evidently outgrown any interest in the life of the mind. Sara's only problem, according to the received wisdom of the Staff Room, was that she might find it all too easy – might be under-extended, and so fail to realise her potential. Everybody was determined that this should not happen, since the merit of Sara's potential was that it would help keep the school full.

There was no need for Ramona to be constantly seeing Sara, in order to know how she was getting on. There was no need for any other reason, either. It was enough that she existed, she and her marvellous aunt. The miracle was not going to become unwrought because they did not have heart-to-heart conversations every day.

Did not? In a strange sense, quite new to her, Ramona

found herself increasingly unable to believe that they did not. She had never had anything approaching a telepathic experience, though many of her schoolfriends said that they had, and her own Great Aunt Ramona said that she had. (It was the not unusual story of a friend in a car-smash on the other side of the world.) Ramona had been dubious about the existence of the phenomenon, so completely was it outside her experience. She had heard about levitation, poltergeists, uncanny foreknowledge; she had heard all too often from Dorothy Venables about people's conversations with poets long dead. She was dubious about all these things. But now she found that she walked and talked with the Cordereys, aunt and niece, though one was two hundred yards away and the other fifteen miles away. Nothing very specific was communicated – nothing like 'Be careful, or you're going to drop that cup', or 'The sauce on the fish at your supper this evening will be beastly'. What was communicated was awareness of the cord at both ends of the cord, awareness of love at both ends of the telephone-line.

It was like a massive daily dose of vitamins. It was like solitary early-morning swims in the pool at Garston. It was like Hector her dog wriggling into her lap when they came home after a walk.

Ramona wondered at the diversities of love. The love she had read about was that of men and women for one another, sometimes requited; there was the love also between comrades, which sometimes (if you were to believe what you read) went beyond loyalty, even unto death, and became something altogether deeper and more central without, however, containing any suggestion of the perverse. At least, Ramona thought not. There were, to be sure, the unnatural lusts of men for men and (even odder to Ramona) of women for women, but she did not think she had ever actually seen anything of the sort going on. There was not much mention of it in the English classics, or, if there was, it was so wrapped up that she had not recognised it.

What of the triangular love of an elderly woman, a

236

young woman, and a schoolgirl? Had anybody written about such a thing? Had it ever even happened before? Certainly no other word was possible for what they felt for one another. Had they, between the three of them, invented a new dimension of love?

Sometimes, across the library or the dining-hall, Sara's eye would meet Ramona's. They would hold the glance for a fraction of a second. Something without a name – something hinted at, perhaps, by Beethoven or Rembrandt – would rush between them.

It was like drinking wine, and it was free.

One person, it turned out, was seriously upset by the abandonment of the clay-modelling project. That was Maureen Maynard. Her messy afternoon in the old tack-room had committed her. She thought it was terrible that the youngest children should not, after all, be making models of rabbits in clay.

'After all our work,' she said to Ramona. 'A whole afternoon just gone to nothing.'

But it was not so much that she resented her hard work going to waste. It was that Ramona had fired her with enthusiasm for the project, and now nothing would put the fire out.

She became quite tedious on the subject. From not having mentioned it at all, she began to mention it constantly. The women in the kitchen shut her up about it, but Ramona did not have the heart to do so.

'It's not just all my hard work gone to waste,' said Maureen, 'it's yours too, ennit?'

Even Norman the odd-job man, who had a kind of kind heart, told Maureen to belt up about clay modelling.

Sara Corderey now openly read books borrowed from her aunt, without shame and without fear for the books. The other girls had no special prejudice against it. It was not what they liked, but it was what Sara liked, so let her get on with it and good luck to her.

It was assumed, if anybody thought about it, that Rosalind Tuck shared this tolerant indifference.

It was therefore a surprise to see Sara reading aloud to four girls, on the grass in the sunshine, one of whom was Rosalind.

The book was Thackeray's *Barry Lyndon*.

'I've never even heard of it,' said Marigold Kent in the Staff Common Room. Hilda Joy pretended that she had heard of it.

Ramona had read Jennifer Corderey's copy before handing it on to Sara. She now had a sense of rereading it, of looking over Sara's little shoulder and sharing with her the deplorable Irishman's adventures.

Rosalind Tuck seemed to be quite interested in what she was hearing.

Amanda Loring's death left a vacancy in the school and in her class which was filled, oddly, a fortnight after the beginning of the summer term. The new arrival was called Joanna Curry. Her father was a parson, working for the British and Foreign Bible Society in Central America. Joanna had been there with him, being taught at home by her mother. Violence made the place unsafe for a girl Joanna's age; it was pretty unsafe for a pale-haired teen-ager at the best of times. Joanna and her mother were ordered home, but her mother refused to go. Joanna was sent to a cousin, and by the cousin to the Malham House School; the choice was as obscure and unsatisfactory as in Sara's case.

Nobody at first much noticed Joanna Curry. It was difficult to notice her. She was so shy and retiring that if your eye fell on her, and moved on, and went back for a second look, it found her gone.

Rosalind Tuck said she seemed dim, and it was impossible not to agree.

Ramona saw the whole situation from her uninvolved

and supervisory distance, and would have grieved: but she was in no mood to grieve. The rest of the staff saw the situation, and used phrases like 'Soon shake down', and 'Only a question of time before she finds her level and acclimatises'. They had seen it all before.

Sara Corderey had seen it all before, with the difference that she had seen it from the inside. She suspected that Joanna Curry was not dim, but only shy and frightened and lonely and homesick. Obviously she could help. But a thing you very soon learned was that only the friendless made friends with newcomers. If you went and talked to Joanna Curry, it could only be because you had nobody else to talk to. Sara was Mightymouse, eccentric but accepted. Not so accepted that she could take that kind of risk.

Rosalind had befriended Sara herself, but nobody could misunderstand that. Nobody could accuse Rosalind of being friendless. Different rules applied. Sara could no more be like Rosalind than Rosalind could be like Sara. Besides, Sara had been around for weeks before Rosalind made her a friend. Joanna had only been there for a few days, if you could say someone was there who was mostly invisible.

Sara was citizen of a country of which Rosalind represented the Presidency. Sara's citizenship was probationary. She would jeopardise it by befriending immigrants.

Probably in a week or two Rosalind would befriend Joanna, and then it would be all right to be seen talking to her.

It happened sooner than that.

It happened in a way that could probably only have happened among teenagers in a boarding school: probably only among girls.

It became evident after three or four days that Mrs Curry, over there in a place with an uncouth name, was a thoroughly competent tutor, and that she had had good

239

material to work on. Joanna immediately and effortlessly occupied second place behind Sara Corderey in the class, the place that Colette Davies would have occupied but for her sea-change. Joanna was four months older than Sara, and younger than any other girl in the class. She was ash-blonde (a kind of blonde completely different from Rosalind Tuck's resplendent ripe-corn gold) with little sharp features and very slim wrists and ankles. She was small but still growing; physically she was just beginning to mature.

Put it all together, put Joanna beside Sara, and Joanna was obviously Minimouse.

It was Rosalind Tuck who thought of the name.

Named, Minimouse suddenly had three dimensions instead of two; she was substance instead of shadow. She turned out to be pretty interesting about the violent, passionate country she had just left, which none of the others knew anything about.

It was all right to be seen talking to her. Sara was seen talking to her. Together they were the Mice, viewed with a tolerance in which there was an element of respect.

Friendship between the Mice had a kind of inevitability. It had nothing to do with Sara being friendless, because Minimouse was already accepted as somebody you could have as a friend. Rosalind Tuck said that hearing the two of them talking was like hearing a conversation in Greek. In her tolerance there was an element of respect. Also, she now had two people available to help her with her homework.

'It is to be hoped,' said Hilda Joy in the Staff Common Room, 'that those two little bookworms don't stick together all the time.'

It was one of the occasions when Hilda Joy broke the rule about talking shop in the Staff Room, the rule which she herself so often restated when other teachers did it.

'They could hardly have a bad influence on one another,' said Marigold Kent.

'No, of course not, but they should mix. Everybody should mix. School is a preparation for life, and there is a great deal more to life than reading books.'

'There is also the aspect,' said Dorothy Venables, 'of their influence on the rest of them.'

This point was generally taken, but not by Ramona, none of whose business this was. Sara now had a friend of her own age who was like-minded and literary; that was all right, and they were all making too much of it. There was no danger that Sara would become engrossed with Joanna Curry to the exclusion of the other girls. There was already a special relationship in Sara's life. She was one point of a triangle. The phrase 'eternal triangle' popped into Ramona's mind, but she pushed it out again as having quite different associations.

Sara's eye continued, often enough, to meet Ramona's. Joanna Curry was not jamming the transmission. She never would. Nobody ever could.

On the first Sunday in which the girls were allowed out for the day, Ramona was on duty. Sara went off alone in her aunt's little car. Joanna Curry had arrived, but Minimouse had not yet been brought to life by Rosalind Tuck.

Before the next free Sunday, plans for outings were discussed in dormitories and dining hall. Minimouse said she had no plans, because the cousin on whom she had been dumped was in Scotland.

'The Mice must go together,' said Rosalind, 'and nibble the same bit of highbrow cheese.'

Everybody thought this was a good idea. Nobody terribly wanted to ask Joanna out, even though she was Minimouse and accepted; and she was probably too shy to enjoy the boisterous parties of uncles and cousins.

'I'd already thought of it,' said Sara to Joanna. 'I think you'll like my aunt, though she terrifies most people.'

'Most people terrify me,' said Joanna.

'Me too, but she won't.'

Sara telephoned her aunt, standing in line for half an

241

hour for the telephone the girls were allowed to use. Jennifer Corderey said she would be delighted to welcome a contemporary of Sara's, but sorry that she would not see Ramona. Why should she not see her too? Because Jennifer already had a guest for Sunday lunch, a one-time colleague, and she could not cope with more than four in the dining room.

Sara assumed that Ramona assumed that the two of them would be going out to lunch with Jennifer Corderey. They had not discussed it since term began, but they had talked at Easter about their Sundays on the lawn. Sara thought she had better find Ramona at once, to tell her she was not asked to lunch. Ramona was not in the library or the staff Common Room or her own classroom. Perhaps she was in her bedroom. It was an awful long way up. They were bound to come across each other in the next day or two, and Sara could tactfully give Ramona the sad news. No – they had not really run across one another for weeks. Sara faced the climb – quite likely useless – to Ramona's room.

'Come for a walk, Mice,' said Rosalind Tuck.

Sara and Joanna went for a walk with Rosalind Tuck and a girl called Patsy Matthews, whose father worked for East African Airways. Rosalind said that both the Mice would grow up to be beauties. She insisted that this was so, and Patsy Matthews, who always agreed with Rosalind, agreed with Rosalind. It was the topic of conversation on that walk.

Ramona and the message for Ramona went out of Sara's mind.

Saturday. The next day a free Sunday. There was still no need for Ramona and Sara to meet and talk. They had met, they had talked, at Easter; they had planned their afternoons on the lawn of Jennifer Corderey's cottage. Since then their eyes had met, and the arrangements were confirmed.

Sunday. Ramona waited in the clump of trees at the

242

bend in the drive. This arrangement, tacitly and almost guiltily arrived at so long before, perhaps unnecessarily persisted. None of them had come out and said that it was no longer necessary. None of them had even mentioned it, since Jennifer Corderey's surprise the very first time. It had become part of their lives, a dot within the magic triangle.

Ramona had dressed up for Sunday lunch in a cotton frock with a light cardigan. There was a tiny trace of mustard-yellow paint ineradicable in the wool of the cardigan. The new Ramona rose above such things. Was she to throw away a Marks and Spencer cardigan, not two years old, because of a trace of yellow in the baby-blue wool?

She had booked out for lunch. On these free Sundays, they needed to know in the kitchen how many people they were cooking for. On a fine Sunday like this it was very few. Marigold Kent was noisily furious about being on duty, even though she would have had a row with her daughter if she had gone away and taken her out to lunch.

Ramona saw Jennifer Corderey, at the wheel of her Renault 4, bumping up the drive towards the school. People were beginning to make noises about the state of the drive. It would not be long before some uncle at the wheel of an expensive import damaged his suspension. The cost of resurfacing was a cause of concern for the Bursar; he had been saying so more and more often.

It was a matter of minutes: a matter of seconds.

The moment came. The car came. There, above and behind the wheel, were the strong, well-loved features of Jennifer Corderey. There in the back seat was Sara, with the broad, sweet smile that promised such adult devastation. There beside the driver, leaning back to say something over her shoulder to Sara, was Joanna Curry.

The car went briskly by. Ramona stood among the trees, knowing that she would get no lunch, unable to believe that she had seen what she had just seen.

CHAPTER TWELVE

Ramona walked down the drive, away from the school instead of towards it. When a car came along, she slipped into the bushes beside the drive. She had to do so many times before she reached the gates. A bramble made a triangular tear in her cardigan. That was not terribly important, since the cardigan was already ruined by yellow paint.

If she went back to the school, they would all want to know what had become of her lunch party. Marigold Kent would want to know. Marigold would demand an explanation, and she would deserve one because of her unfailing goodwill. Ramona could not face Marigold's goodwill.

Lunch at the cottage was a success.

The little Joanna, at first so unpromisingly taciturn, was warmed into opening her petals just as Sara had been, the previous autumn. Jennifer's one-time colleague was a help: it was a fortunate chance that she had once worked in what was then British Honduras. Jennifer and Sara pushed the others out onto the lawn so that they could clear away lunch; they had Latin America to talk about.

'I hope Ramona wasn't too disappointed?' said Jennifer to her niece.

'So do I,' said Sara.

'Didn't she say anything?'

'No,' said Sara truthfully.

Sara felt guilty. She had simply forgotten to tell Ramona. But surely Ramona would have expected her to come and confirm the arrangement, if the party was still on, if she was still invited? Wouldn't anybody? If Sara didn't come and talk to her about it, wouldn't that mean she was going out alone, or with somebody else? Ramona couldn't simply have assumed an invitation which had never actually been made? They had discussed it vaguely at Easter, but nobody had actually come out and said, 'We're expecting you for lunch on May 23rd.'

Ramona might be a bit bored with the Cordereys, especially as they knew nothing about painting.

Probably Sara had bored Ramona, by talking too much about herself at Easter. That was why she had seized on the art books with such relief, just to have something new to talk about. And of course that was why Ramona had not said anything to Sara, or come anywhere near her, since the beginning of term. Sara was annoyed to think how boring she must have been; she made herself a vow that she would never again talk so much about herself.

Aunt Jennifer could be a bit boring. She did bang on and on about books, as though nothing existed outside the covers of books. It might be the result of her never having been married, or it might be the cause of her never having been married.

Sara loved and respected her aunt, but she was very sure she did not want to be a spinster herself.

Ramona was still quite young enough to get married, but Sara did not think it would happen. She never saw anybody. It would have made no difference if she met every bachelor in London and Paris and New York.

Sara did not know what she wanted out of life. All her options were completely open. But she knew she did not want to end up like her Aunt Jennifer, or like Ramona.

They stacked up the lunch things on the draining-board, and went out to join the others on the lawn. There was the table, on which they might later have tea. There was a bird's mess on the table. Somebody would have to scrape it off before tea, and even then the memory of it would remain, so that you would not put a piece of cake on the table. They had talked about bringing those art books out, and looking at them on the table. It was a very bad idea, precious books which were somebody else's property. Probably they would never have brought the books out, when it came to the point. It would have been a choice between staying indoors and not looking at art books. Probably Ramona would have chosen staying indoors so that she could look at the books; Sara would have been obliged by good manners to have stayed with her. The books were lovely, but it was better to be out of doors.

Sara sat on the warm grass, which a man was coming to mow the following day. He would mow away the heads of the daisies. There were a few bees on the daisies; Sara was careful not to sit on one. She could not picture Ramona sitting on the grass. She could not picture herself, when she reached Ramona's age, not sitting on the grass. It was a different sort of person. Sara told herself that she did not assume that she was a better sort of person than Ramona, but she was a different sort.

Half listening to the others, Sara divided the world into people who sat on the grass and people who didn't. Aunt Jennifer didn't. Joanna Curry did now, but she might turn into the sort of person who didn't. Her own parents did, or would have if they were somewhere where there was any grass. Of all the teachers at Malham, Marigold Kent was the only one you could imagine sitting on the grass. Rosalind Tuck would always sit on the grass, even if she was wearing a ball-gown from Dior, which she probably would be most of the time. Rosalind had her faults, but she was a firm friend and she sat on the grass.

Ramona was sitting on grass, on the dusty grass of a bank beside a lane. She was two miles from Malham House, on the way to nowhere. She did not think the dry grass would do any permanent damage to her cotton dress. She had seen no one and no one had seen her. No one would know how she had spent the day, doing absolutely nothing, her head absolutely empty.

The only positive thing that she felt was hunger.

Rosalind Tuck had been asked out to lunch by a girl called Yvette Wilson. Yvette was an imitation Rosalind Tuck whose father worked in Dubai. Her Uncle Eddie, though, burned all the way up from New Malden in his Datsun, once or twice a term, to take Yvette out. He brought his wife, Yvette's Aunt Gwen, and their seventeen-year-old son Darren. They also brought, on this occasion, Darren's best friend Simon, whom Yvette had met in the holidays. It was a coup for Yvette to have persuaded Rosalind out to lunch. Rosalind would impress Darren, and Yvette thought Darren would impress Rosalind. If that was how it worked out, Simon was left for Yvette.

They went to the usual hotel, near the museum and art gallery, to which they did not go. It was a squash with six of them in the car. They made a big joke of people sitting on other people's laps. Darren contrived that Rosalind sat on his lap, although Simon showed signs of wanting Rosalind on his own lap, instead of Yvette. They made jokes about all sorts of things. Eddie was full of jokes (from the first, Rosalind was told to call them Eddie and Gwen). Gwen laughed at all Eddie's jokes; Rosalind laughed at some of them, because she was being bought an expensive lunch.

Rosalind was bored before the end of lunch. Darren and Simon started making eyes at her from the word go, which would have been all right if they had both been quite different. But they were creeps. Eddie started making eyes at her, too, after his third Bloody Mary. Rosalind wondered who was going to drive back. Her own father sometimes had one too many, but not if he was going to drive.

They thought making a lot of noise was proof that you were having fun. Yvette caught Rosalind's eye from time to ime, with an expression that said, 'Isn't this fun?' Rosalind smiled back because of the expensive lunch.

Eddie was fairly rude to the wine-waiter.

It came to Rosalind that she was not really one of these people at all. She was embarrassed to be seen with them. Her own father had not had an expensive education, but he knew enough to be considerate to servants. She felt glum when she thought of the drive back, sitting on Darren's lap or Simon's or even Eddie's. Any one of them would think that a long, noisy lunch was enough to turn you into an intimate friend. You could do all sorts of things with your hands, to a girl on your lap, when there were four of you in the back of a car. Rosalind had been there. Sometimes she hadn't minded at all, quite the reverse; it just depended whose lap you were on.

In the event, Rosalind sat on Darren's lap on the way back to Malham. She kept slapping his hands away, but they kept creeping back. Gwen and Yvette and Simon all thought it was hilarious. Eddie seemed to be safe to drive.

Rosalind got thankfully out of the car at the moment when the Mice got out of Sara's aunt's car. Sara's aunt looked pretty grim, but she was probably interesting. Nobody in a million years could call the Wilson family interesting. The Mice had had a more interesting time, a better time, than Rosalind. She envied the Mice.

She owned the Mice, and took possession of them.

She said, 'I don't want to sound bitchy. It's not Yvette's fault. But that lot are the pits. I can't talk about anything much, but they can't talk about anything at all.'

'You said they shouted all the time,' said Joanna.

'Yes, but not about anything. Just about cars, and stupid jokes, and whether I was flirting with one creep or the other. I wish I knew a completely different lot of people, but what can you expect in a dump like this? Ouf, I've eaten too much and sat all day in a stuffy hotel. Let's go for a walk.'

Ramona came up the drive at a time which was feasible if

she had been spending the day with friends. She came openly. Her friends had dropped her at the bottom of the drive, at her own request, because she wanted to stretch her legs and shake down the clotted cream she had eaten, with sponge cake and strawberry jam, for tea.

She saw Sara Corderey and Joanna Curry and Rosalind Tuck.

She heard a laugh. It was not Sara's laugh, which she knew – a sort of gurgle punctuated by squeaks. It was not Rosalind's laugh, which she knew – a derisive yowl. It was a high, clear, girlish laugh, surprisingly strong, unbridled, a laugh which could not be called a gurgle or a yowl but could only be described as a laugh. By the process of elimination it was Joanna's laugh, which Ramona was sure she had not before heard.

What were they laughing at? Who were they laughing at? Who, between them, had they hurt and humiliated for their own amusement?

The bear thought it had escaped from the pit. The bear was wrong.

Rosalind Tuck was refreshed by her walk with the Mice. It was good to be with people who talked about something, even though half the time she did not understand what they were talking about.

Rosalind had always been aware that there was a world outside the one where she lived, a world inhabited by teachers and culture-vultures, in which she had no desire to set foot. Now she had friends who were citizens of that world, and she would have liked to visit it. There was no way she could get a visa. She was as thick as a plank. Her father was pretty bright, but her mother could only add two and two if the neighbours told her how, and Rosalind had inherited her mother's brain. This had been obvious from her first days at nursery school. She had never much cared; she preferred what she had. Now she was not so sure. The Mice got things out of things that Rosalind couldn't get anything out of. They were going to look all

249

right, too, if somebody told them what to wear. They had the best of all worlds. Rosalind felt cheated.

They talked a lot, but they did not hog the conversation. They were good listeners, when Rosalind wanted to talk. In that way they were like everybody else. In a lot of ways they were. They were not freaks, after all. Rosalind wondered if she were not the freak.

In the distance Rosalind saw The Moaner. The Mice were too absorbed in the nonsense they were jabbering, but Rosalind saw The Moaner dodge out from a clump of bushes and dodge back into it again. Rosalind wondered vaguely why The Moaner was playing hide-and-seek on a Sunday evening.

On balance, and without deep interest, she rather liked The Moaner. She admired the guts the woman had shown after Amanda and Colette had covered her with that ghastly dye. Rosalind had never understood why the two of them had been to such trouble to do something so puerile. She faintly regretted the practical jokes she herself had played on The Moaner, though they had been fun at the time. Pouring all that water on The Moaner's bed – what did something like that achieve? It was something a six-year-old might do. Being in such a rage after the silly row about the paperback cover – that was like a six-year-old, too. Tearing the page out of Sara's aunt's book was another matter. Rosalind would not have admitted to that to anybody. It seemed a very good joke at the time, and everybody thought it was a very good joke at the time. Everybody thought the rubber knickers were a very good idea at the time, though when Colette Davies suggested them Rosalind was not very keen.

She had laughed when she heard about the yellow paint, but now she did not know why she had laughed. It was a bloody thing to do to somebody. The Moaner must have shown some guts about that, too, because nobody ever heard a whisper about it.

They all thought The Moaner's fat book was a diary. Somebody said The Moaner herself had said so. Rosalind remembered saying it would give them a giggle to read it.

It wouldn't have, even if the 'diary' really had been a diary. More to cry over, probably. It was absolutely stupid of poor old Amanda to go and nick the book out of The Moaner's room. Amanda's death was the most horrible thing that had ever happened to Rosalind – the only horrible thing that had ever happened to her – but the reason was absolutely stupid. Amanda had only done it as a way of sucking up to herself, Rosalind. Rosalind didn't mind being sucked up to, if the person meant something and if it was done in a sensible way. The Mice sucked up to Rosalind a bit, but they meant something and they did it in a sensible way, by just talking. Amanda meant something, though you had to know her a bit before you saw it, but what she did was bloody silly. Rosalind was truly sorry for Amanda's parents, who were like people sleepwalking.

'That book you were reading aloud, Mightymouse,' said Rosalind. 'About the Irish yob who got mixed up in a war – '

'What about it?'

'Would your aunt mind if I borrowed it after you've finished it?'

'No, of course not, but I've got some others you might like better.'

'I'll be guided by you,' said Rosalind. It was a phrase she had picked up from her father. He used it to wine-waiters in restaurants. He liked wine, but he admitted he knew nothing about it. That did not make the waiters despise him but, on the contrary, respect him. It was very different from Eddie Wilson.

Sara lent Rosalind *The Pickwick Papers*.

Rosalind had a feeling that she was sucking up to the Mice. She had never sucked up to anybody before; she had never thought she would need to. She had always been at the receiving end of any sucking up that was going. But this was a special case, and it might turn out to be worth it.

*

251

Ramona saw Rosalind Tuck crossing the main hall towards her form-room, with a big book under her arm. The book was wrapped in brown paper, and Ramona thought she recognised it.

'Rosalind!'

'Yes, Miss Charnley?'

Rosalind turned, her eyebrows raised. Her face expressed nothing except enquiry. A shaft of sunlight, as though waywardly, caught the ripe-corn gold of her hair. She really was a beautiful girl.

'What book is that?'

'It belongs to Sara Corderey's aunt. Sara lent it to me, if I promised to look after it very carefully, which I did and am.'

'I don't believe it.'

'I know it looks funny, seeing me with a book. I can actually read, if the words aren't too long. You can ask Sara.'

'Yes,' said Sara. 'I asked my aunt, on the telephone. She's very pleased that other girls want to read her books, as there's nothing worth reading in the library. She won't be pleased if the books get damaged, but Rosalind's promised.'

'And you believe her?'

'Yes, of course.'

Between the three of them, they had put Ramona in a false position. Ramona acquitted Jennifer Corderey of deliberate complicity.

But Ramona had been excluded from the lunch party. Jennifer must have known about that. It must have been on her instructions. She was fed up with ceaselessly entertaining Ramona, who could make no kind of return. Probably all that talk about painting had put the lid on it.

*

252

Evening Study Period. The Moaner was in charge. There was no trouble of any kind. A lot of the girls were coming up to O-levels. There were several girls, besides Sara and Joanna Curry, trying to work hard after years of lethargy. The last thing they wanted was disturbance, distraction.

Nobody wanted to upset The Moaner, either. She had mysteriously become almost popular. Her nickname derived only from her name. You couldn't see the purple dye on her face any more, but you couldn't forget it. You couldn't forget the guts The Moaner had shown about that, as Rosalind Tuck said to everybody.

Rosalind was reading *The Pickwick Papers*. She had been encouraged in doing so by her tutor Hilda Joy, in preference to learning anything about which she might ever be examined. There was no way she was ever going to pass any examination, so she might as well use the time acquiring some culture. Hilda Joy said so in the Staff Common Room; it was generally surprising, as she herself had never acquired any culture.

The electric bell sounded. Babel, and a rush of bodies. Sara stopped to talk to Rosalind, who was still reading, oblivious of the tumult round her. Rosalind smiled at something Sara said. She turned back to the book. The library was almost empty.

Sara left Rosalind to the book; she had other things to do.

In the door she turned and said, 'See you later, Alligator.'

It was a silly sort of thing to say, something out of an old, old song, something you found yourself saying, friendly, beyond that almost meaningless.

'In a while, Crocodile,' said Rosalind, glancing up from her book.

Ramona heard. She misheard.

Sara disappeared.

Ramona found that her hands were shaking, and she felt that her face was twitching.

253

Rosalind was now the only other person in the room. Rosalind was looking at her oddly.

Ramona made it to the door, and out into the hall. Whispers followed her, the whispers of the previous term.

Hector, her loved and loving Hector, had been murdered.

Everybody said the tractor-driver was not to blame, but that was silly. Of course he was to blame. Who else could you blame? He was the murderer of Hector, and he had taken the light out of Ramona's life.

Such a thing could not go unpunished. That would have been unfair and unjust. Ramona was brought up to fairness and justice. Her father said his whole business was built on fair dealing. Sometimes her parents showed a bit of unfair favour to Persephone or Patrick, it was true; but sometimes Great Aunt Ramona showed a bit of favour to Ramona, so that balanced out.

Justice. It meant that if you were caught doing something wrong, you were punished. It meant exactly that, neither more nor less. Her father had said, 'I'll see justice done if it kills me', meaning that a man who had bumped into his car must be made to pay for the damage. The worse the thing you did, the greater the punishment. Anybody could see that.

The punishment was supposed to fit the crime. That was another thing her father said. Patrick once, in a fit of temper, knocked over a bottle of wine and smashed it on the flagstones of the kitchen. He did it deliberately. Their father made him sweep up all the broken glass, and then scrub and scrub the floor until all the red stain was scrubbed away. It took him a long time and he hated it. Ramona was sorry for him at the time, but the lesson struck home and stayed. The punishment fitted the crime.

This crime was murdering, with a tractor, the creature most loved and lovable in the world. It was obvious what punishment fitted that crime. Nobody who thought about it sensibly could fail to see the obvious punishment. It was only fair. It was justice.

Ramona had to wait quite a long time until just the right moment arrived. She was impatient, but she made herself wait. She waited and watched. The moment came. The tractor-driver's wife was in the garden at the back of their cottage, hanging up a lot of washing. The baby was in a play-pen in the cottage – Ramona had seen it there. The tractor-driver was backing his murder-weapon, his trailer loaded with logs.

If the baby made any noise, Ramona did not hear it because of the noise of the tractor. If the wheels of the trailer running over the baby made any noise, she did not hear that either. She was quite glad. She would not have liked the noise, but she would have stood it in the interest of justice and fairness and making the punishment fit the crime.

There was no point in ever telling anybody about this.

What punishment fitted the crime of treachery? In wartime, traitors were shot. Ramona's father had known of a case. It was one of his stories.

This was wartime.

Crossword puzzles. Waiting and watching. Ramona had done it before and she was very sure she could do it again.

There were still six weeks of the summer term.

And then Sara herself mixed everything up by giving Ramona a message from her aunt: would Ramona come for lunch the Sunday after next?

Ramona was thrown off balance by the invitation. She mumbled something about looking in her book, as though, in the welter of her luncheon invitations, she could not remember whether or not the Sunday after next was free.

She said she would let Sara know. Sara nodded and smiled, pretending to be friendly.

*

As far as Ramona knew, the situation was without precedent among civilised people.

Chicago gangsters in the days of Prohibition, she thought, would go out to lunch and blow a fellow-guest's head off with a sawed-off shotgun. That was a memory of old black-and-white films on the nursery TV at Garston. Nanny loved Jimmy Cagney. She put her hands over Ramona's eyes when anything nasty was happening. Something very nasty was happening now, and Ramona was forced to look at it.

Campbell of Something, a rough tough man, killed all the MacDonalds of Glencoe, although he was their guest at the time. They were thieves. They had stolen his favourite horse, and he even knew what stable it was in. Ramona's father had told her the story. He was rather on the side of the Campbells, but he admitted they had had a bad press. Ramona did not contemplate massacre.

Some of the later Roman emperors killed people they sat down to lunch with. The Borgias did, too, and King Henry VIII of England. He must have had lunch a lot of times with Anne Boleyn and Katherine Howard and probably Sir Thomas More. Ramona thought they did not call it 'lunch'.

She decided to refuse the invitation, on moral grounds, and tried to think of an excuse which Sara would believe. Sara would not believe another invitation already accepted. Ramona had told Sara all about herself, far too much about herself, in the days when she trusted her. If she were to be on duty, the notice board in the main hall would say so. She could not predict a splitting headache ten days off, not credibly. She had been genuinely and visibly anxious to come, all the other times she had been asked. She had let herself believe that she had enjoyed herself, and that she wanted to come again. She was hoist with her own petard, a phrase the meaning of which she was half-sure she had once known.

She had to accept the invitation, because she could not think of a single reason she could give for refusing it. Sara pretended to be pleased, and said that her aunt would be pleased.

Joanna Curry was not coming. She was going out with somebody else. It would be just the three of them, as so often before.

The prospect of lunch would have been distracting, if Ramona had let it distract her. She refused to be distracted. Her old virtue of thoroughness still held.

The crossword. Watching and waiting. The whispers down the corridors were distracting, but they were also a spur.

She mocked herself for the pipe-dream of the first weeks of the term. Rebirth, the Summerlands – girlish twaddle, the self-delusion of an eleven-year-old. Ramona was adult, although she was aware of inexperience in many areas. She was old enough to face reality, without Nanny's hands over her eyes. Part of the reality she faced was that she had suffered from a delusion, a green-gold mirage in the midst of the howling desert.

She would give the desert something to howl about.

Different fish were lured by different ground-bait, or rose to different flies if you did Ramona's father's kind of fishing. There were big single hooks and little treble hooks, and furs and feathers and tinsel, but ultimately the knock on the head was the decider, the bash at the base of the skull with a six-inch club called a 'priest'. As a child, Ramona had been a bit shocked that the weighted staghorn truncheon with which her father killed salmon was a 'priest', but now she saw the wry black humour of the traditional name.

Ramona gave thought to the form her own 'priest' would take.

Lunch at the cottage did not live up to the past.

Jennifer Corderey wondered if the fault lay in herself. She thought not.

257

Sara was growing up all the time, a little more interesting, a little more a personality in her own right, every
time Jennifer talked to her. The school might not be the
best in the world, but it was not doing so badly by Sara.
The fault did not lie there.

The one who was different was Ramona. It was not
something you could put your finger on. She looked a little
wan, perhaps, a little short of sleep or vitamins. She talked
normally and sanely. She was not uproariously witty, but
she never had been. She did not start at sudden noises,
and there were no black circles under her eyes. She was a
house with all the curtains drawn shut, all the blinds down;
sightless and secret. She had been so when Jennifer first
met her; then, one by one, the curtains had been opened
and the blinds raised, revealing to Sara and to herself
the sunny, well-furnished, welcoming, cultured interior.
Jennifer supposed that, of course, they had not seen into
every corner. You were not supposed to see every secret
corner of a person, any more than you were supposed to
see every private detail of the back premises of a house.
They did not pry, and Ramona did not thrust herself down
their throats. All the same, they got to know her better
than one got to know most people, and Jennifer guessed
that Ramona showed more of herself to them than to most
people.

Not that day. She was upset about something. She did
not say anything about it, and Jennifer decided not to ask.

She did say something to Sara about it, when Ramona
had gone indoors and was out of earshot.

'I know, I've been thinking the same,' said Sara. 'I
can't imagine what can be wrong. From what I've heard,
Ramona's having a better time at school this term than
she's ever had before.'

'Better in what way?'

'Easier. Nobody taking advantage of her or playing practical jokes on her.'

'Did they do that?'

'You surely remember that purple stuff.'

'Do you know who actually did that?'

'No. I thought I knew who'd done it, and I thought I knew why. But I was quite wrong. I'm a hundred percent certain it wasn't the person I guessed. I'm glad about that, because it's somebody I rather like.'

'I wish I knew what was troubling Ramona. I wish there was some way we could help.'

'So do I,' said Sara.

Ramona rejoined them, with an air of reluctance to do so.

Jennifer had the idea of bringing out one of the coffee-table art books, in the hope that it might rekindle the spark in Ramona that seemed to have been snuffed out. She spread a clean cloth on the garden table. She said the sun would not crinkle the pages of the book nor fade the illustrations.

'I've brought the Flemish one,' she said, 'because we only had time to glance at it before.'

It seemed to Jennifer that the old spark did reappear, in Ramona's eyes, behind those thick spectacles. But her voice sounded bored as she leafed through the book, and the spark died in her eyes.

It was obvious to Ramona that Jennifer Corderey was numbered with the enemy. Ramona had wondered about this. In a way it was reassuring: it was tidy. Not so guilty a culprit, and so not the ultimate punishment. Ramona thought she would again be pretty neatly fitting the punishment to the crime.

It was the book on Flemish painting that made the whole thing clear. Ramona's enthusiastic teacher, all those years ago at school, had had an almost single-minded passion for the Italian Renaissance, and that was what she taught them about and what they were taken to see. English art, especially of the eighteenth century, was the other area they were well exposed to. From her father, Ramona also knew a good deal about early nineteenth-century English sporting art. The French eighteenth century had passed her by, but she had been happy with the book about it.

259

For one thing, she could pronounce the names of the painters.

But the Flemish book was calculated to humiliate her, and in front of Sara. The names were grotesque. She had no idea how to pronounce them. How were you supposed to pronounce 'Pieter de Hooch'? And among the pictures she was all at sea. All those harbours, those flat landscapes, those bowls of fruit, those soldiers drinking in the back rooms of taverns. They were completely unlike the paintings she knew about, Raphael and Titian, Gainsborough and Romney, Herring and Sartorius. She did not know how to compare a still-life with a tavern scene. She was tricked. She was made to make a fool of herself. And in front of Sara.

Sara's punishment would punish Jennifer Corderey, just the right amount, in just the right way.

Sara was as puzzled as her aunt, and as distressed.

What she had said was true – even within the nine months of Sara's experience, Ramona was more popular and had more authority, as though she had suddenly grown up. She had been baited and victimised, but no more. Nobody wanted to do that any more. Rosalind had done one or two pretty beastly things, but not any more. Rosalind had borne a stupid, childish grudge. She had outgrown it. Sara was two years younger than Rosalind, but she saw that Rosalind had been very, very childish when they first knew one another. Her adult sophistication was a false skin, made of plastic. She had been growing up fast, in front of Sara's eyes, and most of the plastic skin had cracked and fallen away.

With a shock, Sara realised that Rosalind had been self-conscious, insecure, unsure of herself when she first came to Malham. At sixteen, she had never been to boarding school before. She was an only child, adored and indulged by pretty uneducated parents. Rosalind's father sounded a very decent man, from what Rosalind said, and of course it was a great thing to be so successful from such simple beginnings. But obviously he was not sophisticated, not cultured at all, as Rosalind herself said. So nothing in Rosalind's life had prepared her for being dumped into a world of discipline, rules, strangers, future examinations. Of course she felt insecure. And as a result, she showed off. She showed off by pretending to have had all kinds of adventures which Sara now knew she had not had; she showed off by smoking, putting on eye-shadow, wearing ridiculous perfume; she showed off by being insolent to the teachers. That was all it really came to. Now that she felt at home, there was no need for any of it.

Rosalind was a natural trend-setter, even though she was not working at it. Therefore it was still the fashion to imitate her. She said she had come to like and admire The Moaner. It became the fashion to like and admire The Moaner.

Yet here Ramona was, in a place where she had surely been happy, bored and silent and obviously wishing she was somewhere else. Aunt Jennifer and herself were not *that* boring, were they? Or had Ramona, in growing up, outgrown them?

From much that Sara had read, Ramona's sullen abstraction could be put down to unrequited love. Catherine Morland, before the rather cheated happy ending of *Northanger Abbey*, had been like that when she went home from Bath. It did not seem terribly likely, but as a theory it fitted the facts.

Ramona had met someone when she went out to lunch, two Sundays before, the day Joanna Curry came to the cottage. Probably it was then. She had fallen in love, and he hadn't, or was already married, or something. 'Men don't make passes at girls who wear glasses', Sara remembered somebody quoting. And Ramona's glasses were exceptionally thick, poor thing.

It was something like that, and Sara was truly sorry for Ramona. But it was still true that Ramona was rather ruining the party at the cottage.

*

261

The noise of the car's engine, the brushing of the tyres on the tarmac, echoed the derisive whispers which followed Ramona along the corridors of the school.

Sara thought Ramona was her dupe – ignorant, a gull, a sucker. In her adolescent arrogance, Sara thought Ramona liked and trusted her.

It made everything very much easier.

It was necessary to keep Sara's delusion going, at whatever cost in self-respect. It had been impossible to do the desirable amount of play-acting at that terrible cottage, but Ramona forced herself to make up for that.

'I'm sorry I was a bit below par,' she said to Sara, forcing a smile, in the main hall before roll-call.

'We did think you were a bit.'

'Next time I'll be my sunny self.'

Sara smiled. She did it skilfully. There was an appearance of gladness, of relief in Sara's smile that might have fooled Ramona if she had not been so thoroughly forewarned.

In a way it was irritating for Ramona to have such insulting assumptions made about herself. But in a more important way it was highly convenient.

That evening, before they went to bed and while they were going to bed, Sara had the sense that there were discussions going on from which she was excluded. High matters were being considered, which she was too young to hear about – debarred from hearing about, perhaps, because she was a Mouse, or because The Moaner had come out to lunch with Aunt Jennifer. Sara saw Rosalind and Colette deep in murmured conversation, their faces serious. Rosalind looked really serious. They both glanced at Sara and then, meeting her eye, glanced away again.

Minimouse, Joanna Curry, was drawn into the whispered conference. She too glanced at Sara, looking not guilty or knowing but worried and puzzled.

262

Sara felt puzzled, too, and a little upset. She was being excluded from something; she did not know what, or why. It was like the first weeks of her first term. She thought things had changed. It was not like Joanna to be part of a gang which excluded her; it was not like Rosalind, either, the person Rosalind had become.

They all said goodnight to Sara with great friendliness.

Ramona's preparations were vexatious but essentially simple.

On the attic floor of the house, as on every other floor, there was a housemaid's cupboard in which brooms and dustpans, mops and dusters had been kept. None of the cupboard doors had locks – obviously not – even Edwardian housekeepers did not keep mops under lock and key. The doors were of their time and type – heavy, two inches thick, not very well-fitting. The door of the attic broom-cupboard was much more solidly made than than the old gimcrack balustrade had been.

The cupboard was a little wider than the width of the door – perhaps four feet wide. It was nearly a yard deep. There were a few shallow shelves, for tins of polish and the like, and hooks for dusters. The cupboard was a foot higher than its door – about eight foot high. Ramona did not know how long it would be before a person in the cupboard were asphyxiated.

Ramona took a bolt from Norman's tool-shed, an ordinary heavyweight bolt that might have been made for a stable. It was one of the oddments that Norman, like all odd-job men, could always lay his hands on. He had dozens of miscellaneous door-fastenings on a particular shelf in his tool-shed – bolts, hooks, latches, doorknobs, locks without their keys and keys with no locks to open. Norman would not miss one old-fashioned bolt.

She took six screws that fitted the screw-holes of the bolt – four for the bolt itself, two for the metal sleeve that the bolt ran into. She borrowed a screwdriver and a gimlet.

263

The pencil for marking the places where the screws were to go she could provide herself.

It took her two days of stealthy intermittent work to fix the bolt to the outside of the broom-cupboard door. Probably it had taken Rosalind Tuck about the same time to drill the hole in the bathroom ceiling. Rosalind was a spent force. Ramona was not. It was harder work than she expected, getting the screws bedded right into the old woodwork. She hurt the palms of her hands.

The bolt was usable but too stiff. She returned the screwdriver to the tool-shed, carefully wiped, and borrowed a little oil-can. She oiled the bolt. It slid in and out, after a few moments, quite easily and silently. She had never attempted such a job before, even in Brewster Terrace, and she looked at the result with pride.

Nobody else would look at it. Nobody would come up to the attic floor. Anybody who did would not see the bolt, dark against dark wood in a dark corner. Anybody who saw it would assume it had always been there. Ramona would say she had no idea whether it had been there or not. In fact the police would realise it had just been put there, by the fresh scratches on the heads of the screws. They would find out that the bolt had come from Norman's tool-shed. None of that would help them in the slightest.

Ramona had a flannel skirt, dating from Garston days, unwearable because it was a schoolgirl's pleated skirt and hopelessly dowdy even by Malham House standards, even by Ramona's own standards. She had worn it sometimes in Bilborough, but nobody at Malham had ever seen it. It was undatable, untraceable, once the label had been snipped off. Ramona cut the skirt into two-inch strips. With glue from the cupboard in her own classroom, glue messily used by her own little pupils, she stuck the strips of flannel to the insides of the frame of the cupboard door. The door became stiff to shut, as the edge of the door pushed against the flannel. It became airtight and soundproof. Nobody would know she had sacrificed a skirt, and nobody would notice the small amount of glue she had used.

264

The salmon-fly was an opportunity to mock and humiliate Ramona. Sara would not be able to resist it. But it was artificial, fur and feathers and tinsel. Hidden inside it was a sharp hook with a strong barb. The broom-cupboard was the landing-net. The 'priest' was in Ramona's hand; it was a heavy, well-oiled bolt from a stable door.

Ramona borrowed a can of white enamel paint from Norman. She did this quite openly. Nobody noticed or was interested, but later she could say, and Norman confirm, that she had borrowed a can of paint. Norman lent her also a half-inch brush, which was soaking in a jam-jar of white spirit.

'For Gawd's sake be careful, Miss,' said Norman, who would have done the job himself, in his own time, only that he wanted to get off to the pub.

He was thinking of the yellow paint. So was Ramona.

Ramona painted the bookshelf in her bedroom. She had to pile her few old paperbacks, and a couple of Jennifer Corderey's books, awkwardly in a corner. She got paint on her hands and a blob of paint in her hair. The painting was perfectly unnecessary. Nobody would know that, not when it was covered with fresh white enamel. The smell reminded Ramona of the yellow paint. These were small things.

'I've done some paintings,' Ramona would say to Sara. 'It's a dead secret, but if I don't show them to somebody I'll burst. But please don't tell anybody. Promise.'

Sara would promise. She would say to her cronies. 'The Bedwetter's done some paintings. I'm going to go and see them. Wait for a bulletin.'

'No,' Ramona would say afterwards, 'good heavens, no. I told Sara I'd done some painting.' She could show anybody who wanted to see it the new white paint on her bookshelf. Norman would know all about it. He had lent her the paint and brush.

Ramona gave her bookshelf a second coat, and returned the paint to Norman with the brush in its jam-jar of spirit.

'What was it you was paintin', Miss?' said Norman.

'My bookshelf,' said Ramona.

Norman looked at her oddly. There was something impertinent in his expression. Ramona turned away from him, from all the muddle of ironmongery that he crooned over like an old hen.

As she walked away, with the dignity she had learned at Garston, she remembered that Norman had seen her bookshelf, recently and often, when he was cleaning up the mess of the yellow paint. The paintwork of the bookshelf had been quite fresh, because it was used only by her and that not much. It had not needed another coat of paint. Norman would have noticed that, because it was habitual with him to notice anything that needed a lick of paint.

It was no business of Norman's. What he thought about Ramona needlessly painting a bookshelf was unimportant. What was important was not what Norman thought but what Sara thought.

Ramona's plan was quite different from the other, which had worked so well and so badly, because of what Sara thought Ramona thought. The fish thought it was catching the fisherman. There was no need of any other groundbait.

Ramona was being more sporting, doing without ground-bait. She was fishing in a manner of which her father would have approved.

Ramona telephoned Jennifer Corderey, on the telephone in the cubby-hole outside the Staff Common Room. Nobody could hear what she said when she shut the door, stuffy as that made the cubby-hole. She had often seen Hilda Joy and others apparently miming animated conversation – she knew the door was soundproof, like the one to the attic broom-cupboard.

'Jennifer, it's Ramona Charnley.'

Jennifer sounded surprised.

'I need your help. I need to consult you. I need your advice.'

That would bring her.

'It's a, well, both a personal and a professional problem. I can't talk about it on the telephone. It's been terribly on my mind. I may have seemed a bit preoccupied when I had lunch with you – it's because I'm so worried. It's a situation I simply haven't the experience to deal with.'

It would be Hilda Joy's double standards. How was Ramona, so very much junior, to protect the girls themselves from Hilda's capriciousness?

'An afternoon,' said Ramona tentatively. 'Wednesday afternoon, soon after lunch? Would that be possible?'

All Jennifer Corderey's busybody goodwill came thrumming down the line to Ramona. The arrangement was made. Jennifer would give Ramona the very best of her experience and advice.

She might be guessing the problem was a man, or she might be guessing it was somebody like Hilda Joy. Either way, she was going to give Ramona her alibi. There was a lovely justice in that.

'A bit preoccupied,' echoed Jennifer Corderey's mind when she hung up the telephone. It was a mild way of putting it. Ramona had seemed a good deal more than a little preoccupied. 'Both a personal and a professional problem.'

It was distinctly odd. All her life, Jennifer Corderey had been consulted, on the widest variety of topics, by family and friends and colleagues. There was something about herself, she supposed, which inspired confidence. People knew she had commonsense, a great width of reading, experience of many cultures and countries; people knew that their secrets were safe with her. But Ramona had not really confided in her, ever at all. History, background, yes, but not hopes, fears, worries, terrors, triumphs. Ramona had all these things because everybody had them: but she had not shared them with Jennifer.

Now, it seemed, she was suddenly about to do so – was so urgently intent on doing so that she effectively sent for

267

Jennifer. And this only a few days after Ramona had spent a day in Jennifer's company.

Jennifer wondered what Ramona really wanted of her.

Ramona took a precaution that she had taken before. She did it more quickly and deftly this time, with the benefit of practice. She took the bulb out of the bracket on the top-floor landing, broke the element without breaking the bulb, and replaced the useless bulb.

'Yes,' said Sara, 'of course I'd love to see them.'

'I've taken over one of the empty top-floor bedrooms as a studio,' said Ramona. 'I've simply amazed myself. I've turned out to be a surrealist. I hope you don't think they're pornographic.'

Sara giggled. The fish was racing after the fly. In a moment it would grab it.

'Here we are,' said Ramona.

She clicked the switch of the landing light. Nothing happened, of course. She clicked the switch up and down, perhaps overacting the instinctive reluctance of a person to accept that a light did not work.

'Blast,' she said. 'Popped again. I think there's something wrong with the socket.'

Sara stood waiting in the near-darkness, not knowing which door to go through.

Jennifer Corderey's car would be bumping up the drive any second. Ramona would have run upstairs only to grab a coat. Off she would go, with Jennifer, the coat over her arm.

'On you go,' said Ramona. 'I'll find a light.'

'But this is only a – ' Sara began.

She was pushed forward into the cupboard. She was pushed across the cupboard, into the shelves, by the door slamming into her back.

Ramona slid the bolt into its socket. She heard, very faint and far away, Sara shouting and beating at the door. She would use up the oxygen quicker if she went on like that.

Somebody would realise during the afternoon that Sara was not to be found. Nobody would begin seriously looking for her, not for two or three hours. Nobody would think to come up here.

Probably Ramona would remove the body. It hardly mattered where she put it. That was a problem for later. The thing now was to get the coat, to get down and out of the building.

'Oh Miss,' said Maureen Maynard, 'that wasn't a nice thing to do.'

CHAPTER THIRTEEN

Ramona stood gasping, utterly astonished. Maureen pushed past her, quite rudely, which was unlike her. Maureen went to the door of the broom-cupboard and pulled back the bolt. At once the door opened and Sara came out. She came out as fast as the cork of a Champagne bottle, one of the thousands Ramona had seen her father open at Garston. Sara was staggering a little. She was wide-eyed and pale, the pallor of her small face evident even in the dark. She stared in visible amazement at Ramona and at Maureen. A greasy cobweb from somewhere in the broom-cupboard had draped itself over her forehead; she became aware of it, and brushed it away with the back of her hand.

Maureen said, 'Get away out of it, kid, before she tries again.'

Sara sped away like a mouse, like one of the Mice. She ran into the arms of Rosalind Tuck, who was standing in the darkness of the passage. Ramona had not seen her, standing there in the shadows; all that Ramona could see of her now was the mane of unmistakable hair.

Maureen and Rosalind had come up together, quietly, following Ramona and Sara. They had reached the landing in time to see Ramona shutting Sara in the broom-cupboard. In the excitement and physical effort of the movement, Ramona had not seen or heard them come up onto the landing.

Rosalind caught and held Sara, embracing her.

'Everything's okay, Mouse,' said Rosalind. 'You're safe.'

'Oh,' said Sara. 'Oh.'

Rosalind kept one arm tight round Sara's shoulders. With the other hand she reached out to the landing light. She clicked it up and down, exactly as Ramona had done, exactly as nearly everybody would have done.

'Never mind about the light,' said Rosalind. 'Everything's okay.'

'I don't understand.'

'Nor do we, really. We've thought about it and thought about it, and talked about it and talked about it, Colette and me and Joanna and so forth. We didn't say anything to you, because you were such pals with The Moaner. You might have said something to her. I expect you saw us muttering in corners. This is what we were muttering about.'

'What is? What's happening? I still don't understand.'

'I didn't understand, either, as I said. That's how it started, me not understanding. It started because I couldn't understand about Amanda.'

'She came up here to get what she thought was a diary.'

'Yes. It was absolutely stupid, but I'm afraid that's what she did. And then she's supposed to have fallen through that railing. How *could* she have?'

'It was dark.'

'Not pitch dark. About like now. There's nothing to trip over. Look! The floor's perfectly smooth. Her eyes were perfectly all right. She wasn't drunk. The passage is about five feet wide.'

'But if she didn't just fall – '

'Of course she didn't just fall!'

'You mean she was pushed?'

'Of course she was pushed.'

'But why?'

'I think it's because The Moaner thought she was me.'

Ramona became aware that Maureen Maynard had hold of her arm. Maureen's brain might be weak but her hand

271

was strong. Ramona did not try to break loose and run away. She had nowhere to run to.

'The Moaner hates my guts,' said Rosalind. 'I'm not sure I blame her, really.'

'Rubbidge,' said Maureen unexpectedly. 'You're not a bad kid.'

'No, I don't think I am, but I can see that I was,' said Rosalind.

'You an' that vanishin' cream,' said Maureen.

'You know I'm sorry about that.'

'Least said soonest mended. I must 'a looked a proper goony. I see the funny side now.'

Sara made a small exploding noise. She was impatient to know what was happening and why.

'There were things that were perfectly obvious,' said Rosalind, 'even to a moron like me. Amanda couldn't just have fallen, from here, from this spot. All the way from that door, and falling hard enough to go through the banisters? She wasn't as stupid as that, poor old thing. She could walk a yard or two without going over a banister. That was one obvious thing. I didn't tell her mother about that. Another thing was The Moaner hating my guts.'

'How do you know she did?'

'Everybody knows she does. It's obvious. Ask anybody. And then there's another thing everybody seems to have forgotten about. Amanda was wearing my coat.'

'So she was,' said Sara slowly.

'I've never worn it since. I couldn't bear to. I've never even seen it since, not after they took it away with Amanda inside it. They offered to clean it and send it back, but I said no, give it to Oxfam. A lot of people saw Amanda wearing that coat. You did. Obviously The Moaner didn't, if she thought it was me in the coat. Anyway, she couldn't have seen Amanda wearing it if she was in that old stable place all afternoon. She said she was and Maureen said she was and everybody knew she was.'

'Then she couldn't have . . .'

'She couldn't have, but somebody did. Listen, old

272

Amanda was a bit of a pudding, not much brighter than me, but nobody could *hate* her.'

'No.'

'Not enough to push her off this landing, not enough to kill her. So I thought it had to be me they were trying to kill.'

'But *who* were?'

'I thought it must be The Moaner, but we knew it couldn't be The Moaner, not if she was with Maureen all that time. So that was the puzzle. In the end Colette and I went and asked Maureen where The Moaner really was that afternoon. That was Colette's idea. I never would have thought of it. I should have, but I didn't. Maureen said The Moaner *was* there all the time, all afternoon, in that stable place. So we went to the stable place, us and Maureen. It turned out Maureen didn't actually see The Moaner, for about an hour and a half, because there's a partition down the middle. But still she must have been there, Maureen said, because there's only one door and the window only opens a tiny bit. So then Norman came along.'

'Norman . . . ?'

'Just snooping. You know how he does. He saw Colette and Maureen and me going into the stable, and he wondered what we were up to.'

'We told him,' said Maureen.

'Maureen told him,' said Rosalind. 'We tried the window, and it does open. Quite enough to get through. So then Norman had a look at the stable, and he said nobody had spent an hour and a half cleaning the part The Moaner was supposed to have cleaned. There were cobwebs all over the place. Somebody had done a bit, maybe, but only a bit. Hardly scratched the surface, Norman said, not five minutes' work. He said it was the first thing anybody would do – brush away the cobwebs so you could see what was what. It might take you half an hour, Norman said. It would take me about a year, but it's the first thing anybody would do.'

273

'It's what I done,' said Maureen. 'An' her not liftin' a finger.'

'She was lifting a finger, all right,' said Rosalind. 'But it was a different finger. I would never have thought of that about the cobwebs. I don't believe Colette would have thought about it. Norman spotted it right away. He was cross about it. He said The Moaner had been taking advantage of Maureen's good nature. But he wouldn't believe she killed Amanda. He had to admit it was possible, but he wouldn't believe she'd done it.'

'I don't believe it either,' said Sara. 'At least, I wouldn't have until . . .'

'Until she locked you in that cupboard. So finally we plucked up courage and we went and saw Hilda Joy.'

'Miss Joy,' said Sara blankly.

'She is supposed to be my tutor. She's supposed to be the person I go to with all my problems. I couldn't imagine a bigger problem than this one, so we went to her.'

'What *did* she say?'

'She thought we were making the whole thing up. She thought I was trying to get back at The Moaner, because it was her who caught me when I hitched a ride on that motorbike. She said we were just stirring up trouble, making mischief, inventing fantastic rubbish. Really it was all just what you'd expect her to say. I don't suppose she mentioned it to The Moaner. She'd think it was beneath her dignity or something. She'd think she was playing our game.'

Dully, as though her brain was travelling through syrup, Ramona noted that Hilda Joy had been told about Rosalind's suspicions, and had done and said nothing about it. By no word or look had she communicated anything to Ramona. Of course not. She would not admit to such an impertinent fabrication on the part of one of 'her' girls, to such a ghoulish misuse of tragedy. The face she had turned to Ramona was her usual one, superiority sometimes tolerant and sometimes not.

'Nobody believed you,' said Sara. 'I'm still not sure if I do.'

'Nobody believed us,' said Rosalind, 'and I wasn't sure Colette truly believed any of it, either, not in her heart of hearts.'

'I b'lieved you,' said Maureen.

'Maureen believed me, but I never understood why.'

'Me doin' all that work, all for nuthin'. Not fair, that wasn't. Norman said so.'

'So,' said Rosalind, 'I went to the cleverest person I could think of, after you. I went to your co-Mouse.'

'Joanna?'

'I wanted her on board, because she's got almost as many brains as you. She didn't believe me, either. Of course she didn't know Amanda. She didn't think I was stirring up trouble, she just thought I was wrong. She thought I was crazy. I couldn't get her to see that it wasn't me that was crazy, it was The Moaner. But at least she was willing to talk about it, not like Hilda Joy. We did talk about it.'

'Yes, I remember,' said Sara. 'Yes, I did see you talking to each other, leaving me out.'

'I'm sure you see why we left you out. It's funny, really. I'd got to like The Moaner, in a way, but she hated my guts. So we thought we'd better watch her.'

'Who watched her?'

'Just me and Colette and Maureen, at that stage. Of course we thought it was me she wanted to murder. We never dreamed it was you. And of course, if we'd guessed it was you, we'd have warned you. As it was, we all thought it was better to keep quiet, in case you warned The Moaner. Anyway, we were watching her, so there was nothing terrible she could do. So we saw her putting a bloody great bolt on the door of that cupboard. That was an absolutely crazy thing to do, unless there was a reason, and we could only think of one reason. We asked Norman about the bolt, and in the end he said he thought he was missing a bolt. He said it was a right liberty, somebody coming and pinching one of his bolts. Then she oiled it.'

'How can you know that?'

'Maureen found it all oily.'

275

'Like a bit o' the van,' said Maureen. 'Like what they do call the dipstick.'

'There's only one way that bolt could have got oily,' said Rosalind. 'At least, we could only think of one. Then she chopped something up and made a sort of pad inside the door-frame. Colette watched her sticking it there.'

'You've left me behind,' said Sara.

'It left me behind, too,' said Rosalind. 'We got Norman to come and look at it. Norman said it could only be to make the door airtight. That was when Norman began to believe us. He believed us a bit more after something about paint.'

'Paint?'

'The Moaner painted something that didn't need painting. That may not be exactly crazy, but it's not exactly sensible, is it? Unless you want to change the colour, and she didn't. She told Norman it was her bookshelf she painted.'

'Her bookshelf was white,' said Sara.

'I know. Norman told me. It's still white. It was white paint he gave her.'

'Airtight,' said Sara. She sounded thoughtful. It seemed to Ramona that Sara only now understood the full implications. Ramona, herself, found herself beginning to face implications.

Maureen's grip had not slackened.

'We showed Joanna the bolt and the padding on the door,' said Rosalind, 'and she had to begin to believe us, too. She said just what Norman said – the bolt could only be to keep somebody in the cupboard, not to keep anybody out of it, and she said the padding stuff could only be to make the door airtight. So that was really the result of the bolt and the painting – it gave us more of a team – Joanna and Norman as well as me and Colette and Maureen. It made it much easier to keep an eye on The Moaner. By that time we thought we knew what we had to watch for – just this cupboard. It was a relief to me, I can tell you. All I had to do was not go into that cupboard. Of course,

276

we *still* didn't guess it was you she was going to lock in the cupboard. Poor Mouse, locked in a cupboard.'

'Not very nice,' said Maureen.

'Anyway, Maureen saw you going off with The Moaner after lunch, going upstairs, all the way up here. I said she wouldn't do *you* any harm, but Maureen said Norman said The Moaner must have gone over the edge, and it was best to play safe.'

'Better safe than sorry,' said Maureen.

'Much better,' said Sara faintly.

'The rest you know,' said Rosalind.

'Thank you both very much,' said Sara.

'Don't thank us. Well, thank us a bit, if you like. Thank Colette and Norman and Joanna. That's where the brain-power was. I wonder where they've all got to? Now that we've won I don't know quite what to do.'

'Nor do I,' said Sara.

Nor did Ramona.

Further thought had increased Jennifer Corderey's feeling that there was something odd about Ramona's sudden and desperate appeal for advice.

She pulled up in front of the school. She assumed that Ramona would be looking out for her, not simply because she so urgently needed to talk to her but also as a matter of politeness. Jennifer sat waiting for Ramona to come out of the front door.

After three minutes it was evident that Ramona was not coming out and had not been looking out for her. Irritation, rapidly growing, was added to puzzlement in Jennifer's mind. It was no little favour Jennifer was doing Ramona, driving all this way immediately after a lunch eaten specially early, when there were dozens of things that needed doing in the garden. Punctuality could reasonably be demanded.

Jennifer at last climbed out of the car and went up the steps to the front door.

In the hall there was a fair number of girls, but no visible member of the staff. Jennifer had acquired the habit of command, like any competent teacher of long experience. She made her presence and her annoyance felt. But none of the girls had any idea where Ramona was, until one of them pushed forward little Joanna Curry.

'Here's Minimouse at last,' said Rosalind. 'What a time you've been. You've missed all the excitement. Where are the others?'

'Colette went off to fetch Norman,' said Joanna, who was panting after running up the stairs. 'I've been with Sara's aunt.'

'My aunt?' said Sara, sounding astonished.

'She came to take Miss Charnley out,' said Joanna. 'She was asking everybody for her. She was a bit annoyed, at being kept waiting. I told her Miss Charnley was up here with you, Sara. I said she must come up. I hope that was right. I didn't really tell her why, because she wouldn't have believed me. She's coming upstairs.'

Decisive footsteps could indeed be heard. It was a considerable climb for a woman of Miss Jennifer Corderey's age, but she was thin and fit. When she arrived at the top landing she was not panting as Joanna had been; but of course she had not run upstairs.

Little Joanna Curry was insistent that Jennifer should go all the way upstairs, that Ramona would be there with Sara and that Jennifer's presence was necessary. Jennifer could make nothing of all this. The child was not incoherent, but what she said was without merit or sense. Jennifer was as puzzled as ever, and more than ever annoyed. It was no way for a girl of Ramona's age to treat a woman of Jennifer's age, to drag her without apology up a mountain of stairs on an errand as yet totally unexplained.

The journey upwards was from light to darkness. Each flight of stairs was a little darker than the one before, and each grew a little darker as it rose. Jennifer was aware of her eyes becoming gradually used to the growing darkness as she ascended.

The scene on the very top landing was therefore obscure but not impenetrable. It had a dramatic grouping so well posed that it might have been deliberate, rehearsed. Jennifer was reminded of something which after a second she identified. It was a scene from a German film, one of those experimental and expressionist films they showed at small cinemas in Chelsea and Hampstead in her student days just before the war. Darkness, menace, significant grouping.

At one end of the scene, just visible, was Ramona, a dim light from somewhere reflected in her spectacles. She was close to, perhaps held by, a big young woman unknown to Jennifer. At some distance stood Sara, her face a pale wedge in the darkness as she turned to look at Jennifer. Beside her, close to her, was another girl, taller, a mane of blonde hair which seemed to glow with its own luminence, as though by a trick of cinematographic lighting. This taller girl's pose was unmistakably protective. Jennifer saw that she had an arm round Sara's shoulders. Joanna stood near them in a posture that suggested she was a messenger or herald. As in those German films, it was impossible in the dark to guess what was going on.

Jennifer saw an evident lamp-bracket on the landing wall, with an evident switch below it. She strode at once over to the switch and clicked it up and down.

'One thing at least is explained,' she said. 'But the cause of this darkness is the only thing I yet understand.'

'Hullo, Aunt Jennifer,' said Sara. 'This is Rosalind.'

'Hullo,' said the tall girl with bright hair.

'Rosalind,' said Jennifer. 'I am so pleased to meet any friend of Sara's. I think I see Ramona over there. Whatever has been going on up here? Joanna dear, whyever did you drag me all the way up those awful stairs?'

'Ramona locked me in the cupboard, Aunt Jennifer,' said Sara.

Jennifer was startled and shocked. She said, 'Good

279

gracious, Ramona. I have always deplored that as a punishment, though I know ignorant mothers still do it to naughty young children. Perhaps it was a joke? Not in your usual good taste, Ramona.'

'No joke,' said Rosalind.

'A punishment, then. Whatever for? What had you been doing, Sara?'

'I don't know,' said Sara.

'It's an ongoing situation, Miss Corderey,' said Joanna.

Jennifer, in the midst of her bafflement and her annoyance, took a moment to be amused by the pomposity of this phrase. She hoped it was not going to become typical of Joanna.

She said, '*What* situation?'

'Miss Charnley trying to murder people,' said Rosalind.

'I don't understand a word you're saying, child.'

The girl called Rosalind began to tell Jennifer a rigmarole about the death of another girl, called Amanda Loring, of which of course Jennifer had heard. What she was saying was not logically organised nor well expressed; its meaning becoming at last more or less detectable, it was to be dismissed as the purest fantasy.

The girl was in earnest. Jennifer tried to examine her face in the dark. A lifetime's experience of deceitful children had taught her to know a deliberate lie when it was offered to her. The girl was not lying; she did seem in earnest. Jennifer thought Rosalind was telling what she thought was the truth.

And it was blatantly absurd. Aware that her psychology was amateur, Jennifer guessed that Rosalind, a warm-hearted creature, had been deeply upset by the accidental death of her closest friend, and wanted somebody to blame. Having grounds, real or imagined, for a grudge against Ramona, she made Ramona the target of her suspicions. Unconsciouslessly she built a platform in her mind, piling detail onto detail to form this fantastic structure. It was understandable enough, forgivable enough. An acute sense of personal loss could drive out commonsense. It had never happened to Jennifer, but she knew of cases.

She listened incredulously, with diminishing patience, to a complex narrative involving borrowed coats, cobwebs, bolts on doors, a person called Maureen and one called Norman, and the utterly irrelevant but repeated matter of a painted bookcase.

She understood that Ramona had been watched, for as much of the time as possible, by a bizarrely-assorted team that had latterly included an odd-job-man and a retarded maidservant; and this was because the watchers had all deluded themselves, or been deluded by Rosalind, that Ramona had carried out one murder and, being in the grip of an obsession, would attempt another.

She looked down the landing towards Ramona, whose face was a pale disc in the darkness, punctuated by the two smaller and paler discs of her spectacles. The idea of that shy, dumpy, art-loving young woman being a murderess was not tenable. Jennifer tried to curb her impatience.

It became obvious to the others, to Rosalind and Joanna and Sara, that Miss Corderey was not taking in a word she was hearing.

Rosalind knew that everything she was saying was exactly true. Joanna had become ninety-eight percent convinced that it was true, by the fact of the bolt and the padding, and by the occasional visible oddity of The Moaner. Sara was becoming convinced, more slowly and reluctantly than the others owing to her erstwhile closeness to Ramona; what weighed with her was the fact of having been locked in an airtight cupboard.

It was impossible to guess what Maureen was thinking. Meanwhile she held onto The Moaner's arm.

Rosalind took her arm from Sara's shoulders, so that she could use both hands to gesture. She gestured passionately.

Passionately she said to Jennifer Corderey, 'Look how

281

wide the passage is! Would *anybody* come out of that door and just dive across, right through the banisters?'

There was a pause. They waited for Jennifer Corderey to speak. All of them knew that she would say she did not believe Rosalind, but none of them knew in what words.

She said at last, speaking slowly, 'I remember the reported account of the accident. The Coroner's Court brought in a verdict of accidental death. The local newspaper quoted a criticism of the condition of the banisters up here. I was worried for you, Sara, since I knew you came to see Ramona in her room. But I thought you had sense enough not to fall through the banisters.'

'So did Amanda,' said Rosalind. 'Quite enough.'

'Even if what you hypothesise contained a tittle of truth,' said Jennifer Corderey, 'which it clearly does not, I do not see how you could hope to prove it.'

'That's what Colette and Joanna say,' said Rosalind. 'That's one of the reasons why we were watching. To catch her red-handed, when she had another shot. Which we did.'

'No,' said Jennifer Corderey. 'You saw her lock Sara in the cupboard. I accept your evidence and Sara's as to that. But you cannot know how long she intended to keep her there. It might have been for five seconds only. It might have been no more than a crude practical joke, or a punishment.'

'The bolt?' said Rosalind.

'Necessary for either the joke or the punishment. Neither joke nor punishment could succeed if the door could be opened from inside, simply by turning the handle.'

'The strips of felt in the door-frame?' said Joanna.

'Ah,' said Jennifer Corderey. She crossed to the cupboard door, opened it, and felt the material with her fingertips. The movement took her close to Ramona, whose face showed nothing.

'Nobody would ever notice the felt, or whatever it is,' said Joanna, 'in the dark like that, in a cupboard nobody

282

uses. And if they did see it, they'd think it had been there for ever.'

'How do you know it has not been there for ever?'

'Colette saw her sticking it on,' said Rosalind.

'There might be many reasons for that.'

'We can only think of one.'

'I can think of others. In my borrowed cottage, the larder door rattles when the wind is in a certain quarter. To prevent the rattling, which kept me awake, I myself cut up a piece of old underfelt which I found in a roll in the garage. I cut the felt into strips and glued them to the inside of the door-frame. The result is incidentally airtight, I imagine, but the purpose is to silence the rattling of the door. This cupboard door is near Ramona's bedroom. I can imagine that it rattled in the night. I daresay it kept you awake, Ramona? The remedy you found is exactly the remedy I found.'

Ramona made no reply. It could be presumed that she was listening, but still her face showed nothing, behind the thick spectacles, in the near-darkness.

'If there were any serious grounds for your suspicions whatever,' said Jennifer Corderey to Rosalind, 'why did you not report them to one of your teachers?'

'We tried that,' said Rosalind. 'Oh, we tried that.'

'I can imagine the response. Sara, I can understand the ridiculous fantasy that brought these others upstairs, and that there might be a dozen reasons for Ramona coming upstairs even at the cost of keeping me waiting, but why did *you* come all the way up here on this particular afternoon?'

'Ramona had done some paintings,' said Sara, 'in one of the empty rooms up here. That's what she said. She wanted to show them to me. She said she hoped I wouldn't think they were pornographic.'

'I should hope so, indeed.'

'Not paintings, painting,' said Ramona suddenly, speaking for the very first time since she had shot the bolt on the broom-cupboard door. 'Bookcase,' she added.

'Norman give 'er paint an' a brush,' said Maureen. 'He were worried, 'cos of same like before.'

283

'She said paintings,' said Sara, 'meaning pictures. I couldn't have got that wrong.'

'The whole perceived meaning changed by the addition or subtraction of an S,' said Jennifer Corderey. 'Curious. I wonder how many other examples there are? It is probably a point raised by Fowler. That misunderstanding would be the easiest possible thing. It has probably happened many times. She said "painting" and you heard "paintings", and thus figured to yourself a series of canvasses.'

'No,' said Sara. 'No, Aunt Jennifer. Ramona said "painting*zzz*". She said "they". She said she hoped I wouldn't think *they* were pornographic.'

'Anyway, how could a bookcase be pornographic?' said Joanna.

'By dint of its contents,' said Jennifer immediately. 'They, plural, meaning books, plural. What books would Ramona have that would fall into that category? Nothing very searing, I imagine. Perhaps the level of Zola. Not in my judgement one of the very great masters, but I admit that in French literature I am a baby.'

'Judgement. Baby,' said Sara in a small, astonished voice. 'I remember . . .'

Jennifer Corderey remembered too.

A moment of absorption, a jab of needle-sharp recollection, a face of stone, a voice of trance.

The Judgement of Solomon. A carving in Venice.

'Solomon would have cut the baby in half. I did that once.'

The conjunction of words, spoken almost without thought in order to give herself time to think, and in a totally different context, had triggered the same unsettling memory in Jennifer and in Sara.

'*Did* you cut a baby in half, Ramona?' asked Jennifer Corderey.

She imagined that nobody had ever had occasion to ask this question before.

'Not literally,' said Ramona out of the darkness. 'I had it squashed by the tractor.' Her voice sounded patient,

284

reasonable; the voice of somebody restating the obvious only because it had passed the listener by.

'My God,' said Rosalind.

Jennifer Corderey prided herself on strict intellectual honesty. It was not a quality with charm or sex-appeal; it was not fun; it was what she had. This was a moment for the most ruthless honesty. She put memory, report and observation together, and contemplated the sum.

The significant memories were probably many, but the one that stood out was the moment of the Venetian carving.

Report? This beautiful Rosalind Tuck was the principal source. She was not a clever girl, but she was a person of obvious goodwill and commonsense. Jennifer had been clear throughout that Rosalind believed the truth of what she was saying. Honesty now obliged Jennifer to take it seriously. Joanna Curry was a clever little thing, not easily fooled. Without absolute certainty she was confirming Rosalind's account. And Sara had been locked in the cupboard.

Observation? It had been and remained difficult to observe any nuance of expression, anything subtle that could convey truth or betray lies, in this sepia semi-darkness. But voices told. These voices had told. Ramona's own voice had told.

It did not add up to instant, incontrovertible proof; but there was a case to answer. It could be put much higher than that; it could not be put lower than that; there was a case to answer.

'Why Sara, Ramona?' asked Jennifer suddenly. 'What had she done?'

'My father,' said Ramona, 'knew of a man that was shot for treachery in the war.'

'Treachery . . .' said Sara.

Jennifer Corderey said slowly, 'Ramona was to have left this building, with me, immediately, in my car.'

'Why, Aunt Jennifer?'

'In order to consult me about a problem that she would not discuss on the telephone. I was surprised by this sudden

285

appeal for advice. There had been nothing like it before. The explanation may be – not must be, but may be – simply that Ramona would have been out all afternoon, far away, in my company.'

'You were here to give her an alibi, Miss Corderey,' said Rosalind. 'Like Maureen.'

'Yes, dear. Perhaps.'

'So then,' said Sara, 'people would think some other girl had shoved me in the cupboard as a joke.'

'If they found you, dear. She might have had some plan for removing the body. In the small hours. I imagine. And then, you see, nobody would have known how you came to be asphyxiated. If, indeed, your body was ever found. If it were not, everybody would assume that you had run away, or been abducted. A massive search would have been mounted. Thousands of people would have been interviewed, and witnesses asked to come forward. Probably, in the end, your body would have been found, and some unknown vagrant would have been blamed.'

'Golly,' said Sara.

'What *did* you intend, Ramona?' asked Jennifer Corderey.

Ramona did not reply. She stared at Jennifer Corderey. She had been right. Jennifer's friendship was and always had been a fraud. She was a central part of the conspiracy. The punishment Ramona had planned for her was not nearly sufficient. It was necessary that Maureen should let go of Ramona's arm, so that she could concentrate on making other and better plans. Maureen's grip did not slacken. She was not much hurting Ramona, but she was not letting her go, either.

Ramona noticed without interest that Colette Davies had come up the stairs, followed by Norman. Ramona remembered, as an event of the remote past, that somebody had said that Colette was looking for Norman. She had found him, then. Norman made straight for the light-switch. When the light failed to come on he made a small hissing sound, like that of a man grooming a horse, a sound which had filled Ramona's childhood at Garston. Norman

286

took the bulb out, shook it beside his ear, and put it in his pocket.

Ramona did not know why Norman was there, or Colette. She did not care. They were irrelevant. Her mind, methodical as always, strove to forget the distractions around her, and began to consider methods of achieving justice, punishment, liberation.

She hardly heard Jennifer Corderey say, 'Well, this all comes as quite a shock. I had myself been surprised by Ramona's recent demeanour. A new secretiveness, a kind of opacity, the shutters closed over the windows of the soul. And then the Judgement of Solomon. I suppose she will be placed in an institution. Perhaps they will allow her books. We had better go downstairs and find a telephone.'

Ramona hardly noticed the journey downstairs, so busy was her brain with planning her next stroke.